HEATHER GRAHAM

LINDSAY MCKENNA
MARILYN PAPPANO
ANNETTE BROADRICK

Snowy Nights

Published by Silhouette Books

America's Publisher of Contemporary Romance

SILHOUETTE BOOKS

SNOWY NIGHTS

Copyright © 2003 by Harlequin Books S.A.

ISBN 0-373-21852-4

The publisher acknowledges the copyright holders of the individual works as follows:

THE CHRISTMAS BRIDE
Copyright © 1991 by Heather Graham Pozzessere

ALWAYS AND FOREVER
Copyright © 1990 by Lindsay McKenna

THE GREATEST GIFT
Copyright © 1989 by Marilyn Pappano

CHRISTMAS MAGIC
Copyright © 1988 by Annette Broadrick

This edition published by arrangement with Harlequin Books S.A.

® and TM are trademarks of Harlequin Books S.A., used under license. Trademarks indicated with ® are registered in the United States Patent and Trademark Office, the Canadian Trade Marks Office and in other countries.

Visit Silhouette at www.eHarlequin.com

Printed in U.S.A.

CONTENTS

THE CHRISTMAS BRIDE

Heather Graham

Dear Reader,

To me, Christmas is truly the most magical time of the year.

We come from Miami, so I grew up in a place where many people said there just wasn't the same Christmas spirit as there was up north.

But when I grew up, my husband and I wound up buying a home in Massachusetts because he has lots of wonderful family there. So now I've had Christmas in the snow and Christmas in the sun.

I've discovered it's just as wonderful a time whether there's a snowman outside or a palm tree. My children are all getting older now (except for the thirteen-year-old— she's not really out in the world yet!) and so Christmas has become that one time when we can guarantee we'll really all be together. Wherever it may be, being together is what counts, what makes the magic. It's truly a time to count one's blessings.

This story was actually written long ago, but I've discovered that the sentiments within it have never changed for me. For people struggling with loss, with the insanity of daily life, the Christmas season can become a time just to stop and remember the fine gifts we've been given—and the greatest, most noble of man's emotions: love.

I hope you enjoy!

Heather Graham

Chapter 1

"And what would you like for Christmas, little girl?" Cary Adams asked. She leaned forward at the table, resting her chin whimsically on her hands as she asked her friend June Harrison the question. Cary's hair, a sleek and shimmering brown, curved around her delicately boned features, and her eyes, a tawny hazel that glittered when she laughed, were as wide and innocent as a child's. Well, it *was* Christmas. Nearly.

"It's not a 'what,' but a 'who,'" June replied with a laugh. "His name doesn't matter. He just has to be tall, dark and handsome. And rich," she added as an afterthought. She grimaced. "It's not that I'm a material girl, but it *is* a material world."

Cary grinned and leaned back. She wagged a finger at June. "Not fair. I can't get you a man for Christmas."

"No? Well, I wasn't expecting one, anyway. But you, Mrs. Adams, deserve one. And he *should* be tall, dark and handsome. And rich."

"What if I prefer a blond?"

June shook her head. "No, I'm sorry. The saying is 'tall, dark and handsome.' Take it or leave it."

Cary laughed and looked around the room.

Despite the fact that it was always held indecently early—at barely a week after Thanksgiving—Cary loved the annual office family Christmas party. She loved the music, the colorful lights, the scent of the holly branches, pine and candles, and today she even loved the snow that was piling up on the sidewalks and streets.

There was another Christmas party held at the *Elegance* office every year, always the night before Christmas Eve. But today's party was Cary's favorite. It was held for the families of the employees. Husbands, wives, children, grandparents and even a few cousins managed to finagle invitations. Every year Jason McCready, the publisher of *Elegance,* rented the ballroom of one of the most prestigious hotels in Boston, and it was pure joy to see toddlers and teens running amok among the handsomely tuxedoed waiters. Champagne, eggnog, beer and wine poured freely for the adults, and Christmas punch—bright red for the season, of course—was in abundance for the underage crowd. There were drawings for huge turkeys and hams, and there was a main prize, too, a microwave oven, a television set, a video recorder or the like. Always the latest, always something that someone would really want. Jason McCready, for all his eccentricities, planned Christmas well for his employees. Everybody went away with something, for there was a draw that he called the seasonal exchange. Each employee drew a name from a hat, someone with whom to exchange a gift. Not that it mattered what McCready called it, for everyone in the office joined in his Christmas party, regardless of their religious beliefs. It was all done with tremendous warmth and goodwill, and though the hall was adorned with a giant Christmas tree and someone was always elected to hand out toys to the children, McCready saw to it that the beautiful and ancient

Hanukkah songs were also played, and no one's beliefs were trodden on.

"Hey, kid, you're awful quiet! This is a party, a celebration, remember?"

Cary blinked, then smiled. June, of the magazine's advertising salespersons extraordinaire, was staring at her pointedly. June was her senior by about five years. At first Cary had resented being called "kid" all the time, but she had quickly learned that June used the word with affection. After a rocky start, the two had become best friends.

"I was just thinking," Cary said.

"Horrors!" June murmured in mock protest. She was a striking woman with a headful of wild platinum hair and soft gray eyes. She had the type of figure that might well have once graced the inner pages of a magazine centerfold, but she was as smart as a whip and knew her business backward and forward. June stirred her Irish coffee. "What were you thinking about? Men?"

"No. Actually, yes. One man. I was thinking that McCready throws a fabulous party—especially since he is...McCready," Cary finished a little lamely.

June smiled and shrugged, and Cary knew her friend understood her completely. Jason McCready was a good-looking man—definitely tall, dark and handsome—and he was very young for his position, still a year shy of forty. But it was said that he had been a dynamo in his early twenties—bright, energetic and full of the ideas that could turn a dying biweekly into a respected glamour magazine. *Elegance* had a section on the finest homes in America, an entertainment division, a special section devoted to current politics and one to current affairs. And there was the "American World" column, Cary's own baby, full of insights into people and more personal events. The magazine had a contemporary flair along with the old, traditional val-

ues that were intangible and yet all important. And that was
Jason McCready's doing.

He was the publisher, and he was also the president of
the board. He was an American success story, and years
back, long before Cary had come into the business, he had
often graced the covers of various other news-oriented
magazines. She could remember one photograph in particular, taken when he had been at Rockefeller Plaza with his
wife.

Oddly enough, Cary reminisced, it had been a Christmas
photograph. And she could remember it so clearly. The
huge annual tree had risen behind them, the ice rink had
stretched out before them, and New York had been decked
out in a fabulous display of colorful lights. McCready had
been in a long black coat that had accented his dark good
looks, and his strong, decidedly masculine profile. His wife,
Sara, had been in the softest white mink, a complete contrast to him with her feathered white-blond hair and eyes
so blue that, even in the picture, their color shone with an
almost unreal light. They had been smiling at one another
in that picture, the look on Sara's beautiful face one of
adoration. And he had gazed at her with a tenderness that
was somehow shattering to the observer; one could almost
touch it. They had been so stunning, a fairy-tale couple.

The next year, though, Cary knew, Sara McCready had
been dead before Christmas.

And Jason McCready had never consented to another
interview. Cary had thought to do one for their own magazine. It had been one of the few times she had actually
spoken with him.

And he had nearly jumped down her throat.

She could still remember the occasion in his office. She
had made an appointment with his secretary, had gone in
fully prepared and with a truly intelligent presentation.

She had walked into his sparse office. White-walled,

peach-carpeted, two prints on the wall, a massive oak desk, a leather sofa, two chairs.

He had never even asked her to sit.

He had remained behind his desk, his lime green eyes sharp and cold and so pointedly on her that she'd felt as if steel blades were stabbing her. He had listened for at least sixty seconds before the pencil he had held idly between his fingers suddenly snapped. Then he'd stood, rising to his full, imposing six-three, and walked around the desk to stand before her. She had nearly cowered, when his palms touched her shoulders. Hard. Forcefully. But not violently.

And he had issued one harsh word to her. "No!"

He had stood there staring at her, a strand of his usually impeccable black hair falling over one of his deadly dark eyebrows. His bronze features had gone tight and white, and the fullness of his mouth had been compressed into a grim line. He'd stared at her as if she were an ancient enemy, and she had wanted nothing so much as to run.

It wasn't courage that had kept her standing there—she was simply too surprised to move. And at last his hands dropped from her shoulders and he turned away. "I said no, Miss Adams—"

"It's Mrs. Adams," she'd interrupted, fighting the tears that welled in her eyes, wondering why it should matter at this particular time that she make such a point about her name.

"*Mrs.* Adams. Excuse me," he said coldly. He walked around the desk and sat again, with something like an air of royalty about his designer-suited form. "Could you leave now, please? I'm busy, and this interview is over."

She stiffened her shoulders, certain that not only had he refused her, but that he had also fired her. "I can have my desk cleared out by five," she said flatly. "I shall expect to see a severance check just as promptly."

Only then did his dark brows arch and a look of fleeting

surprise pass over his hard and handsome features. "Why on earth should you clean out your desk, Mrs. Adams?"

She hadn't wanted to falter, but she had. And she knew that crimson flamed in her cheeks. "Mr. McCready, it certainly sounded as if you were annoyed and no longer cared to employ me."

"I *am* annoyed, Mrs. Adams, but I do not fire people simply because they annoy me upon occasion. I find your work excellent. I merely wish that you would vacate my office and refrain from mentioning such an article in the future."

She was still staring at him blankly. She had often wondered if the man read anything that went into the magazine anymore. Apparently he did.

"Is there anything else, Mrs. Adams?"

"No!" she exclaimed. But she didn't move, and she was stunned to hear herself speaking again. "Mr. McCready, this is your own magazine! Why won't—"

He was on his feet again. And, oddly enough, she felt as if she had his attention. Really had his attention, and not just his anger.

"Because I cannot talk about my personal life, and that is that! Do you understand?"

"All right," Cary agreed. He was still staring at her. She felt tremors, hot one minute, cold the next, racing along her spine.

For the briefest moment she saw what might have been a glimmer of anguish in his eyes. And she knew, intuitively, that he was thinking about his wife. He had nothing to say without her in his life anymore.

"I'm sorry—" Cary began.

"Don't be!" he interrupted her.

The words were soft, the emotion behind them vehement. And Cary found herself speaking again despite them. "Mr. McCready, you loved her very much. I can see that. I'm sorry. So very sorry. But you're not the only one who has ever lost someone they love. Perhaps the article is a bad idea. But you should talk to someone. You should...''

Her voice trailed away. He was staring at her with ice-cold fury in his eyes.

"Are you quite finished, Mrs. Adams?"

She nodded. His life was none of her business.

"Perhaps you'd like to get back to work then?" he suggested pleasantly.

She spun. She did not thank him for his time. He hadn't willingly given her any. And she didn't need to thank him for not firing her. Her work was good; that was what mattered. He just wanted her out of his office.

"Mrs. Adams!"

She looked at him.

"I beg your pardon," he said. "I really do beg your pardon." His voice was soft. And, seated behind his desk, his hands folded, his hair so dark and his eyes so startlingly green, he was striking—and more. He was appealing. She gritted her teeth, startled at the temptation to walk to him and slip her arms around him. To offer him some comfort.

It was an illusion. McCready wanted nothing from her. And there were no weak links in his armor. He just wanted her to leave his office.

She obliged him.

And she had never ventured back in.

"He still throws a very nice Christmas party," she commented idly, then cast June a mischievous smile. "Almost as if he still believed in the Christmas spirit. Ho, ho, ho."

"You almost make it sound as if you still believe in it yourself," June said sagely, eyeing her friend across the table.

Cary felt as if her heart slammed against her chest, and it was suddenly difficult to breathe. That hurt. She tried. She tried very hard every Christmas. She had learned to smile and laugh a lot. For her family, if not for herself. She had done very well, or so she had thought.

She had gotten past the shock and the agony and the feelings of utter rage, of helplessness. She had found her own apartment, she had become independent and she had managed to build a new life, filled with her son's school activities, her work and visits to her in-laws and her family. It wasn't in the least fair that June should attack her about her Christmas spirit.

But June wasn't really attacking, nor was she going to persist in that vein. She tossed her wild mane, licked her swizzle stick and used it to point toward the large, intricately decorated cardboard house where Santa was seeing to the little ones. "Jeremy is playing Santa this year, isn't he?" she asked.

Cary nodded. "Padded to the gills, complaining black and blue and having the time of his life. Danny should be just about up to him now. I wonder if he'll recognize Jeremy."

"Let's go see," June suggested.

They rose and threaded their way through the gaily dressed crowd, stopping to call a greeting here or there. Just as they reached the line leading into the house, Cary came to a halt, smiling. It was just about Danny's time to go in to talk to Santa. The little girl in front of him had just been escorted through the bright red curtains. Through a tiny crack in the cardboard, Cary could see Jeremy give Santa's long-legged and beautiful helper a little pinch where the short-skirted elf outfit left her thigh bare.

"Santa is a lech," she told June with a sigh.

"And Isabelle loves every minute of it, I'm sure," June assured her.

Isabelle, Santa's helper, was the newest college student to take a job in the mail room. And her smile clearly indicated that she was having a good time.

Danny, Cary's eight-year-old son, turned suddenly, sensing that she was there. His freckled face broke into a wide grin at the sight of her, and she felt a sudden, quick pounding of her heart. Danny looked so much like his father. The clear, sky-blue eyes, the blond, almost platinum-streaked hair, the pale spatter of freckles over the bridge of his nose. He was a cute kid, she knew, not just because he was her own. Most kids were cute, she assured herself, but with Danny, it was more. There was something about his eyes...a wisdom in them. Even a compassion. Danny had never grown bitter, even when he had understood what had happened to his father. He had only cried.

He still cried at night, sometimes.

But he had never allowed his father's death to warp his feelings toward others, or even toward life. He had grown older long before his time. Yet it had given him a charm and a sense of responsibility, rare for his age. Talking to Danny was sometimes like talking to a teenager or a young man ready for college.

"Mom! Come on up!" he called to her.

"Go on," June told her. "I'll wait for you by the exit from Santa's hut."

Cary grinned. "All right. I want to get a peek at Danny with Santa if I can, and see if Jeremy holds up."

June nodded. Cary excused herself, as she wended her way through the parents and children to reach Danny. Isabelle offered her a wide friendly smile. "Hi, Mrs. Adams. Is this one yours?" she asked, indicating Danny.

Cary nodded. "He is. Danny, this is Miss Isabelle LaCrosse. She works with us now. Isabelle, my son, Daniel."

Danny solemnly shook hands. "And I thought you were really an elf!" he said with a soft sigh.

Startled, Isabelle stared at Cary, who shrugged, hiding a smile. "He likes elves," she explained lamely.

Isabelle peeked behind the curtain. "I think Santa is ready for you, Daniel. Come on in. Mrs. Adams, if you'd like…"

Cary saw a break in the red curtain where she could discreetly spy on Santa and her son. She offered Isabelle a wide, engaging smile and slipped closer while Danny marched in to sit on Santa's lap.

"Well, ho, ho, ho, it's Mr. Daniel Adams, so it is!" Santa said. Cary watched her son's eyes widen with surprise as Santa addressed him so familiarly.

Jeremy, she decided, was perfect. He was padded wonderfully, and the suit was great. A big snowy beard covered his chin, with a swooping mustache attachment that hid the whole lower half of his face. The red and white Santa hat fell over his forehead, and little gold spectacles sat on the tip of his nose.

"Yes, sir, Santa," Danny said with a certain awe. He had told Cary that he had no intention of sitting on Santa's lap, that he was a big boy. He had meant to stand and talk to Santa man to man.

But he was quickly up on Santa's lap, and he seemed to have no idea at all that he was talking to his mother's cousin.

"I know that you've been just as good as gold this year, Danny. So tell me, what would you like for Christmas?"

Danny hesitated. Cary frowned, watching him. "What would I really like for Christmas?" Danny asked softly.

"Yes, son, of course. What would you really like for Christmas?"

"I believe in Santa, you know," Danny said quickly. "I believe in God and Santa and miracles, especially Christmas miracles. And I know you can help me, Santa—Mr. Claus, I know you can!"

"Danny, I—"

"I'd like a father, Santa. Oh, not a real one! I know you

can't bring my dad back. He lives up in heaven, with God, because he was a great dad. God can't give people back once he takes them. And it isn't for me. I'd like someone for my mom. She tries not to show it, but she's so unhappy, and I can see it. I don't think she knows I can see it, but I do.''

''Danny—''

''She's a great cook, and a good housekeeper. She makes neat chocolate chip cookies. And she's a writer. She writes all about other people who need help, and sometimes the things she writes get help for them. She's been really good, Santa. Please.''

She felt her heart—she could have sworn that she actually felt her heart—swelling. Tears welled behind her eyelids, and she almost choked on them. She swallowed. Hard. A smile slowly curved her lips. I love you, Danny, she thought.

''Look Danny,'' Santa said, managing to interrupt him at last. ''I—I'd like to make you a promise, but I can't. You see, grown-ups have to—well, they have to find people that they like themselves sometimes.''

''I know you can help me,'' Danny said stubbornly.

Santa opened his mouth, then closed it. Danny had a stubborn streak in him. And this Santa knew it very well.

''I'll tell you what, Danny. I'll see what I can do. But that's not an easy Christmas order. It's absolutely the hardest. You may have to give me more than one Christmas to fill that wish, all right?''

''But you'll work on it?''

Santa sighed. ''I've *been* working on it,'' he muttered, then smiled. ''Of course I'll work on it. Hard. I promise.''

''Thank you,'' Danny said simply. ''I'll help you. I'll wish on the North Star every night.''

Santa nodded. ''And what about this Christmas?''

"Oh, well, I'd like that computer made especially for kids my age. The one they have at school."

Cary almost muttered an expletive out loud. Danny would never say he wanted anything. And now he was asking for something she could never afford. She knew the computer he was working with at school. It was a wonderful invention, with talk-it-through word processing and talk-it-through graphics for math and art projects.

I'll bet I could even straighten out my income taxes with it, she thought wryly.

But, unlike many other computers, this one had yet to come down in price. The whole outfit cost thousands, and she didn't know if she could manage the payments even if she bought it on time.

Jeremy obviously didn't know the price of the computer. "That's easy!" he assured Danny. "I can definitely work on that one!" He set Danny on his feet and reached into the big red bag by his high black boots. "For the moment, my boy, I've got a remote-control car for you, how's that?"

"Great, Santa!" Danny said. "It's great, honest, just great. And thanks, thanks a lot."

Danny escaped through the curtain, Jeremy started to summon Isabelle to lead in the next child when he happened to look up and notice Cary standing there. He stared at her for a second, then crooked his finger toward her.

"Come here, Cary Adams!" he commanded.

She stepped forward. "Sorry, I was eavesdropping. I couldn't quite—"

She managed to swallow a little squeal as he wound his arms around her and pulled her onto his lap.

"I hear you've been a very good girl," he told her, and winked.

"Would you quit that, you lech, I'm your cousin!" she protested, laughing.

"Second cousin," he reminded her, and sighed.

"Close enough, so behave."

"Well, you heard your son, Mrs. Adams," he told her. "He wants someone for you. And I've tried and tried—"

"Jeremy, you're a dear, and I love you with all my heart, and you know it. And you know, too, that you aren't a bit serious about me—"

"I could be, if you would just get over this relative bit," he said jokingly.

"Jeremy—"

"What about that electrician who was built like a body-builder?" he demanded darkly.

She had to smile. "Sorry. He wore his boxer shorts up to his boobs."

"The lawyer from Concord?"

"He was cross-eyed, I swear it."

"Cary," Jeremy told her sternly, "no one is going to be Richard. That lawyer was not cross-eyed."

She caught her breath and stared into his eyes, seeing his concern and love. She exhaled slowly. "I know no one will be Richard, Jeremy. Honestly, I know that. But he— he would have to live up to Richard, can you understand that?"

He started to nod then maybe he realized that she was very close to tears, so he shook his head vehemently. "Mrs. Adams, your boy has been very good all year. And I think—"

"I think you got me into a lot of trouble!" Cary interrupted him.

"Me?" Jeremy said in mock distress. "I have been an absolute angel!"

"Jeremy, you've never been an angel, but that's not what I'm talking about."

"Oh?" he murmured, wounded.

"You promised him a father!"

"Hey! I gave you a few years."

"Thanks. That was really swell of you."

"I do try to please."

"And then, on top of that, you promised him a gift I can't possibly afford!"

"What?" For a moment, Jeremy was serious, frowning. "I thought computers prices were coming down!"

"They are—but not the setup Danny wants. It costs thousands, Jeremy."

"I'll help—"

"Like hell you will. I don't take charity from the family, Jeremy, and you know it."

"Hey! I have every right to buy my little cousin a Christmas present."

"Sure. And if I ever manage to afford that system, you can buy him a game or some software."

"Stubborn, stubborn, stubborn," Jeremy insisted. Then his eyes brightened. "We might get Christmas bonuses."

"That much?"

"Maybe. After all," he teased, lightness returning to his voice, "you've been a good girl yourself. Too good. Atrociously, boringly good. So I'm going to sprinkle you with Christmas dust. And the next man you see is going to be the man of your dreams. Rich as Midas, sleeker than a Mercedes Benz, tender, gentle and kind. Tall, dark and handsome. Danny's Christmas present—and yours. And the Christmas dust is going to make you run right out and be bad with him. How's that?"

She was laughing. "The next man I see will probably be old Pete from the mail room, he of the ten children and eighteen million grandchildren. But hey, knock yourself out. Sprinkle away with Christmas dust. Maybe I'll at least find a suitable date for the adult Christmas party. What do you think?"

"I think that your time's up," Jeremy said. "If the one

adult I get on my lap all day can't ask for one lousy, decadent present, you may as well stand!''

Laughing, she found her feet. ''I'm telling you, Santa
sure isn't what he used to be,'' she said with mock horror.
She started toward the exit when she stopped short, suddenly aware that someone was blocking the red-curtained
exit door.

Someone big. She couldn't see who it was right away,
because the flare from the Christmas lights was in her eyes.
All she could catch was the form, tall, imposing, totally
blocking the exit. Dark. Even forbidding.

For a moment her heart fluttered, and she didn't know
why. She felt an acute sense of unease.

How silly, she told herself. She didn't know why she
was so startled by the masculine figure in the dark tux.

She took a step forward, then realized who the man was.
She should have known him instantly from his height alone.

It was none other than their host himself. Her boss. The
illustrious Mr. Jason McCready.

There had been rumors that many a female at *Elegance*
had foolishly cast away her heart and pride on his behalf.
McCready wasn't interested. He never dated his employees,
and when he made his necessary social appearances with
women, they were never the same from one occasion to the
next. Still, Cary knew that June found him irresistible.

That was undoubtedly because June had never ventured
into his office with a story proposal, Cary decided.

She took another step forward, deeply irritated with herself. Then she paused again, because of the way he was
staring at her.

Once again it seemed as if those green eyes sliced her
like steel blades. The scent of him slowly curled around
her; it was subtle, but very masculine and...alluring, she
had to admit. He was compelling, standing there. So tall,
so dark, his shoulders broad, his hips lean. She wondered

about his chest. It would be deeply muscled, she was certain. Hairy, or sleek and bare? Hairy, she was sure. Darkly hairy, with a narrow whorl that drew a line from his chest to his…

She jerked her head up and stared into his eyes, horrified. He stepped back, lifting the curtain for her.

"Mrs. Adams?"

She gritted her teeth and started forward. She had meant to see him sometime during the day to thank him for the party, but now she couldn't seem to muster up a thank you. In fact, she couldn't seem to speak at all.

"Mrs. Adams!"

She looked up and realized she was very close to him. Close enough to see the texture of his tux, the snow-white pleats of his shirt. The angles and planes of his face, the sensual fullness of his mouth.

"Yes?" she managed.

"I had intended Santa's lap for those children among us who are under, say, fifteen."

How long had he been standing there? How could she explain?

She didn't know if he was seriously angry or if he was teasing her. She still couldn't find a reply. Nor could she seem to tear her eyes from his.

"Mr. McCready, I…"

He smiled, which made him seem more striking, younger. Almost touchable. Her voice died away as he stared at her.

"I do not want your desk cleared out by five, Mrs. Adams," he said softly. "I still find your work exceptional."

"Thank you," she managed. He was still staring at her. She couldn't smile; she couldn't speak. He didn't expect her to. He was just watching her.

She turned away at last and fled down the steps, hurrying toward June. Just as she reached the bottom step, she realized a little girl was waiting on the landing, waiting for Cary to move so she could run up the steps herself.

But the girl waited politely, with a beautiful smile. She must have been about six or seven, and she had light blond hair caught up in pigtails tied with red ribbons. She looked like an angel, delicate, sweet, with a haunting, wistful smile that instantly tugged at Cary's heartstrings.

"Is Santa free now?" she asked Cary.

Cary heard June's laughter, and she blushed. Then she returned the little girl's smile. "Yes, Santa is free, I think. Of course, there is a line around the other way. I'm not sure—"

"Oh!" the girl cried, stricken. "I have to leave, you see, and my father said it might be okay to slip around this way. But it would be rude to take someone else's place."

"Angela, it really is okay. We'll be quick, and the others will understand," came a deep masculine voice over Cary's shoulder.

She turned in dismay. McCready again. But this sweet, delicate little child couldn't possibly be his daughter....

Yes, she was, Cary realized. She stared from McCready's gaze to the little girl's wide eyes. "Excuse me," she murmured lamely. "Honey, if you have to leave, I know Santa will be thrilled to see you, and no one will mind at all."

Angela McCready smiled again. "Thank you." She started up the stairs, then turned back. "It was nice to meet you, Miss..."

"Mrs. Adams. Cary," Cary told her. And once again that smile crossed the little girl's lips.

"Mrs. Adams!" Angela McCready exclaimed happily. Cary arched a brow, and Angela continued quickly. "You must be Danny's mother."

Cary nodded, still confused.

Angela enlightened her. "We sat together for the magic

show. And he taught me how to do a trick. He's really wonderful.''

"Yes, well, I rather think so myself," Cary agreed.

"I hope I see him—and you—again," Angela McCready said.

There was such hope on her face that Cary couldn't disappoint her. "I'm sure we'll meet again," she said.

McCready's eyes were on her, sharp, unfathomable. Cary felt herself growing warm. But then he and his daughter disappeared into the cardboard Santa hut, and Cary turned away.

It had all happened in a matter of moments, she realized. Running into McCready, meeting his daughter, sitting on Jeremy's lap...

Jeremy and his Christmas dust! she thought with disgust. So much for Jeremy's prophesies.

"Danny's watching the puppeteer. I told him it would be all right," June said. "Let's go for a glass of that delicious champagne. I don't get to indulge in the really good stuff all that often."

"Champagne sounds wonderful," Cary agreed. She was parched. More parched than she could remember being. Except for the time she had gone into Jason McCready's office with her notebook and great expectations.

They walked to the champagne table, where a polite bartender helped them both. Cary toasted June, then raised her glass and sipped her champagne.

The next man you see, Jeremy had told her. She didn't want a man for Christmas. Sometimes she wondered if she would ever want another man in her life.

And then sometimes...

Sometimes she was lonely and frightened, furious with Richard for leaving her, and sometimes she ached because he had taught her that love could be so very sweet, and then he had been gone, leaving nothing in her life except for the pain and the blackness and the void. She had tried to date, but she had always backed away quickly. Because...

Because no one had ever touched her in the same way. No one had ever made a kiss seem natural. No one had ever seduced her to where she could forget...

"Cary, are you still with me?"

"What? Oh, I'm sorry." She realized she had been ignoring June. They were sipping champagne. It was a party. And she was having a good time. Well, she was almost having a good time.

She started to smile. Jeremy. Santa. Where would she be without him?

Him and his prophesies!

The first man she had seen hadn't been old Pete from the mail room after all.

She suddenly choked on the champagne.

No, it had been someone much worse.

Jason McCready.

Tall, dark and handsome. And rich. Just like June had ordered...

Cary swallowed more champagne.

No, no, no...

So much for Christmas dust and miracles!

Chapter 2

Jason McCready had a headache. One that pounded viciously at the back of his skull as he drove toward his house.

He knew he was disappointing Angela by leaving the party so early, but he'd really wanted to go home.

The party had really been Sara's baby.

Oh, he'd always had a Christmas party. And he'd always tried very hard to do right by his employees. He hadn't been born to money, nor had he inherited the magazine. He had built it. He knew what it was like to work hard. And more, he knew what it was like to dream.

And once he had even known what it was like to hold magic in the palm of his hand. There had been a time when he had had everything.

He'd had Sara.

Sara had loved Christmas. She'd loved winter, the snow and the clean, cold air. She'd loved the bright lights and the decorations, the Santas in the stores and on the street corners, the specials on television. Just sitting with her before a fire had meant more than anything in the world to him. He'd really, truly had everything.

But that had been before the December night when a drunk driver had plowed into Sara's silver sports car with enough speed to kill her instantly. The only miracle had been that she had just dropped Angela off for a Christmas party, and so he was left with his very young daughter when he had been bereft of his wife.

But others had handled Angela for him then. In his grief, he realized now, he had deprived her of two parents instead of one. It had taken months for him to rouse himself enough to care for Angela. And now he was trying very hard to make it up to her.

"Can he, Dad?"

"What? Sorry, darling. I guess I wasn't listening," Jason apologized. The traffic was bad tonight. Fresh snow had made the streets slippery.

"Danny. Danny Adams. Can he come skiiing with us?"

"What?"

"I said—"

"No, no, I'm sorry, I did hear you, I just..."

"He was so nice, Dad. He—he made me laugh. And he understood when I—"

Angela broke off speaking.

"He understood what?" Jason asked her curiously. He braked quickly for a red light. On a street corner, a Salvation Army volunteer was waving a bell that clanged away, chiming out the Christmas season with a cheerful vengeance.

Why did he feel the loss so much more keenly every Christmas? Jason asked himself. It was a time for peace, a time for faith.

"Nothing," Angela murmured evasively. "He's just— he's just great. Couldn't we ask him, please?"

"Honey, his mother is one of my employees. I don't know if I should bother her with this." His mother wasn't just an employee. She was Mrs. Cary Adams, and since he'd been watching her for quite some time now, he could almost guarantee she would tell him no.

Angela didn't seem to see it that way. "His mother was very nice, and I don't think she'd be bothered at all," Angela said stubbornly.

Why shouldn't he ask a friend along for Angela? Guilt plagued him. He hadn't thought how lonely things must become for her now and then. She had the run of the lodge, of course, but it was true. She had no special friends.

Except for now. She was crazy about this Danny.

Jason had to admit that the boy seemed to be a special kid. There was something in his smile. It was nice. It was open, generous. He'd taken a few hard knocks himself, but he'd come through with that great smile. Jason knew about Danny Adams's life because he'd made a point to know something about Cary Adams. He'd done so the day she'd come into his office—and walked out of it with her head held high.

He would never forget that day. Just as he hadn't been able to forget Cary Adams.

She was petite. She had a smooth, soft, melodic voice, but she had a certain essence of steel about her. When he thought about it, he realized that she was a very beautiful woman, with her sweeping dark hair and richly lashed hazel eyes. They burned when she was indignant or angry. He smiled. She wasn't flashy. She was nicely, quietly sophisticated. Something wild or ornate might draw a glance first, but once a person's eyes had fixed on her quiet elegance, they were compelled to stay.

It wasn't her looks that had drawn his interests, for he lived in a world where women were often beautiful and sophisticated. It had been her determination in coming to him, her staying power when he had refused her.

And then it had been the way she had gazed at him with glimmering gold eyes as she had told him bluntly that he wasn't the only one who had ever lost someone. And he had been in a rut, one hell of a rut of self-pity. She hadn't lifted the weight of the world from his shoulders, but her anger had done something, and since that day, life had been a little bit better. He'd made sure it was better. She'd made him see that it was something he had to do himself.

That was why he knew about her. He'd had her personnel file on his desk within five minutes, so he knew that Richard Adams had walked into a burning building because he had heard a child crying, and that he had never walked out again.

"Daddy?"

He sighed. The very beautiful Mrs. Adams might have cast accusations at him, but she had a few failings of her own. He could almost guarantee that she would turn him down. She had the defenses of a porcupine.

"I'll try, Angela."

"Oh, thank you, Daddy!" She threw an arm around him and kissed him.

"Hey! There's traffic out tonight!" he warned her.

"Sorry, Daddy!"

But he caught the look in her eyes. She was smiling. She was radiant.

He'd never seen her so happy or so excited.

Jason tightened his jaw. Somehow he was going to have to get Mrs. Adams to agree to let Danny come with him.

Even a porcupine had to have a chink in its armor somewhere.

It was the very next Monday that Cary found herself summoned to McCready's office.

She had been looking through the photographs for a Valentine's Day special when she sensed someone watching her. Gazing up, she was surprised to find June staring at her with a look that combined excitement and anxiety.

"What is it?"

"McCready's office," June said nervously.

"What?"

"You're wanted. In McCready's office."

Cary's heart lurched. Was she being fired after all? Perhaps he really had been angry to see her sitting on Jeremy's lap.

"Now?" she murmured. Of course now! She rose from her desk and stared at June. Was this how people felt when they walked to the gallows?

No, no, this wasn't that bad! Even if he was firing her, it wasn't anything as terrible as walking to the gallows. She was talented! She would find a new job....

Just a month before Christmas. Danny would never get his computer.

He couldn't be firing her! Not right before Christmas!

But despite his wonderful parties, McCready didn't have any Christmas spirit. His spirit had been buried with his very beautiful wife.

"I'm here for you," June said to her softly.

"I'm fine," Cary muttered. She lifted her chin, squared her shoulders and walked from her office to the elevators. She stepped into an elevator and punched the penthouse-level button. Her fingers were trembling, she twisted them together.

Stepping off the elevator, she saw Billy Jean Clanahan, McCready's attractive and sophisticated secretary. She expected to see pity in Billy Jean's eyes, but there was none. Instead Billy Jean greeted her with a wide grin. "Oh, good, you're here!" She lowered her voice. "He was getting so anxious in there, I thought he was going to head down and accost you in your own office! Go in, go right in!''

Cary had little choice, for Billy Jean was prodding her toward the door.

She was pushed forward, and a door closed behind her. McCready's dark head had been bent over the papers on his desk, but it rose instantly. His unfathomable green eyes were on hers, as he stood and walked around the desk, offering her his hand. ''Mrs. Adams! Thank you for coming so quickly.''

She wasn't aware that she had offered her hand in return, but his fingers were folding around hers, and she was aware of an electric tension and tremendous strength. And a startling heat.

She drew her fingers away quickly.

''Sit down, Mrs. Adams, please.'' He pulled out one of the chairs for her, and she sat, very aware of him behind her. He was always impeccable. It was a natural thing with him. And he carried that handsome, subtle scent of aftershave. She suddenly felt a warm flowing sensation cascading all the way down the length of her spine. Her fingers curled around her chair, and she caught her breath. She thought that she would leap up and scream, except that he came in front of her and leaned on the corner of his desk, crossing his arms over his chest.

''I have a favor to ask of you,'' he told her.

She wasn't being fired. No one fired an employee this way.

She exhaled, then gasped in new air. He was staring at her curiously, and she struggled for an appearance of composure. ''A—a favor?''

''Yes. And may I add from the beginning, Mrs. Adams, that your agreement or disagreement will have no bearing whatsoever on your position here.''

He was smiling again, she thought. That secret smile of his.

She felt herself flushing, and she sat more primly in the chair, her eyes lowering despite her determination. "I didn't think—"

"Yes, you did think," he said, and she was startled when he laughed. She looked into his eyes, and she was further surprised by the light of humor in them. "You thought that I had decided to fire you because you had been sitting on Santa's lap. Taking time away from the children. For shame, Mrs. Adams."

"Mr. McCready—" She started to stand, utterly humiliated. But his hands were on her shoulders, and his laughter was surprisingly warm and pleasant, even compelling, as he pressed her into her chair. "I understand that you and Jeremy are cousins, right?"

Cary wet her very dry lips. "Yes. But if you—"

"Mrs. Adams," he said as he walked behind his desk, "do you remember the last time you were in this office?"

Of course she remembered it. She would never forget. She was surprised, however, that he had remembered it.

"Yes, Mr. McCready, I do remember," she said with grave dignity.

He was still smiling. "Well, you made a rather personal remark to me. You told me that I wasn't the only one who had lost someone."

Cary felt as if she were strangling. More than anything, she wanted to get out of his office.

"Look—" she began, standing once more. "I'm sorry, I really had no right—"

But again he was before her. "Ah, but you took the right! Mrs. Adams, will you please sit?" She wasn't going to have a chance to rise this time. Casually seated on the edge of the desk before her, he kept his hands on her shoulders. She looked at him, and to her great distress, she felt a heat like the warmth of the sun come sweeping over her. She didn't remember ever being this aware of a man. There was little help for it. His bronzed hands remained on her shoulders. The fabric of his suit was nearly close enough for her to feel the texture. And she could feel that electricity emanating from him, the leashed but still powerful energy.

"Mr. McCready—"

"You saw fit to comment on my personal life, so I think that maybe I have the right to comment on yours. You are sensitive, Mrs. Adams. Very, very touchy. I've never met anyone so defensive, so quick. Will you please relax! Your work is very good, and I admire you very much as a person."

Stunned, she stared into his eyes. "Then..."

"I'd like to borrow your son."

"My son!" she repeated.

"Just for a week. And you have every right to say no, as I explained before. But I'd look after his welfare as if he were my own."

"What are you talking about?" Cary demanded in confusion.

"I'm going on a ski trip next week. Half business, half pleasure. Angela is coming with me. She was entranced with Danny at the Christmas party."

"Oh!" Cary murmured. This had nothing to do with her job. Nothing at all.

And for once McCready was looking at her anxiously. She'd never before seen anything that even remotely resembled anxiety in his eyes.

Something did matter to McCready, even if his wife was gone. Angela mattered.

Dismay filled her. "I really am sorry—"

"It would be a wonderful experience for him. As I said,

I'd see to his safety at all times. Mrs. Adams, I'm aware that you do not particularly like me, but Angela has not been so enthused since…well, it's been a very long time. She hasn't been so excited about anything since her mother died. If you feel some bitterness for me, I implore you, think of the children.''

Cary shook her head. ''No, no! It isn't anything like that at all. It's just that—Danny is diabetic. He is very good with insulin shots himself, but he's still…he's still a little boy. And when he's away, when he becomes involved in playing, he can forget. Really, Mr. McCready, I'd love him to be with Angela, she's a beautiful child. If I could let Danny go, I would.''

She was touching him, she realized. While she had been speaking, she had let her hand cover his to emphasize her sincerity.

She jerked her hand away, and her eyes fell from his. ''I am sorry.''

He moved, first walking around behind her, then behind his desk. He sat and idly tapped a pencil against his blotter. ''If that's your real reason, there's no problem at all.''

''I beg your pardon?''

''You can come, too.''

''Oh, but I can't. Really, I can't.''

''Why not?''

''Well, I have work here—''

''You can work in New Hampshire.''

''But I may need things that are here—''

''They can be expressed or faxed.''

It was so simple for Jason McCready. Everything was always at his fingertips. Well, she wasn't.

''I'm sorry.''

''Oh,'' he murmured. ''Well, if you're involved with someone…''

"No, no, it's nothing like that!" she protested. Then she was furious with herself because she had just admitted to this man that there was no one in her life.

She stood up. "Life just isn't like that!" she exclaimed. "You don't live in the real world! No one else can just snap their fingers and have whatever they want!"

He looked at her with a slow, rueful smile curving his lips. "I do live in the real world, Mrs. Adams. I once swore to God that I would trade anything I had if Sara could just breathe, just speak, one more time. It didn't happen. I'm very aware that the world cannot always move my way. There were two reasons I pulled it all back together, Mrs. Adams. This business, for one. Almost a hundred people are dependent on it for their livelihoods. And I held it together for my daughter. I'm not doing anything terrible here. I'm asking you and your son on a week's skiing trip, and you might just forget yourself long enough to allow the both of you to enjoy it!"

Cary didn't know what was disturbing her so much. She leaped to her feet. "I'm sorry!" she snapped again.

And then she spun and hurried out of the office as fast as she could.

June was eagerly awaiting her downstairs, but Cary couldn't talk to June. She rushed past, shaking her head and casting her friend a look that promised she would explain later.

"Were you fired?" June called as Cary hurried by.

"No!" Cary said. She closed the door to her office and leaned against it, looking at her hands. They were shaking.

What was wrong with the idea? Jason McCready had asked her and Danny on a nice trip. She should be grateful and go. Skiing in New Hampshire. It would be beautiful. The snow would be all over the ground. The lodges would all be decked out in their Christmas finery.

She closed her eyes. She knew why she had said no. She didn't want to be somewhere like a beautifully decorated ski lodge. Not with Jason McCready.

Because she found him way too interesting. She had liked him better when he had been entirely cold and distant. She didn't like seeing into any part of his personality.

She was becoming more and more aware...

Of him as a man.

The phone on her desk starting ringing. She walked over and picked it up.

"Cary Adams here."

"Please?"

The voice was low, deep and very rich. And she was startled when she felt a smile curve her lips.

"It's just not possible. I'm sure that it's very crowded this time of year. I'll never be able to get accommodations—"

"Yes, you will."

"It can't be that easy—"

"Yes, it can."

"But—"

"Mrs. Adams," he murmured wearily, "I own the lodge."

"Oh," Cary replied softly.

"Well?"

"I..." She hesitated again. There seemed to be every reason in the world for her to go. Danny would be delighted. And she would please Angela McCready, and Angela seemed like such a sweet little girl. There was no reason at all that she shouldn't go.

Yes, there was. McCready himself.

He hadn't made any illicit overtures toward her, she reminded herself dryly. He hadn't made any overtures at all.

Still, there was something...

"Mrs. Adams?"

"All right. All right, we'll come."

"I'll pick you up at your house on Sunday morning. Nine o'clock. Is that all right?"

Her palm was damp, Cary realized. "Yes," she said. Sunday morning.

What had she done?

Sunday morning came, and Cary waited anxiously for nine o'clock to come. How did Jason McCready travel? Would he pick her up with an entourage? In a limo? Maybe a Mercedes. No. A Rolls.

"You all right, Mom?"

She was looking out the apartment window, and she would have been chewing her nails if she hadn't already donned her gloves. Bless Danny. He thought it was the most natural thing in the world that her boss should have invited them on a ski weekend. Oh, the innocence of children!

But then, she had been the only one to see anything at all wrong. June had been ecstatic. "He likes you, kid, he really likes you!" And then, in the middle of Cary's office, she had loudly said "Hmm! He's definitely tall, dark and handsome!"

"And a recluse. And deeply in love with his deceased wife," Cary had remarked flatly.

"Well, look at that, will you? You're deeply in love with your deceased husband, he's deeply in love with his deceased wife. What a couple."

"We're not a couple at all. I'm certain he'll have a date up there for...well, for some function. I'm just going as...as..."

"The nanny?" June had suggested drolly.

"Right. The nanny," Cary had agreed sweetly, making a face.

"Well, we did order tall, dark and handsome for Christmas. And he's rich, too."

"*We* didn't order tall, dark and handsome. *You* did," Cary had reminded her.

"That's right. According to Jeremy, all we needed to find for you is someone who doesn't wear his boxer shorts pulled up over his belt."

"Would you get out of here, please?" Cary had moaned.

"Hmm," June had speculated again. And Cary had thrown her out of her office as nicely as she could.

But now that the time was coming nearer and nearer, Cary was nervous. She might have been invited because of Danny, but Jason McCready had never suggested that she was along to play nanny for the children.

But then, she wasn't one of his real guests, either. So where did that leave her? And why did she care so much?

She leaned her forehead against the windowpane and felt the searing cold come through. Her stomach was in knots, she was so nervous.

Too sensitive. And defensive. She had to relax. Well, she would try.

A Jeep Wagoneer pulled up to the curb as she stared out the window. Her eyes widened when she saw the very tall figure of Jason McCready slide from the driver's seat.

He was in blue jeans and a leather jacket, hatless despite the cold. He looked up and managed to find her face right there in the window. His dark hair was out of order, lifted by the wind, falling over his forehead, and his eyes were very bright. Instinctively, Cary wanted to withdraw. But he had seen her, and he was smiling. Then he waved, and her heart turned another little somersault, because she suddenly realized just how attractive a man he was.

She smiled. So much for the Rolls, the limo or the Lincoln. He'd come in a Jeep.

"He's here!" Danny shrieked delightedly.

"Yes, yes, he's here. Grab your bags, Danny. And don't scream quite so loudly, or we won't last the first day!" she advised him. But Danny wasn't chastised. He cast her a lopsided grin, his eyes alight with pleasure. He scooped up his duffel bag and headed for the apartment door, casting it open just as Jason McCready appeared before it.

"Well, I was about to ask if you were ready or not, but it appears that you are," he told Danny.

"Yes, sir! Thank you, sir! I'm ready. This is great! Just great. Did I say thank you?"

Jason McCready seemed pleasantly amused. "Yes, you did. And I thank you for coming. Angela is very excited. She's in the car. Want to take your things and run on down? I'll get your mom's bag."

Danny ran out, and Cary found herself face-to-face with Jason McCready. She moistened her lips, alarmed that she was so nervous.

It seemed that she stood there forever, feeling those green eyes touch down on hers. And despite the cold of the day, she felt a warmth creeping swiftly through her.

"Is that your only bag?" he asked.

"What? Oh, yes, that's it, thank you," she murmured.

He collected her bag. As he did so, his eyes swept the apartment.

She loved antiques, and they fit well with her building, a three-storied federal brick that had been built in the early eighteen hundreds. The parlor was a compilation of Edwardian and Victorian pieces she had lovingly stripped and stained and polished herself. A braided rug covered the floor before the fireplace, and a deep old leather sofa was covered with an afghan. Little copper pots and other bric-

a-brac decorated the buffets and cabinets. Blue and white
Dutch patterned draperies hung at the windows. It wasn't
contemporary; it probably wasn't in the least what Jason
McCready was accustomed to. But it was a warm and very
inviting room.

He didn't comment on it, only said, "Ready?"

"Yes."

He smiled. "You're not going off into a den of lions,
you know."

She arched a brow and stiffened. Jason McCready's
smile deepened. There was no way, of course, that she
could know that he was thinking that the spines of his little
porcupine were already bristling away.

Cary hurried through the door.

She also didn't realize that, as she brushed by him, he
breathed in the clean scent of her hair. Or that the subtle
charisma of her perfume trailed sweetly through the air.

She was just too aware herself. Of Jason McCready. Big,
so very tall in her antique doorway, his shoulders excep-
tionally broad and attractive in the leather jacket.

She would certainly have no complaints if she was dating
this man, she thought. His underwear was not pulled well
over his belt line. His belt line was perfect. All of him was
perfect.

That wasn't fair. She knew a lot of attractive men, and
she had been teasing about the underwear. It had very little
to do with looks. McCready's appeal was all in his eyes,
in the little line around them, in the richness of his voice,
in his rare smile....

And then she nearly gasped aloud. She wasn't dating
Jason McCready. She was accompanying her son on a trip
to the man's ski lodge!

With her cheeks flaming, she hurried down the stairs. By

the time she reached the streets, she thought she had regained a little of her composure.

The kids were already in back, chatting away. Angela leaped from her seat while Jason packed Cary's bag in the rear of the vehicle. She threw her slender little arms around Cary, so giving, so trusting. "Thank you! Thank you so much for coming. Daddy said you might not let Danny come along, but I knew you would. I'm so glad that you're going to be with us!"

"Thank you," Cary murmured. Jason was coming round to open her door. She stared at him, and he shrugged. She hadn't realized that he knew her well enough to warn his daughter that she might very well refuse.

The passenger door was open, and he was waiting. She slipped into the Jeep, and the door closed behind her.

Jason McCready went around and slid into the driver's seat. A plaid thermal blanket lay on the seat between them. He flashed Cary a quick smile. "It's a long drive. About three hours. Just in case you get cold."

"Thanks," she said.

There was very little traffic, even in Boston. The kids chatted away while Jason expertly steered the large vehicle through the narrow streets, past the Common and toward the turnpike.

"Do you ski?" he asked Cary. She shook her head. He shrugged. "Well, we can solve that in a week."

Her heart skipped a beat. "Really," she murmured. "You don't have to worry about entertaining me. I'm just along for Danny. I'll be all right."

She nearly jumped a mile when his arm stretched out across the seat and his fingers curved around her neck. He flashed her a very quick smile.

"Relax, Mrs. Adams! It *is* a ski lodge. It's where people

learn to ski. And you and Danny are both my guests, I'm very much hoping that you'll enjoy yourself.''

The most absurd sensation swept through her. Tears stung her eyes, and she suddenly longed with all her heart to move closer against him. To lay her head on his shoulder. To relax...to feel his fingers, warm and sure, working away the tension at her nape....

His hand fell away, and she blinked. Hard. Then she managed to smile. ''Thank you, Mr. McCready.''

''Dad's name is Jason,'' Angela suddenly volunteered from the back.

''Yes, I know,'' Cary said.

''Mom's is Cary,'' Danny offered in turn.

Jason grinned, meeting Danny's eyes in the mirror. ''I know, son, but thank you.''

''Well, if you both know,'' Angela said with exasperation, ''why do you keep up with this Mr. and Mrs. business?''

Cary, smiling, shifted in her seat to see the wide, expectant eyes of the children. ''He's my boss,'' she told Angela.

''And she's one of my employees,'' Jason explained.

''That doesn't change your name, does it?'' Danny asked innocently.

''No, it doesn't,'' Jason said. He glanced quickly at Cary. ''I can live with Cary, if you can handle Jason.''

''I think so. It's simple. Two syllables. I should be able to manage it.''

The Jeep sped along the highway. Cary realized that she had actually known Jason McCready for about three years. And now, within a period of fifteen minutes, they were suddenly on a first-name basis.

And she still felt warm. Very, very warm—despite the cold of winter....

Chapter 3

The ski lodge was beautiful.

The place looked like an alpine château, all wood and angles, with beautiful carvings. The reception area in the front boasted a huge stone and wood fireplace that was decorated with Christmas stockings and ran nearly the length of the wall. All around the fireplace were leather sofas and chairs, arranged for small and large gatherings, all offering warmth and intimacy. Hot and cold drinks were served in the area all afternoon, with mulled wines and exotic coffees the specialty for grown-ups, and hot chocolate with whipped cream and chocolate shavings the main offering for the smaller fry.

Jason McCready explained all this to Cary as they stood in the entryway together. He had pointed out the nearly twenty-foot-high Christmas tree in the lobby to Danny when a young blond man came hurrying forward to welcome them. He was anxious to please Jason McCready, Cary decided, but there was also a warmth in his eyes and a pleasure in his voice that could mean only one thing— he liked his boss.

"Mr. McCready, you're here! No bad traffic, I hope. Did the weather slow you down?"

Jason shook his head, drawing off his gloves. "No, Randy, the trip was fine. We got off the highway to take a look at the Basin." He smiled at Cary as he explained. He'd mentioned the Basin when they had stopped for pizza for lunch. It wasn't far from the lodge, just before a little town called Franconia's Notch. It was one of the most exquisite places Cary had ever seen, with falls and rivulets racing over rocks through the snow to reach an otherwise tranquil spot where the water hurtled down with a noise like thunder. A lot of the shallower water was freezing over, but Cary assumed that the place would be beautiful in any season. Thoreau had thought so, too. According to Jason, he had been a frequent visitor to the area, and some of his words were now immortalized at the spot.

The area had been exciting to see. And more so, perhaps, with Jason McCready. Because of the ice, he had kept a steady hand upon her elbow as he had led her along, the children racing ahead. He had watched her in silence as he had shown her the place, and when she had spun with pure wide-eyed pleasure, he had seemed to read her thoughts.

"It's almost like Camelot! In summer, everything is green and lush, and there are wildflowers everywhere. In fall, the colors are simply fantastic. In winter, it's a crystal palace of ice, just as you see. And spring brings the water rushing down at a greater crescendo, sweet and clean, the flowers just budding and the return of the birds..." His voice had trailed away, and he'd shrugged. They had stood gazing at each other. He hadn't seemed to need a reply, but she had never seen him so animated, nor had she imagined that he might feel so poetic about any place.

"It's wonderful. Just wonderful," she'd murmured, and

then quickly added, ''thank you for taking the time to stop for me—and Danny, of course—to see this.''

''The pleasure has been all mine, Mrs.—Cary,'' he'd said softly. Then he had turned and walked away, leaving her to follow on her own.

And she had wondered if he had come there often with his Sara, and if the place had awakened memories.

In the car he had remained quiet. And he had winced when Angela had begged him to play Christmas carols on the tape player. He had caught Cary's glance and tried to smile.

He had played the tape, just as his daughter had asked, but he hadn't joined in any of the songs.

Now, however, he was as polite and easy as could be. He turned, catching Cary's hand and drawing her over to meet the younger man. ''Randy, this is one of my top writers, Cary Adams. Cary, Randy Skylar. And this is Cary's son, Danny.''

Randy shook her hand and grinned broadly. ''Mrs. Adams, it's wonderful to have you.'' His gaze returned quickly to his employer. ''I've readied the suites in the rear, just as you asked. Would you like something sent up?''

''I'm afraid I have a meeting with the sales staff right away,'' Jason said. ''But, Cary, perhaps you and Danny would like something?''

She started to shake her head, but then she thought about the children. ''Angela, why don't you come with us to our room for a while? That way we can have Randy send us all some hot chocolate while your dad is busy.''

Angela smiled shyly. ''I'd like that. May I, Dad?''

''Well, maybe Cary and Danny should have a little time to settle in first—''

''It's fine, really,'' Cary said, interrupting him. She almost added, We're only here for Angela, but she didn't want Angela to feel that she was a burden, because she wasn't at all. "I'm not tired, and I can throw things in drawers in a matter of minutes."

Jason shrugged. "Fine, then. I'll see you all later for dinner."

He left the three of them with Randy, who escorted them to the room Jason had reserved for her and Danny.

The door to their room was certainly ordinary looking. It was a plain wooden door that opened from the balcony that ran the length of the wall above the Christmas tree. But once that door had opened...

The room was massive, yet cheerful and warm, with its own fireplace against a wall of granite. There was a white leather sofa standing on a raspberry carpet, and beyond a curving pine bar was a full kitchen that appeared to be equipped with all manner of conveniences and utensils. There were two doors leading from the main room. Cary glanced at Randy, then strode across the parlor area to the first door. Opening it, she discovered a bedroom with a huge queen-sized bed covered by a massive quilt. Even here, there was a fireplace. And to one side of the fireplace, set into a small field of white tiles, was a huge Jacuzzi.

Cary left that room behind and hurried on to the next. It was smaller, and it was missing the Jacuzzi, but it was every bit as warm and as nice.

These rooms had been designed as family getaways, she decided. The suite provided a romantic seclusion for adults, while children could be just steps away....

The lodge was his. He had probably designed it, too, Cary thought.

She walked to the main room, and she must have been frowning, because Randy was quick to question her. "Is anything wrong?"

"No, no, of course not. It's just that..." Angela was

staring at her anxiously. It's just too nice! she wanted to shout. She hadn't really been invited on this trip—Danny had been the intended guest. And now here she was. In the absolute lap of luxury and feeling very uncomfortable.

"I'm just afraid that I'm taking space from...from another guest," she finished lamely.

"Oh, but you're not!" Angela assured her. "There are two of these suites here. My dad and I have the other. See—it's through that door over there. He never rents out these rooms. Never. They're always for guests. Really. I hope you like it."

"I like it very much," Cary told Angela, but her discomfort was growing. She suddenly felt very much like the governess.

"Come, Mrs. Adams," Randy Skylar told her. "You haven't seen the half of it yet!"

He led her through the main room and pushed open French doors that led to a balcony. From there, plate glass stretched above her. Below her, swathed in mist, was an indoor pool. A swirling whirlpool sent water cascading over a rock fall into the pool.

Beyond it, the mountains and the ski slopes were visible through the plate glass. It was breathtaking.

Cary heard laughter and looked through the mist. Some guests had left the slopes to sink into the warmth of the heated pool. Children played on the steps. And a pair of lovers, perhaps the parents, laughed together, the man in the water, the woman stretched out on the tiled rim of the pool beside him.

A knot twisted in Cary's stomach, taking her unaware. Once she had been like that. She could close her eyes and remember when she and Richard and Danny had taken vacations and left their cares behind.

"Hot chocolate has arrived!" Randy announced. Cary

turned. A young woman had appeared, pushing a cart holding a silver pitcher of hot chocolate and a plate of Oreo
cookies.

"This is living!" Danny announced happily. Then he
looked at his mother, remembering that he needed to be
very careful with Oreos—their sugar was high, and that was
bad for his diabetes. "Can I have some?"

"Yes, of course. A few," she told him, smiling. She
made a mental note to test his blood sugar level and give
him his insulin as soon as they were alone. They had a
small machine to do the testing, and he was accustomed to
receiving his insulin three times a day. Even at his age, he
knew how to do it himself, and Cary was proud of him for
that, but he was still young, and she liked to be there to
oversee things.

But right now, she decided, he could have a few Oreos.

Cary smiled at the children. Danny was still watching
her. "Why don't you two dig in, and then get into your
suits? We'll swim and shower and change, and maybe then
your father will be ready to join you again, Angela."

Angela, delicate and pristine even with an Oreo in her
hand, gave Cary a beautiful smile. "Oh, he will be. He's
always on time, and he never lies."

"Well, how commendable," Cary murmured. She of-
fered the two another smile, thanked the maid and Randy
Skylar, then disappeared into the master bedroom. As
Danny had said, this was living.

She just couldn't accept this kind of hospitality. It was
too much.

She stretched out on the bed and closed her eyes. It
would have been so nice if she could have come to such a
place with Richard.

In her mind's eye she saw the pool and the snow-covered
mountains beyond the glass. She saw a fire burning, and

she saw herself, her head resting against the shoulder of a dark-haired man.

She bolted up, setting her hands against her flushed cheeks.

Richard had been blond. As light as Danny. The dark head in her daydreams had belonged to another man.

Jason McCready.

She groaned softly and buried her head in her pillow. And she didn't rise until Danny came in to tell her that their luggage had been brought up, so they could change for the pool.

After their swim, Angela went through the connecting door to the suite she shared with her father to change. An hour later she knocked at the connecting door and Cary let her in.

"Has anyone ever told you that you are really beautiful, Miss McCready?" Cary asked her, smiling.

Angela blushed, her cheeks as rosy as her red velvet dress. "Do you really think so?"

"Indeed I do."

"You're very beautiful, too."

"Thank you."

"I told my father that."

"Oh," Cary murmured.

"Yes, she did, but it wasn't at all necessary," came a rich male voice over Angela's shoulder.

Jason was freshly showered and shaved, his hair was still damp, and he was very handsome in a black dinner jacket and red vest. Cary, uncertain of how to dress, had chosen a soft white knit that gently molded her body until it flared slightly into a wider skirt just below the knees. Only the back was low and in the least daring, and she had hoped that her choice would suffice whether she found herself in casual or dressy surroundings.

"I already knew how beautiful you are, Mrs. Adams," Jason assured her.

She felt a flush rising to her cheeks, as red as the color that stained Angela's fair face. But she wasn't young, she told herself. And she wasn't the least bit innocent. She had to acquire a backbone where this man was concerned.

"Thank you. May I return the compliment?"

"You think Dad's beautiful?" Angela inquired, giggling.

"You mean he's not?" Cary said lightly.

"Oh, no!" Angela told her gravely. "He's handsome. Very, very handsome."

Tall, dark and handsome! an inner voice taunted Cary. Ah, but tall, dark and handsome had been June's order for Christmas. Cary had just wanted a man who didn't pull his boxer shorts up to his earlobes.

No. She hadn't wanted a man at all. Jeremy was the one who had wished that upon her. Jeremy and his darned Christmas dust!

"Well, we've got reservations at a place up by one of the other slopes," Jason said. "Not that the restaurant here isn't marvelous—it is. But the week may grow hectic, and you may eat here frequently, so I thought I should get you out while I could. Is that all right?"

"Certainly. It's very thoughtful," Cary told him. "But you really don't have to worry about Danny or me—"

"Tsk, tsk, Mrs. Adams. I realize that I don't *have* to worry. I *choose* to worry. May I?"

There was that smile again. One that was open and honest. The smile that made her feel warm. That made candlelight seem to dance and flicker down the length of her.

Cary nodded, consenting as graciously as she could.

Dinner was wonderful. The owners of the restaurant had

managed to combine moose and elk and deer heads on very rustic walls with a certain amount of elegance. Cary had her first beefalo steak, and a delicious salad. Conversation with Jason McCready was proving to be easy and natural, and throughout the meal she was surprised by the range of topics they covered, from the best qualities for grammar school teachers to the situation in the Middle East. And with Angela and Danny there, Cary also found herself laughing through the meal as Danny described the very best way to spit on a ball to give it a fast curve, and Angela sang camp songs that might have repelled a hungry bear. So much for elegance.

When they left the restaurant, it was late. The children were barely in the car before Cary turned and realized they were fast asleep, one slumped on the other.

Jason was silent for a while, and Cary felt her eyes flickering shut. Then Jason suddenly spoke.

"The kids are out?"

"Fast asleep," she assured him.

"I just wanted to say thanks. Thanks very much for coming."

"Thank *you.* The suite is beautiful. Too beautiful. I think I would have been happier with something, er, smaller."

She saw the slow curve of his smile. "Mrs. Adams, you are worth it."

"Well, thank you," Cary murmured. He didn't reply. The motion of the car as it sped through the night mixed with the warmth of its heater, and her eyes kept closing. Then they closed one final time and she couldn't quite get them open.

It startled him when her head fell on his shoulder. Jason almost jumped, but he managed to hold still. The soft, sweet scent of her hair teased his nose, and for a moment he held his breath.

A poignant anguish stole slowly over him, seeming to seep into him like water over porous rock.

It had been so long....

Sara had fallen asleep on him like that.

He'd been out a number of times since her death. And though he was certain that he'd always been courteous, he knew, too, that he'd always been distant, and he'd seldom seen any woman more than once. According to a number of tabloids, he'd become a very eligible bachelor, but in his heart, he knew he would never be that. He couldn't retain his interest in anyone; he couldn't look at beauty with more than a casual eye. He hadn't really dated; he'd had arrangements, and that had been that. Strange, because he had been intimate with some of those women, but...

He'd never come so close that one of them might fall asleep on his shoulder.

And Cary was certainly the only woman he would allow to be there.

He didn't know why. He did know that he hadn't thanked her just for Angela. He had thanked her for himself, as well. It had been years since he had really laughed. Years since he had been anxious for a day to end so that he might see someone—other than Angela—again.

Her hair brushed his chin. Soft and satiny, so warm with its rich brown depths. Like silk, it teased over his flesh. His fingers tightened on the wheel, and he clenched his jaw as he felt sudden, volatile stirrings of desire rise hard within him. His initial anguish had faded away. The present—and this woman—held all his attention. He couldn't remember wanting anyone quite this way. It was ironic.

She was probably the one woman who would not want him.

She made a soft sound in her sleep as she curved against the warmth of his body more comfortably. Her fingers curled over his shoulder. And then her hand slipped and fell to his thigh.

He clamped down on his jaw even harder.

Cary awoke when the car jerked to a halt. Almost instantly, she was sitting upright, wondering how she had been sleeping.

But Jason McCready was already out of the car, and she didn't know whether to apologize or not.

"This is it," he said curtly. "We're here." For once on this trip, he wasn't being terribly polite.

"Yes. I'll, uh, I'll just get Danny."

"I'll get Danny. He's a lot heavier than my daughter. You carry Angela. If you think you can."

"Well, of course I can—"

"I meant that you're so tired yourself. And hell, you're not a lot bigger than either of them."

"I can manage," Cary said irritably.

"Yes, yes, you can manage." Jason quickly had Danny in his arms. She bent down for Angela, and his next words seemed to slap her right in the face. "Have I ever told you that you remind me of a porcupine at times?"

With her young burden in her arms, Cary stiffened and swung around. "What a lovely comparison. Thank you so much, Mr. McCready."

"I didn't say that you looked like a porcupine, Mrs. Adams. You're a very beautiful woman, and you must know that. Even though your husband hasn't been around for a long time to tell you, I'm sure that other men have. Or maybe not. With those porcupine bristles of yours, maybe no one has managed to get close enough."

"Thank you again. You do have my life right down to a tee, Mr. McCready. And with all the women you date! Don't you dare judge me!"

Cary delivered the last statement with her nose in the air, then turned quickly on her heel and headed for the lodge.

He was right behind her. "All the women I date?" he inquired.

"Ah, yes, if it's Tuesday, it must be a redhead," Cary said sweetly as they reached the door to the lodge.

"I didn't know you had been paying so much attention to my dating habits," Jason said.

Cary wasn't able to reply. Randy Skylar was there to open the door for them. "Let me take her," he offered Cary, and without giving her a chance to refuse, he swept Angela into his arms. Cary followed the two men up the stairs to the suites, forcing a smile to answer Randy's polite questions about their dinner.

Jason laid Danny on his bed. Randy had taken Angela into Jason's suite, so Cary and Jason were left alone to stare at one another, the sprawled and comfortable body of Cary's son between them.

"Good night, Mrs. Adams," Jason said softly.

"Good night," Cary murmured. "Thank you for dinner. It was lovely."

His slow, rueful smile curved his lips. "Yes, it actually was." Then he brushed by her and left. And, oddly, Cary could feel the entire length of her side where he had touched her so lightly and so briefly. It was so much warmer than the other side....

Funny, she had been so tired. But even after she had tucked Danny in and changed into a comfortable flannel gown, she couldn't sleep at all.

She pulled the pillow over her head, gritted her teeth and willed sleep to come. But for the longest time it didn't.

She kept feeling the warmth of her side and wondering how closely she had leaned against Jason McCready when sleep had come so easily in his car.

* * *

There was a note beneath her door in the morning. It was handwritten, and she recognized Jason's handwriting from the Christmas cards she had received over the last few years. It was a broad, large script, very legible, and somehow like the man, firm and powerful. The message was brief but courteous. He was tied up for the day, but she mustn't feel that she needed to tend only to the children. There were programs for them all morning, movies, lessons on the bunny slopes, whatever. She was welcome to spend her day however she chose, and she shouldn't worry. His staff were wonderful with children.

Cary didn't mind spending her time with the children, but she did have an article she wanted to edit, and with a magazine's deadlines, time could be very precious. She decided to have breakfast with the kids, then work for a while, then go down to the bunny slopes with them.

The day worked out as she had planned it. They breakfasted in her suite; then Angela and Danny traipsed off to see cartoons. Cary started to work in front of the main fireplace in the suite. She wondered if she would be able to concentrate, but to her great pleasure, she found that the comfort of the lodge and the snap and crackle of the fire were definite pluses. She didn't dig her nose out of her manuscript until two o'clock, when she had accomplished everything she had wanted.

Pleased, she dressed in her own best rendition of a ski outfit—clinging knit pants, a warm wool sweater and a windbreaker—and went in search of the children. They were just finishing lunch, and both were pleased that she was going to join them on the bunny slopes.

"I don't ski," Cary told Angela. "That puts me on the bunny slope with you and Danny. Except that I'll bet that you can ski."

Angela could ski. Beautifully. But she spent the afternoon with Cary and Danny and the young ski instructor, laughing delightedly as Cary and Danny struggled with the equipment and a new sense of balance. Cary, overwhelmed at first by the heavy boots, the skis and all the safety tips she was being given, swore she would never be able to manage. But by early evening she was delighted. She was managing the slopes. She was skiing! And she was thrilled with the rush of pleasure and exhilaration that negotiating the small slopes brought her.

She was also cold. She and Danny and Angela headed into the lodge. The children had hot chocolate; she decided on an Irish coffee. It was very good, but since she hadn't bothered with lunch, the hot drink seemed to hit her like lead.

She and the children decided to have dinner in the suite. And by the time they finished with the delicious linguine, the kids seemed willing enough to go to bed. Angela slipped through the door into her own suite. Cary hesitated, told Danny to get ready for bed and followed Angela into Jason McCready's private quarters.

His suite was obviously never rented out. It had the same view of the pool, the same handsome pine walls and deep plush carpeting. There was more of a feeling of home to his rooms. There were beautiful mountain prints on the walls, and a cabinet filled with curious sculptures and knickknacks. A handsome oak secretary was covered with papers, and on a coffee table before the sofa were several issues of *Elegance* and other magazines. On a side table was a picture frame. It contained the perfect family photo. Jason McCready surrounded by the two women he loved, a much younger Angela and Sara, both with their beautiful blue eyes and angelic halos of soft blond hair.

Cary suddenly felt as if she was intruding, and she almost backed away. But Jason McCready had never given her any decrees about not entering his private domain, so she hurried through the living room to tap at one of the bedroom doors. "Angela?"

"Cary? Come in."

Angela was already in her red flannel nightdress, her hair flowing down her back, her eyes wide and bright. Looking at her, Cary felt a peculiar rush of emotion, her heart tearing for Sara McCready. She's so beautiful, Sara! Cary thought. If only you could see her!

"I just came to…to see if you wanted to be tucked in," Cary told her.

Angela's eyes widened. "Yes, please. Thank you very much."

So Cary tucked her in, kissed her on the forehead and promised to see her bright and early the next morning. She went to her suite and tucked Danny in, then changed into her flannel gown. But once again, as exhausted as she should have been, she couldn't sleep. She got out of bed, made herself a cup of tea and wandered to the balcony overlooking the pool and the mountains beyond.

To her surprise, there was activity by the pool. She first recognized Barney Mulray, a salesman from Ohio whom she had met at a convention. Then she realized that the pool was full of *Elegance* salespeople.

And at the far end was Jason McCready.

To Cary's growing dismay, her first thought was that he looked wonderful in a bathing suit. He was bronzed, lean and very well muscled. His chest was covered by a handsome and provocative mat of dark hair. And from the breadth of his shoulders to the clean, lean line of his hips to the powerful thighs below his black bathing suit, he was perfectly formed.

Someone else thought so, too. There was a little young redhead, with a chest that didn't quit, sitting near him. She was talking to him, and Jason was responding. But then Barney called to him across the pool, and Jason was just as quick to respond to Barney. Cary leaned a little over the balcony, trying to hear their words.

"Come on, time for a drink," Barney encouraged.

Jason shook his head. "No, thanks. I'm about to head up to my room. I want to check on Angela."

Other encouragements were called to Jason, who shook his head. The people began to trail out of the pool. All but the redhead. She leaned closer to Jason—with that chest that wouldn't quit.

"Really, Jason. Just one drink. Come on. It's early."

"Trudy, thanks," he said, his voice firm. "But I'm tired. I'd like to be alone now, please."

Not even Trudy would dare to argue with such a tone, it seemed. She rose with a shrug and moved off with the others.

The pool area was suddenly very silent. Only Jason remained at the far end, his eyes closed. Again Cary felt as if she was intruding. Well, she *had* been intruding, eavesdropping. She started to move away, but right then his eyes flew open. Right to her.

"Ah, Mrs. Adams!" he called softly.

"Hello," she called back uncomfortably.

He smiled. Just like the cat who had caught the canary. "Did you have a nice day?"

"Yes, lovely, thank you."

"The kids?"

"They're fine. They're sleeping."

"Angela?"

"She's fine. I...I tucked her in."

His eyes widened a bit, she thought, but she didn't know with what emotion—pleasure that she would do so, or annoyance that she would presume to come so close.

"But you're wide-awake, I see," he commented.

"Yes, well, I was going in—"

"Don't. Come down," he commanded suddenly.

Cary hesitated. She should go to bed. She shouldn't go down to him. She felt as if little rivers of water were already dancing down her spine.

This was when memory usually kicked in. When she would remember Richard's smile, his laugh, when she would feel so cold and empty...

But this time she didn't see Richard's face before her. She was caught by the powerful, handsome face of the man in the pool below.

"I just heard you say that you wanted to be alone," Cary murmured.

"Did you?"

Cary flushed. "Yes," she admitted.

"Well, I did want to be alone—then. But I would very much appreciate your company now. Please, come down. The water is wickedly warm."

Much, much more than the water was wickedly warm, Cary was certain.

But suddenly she ached for a taste of that warmth. Just a taste. Jason McCready never offered anything more. And she could never take anything more.

But tonight...

Indeed, the wicked warmth seemed to sweep right up and curl around her. She moistened her lips, still hesitating.

"Cary?"

"I'll be right down," she promised.

And to her amazement, she got quickly into her suit and made her way to the pool. To the warmth.

Chapter 4

By the time she reached the pool, Cary was wondering why she had come. Jason McCready was no longer at the end of the pool, and she felt rather foolish standing there, looking around for him.

"In here, Mrs.—Cary."

He'd moved to the Jacuzzi. And he'd watched her arrive. For some reason, that disturbed her.

And there was more to disturb her. There was a tray by his side as he slowly leaned back in the hot swirling water with his eyes on her. There were two glasses of champagne on the tray, and a dish of bite-sized cheeses and shrimp and crackers.

Cary stiffened and tightened the belt on her terry swim robe. But then she heard his husky laughter, and her flesh warmed. "Your quills are bristling, Mrs. Adams."

"Are they?" she said, looking disapprovingly at the champagne. "Was this for my benefit?"

"It was."

"Well, you shouldn't have."

"Why not?"

She waved an arm to indicate nothing—and everything. "Because it's just too...practiced. As if you were going to..."

"Going to what?" He picked up one of the champagne glasses and took a sip.

"If you don't know—"

"If you're assuming that I intend to seduce you, don't you think you're being just a little presumptuous?"

"Oh, my Lord, this whole trip was a mistake. I just knew it—" Cary began, turning, intending to walk quickly away.

But she didn't quite manage it. Jason McCready was out of the Jacuzzi and standing before her, dripping wet, very masculine—and entirely imposing.

"It was a mistake because Danny is having such a miserable time?" he demanded. "Or is it a mistake because you're suddenly afraid of me? Why, I wonder? I'd admired you because you seemed to be the one person who wasn't afraid to say what she was really thinking."

"I'm not afraid of you!" Cary snapped quickly.

"Then?"

"Then...why did you invite me down?" she blurted.

He smiled. And there was a gentle humor in his eyes. "I like you. You're my guest here. I've been dealing with business all day, and you've been with our children. I thought it might be nice to talk. And, since it's late and it might also be nice to unwind, I ordered champagne and a snack. I thought you might enjoy it. And you just might, you know, if you let yourself."

She wasn't sure exactly why she felt like such a fool. Maybe she really had been presuming too much. Maybe he didn't find her attractive in the least.

Most probably he was simply stating the truth. And she had been acting like a porcupine.

Her fingers were still knotted over the belt to her robe.

Her lashes fell over her eyes. "Is there cocktail sauce for the shrimp?"

"Yes."

"Well, all right, then."

She couldn't quite meet his gaze, so she turned, slipped off the robe and stepped into the Jacuzzi. The steaming heat was wonderful. It seemed to reach into all her muscles and smooth away her tension. Jason McCready stepped in, keeping his distance, sitting across from her. He offered her a glass of champagne. She thanked him, and he leaned back, sipping his own.

"How was your day?" he asked her.

"Great," she said. She told him how the three of them had spent their time. He asked her questions all the while, and it was more the tone of his voice than the warmth of the water that relaxed her. Before she knew it, she was leaning closer and closer. She had consumed half the shrimp, while he had politely preferred the cheese.

And she had allowed him to refill her champagne glass twice.

But when she had finished recounting the day, there was a sudden silence. Jason was leaning back, his head resting on the rim of the Jacuzzi, his eyes half closed.

"Did you...did you design this place?" she asked him.

His eyes opened slightly. They seemed to cast a searing heat as they swept over her. "Yes."

"I thought so. It's so well planned—" She broke off, willing herself not to flush, because he was staring at her so hard. "You designed it for Sara," she heard herself say.

He shrugged. "Yes."

"Then it must bring back painful memories for you."

He shook his head. "My memories aren't painful. And what difference does it make? According to you, I'm a dating machine."

"Well, it's foolish," she told him.

He shrugged again. "It's better than what you do."

"And what do I do?"

"Start off with your quills bristling."

"I don't—"

"Did you know that I'm fairly good friends with your cousin Jeremy? Second cousin, actually, isn't it?"

Cary inhaled and gritted her teeth. Jeremy! What had he been saying about her?

"He says that you've gone out three times in three years. And that each time you acted like an ice princess."

"An ice princess!"

"Yes, an ice princess. And that you never had any intention of enjoying yourself. At least I try."

"I try, too," Cary protested.

He sipped more champagne, watching her. Now he didn't look so much like the cat who had eaten the canary. His eyes were still lazy, half closed, but very green as he stared at her.

"Would you quit that!" she snapped.

"Quit what?"

"Well, I may remind you of a porcupine, but at this moment you very much remind me of a crocodile. So laid back and ready to snap my head off at any moment."

He laughed and leaned toward her. "I'm not going to bite your head off."

He was close to her. Very close. She could see the water beading on his shoulders and chest, and she was very tempted to touch one of those little beads. She was even tempted to move closer, to taste one of those little drops of water, to put the tip of her tongue against his flesh.

"The...the life you're living is very wrong," she told him primly. She couldn't draw her eyes from the water...or from his chest. Think! she warned herself. Remember.

"Is it?"

She heard his whisper, and then she knew that they were even closer. She felt his thumb and forefinger stroking her cheek, lifting her chin. And then she felt his lips on hers.

The rushing warmth of the water seemed to sweep through her like a fever, to touch her mouth, her body, her soul, with the same sweet fever. She had never imagined kissing any man besides Richard.

She couldn't imagine not feeling the touch of this man....

He did not seduce; he did not coerce. He gave so much with the hungry pressure of his lips. They molded to hers; they brought a fantastic warmth, a burst of emotions and sensations to fruition within her.

Maybe she had always known that he would kiss like this. With no hesitation, with a sheer provocative mastery. Maybe she had known that his tongue would move, hauntingly, drawing sensual patterns over her lips, delving between them, seeking the deepest recesses of her mouth, bringing a surge of sweet desire, latent so long, rushing like a cascade of wild water through her.

A sound escaped her, soft, like a moan. A sound of pleasure. Perhaps even a sound of desire. She could never accuse him of seducing her. His first touch had been so light. Even that kiss had provided every opportunity for escape. Perhaps at that point it was she who seduced him. For it was her arms that were the first to curl around his neck. It was she who floated against him as the swirling hot waters of the Jacuzzi lent them aid, seeming to fit their bodies so closely together.

He kissed her again. And again. His fingers traveled down her back, stroking her flesh, her form. She pressed against his muscled body, torn by memory, awakened by it. She was never anything but aware that he was a different man, a very different man, from the one she had married, the one she had loved. But for once her senses were swept away. She wanted this man, and the sensations were so acute and demanding that she didn't want to care about anything else.

She was in his arms, on his lap, yearning for more and more of his touch. His lips rose a fraction of an inch above hers, and he whispered softly, "I think we're both relaxed at last."

"It's the Jacuzzi."

"No, because not all my muscles are at ease," he told her.

Her eyes widened, and she might have been awakened to exactly what she was doing. But he kissed her again as his fingers caressed her cheek, her chin, her collarbone, and his arms tightened around her. The hot whirl of the water was not something outside her anymore, but something that was a part of her.

His lips rose from hers again. "We can't stay here."

"No," she whispered.

"I want this to go on." Again he offered her every escape.

"I know."

"Is it the champagne?"

"It helps, I'm sure," Cary admitted.

She felt him stiffen. He would walk away now, if she chose. But she didn't choose. She moistened her lips and tightened her arms around him. "Please..." she murmured.

He didn't make her say more. They stepped from the Jacuzzi and walked across the pool area to a door that led to a private stairway. It led, she realized, from the pool area straight to his bedroom.

One light was on. It cast a soft, dim glow over the black comforter that covered the large bed, the mountain prints on the wall, the black and brass and glass of the furniture.

Cary saw very little of it, for she kept her gaze on Jason McCready, on the green eyes that remained locked with hers. She shivered suddenly, violently, for despite the heat indoors, she had come wet from the Jacuzzi into the air, and now her flesh was chilled. Not for long. For when he had laid her down, he covered her with the warmth of his own form. His kiss seared her with heat again, and his caress became a touch of fire.

Once more, his gaze caught hers, and he offered her a last escape. "Will you stay?"

She wanted to speak, but she couldn't. She nodded, closed her eyes and wound her arms around him, burying her face against him.

"Open your eyes," he commanded her, drawing her away. And she did so, meeting his gaze. "Tell me that you want me. Say my name."

"I want you."

"My name."

"Mr. McCready."

"My first name!" He laughed, and she smiled.

She managed to whisper, "Jason. I want you, Jason."

Then he asked nothing more of her, and the magic began.

He touched her...just where she longed to be touched.

And he kissed her...just where she longed to be kissed.

Fires rose in the night, the flames sending little licks of sensation to tease and torment and bring sweet pleasure to her. She saw his eyes in the dim magical glow of the night. And she saw his hands, so bronze, so large, so masculine and wonderful, against the pale hue of her own flesh.

And she kissed him. Touched the bare skin of his shoulder with the tip of her tongue, just as she had dreamed of doing.

It had been so long. So achingly long...

And what he offered her was good. So beautifully, perfectly good.

For he made love. He took nothing that he didn't give. He demanded; he shared; he held her; he caressed her. He touched her…so tenderly. And so passionately.

Almost as if he could love her.

And when the sweet whirl of heat and fever rose from pitch to pitch, when the cascade of need and hunger and wanting came swirling to a peak, it burst upon them both with a volatile climax.

The sensations were so strong, so sweet, that Cary's world went black. And when the light came again, she was still trembling, still drifting. Held in his arms, she shook time and time again with the aftermath of pleasure.

And shock.

It wasn't that she was suddenly horrified by what she had done. She had done it with her eyes wide open.

But she had done it without thinking. And though she still lay in his arms with the soft glow of the night a sweet shield around them, the garish rays of daylight would come streaking down upon her tomorrow, and she would have the future to live with.

She bit her lip, thinking that her suit was lying by the bed. Was there any way to slip into it without feeling awkward? Should she say thank you very much what a wonderful time and try to slip casually to her own room?

Good God, how could she ever go to work again? She had to quit! Unless he fired her. No—it was getting so close to Christmas. She couldn't quit. Danny wanted a computer.

She was thinking about a computer at a time like this?

She started to move, but his hold on her tightened. ''I— I have to go back,'' she said in near panic. ''Danny will be waking—''

"At one in the morning?" he said. Those eyes of his were on her again. And he was smiling.

"I have to go back," she said stubbornly.

He kissed her lips. Then he moved away, rising on one elbow. He watched while she donned her suit, then comfortably slipped into his own. "I'll walk you down for your robe and back to your room."

"You don't have to."

"I said I'll walk you back."

Cary's suit was still soaked, so cold after the warmth they had shared! As she hurried for the door to the stairway, she brushed by the bedside table, looking down as she struck it with her thigh.

And she stared at the picture. The picture of Sara McCready. Smiling so beautifully.

Oh, God. But Jason didn't seem to notice. He moved past her, opening the door, then starting down ahead of her. He found her robe by the pool and set it around her shoulders, then smiled. "You're shivering."

"I'm cold."

"You could have stayed warmly by my side."

"We both have children."

"We had more time."

"No." She shook her head, backing away from him.

"Cary, if you regret anything—"

"No, I don't regret anything. It was wonderful. You know that. I mean..." Oh, she wasn't good at this; she wasn't good at all. She might as well be honest. "It was my first time since...Richard. And maybe I will be able to start seeing people again now. Thank you. But I need to be alone."

"Cary—"

"I have to go!"

"Wait!" he said demandingly.

Why was she feeling such a swift rise of panic and handling things so poorly? "I have to go! And I don't care
what my leaving means. Even if you fire me!"

His jaw went very square. "Cary! I'm not firing you!"

The panic left her suddenly. But she still needed to escape. "So I don't have to clean out my desk," she murmured. She wanted to laugh, wanted to cry. She wanted to
throw herself against him all over again.

But most of all she wanted to be alone. Alone to deal
with the sudden anguish that seized her now. She couldn't
let him walk her back. She turned and ran from the pool
to the steps that led to the balcony, then back to her own
room.

She spent the morning desperately trying to feel and act
normally.

She must have done a better job than she had expected,
because neither Danny nor Angela seemed to notice anything amiss. Cary didn't know where Jason was; she hadn't
gotten a note from him, and he didn't appear at the table
when they went down for breakfast.

To Cary's dismay, he did appear at the bunny slopes that
afternoon. And although he had a meeting scheduled, he
just brought the meeting to the bunny slopes with him. Cary
recognized a number of the sales staff. They had looked a
little dazed at the locale he'd chosen, but nobody was about
to say anything.

Cary thought the whole thing was ridiculous. Especially
when she skied down the little slope and, despite her very
best efforts and determination, ended up on her hind end
in the snow. Jason was there, smooth and sleek and infu-
riatingly comfortable on his skis, to assist her. "We're going to talk tonight," he told her briefly.

"No! The children—"

''The children are going to the lodge's kids' dinner club. They're going to have hot dogs and play games and pop popcorn to string on the tree. And they're going to sing Christmas carols and make Christmas gifts and have a great time. It is the Christmas Season! Have a little spirit!'' he told her. ''Be ready at six.'' By then he had her on her feet and was gliding away.

She couldn't begin to move so quickly. She could hardly move at all.

''Be ready for what?'' she demanded.

But Jason McCready either didn't hear her or didn't intend to answer.

Danny left early for the kids' dinner club. That gave Cary time to bathe and dress carefully. She didn't know where she was going, so she chose a black velvet dress that she hoped was both concealing and elegant. She wasn't going to run away tonight. She was just going to explain that they couldn't go any further. Because...

Because she needed her job. And she couldn't bear for things to be awkward.

And because she didn't want to be one of his long string of women.

And that was the real rub, she admitted, seeing her features pale in the mirror as she slipped on her little pearl earrings.

Why? What did it matter? she asked herself. He was good for her. He would open up the world that she had closed away, and then she could go on.

No. She couldn't.

Because she cared about him, she admitted. Because he had fascinated her from the start. Because no one else could draw the things from her that he had drawn so easily. No one else could make her forget Richard.

She hadn't forgotten Richard.

Yes, she had. For those precious moments in Jason's arms, she had forgotten.

She closed her eyes. He had made her say his name. But he had never spoken hers.

There was a knock on the door to the suite. Cary grabbed her coat and hurried out. She didn't want him coming into her room.

His room, really. The whole lodge was his.

She was breathless when she threw the door open and saw him. His eyes were bright. He was still angry, she thought.

And in jeans and a leather jacket, he was far more casually dressed than she was.

"Oh! I'll change," she murmured.

"No, it doesn't matter. It doesn't matter at all. Not where we're going. Come on."

"Where *are* we going?" Cary demanded.

He could move so quickly when he was in a hurry. He had her by her elbow, and he hadn't answered her question. In front of the lodge there were too many people around, all greeting Jason and nodding to her, for her to say anything. But finally they were in the Jeep, and she repeated her question. "Where are we going?"

"There." He pointed to a structure just up the hill. Cary sighed. For a man who wanted to talk, he was extremely untalkative.

And she still had no idea where they were going.

The ride was too short, and yet it was also interminable. As soon as they entered the wooden building on the hill, she realized it was a private château, and that someone had readied it for their arrival. A fire was burning in the grate, and a delicious aroma was wafting from chafing dishes on the rustic table.

Jason removed his jacket, casting it onto one of the couches. He didn't take her coat, but walked straight to the table, lifting the cover off one of the dishes. "Beef Stroganoff. And, let's see, a very nice white burgundy. Have a seat."

He pulled out her chair. Cary still had her coat on. "Jason, I never agreed to a private—"

"Did you want to discuss our sexual relationship publicly?" he demanded.

"We don't have a relationship!" she insisted.

He smiled. "Fine. Sit down and tell me why."

Exasperated, Cary groaned, doffed her coat and then took the seat he had pulled out for her. He poured the wine, then sat opposite her. His eyes met hers as he lifted his glass to her.

"Well?"

"I just can't see you anymore," she said.

"Why not?"

"You're my boss, for one thing."

"We're nowhere near work."

"But we will be."

"This has nothing to do with work, and you know it."

Cary sipped her wine. "All right. All right—you need another reason? I don't care to be one of the crowd."

"The crowd?" One brow shot up. "Really, it isn't that bad, is it?"

She flushed. "I just don't—"

He leaned across the table. His fingers closed over hers. The warmth was electric. Seductive...frightening.

"I enjoy you. I like you. I admire you."

"You're lost, sunk, in your memories!" Cary told him.

He smiled ruefully. "I am? All right, then, Cary. We have everything in common. You're in love with a ghost, too. But admit it, you're having fun with me. You opened up. You didn't do anything casual or careless last night. You made love with me! And that's a hell of a lot more than you've managed before!''

She jumped up, and his wineglass slammed down. ''At least I'm not always trying to run away!'' he exploded.

But you're not in love with me, either! Cary thought. And then she paused at the awful realization that maybe, just maybe, she was falling in love with him. It had started when he had picked her up for the week....

No. It had started before that. It had started with the fascination she felt each time she saw him.

And now...

''Give it this week,'' he said.

''What?''

''You're having fun. Hell, you're even having sex. Give it this week. Then, if you want to stop, we will. We can go back to work and never even nod in the hallways.''

She should have said no right then.

He had brought her here, to complete privacy. To complete intimacy. But he would take her home if she wanted. She knew that. She had only to say the word.

But...

She liked the lodge. She liked being with the children. And she liked being with him. She liked his slow smile, his laughter, and she even liked seeing the weariness slip from his eyes.

And she liked his chest. Naked.

The rest of the week...

It was almost Christmas. She owed it to herself.

She sank slowly into her chair. ''We'll have dinner,'' she murmured.

And they did. Just dinner. But then it began to snow, and they stood at the window and watched the snowflakes falling. Then they sat before the fire and started to talk about baseball and all the things that little girls needed, and children in general.

Suddenly they were stretched out on the floor beside the flames.

And Cary knew that she wanted to make love. Again.

The flames in front of them, and between them, began to climb higher and higher.

Outside, the Christmas lights flickered red and green.

And Cary knew that she had given herself a bigger Christmas present than she had known. She had given herself laughter and a little bit of Christmas spirit....

And even a little taste of peace.

Chapter 5

The week passed in a whirl.

And while it was happening, Cary had to admit that it was the best time she could remember having.

For one thing, she became a passable skier. Between Jason and Angela, she had plenty of help. And plenty of laughter each time she or Danny pitched into the snow.

The laughter. Perhaps that was what she would remember the most. Or maybe it was the warmth, the quiet evenings. Or maybe the sheer excitement of feeling alive and aware and sensual again.

He told her to relax, to try to have fun.

And she did. They swam; they skied; they ate. They spent time with the children, and they spent time alone. They took lazy walks, and they played in the privacy of the Jacuzzi in Cary's room. They listened to the endless hum of Christmas carols heralding the season, and they went on sleigh rides with bells jingling.

Danny had the time of his life.

But the week came to an end, and though Jason acted as if nothing needed to change because they went back, Cary

knew that it would. The week had been a fantasy. Now
they were in the real world. It was an uneasy feeling, and
as she lay awake the Sunday night before she had to go to
work, she regretted what she had done even as she dreamed
about the days gone by.

And then there was Jason.

Courteous, charming. He'd made her laugh so easily.
And she'd never imagined a more tender or exciting lover.
But now it was time to remember that he moved swiftly,
that no matter how easy he had been to be with, he was
still in love with Sara, and if he thought that Cary was
coming too close, he would move on.

She slept very little that night.

Monday morning passed by without her seeing him. She
had lunch with June, determined that she wasn't going to
give anything away. Nothing. And despite June's persis-
tence, she stuck to her story that it had been a nice week,
that Jason had been charming, that Danny and Angela had
enjoyed a great time—and nothing more.

She thought she would see Jason sometime during the
day, but she didn't. And she didn't know whether she was
anxious, or very, very glad.

A second day passed without her seeing him, and then
a third and a fourth. She lay awake at night, tossing and
turning. She remembered his every touch, and she clenched
her teeth tightly, thinking how ironic it was that she had
finally fallen in love again.

With a man who not only couldn't love her, but didn't
even want to see her again.

She had warned herself. Again and again, she had
warned herself.

By Friday she had stubbornly convinced herself that she
was not going to go from living in one kind of hell to living

in another. If he asked her to dinner, to a show, to coffee—to anything—ever again, she would refuse.

To make matters worse, June plagued her at lunch every day. And it was the Christmas season. Everywhere she turned, people were singing about tidings of joy.

"Maybe you'll have a date for the pre-Christmas Eve party," June teased her at lunch on Friday.

Cary clenched her teeth. "June, I had a nice time last week. I enjoyed both the McCreadys. That's all."

"And did the McCreadys enjoy you?"

"June, drop it," Cary said warningly.

But it was when she returned to her office after lunch that she found the computer. And, as it happened, June was with her.

"It's that system that Danny wanted so much! The one you thought you couldn't afford!" June exclaimed. "How did it get here? Who would have...oh!" She stared hard at Cary, then she started to laugh. "I guess one McCready did enjoy you. Very much."

"June!" Cary gasped.

"Oh, kid, I'm sorry, I didn't mean anything by that. Except that you must have...well, I mean, you must have had a really good time. And *he* must have had a really good time, too. Oh, I'm not making this sound any better, am I? Gee, I wonder how many other people saw this come in here?"

Damn Jason McCready. He'd forced her into falling for him, then ignored her....

And then managed to turn her into the most delectable piece of office gossip in months.

Cary's cheeks were flaming, and she couldn't think of a single word to say to June. She probably shouldn't accost Jason now, in his office. His secretary would hear her, and the staff would probably be buzzing by the end of the afternoon.

Damn Jeremy and his Christmas dust! Cary thought furiously. The computer was in her office, and it must look like some kind of payment for services above and beyond the call of duty. Well, nuts to timing! She strode out of the office, down the hall and to the elevators. And she didn't wait for Jason's secretary to announce her, she waved and went right through the door.

Jason had been expecting to hear from Cary. He'd been waiting for a call.

This past week had been bedlam—absolute bedlam—and he'd played catch-up from morning until night. He'd driven by her apartment on his way home from work twice, but it had been late, and when he'd been about to go up to see if she was awake, he had been amazed to find his hands trembling, and he'd driven home instead.

Early this morning, he'd thought of the computer. He hoped it was the right one and that she would tell him how much it would mean to Danny. The boy had talked about it often enough on the trip, telling Angela all the wonderful things he had been able to do on it in school.

He wanted to talk to Cary. He wanted to hear her voice again. From the minute he had left her at her door, he had missed her. Missed the gold in her gaze, the curve of her smile. He missed the simple beauty of her face and the lithe, sensual beauty of her form. He missed being near someone who shared his love for children; he missed the way she could laugh at herself when she landed in the snow. He missed her eyes, steady and sure when she told him something she was determined he should hear. And he missed her sighs and her whispers and the wonder in her eyes when they made love. Just remembering made an ache rise hauntingly within him.

He had lain awake all night thinking about it, and he had awakened that morning amazed to feel an aching in his heart. He wanted the week back. He wanted to be with her. For the first time in five years he had been happy. He hoped the computer would make her happy, too.

Apparently it didn't.

He was amazed when she stormed into his office, her eyes gleaming with fury, her beautiful features as tense as iron. There was a pencil between her hands. And even before she began to speak, it snapped.

"What the hell are you doing to me?" she demanded.

Defensively, he was on his feet. He walked around the desk and perched on the edge of it, his arms crossed over his chest. "What on earth are you talking about?"

"The computer!"

"It's for Danny."

"Oh, it's for Danny! But it's also for me. And I can't afford it. And I don't want things from you that I can't afford. It looks like a—a payment!"

"A payment!" Jason roared.

"Everyone must know now that…that…"

"You're sleeping with me?" Jason suggested. He said it as if it were something evil. But it had meant everything to him. It had meant salvation.

"But I'm not 'sleeping with' you—it's not some ongoing thing!"

"There was no payoff intended, Cary, and I can't believe—"

"Oh!" she ground out with exasperation. "I *am* going to have to quit—"

"Why?"

"Don't you see what you've done? My position is untenable. I just became another of your casual associations, but I have to appear here every day—"

"I wasn't sure that we were involved in any casual associations," he said, his eyes narrowing angrily. "I intended to call you this afternoon—"

"Did you? No! No, it doesn't matter. It can't go on, don't you see? I can't work here and have everyone looking at me as if I were...as if I were one of your women," she finished flatly.

"It was good between us," he said harshly. "Everything was good."

"*Was!* It's over. I will not see you again!"

He was still. Dead still. Absolutely silent and tense. Then he spoke softly. "All right. I'll marry you."

Cary was so startled that she fell silent, gaping. Then she felt tears stinging the back of her eyes. *All right, he'd marry her?* It sounded as if he had come to a compromise on a business proposal. And he couldn't mean it. No matter how...good...it had been between them, he was striking and rich—no, no, how could she forget? He was tall, dark and handsome and rich. Damn June and Jeremy and Christmas dust and the Christmas season! He didn't mean to marry her; it was just something that had come out of his mouth to stall her.

She shook her head. "You can't mean that. It makes no sense. And if—"

"I mean it with every breath in me." He strode toward her, pausing half an inch away. "And it makes perfect sense. You're the one who said we had a lot in common. So we're both really in love with ghosts. I understand you, you understand me. We share something."

Cary shook her head. She didn't understand the pain she was feeling. He did mean it. He would marry her. Just to keep her near. She should have been flattered. Instead she wanted to cry. "I don't need anyone to marry me. You certainly don't have to do anything like that. I can do very well on my own—''

"Yes, yes, I know. But you can do better with me. And I can do a lot for Danny that you can't do."

"I'm a good mother—"

"But you're not a father."

"This is insane."

"Angela loves you. And I do flatter myself that Danny is fond of me."

His hands were on her shoulders, his eyes burning into hers. They were compelling, demanding that she bend to his will.

Excitement began to seize her. She could marry him. He'd offered her something that he hadn't offered any other woman. There was something missing, but what she would have would surely be better than loneliness. She was falling in love with him. And perhaps that would be enough.

"Do it," he insisted.

"I..." She jerked free from him suddenly. "I have to go!" she said.

"I'll be home tonight. Get someone to watch Danny. Come see me. I'll want an answer."

She left his office.

She spent the afternoon in misery. Jeremy popped his head in, and it was apparent that he and the entire office had heard about the computer. "Wow! Just imagine what you could get if you went away with him for a month!" Jeremy teased.

Cary felt like hurling her desk at him. "Get yourself and your Christmas dust out of here!" she warned him furiously.

Jeremy couldn't be gotten rid of that easily. He came in and sat on the edge of her desk. Frowning, he looked into her eyes. "Cary, I didn't mean anything."

"Never mind!"

"Cary, I really didn't mean anything. And neither did Jason, I'm certain."

"He's careless! He's accustomed to having everything at his whim, and he's accustomed to money—"

"Cary, he was an orphan. An abandoned boy who grew up on the streets more than off them. He worked his way up to everything he has. He isn't careless."

Cary stared at her desk. She hadn't known anything about his past. He never talked about it. Maybe he had walked the hard and rocky road once, but that had been years ago. Perhaps his career had been admirable. Okay, so he was admirable, and that was how he had managed to slip into her heart. That was why she cared so much.

But it was also true that he thought he could snap his fingers and she would snap to attention.

Well, she wasn't going to.

At nine o'clock that night she was on her way to his house in Cambridge. So much for her best intentions. But as the cab carried her along, she convinced herself again that she would say no. In very certain terms.

The house was beautiful, old and furnished with antiques. She was escorted to an eighteenth-century drawing room where Jason was sipping brandy and evidently waiting for her.

She felt awkward as she walked in. And he had no polite chitchat for her. He simply stared at her, waiting.

"How's Angela?" she asked.

"Fine. Sleeping."

She nodded. "Jason, I can't—"

She didn't see the disappointment in his eyes. His lashes shaded them too quickly. "I really can't do this. I can't do this to you—"

"Do it to me? Cary, I want you!"

"And it seems that you're willing to pay a tremendous price. Jason, I don't—"

"The price doesn't matter, Cary. It's Christmas. You're what I want more than anything in the world."

This year, Cary thought.

"I will do my best to give you anything that you want," he said harshly.

"Jason, it's just that—"

"Cary, you don't want to be one of a number of women. I'll make you my wife. I can give Danny anything in the world. The best schools, anything he wants. A guaranteed future. No worry for you. Cary, it's Christmas! And I can give you and Danny every Christmas gift in the world."

"But there's nothing that I can give you!"

"Damn it, Cary, give us both a break! You'd be giving Angela and me a real home!" he exclaimed.

She felt her fingers curl. It was a business proposition. Pure and simple. But it wasn't such a bad proposition.

"All...all right," she told him.

"Done!" A handsome smile slashed his face. In seconds he was across the room. He took her hand, and before she realized what he was doing, he had slipped a diamond on her finger.

It was beautiful. It was large, but it wasn't decadent. It was surrounded by tiny emeralds, and it fit right beside her old gold band.

"Jason, I can't—"

"It's an engagement ring! It seals our promise."

And it fit. It fit her just right, the band snug and warm around her finger. "A ring and a kiss," he told her softly. And she was suddenly in his arms.

The kiss too, was filled with promise. Her anxiety and emotions knotted together, and when his kiss deepened, she found a sweet escape in the growing sensation. It had become so natural to be with him. So natural, so beautiful to feel his touch. To know this wonderful, spiraling desire...

She saw his room that night. Saw his large oak wardrobes and dressers, his massive, white-tiled bath, his king-size bed. She lost herself in that bed, in the soft, warm, sinking comfort. She acutely felt his every touch. The sweep of his hand, the pressure of his body, the passion of his being. She rode with him and flew with him, and when it was done, she was once again left shaking with the wonder of their lovemaking.

And once more feeling the growth of tears behind her eyes.

She lay on the soft sheets, feeling his arms around her, and from somewhere she heard the promise of a Christmas carol on the air.

Christmas...

It was for giving, for believing. It was for miracles. It was for faith.

And to have Jason, well...

But there was something missing. And as she listened to the distant beauty of "Silent Night" filling the darkness, she knew what it it was. Love.

He touched her. Touched her shoulder. And his kiss burned into her flesh.

Once more, she thought. She couldn't resist having one last time. And so she moved into his arms, meeting his kiss with warmth, with magic, with a prayer.

Later, while he slept, comfortable, handsome as a boy, his dark hair tousled, she rose and dressed quickly.

"Where are you going?" Lazy green eyes were on her.

"Home. Danny is there."

"I'll take you."

She shook her head. "No, please, it isn't late. I'll be all right."

But she was beginning to know Jason McCready. Even if this had been a casual date, he would still have seen her home. The man she loved had manners.

He took her to her apartment door and paused there. "I smell popcorn," he murmured.

"June and Danny. I'm sure they're making strands for the tree."

He placed a hand on either side of her head. "I love your apartment. Did I ever tell you that?"

She shook her head, wondering if it could be true. His house was so magnificent. "I love your house," she told him.

He smiled. "Good. Maybe you can change it, and I can love it, too." He leaned down and kissed her, and she wanted to pull away, but she couldn't. She clung to him, letting the magic wash over her.

She walked into her apartment, where June and Danny were indeed busy with popcorn strings.

"Hi, Mom!" There was excitement in Danny's eyes. He knew that she had been with Jason.

"Hi, honey." She kissed him on the top of his blond head, her resolve weakening. It would be so good for Danny. Maybe she was thinking like a fool.

No, it would be wrong to marry Jason. She couldn't do it. She had told him that she would, but she couldn't. And she couldn't see him again. Not under any circumstances. Because every time she saw him, she wanted him. For Christmas.

For always.

"Bedtime," she insisted to Danny, and she finally managed to get him tucked in.

June was not so easy. "Well? You're upset. You're going to cry. Oh, that creep! He told you it was over!"

Cary shook her head. "No, he asked me to marry him."

"What!" June gasped. "Oh, how wonderful!" She
started to dance around the room with a pillow, but then
she paused. "You did tell him yes, right?"

Cary sighed. "Yes, I did. But I'm afraid I'm not going
to. I'm—I'm going to resign tomorrow. I'm not going back
to the office. I'll finish my present assignment, and you can
take in all my paperwork."

"What!" June stared at her as if she had gone insane.
She argued with Cary, pleaded with her.

Cary slipped the diamond from her finger and placed it
in June's palm. "Take this back, too," she insisted.

"Oh, Cary, you can't possibly dislike him or be angry
with him—"

"I don't dislike him and I'm not angry with him," Cary
said. She smiled. "Actually, I love him."

Cary knew that June didn't understand, but Cary wasn't
going to give her an explanation. She ushered June out and
hurried to her bedroom, where she turned on the radio.

Someone was playing "Silent Night" again.

Cary laid her head on her pillow and indulged herself in
a cascade of hot tears.

Jason McCready was on top of the world.

Indeed, the world was beautiful. For the first time in
years he couldn't wait for Christmas. The pain had been
miraculously lifted from his heart, and he loved all the
things that had once hurt so badly. They would be married
before Christmas, he decided. He'd forgotten to ask Cary
to help Angela with a Christmas dress, something special
to be worn to church. She wouldn't mind, he was certain.

Sitting at his desk at work, he leaned back and closed

his eyes. He laced his fingers behind his head and wondered if Danny needed a new baseball bat, or maybe a glove. Or maybe he had an attachment to his old one. Danny liked collecting baseball cards. He had told Jason that in New Hampshire. There were all kinds of baseball card shows they could go to together.

His secretary buzzed him and announced that June was waiting to see him.

"Send her in," Jason said.

As soon as he saw June he felt a foreboding. He knew immediately, beyond a shadow of a doubt, that something was very wrong.

"Mr. McCready, I…" Her voice trailed away.

"June, I have always hoped that all my employees would feel free to come here and say whatever they had to say," he told her patiently.

She went very pale.

"June?"

"Oh, Mr. McCready, I hate being here," she said. "But I…"

She stepped forward, and she put his diamond ring on his desk. He stared at it, and then at her.

"Cary is quitting," June said in a rush.

He paled, amazed at the assault of pain that swept over him.

"She couldn't tell me herself?"

June moistened her lips. "I think she was afraid to see you again. Afraid you wouldn't really listen to her. Not that I understand her myself."

Jason stared at the ring, then stood, slipping it into his pocket. He walked to the window.

"She's going to finish up all her work. She just isn't going to come in anymore," June said quietly.

His back was square and straight as he stared at the

street. "This isn't like her," he said. "Cary Adams has always had a talent for stating her mind."

She did have that wonderful talent, he realized. Since that day when she'd come here and told him exactly what she thought of him, she'd been changing his life. So subtly, at first. She'd just made him watch her. Watch the sunlight in her hazel eyes. Watch her movement in the hallways. Dear God, he'd come to love her smile.

Christmas bells rang below him. Bright lights in green and red were coming on as the early darkness of winter descended.

A bleakness settled over him. The future was empty without her. Suddenly it hit him like a brick as he realized what his despair meant.

He loved her eyes; he loved her hair. He loved her laughter, and he loved her spirit and her mind. He loved the trusting way she looked at him when they lay entwined together. He loved *her,* he realized.

And she wanted none of him.

June realized that he wasn't saying anything. He was just standing there, his shoulders squared in misery as he gazed at the snow. June wanted to touch his shoulders in comfort.

And she wanted to give Cary a good shaking for hurting him so. What was the matter with that woman?

"Cary is usually very determined to handle her own affairs. I suppose she thought it would be easier if she weren't involved this time," June said. Why hadn't Cary gotten Jeremy to come up here? He and McCready were friends, and although June had always liked her employer a lot, she was in a wretched position at the moment. "It's so much harder when you love someone. Though, for the life of me, I can't understand—"

"What!"

June broke off, stunned, frightened by the harshness of

his tone. She couldn't remember what she had been saying.
"I—er—"

"What did you say?"

"What did I say?" June repeated. "Oh. I don't understand Cary. I don't know why on earth she's doing this. She loves you, and—"

"That. That part. Say that again."

"I said she loves you—"

"How do you know that?"

"Well, she said so, of course—"

Once again June broke off. He was striding across the room to her, and he was moving so swiftly, and with such power, that she almost cried out and leaped away. She didn't get a chance to.

His hands were on her shoulders. She was lifted off the floor, and his lips brushed her cheeks.

The bleakness had fallen from him like a cloak of darkness.

She loved him. And he loved her. And as he broke into a broad grin, he suddenly understood. They'd both been too lost. Lost in the past. Lost in pain that they hadn't managed to let go. And then, like a fool, he'd offered her everything in the world. Everything except what a woman like Cary wanted. Love.

"She *is* going to marry me. Thank you, June, but you don't need to stand here stuttering anymore. She *is* going to marry me."

And then, while June stared openmouthed, he walked past her and out of the office.

By late afternoon Cary had decided that Jason had graciously accepted both the return of his ring and her resignation.

She allowed herself another good cry, then decided she

had to try to stop or else she would spend the rest of her days in tears. But it was hard. So hard…

She looked at the phone time and time again, thinking that she should call him. And then her cheeks would flame, and she would be ashamed, because she hadn't gone to see him herself. She should never, never have sent June to face her own particular lion for her.

But she had been afraid to see Jason McCready. Because if he pressed her, she just might want the magic so badly that she would reach for it, even though it was wrong.

Danny came home from school, and she wondered if she should talk with him yet. She had only told him that she was taking a day off from work—she hadn't told him she had quit her job.

After all, it was Christmas.

It wasn't right to be so miserable.

She didn't say anything to Danny, so he spent the night talking about Jason, and about how wonderful it had been at the lodge, and how he hoped that they would get together again soon.

Cary nearly screamed.

At ten she went to bed. She lay staring at her ceiling and willed herself to go to sleep, but sleep wouldn't come.

Tears would. They were just starting to well in her eyes when she heard the first thump against her window. She jerked up, wondering what on earth could be going on. A second thump hit the window, and she jumped up and raced to it, her heart pounding.

Two stories below was a figure standing under a lamppost. And even as she watched him, another snowball came flying at her, thumping against the window.

Her eyes widened in amazement. Jason McCready, hatless and scarfless, was standing on the sidewalk, grinning at her and throwing snowballs.

She threw open the window, shivering against the sudden cold.

"Jason! What are you doing down there?"

To her utter amazement, he began to sing. "I'm dreaming of a white Christmas..."

His voice was good. Very good. Rich. He could croon out the tune with almost the same appeal as Bing Crosby.

The window next to hers suddenly flew open. Mrs. Crowley, from the apartment beside hers, looked out. "What in heaven's name is going on?"

"Jason, hush!" Cary pleaded.

"...may your days be merry and bright..."

Another window burst open. It was old Mr. Calahan from the apartment below hers.

"Hey, not bad!" Mr. Calahan said, chuckling. "How about 'Deck the Halls'?"

"Jason, please, what are you doing?"

"Trying to get your attention."

"Well, you've got mine, young man," Mrs. Crowley informed him. All bundled up in her thick robe, she was a cheerful picture, with her red cheeks and bouncing pink curlers. Jason grinned at her.

"I came to ask Cary to marry me again. I just wanted her to know that I have lots of Christmas spirit. She thinks she knows all about me, but there are a lot of things she hasn't realized."

"Jason!" Cary cried in horror. "I told you I can't marry you—"

"Why not? Specifically."

Mr. Calahan craned his neck. "Yes, why not? Specifically."

"Jason!" Cary cried, mortified.

"That's all right. I already know," Jason told Mr. Calahan and Mrs. Crowley. But his eyes, green, bright and with such a tender expression, remained on Cary. She felt her heart beginning to ache and her limbs to burn.

"I asked her for all the wrong reasons, you see. I said that we'd be good together. That we'd be good parents for each other's children. That we'd keep each other from being lonely. I have a nice business, and I told her that I could take care of her."

"That doesn't sound so bad to me," Mr. Calahan said.

"Go on!" Mrs. Crowley insisted.

Jason smiled. A beautiful, slow, crooked smile that filled his face with wistfulness and longing. "I want to restate my proposal. I want to tell her that I want to marry her for just one reason. For the most important reason in the world. Because she brought light back to my world. She made my every hour worth living. Because I love her with all my heart."

"Oh, Jason!" Cary whispered.

"How romantic!" Mrs. Crowley clapped her hands.

"Well, tell him yes, young woman!" Mr. Calahan commanded. "Tell the poor fellow yes before he expires out there!"

"Yes! Yes!" Cary cried. "Stay there. Stay right there! I'll be right down!"

He could have come up, but she wasn't thinking clearly. And so Cary rushed down the stairs and into the snow, where she threw herself into his arms.

"Oh, Jason! Really? Can it be true?"

He cradled her chin. "Yes, it's true. Cary, I do want to give you things. I want to give you and Danny everything I can. I want to make you happy. I want you to keep working, if that's what you want. And I know that Angela and Danny will be delighted. But, Cary, I do love you with all my heart."

"Jason! I love you, too."

"Kiss him!" Mrs. Crowley called out.

"Are you still eavesdropping up there?" Mr. Calahan demanded.

"Oh, shut up, you old goat!"

"Hmph! All right, young lady, you go ahead and kiss him. And come inside! That way we can all get some sleep."

Cary decided to oblige. She stood on her tiptoes and kissed him. Long and hard.

Mrs. Crowley sighed. A window closed.

And suddenly little flakes began to fall. Beautiful, intricate little snowflakes. It would probably be a very white Christmas.

Jason's lips parted from hers. Cary caught his hand, and they rushed up the stairs.

Once inside her apartment, she was in his arms again. And when the kiss at last seemed to end, she leaned against him, dazed, amazed, dazzled, and then worried and afraid all in one.

"Jason, this still isn't quite fair. You've given me so much already. What will I ever give you?"

"What I want for Christmas most of all."

"And that is?"

"You," he said. "In a red ribbon. And nothing else. Just you."

She smiled shyly, and he kissed her again. Then he broke away. "Maybe something else, too."

"What?"

"I always imagined a wonderful family, a big family. I grew up alone, and somehow that makes you really love kids. We have a great boy, and a great girl, but maybe we could go for two more somewhere along the line. If you're willing. What do you think?"

"I think kids are just great," Cary whispered.

He already knew that.

"So will you marry me?"

"Yes, Jason, yes. Oh, yes, I'll marry you."

"Wow. Oh, wow! Wow, oh, wow, oh, my!" came a little boy's voice.

Danny was up. And Danny had been unabashedly listening to the whole thing.

"Really?" Danny said.

"You're supposed to be in bed," Cary said.

"Really," Jason told him, grinning.

"When?" Danny demanded. "It has to be by Christmas."

"Danny!"

"By Christmas it is," Jason agreed.

And they *were* married by Christmas. The ceremony was on December twentieth. Danny and Angela were both there, along with Jeremy and June and the entire staff of *Elegance*.

They were holding off on a honeymoon because they didn't want to leave for the holidays. Jason and Angela planned to stay with Cary and Danny at her apartment until New Year's Day; then Cary and Danny would move into Jason's house.

And make it a home, Jason knew.

On Christmas Eve they all went to church. And when they came home, everyone sang carols and set packages around the tree.

But once the kids were tucked in, Jason turned on the Christmas lights and was startled to find a note to him hooked on the tree.

"I have a special gift for you. My room. Five minutes."

Curious, intrigued, Jason waited the five minutes, then rushed to Cary's bedroom.

And there, curled up on an expanse of snowy sheets, was his wife.

His gift, his greatest Christmas gift ever.

His wife.

And she was decked out beautifully in nothing—absolutely nothing—but a big red bow.

He paused just a moment, breathing out a prayer. Thank you, God.

And then he walked forward, laughing, and swept his Christmas gift tenderly into his arms.

Epilogue

It was very late, but Danny slipped out of bed anyway. The house was quiet; everyone was sleeping at last.

He ran to the Christmas tree. He was so startled that he paused, his mouth a large O.

He had expected gifts. But he hadn't really expected so many.

And he certainly hadn't expected to find his brand new computer, all set up, with a big red bow on it, just awaiting his touch.

He closed his eyes and opened them again. The gifts were all still there. Wait till Angela saw...

But Angela already knew about the gifts, he was certain. And she would be excited, and she would be pleased, because she was Angela, and she was just great, even if she was a girl. His sister now. They'd both been very lucky this Christmas. They'd already gotten the things that money just couldn't buy. He had a new father. Jason McCready would never replace his real dad, just like Cary could never replace Angela's real mom. But both were the second best thing. And they both had the very gift in the world to give. Love.

Danny knew that Jason would always be willing to leave work early to throw a baseball. And Angela would have a mom to take her to her Brownie meetings, and Cary would fuss over her hair, tie it up in those pigtails and dress it up with barrettes.

Danny found himself shaking suddenly. This was just the best Christmas in the world.

He took a walk across the room, going to the beautiful little crèche that his mother had set up. He reached over and very carefully fingered the little Christ figure, then walked to the window.

He could just see the North Star. He knew which one it was because Jason had shown it to him. "Hello," he murmured. He cleared his throat. That wasn't how you were supposed to pray. "Dear Lord," he began again softly. "I just wanted to say thank you. I—well, I do believe in the Christmas spirit and miracles, but I know that the Santa I spoke to was my cousin Jeremy. So I know that everything I got—all the miracles—was because of you." He smiled. "A new dad, and a computer!" Maybe you weren't supposed to joke with God. No, God would understand, he decided. But his smile faded anyway. "Thank you so much!" he whispered earnestly. "Once you gave us all your Son. And now you've given me a dad, and Angela a mom. And I have a sister, and she has a brother. And Mom has Jason, and Jason has Mom. It *is* a miracle! Thank you!" He stopped because he didn't have any more words that could express how grateful he was.

The North Star seemed to sparkle suddenly with a dazzling light.

And then it began to fade.

Danny stared at it for a while, then he smiled. The star was fading because it was Christmas. Christmas day.

He let out a wild whoop and went running for Angela's door. "It's Christmas, sleepyhead! Wake up!"

Angela, with her eyes barely open, appeared in her doorway in a fluffy robe. "It's so early!" she breathed. "Can we wake them up?"

"Sure. We're kids. And it's Christmas," Danny told her.

Cary awoke to the children's shrieks of delight, yet she was afraid to open her eyes.

Knowing that the kids would be up early, she and Jason had put on pajamas before they fell asleep. His arms were around her tightly; she was pulled against him so that his chest met her back, and they were curled together like a little pair of mice. She felt him, felt all his warmth, and didn't dare open her eyes. She didn't want him to be a Christmas dream.

But he wasn't. She was his wife. She was in love with him, and miraculously, he was in love with her. No gift could be greater.

"Mom!"

"Dad!"

It was Danny who called her name, and Angela who woke Jason. Yet when the two came flying into the bedroom, it was Angela who landed on her, and Danny who tackled Jason.

"Whoa, hey, what is this!" Jason protested gruffly. But he was laughing.

"It's Christmas!" Danny announced indignantly.

"Wow, you mean we might have missed it?" Cary said, wide-eyed.

"Mom!" Danny moaned. "Will you two please get up!"

"I'll make coffee," Cary volunteered to Jason. Then she smiled and slipped out of bed. She winked at the kids as

Jason tried to fall back asleep, and as she left the room, she could hear a burst of laughter as the two attacked Jason, tickling him mercilessly.

And apparently Jason was just as merciless in return.

Coffee and cocoa were ready when they all traipsed out to the living room. Cary seated herself by Jason's side, comfortable in the crook of his arm, as the children opened their gifts. There was paper everywhere. And she was pleased to see that Danny was as impressed with the small things as he was with the wonderful new computer. And Angela, bless her, was thrilled with her gifts, too, even though she'd grown up with everything money could buy.

And Jason McCready, the self-made man, seemed more touched by Danny's home-made Christmas card than by any gift he might have received.

Cary had just stepped over some of the paper to get more coffee when the doorbell rang. She arched a brow to Jason.

"Don't look at me," he told her. "It must be your cousin Jeremy."

And it was. Except that he had run into June in the doorway, so both of them were standing there arguing, with their hands piled high with boxes for the children.

The two were quickly inside, and there was more mayhem as the children kissed them and thanked them for their gifts. Jason poured the coffee while Cary supervised the gift giving. Pandemonium seemed to reign for quite a while; then at last the room grew quieter. "I wanted to know if I could take the kids to the Parade of the Elves. It's not far from here—I'd only need to steal them for a couple of hours," June said.

Jason seemed uneasy. "June, I know it's Christmas, but it might be a little wild out there today. Are you sure you want to take the kids by yourself?"

"Jeremy will come with me," June said.

"I will?" Jeremy began. June kicked him. He stared at her indignantly, then he seemed to realize that June was trying to give the newlyweds some time alone. "Oh, I will. Of course." He cast June a look of stern reproach as soon as he thought Cary was no longer looking. Cary hid a smile. She was certain that Jason hadn't been aware of anything.

"I don't know…" Jason began with a frown, looking to Cary.

"The kids will be fine. And I'm sure they'd love to go," she said demurely.

Within minutes, it seemed, she had the kids dressed and ready to go. June and Jeremy were waiting at the door.

June and Jeremy. Hmm, Cary thought. Why not?

Jeremy paused to give Cary a kiss goodbye on the cheek, and she fluttered her fingers over his head.

"What was that?" he asked her.

"Christmas dust."

"What?"

"Never mind. Just go on and have a good time. And thank you."

"Sure. We'll see you later."

"Christmas dinner is here," Jason advised over Cary's shoulder. "I'm doing the stuffing."

"I'm doing the stuffing!" Cary protested.

"No, you're the turkey and the vegetables and the mashed potatoes and the pies. I'm the stuffing."

Cary laughed as his arms came around her. She shrugged. "Whatever. Christmas dinner is here. Just be back by then, okay?"

"Got ya," Jeremy agreed. June was telling him to get a move on. He rolled his eyes. "Is she coming for dinner, too?"

"Yes."

"Great."

"Christmas dust," Cary repeated.

Jeremy frowned with confusion, then the foursome left.

Oh, well, there was always next Christmas, Cary thought.

She turned in her husband's arms. His lips found hers, and when he kissed her deeply, she felt the familiar thrill sweeping through her.

Jason looked at the door again. "Are you sure they're going to be all right?"

"Yes, I'm sure!" She caught his hand and, smiling, pulled him over to the couch. "June and Jeremy only look flighty, honest. I couldn't trust the kids more with anyone else. And besides, I have another gift for you."

He grinned, cocking a dark eyebrow.

"Oh, yeah?"

She nodded.

"Where's the box?"

"There isn't exactly a box," she said. Her fingers still entwined with his, she started for the bedroom.

His brow arched higher. "Is it a foot massage?"

Cary laughed. "Maybe..." She stood on tiptoe, quickly kissed his lips, then began to whisper. He could still make her feel so shy at times.

"Remember when I told you there was nothing that I could give you that you didn't have? And you said that yes, there was—me. Well, you've got me."

"A gift I will cherish all of my life," he promised her tenderly.

She flushed. "Thank you. But you also said you'd like four kids—if I was willing, of course—and that I could give you the two that were missing."

"Yes?"

"Well, I thought that we could get started. We're alone, we're awake, we're aware..."

"And we're just as eager and as willing as can be!" Jason said, laughing.

He lifted her off her feet and into his arms. And then he was kissing her, deeply, richly, warmly. She felt herself coming alive, trembling, quivering inside.

The kiss seemed to last forever, but when he broke away, Jason paused, holding her tightly, tenderly.

And she realized that he was looking out the window. The North Star was still visible, a faint little flicker against the day that had dawned beautifully blue.

Cary felt a new trembling seize her. Thank you, thank you! she thought in silence. Thank you so much.

Jason's eyes met hers. She smiled. "I was just thinking..." he began.

"So was I."

"I'm so very thankful that I have you."

She nodded. "And I'm so thankful for you. And for Christmas miracles. And Christmas dust."

His grin broadened wickedly. "Christmas dust? That's one you'll have to explain."

"Oh, well, you see—"

"Later," Jason said firmly.

He carried her into the bedroom and laid her down. Then his lips touched hers, and she was in his arms, and very soon the day was exploding into a new splendor of excitement and wonder and enchantment. After the soaring and the magic and the ecstasy, the peace and the contentment remained, and his arms were locked around her.

"We have to get to the turkey," he mumbled lazily.

"Yes, we have to get to the turkey," Cary agreed.

But he didn't move, and neither did she. He might not know about the Christmas dust, but he did know a lot about Christmas miracles.

Indeed he did. He arose at last, pausing to kiss her on the nose.

"Miracles!" he whispered softly. "Thank God for them, and for you—my Christmas miracle!"

He kissed her again, then pulled her from her cocoon of covers.

"Someone really does have to see to that turkey! Unless you want to test our luck and see if any elves will appear to cook it for us?"

Cary grinned. No elves were coming. They already had their Christmas miracles. "I'm doing the stuffing," she told him. "You can be potatoes."

"You be the potatoes!" he charged.

She laughed, found her robe and hurried down the hall, then she opened the kitchen door very carefully.

After all, it was just a matter of belief.

There might be elves in her kitchen after all!

* * * * *

ALWAYS AND FOREVER

Lindsay McKenna

* * *

To the women and men of our military services
who have sacrificed themselves for us.
We honor, salute and respect your gift of freedom to us.

Dearest Reader,

When "Always and Forever" was first published in 1990, I considered it a tribute to those who took part in the Vietnam War. Shortly after it was published, we went into the first Gulf War. Now, as I write this letter, we are in the middle of the second Gulf War. How I hope for world peace someday soon.

When I wrote this story, I wanted to show that love, patient love, even from afar, can help to heal the wounds created by war. I hope you enjoy meeting Gale Taylor and fighter jock Kyle Anderson.

Because I was a navy veteran during the Vietnam War and most of my friends were marines who went over there, I have a unique perspective on how war changes us. I lost half my friends in Vietnam. And when the friends who survived came home, I saw the ravages on their souls the war had produced.

We should not forget the heroes, both men and women, from Vietnam. They gave everything, and this is my way of honoring their sacrifice for all of us.

Warmly,

Lindsay McKenna

Chapter 1

December 24, 1973
Castle Air Force Base, California

Captain Kyle Anderson jogged up the sidewalk toward Captain Mike Taylor's base home. Was he too late? Kyle was supposed to go with his best friend, who was getting married tomorrow, to pick up their Air Force dress uniforms from the base cleaners, but he'd overslept. Damn!

Rubbing his smarting, bloodshot eyes, Kyle rapped his knuckles sharply against the door. Tomorrow, Mike was marrying Gale Remington, an Air Force officer he'd met a year ago. On Christmas Day, of all things. It was like Mike to do something romantic like that.

Kyle's breath was coming out in white wisps as he stood restlessly, hunched down into his dark blue wool coat, waiting to see if Mike was home.

"Mike?" His voice carried impatiently as he waited at the door, knocking even more loudly. Looking around, Kyle realized he was probably attracting the attention of every Air Force wife in base housing. They'd probably be looking out their windows to see who was shouting at 0800.

He'd overslept because of jet lag. Four days ago, Kyle had flown to Castle A.F.B. from Udorn, Thailand, where his fighter squadron was based, to be best man at Mike's wedding. But because of time-zone changes and the need to unplug physically and emotionally from the duties of a fighter pilot in Vietnam, Kyle was exhausted.

The door opened. Kyle grinned, expecting to see his friend from boyhood. Instead, he saw Gale, Mike's beautiful fiancée. His smile slipped considerably in surprise, his eyes widening as she opened the screen door.

"Hi, Kyle. If you're looking for Mike, he took off about fifteen minutes ago for the cleaners."

Pulse skyrocketing, Kyle drew in a shaky breath. He stood there, tongue-tied. Ever since he'd been introduced to Gale three days ago, his world had been out of control like a jet in a flat spin. The moment he'd looked into her incredible forest-green eyes, something wonderful, something terrible had happened to him. Once, twenty-five-year-old Kyle would have scoffed at the idea of falling head over heels for any woman on first sight. But he wasn't laughing now.

Placing his hands on his hips in a typical arrogant jet-jockey gesture, he covered his reaction to her. "Hi, Gale." God, did she realize what she did to him? It was agony to be around her because he wanted to simply absorb her, lose himself in her sunny smile, and stare into those dancing eyes that held such sparkling life in their depths.

Gale smiled shyly. "Mike said you might be late. He'll pick up your uniform." She forced herself to look away from Kyle's hawklike blue eyes that were large with intelligence. If there was such a thing as brazen self-confidence, Kyle possessed it. His stance was cocky and unapologetic. He was a proud eagle standing before her, knowing he was the cream of the Air Force pilot crop because he was an Academy graduate. Her pulse was doing funny things and she tried to ignore it. Since meeting Kyle, an exhilarating force swept through her whenever she thought of him or saw him. When Kyle looked at her with that burning intensity, she felt shaky, her carefully mapped out world falling apart.

"I overslept," he said with a laugh. He wasn't going to admit to her he couldn't shake the jet lag. Gale looked vulnerable and pretty in a pink long-sleeved blouse. The red apron tied around her waist and the dark brown slacks showed off her slim figure. She didn't look like a captain or a meteorologist, but she was both. Her hair, a pageboy of shifting brown color interlaced with gold and a few delicate strands of burnished copper, barely touched the collar of her blouse. He had to get away. It wasn't good to be here alone with her. God knew he'd taken great pains *not* to be alone with Gale—because he hadn't known what he'd do if he was. She affected him deeply.

It wasn't Gale's fault. She was hopelessly in love with Mike. Kyle rationalized his attraction to Gale by telling himself that because she was Mike's fiancée, he naturally liked her. "Look, I'll come back later," he said, his mouth growing dry.

"Nonsense, come on in. Mike's due back in less than half an hour and he wants you to stay for breakfast. Why go all the way back to the B.O.Q. just to come back later?"

Hesitating, Kyle glanced at the watch on his wrist. A half hour. It would look stupid to leave if Mike was going to be back that soon. "Well..."

Gale stepped aside, looking up at him. A large part of her wanted him to leave because in his presence, her emotions vibrated with a strange yearning she'd never experienced. But etiquette dictated differently. "You look tired. Come in. I've got a pot of fresh coffee." She knew Kyle had flown from Thailand to attend the wedding. The strain of what the war had done to him showed on his lean face, around his eyes and in the set of his mobile mouth. Heat fled through her, sweet and unexpected, as she stared at him.

She knew that, like every other arrogant, self-assured military pilot, he wasn't going to let on he was tired, much less exhausted by the war or the flight home. No, Kyle was like his fellow pilots: his callous, cocky exterior hid a vulnerable interior that was rarely shared with anyone. From the moment she'd met Kyle, she'd sensed a warmth and gentleness beneath that facade, and for some reason, Kyle's ebullient, joking presence had been able to lift the fear from her heart. Thirty days after the wedding, Mike, too, would leave for Thailand and become a part of the war. Gale feared losing her young husband.

Taking off his garrison cap, Kyle gave a nod. "Tired?" he teased. "You know us handsome, unabashed jocks aren't fazed by such things." He stepped into the warmth of the small living room. He could smell fresh coffee in the air and inhaled the scent deeply. And bacon was frying. His stomach growled, but he was also hungry in a different way. After he shed his coat, Gale hung it in the hall closet and beckoned him to follow her to the kitchen. He spotted a small Christmas tree, all decorated, in the corner of the living room. The lights blinked merrily, reminding him of the joyous holiday season.

"I promised Mike I'd have breakfast waiting for him when he got back." She smiled and pointed to the table. "Sit down. I'll get the coffee."

A bright red cloth covered the round table, and a Christmas decoration sat in the middle of it. Gale's thoughtful touch, Kyle was sure. "Thanks," he said. Tensely, he sat down and watched Gale move to the stove to pour his coffee. Mike had lived alone here for a year, and from the letters Kyle had gotten from him, he'd thought the house would be cold and barren. It wasn't with Gale present. The place had a light feeling with the winter sunshine filtering in through the kitchen window, embracing Gale's slight form and making her look radiant. Like a starving man, Kyle watched each small movement she performed. There was a sureness and grace to Gale he'd never seen in another woman.

Rubbing his eyes, Kyle tried to figure it out for the thousandth time. What was it about Gale that had thrown him for a loop? He couldn't want her, couldn't be fantasizing about kissing her or having her for himself when Mike was going to marry her. What the hell was wrong with him? It wasn't as if he didn't have his choice of women. Maybe it was the war. He hadn't been the same emotionally since he'd started flying the dangerous missions, although he never discussed that with anyone. Not even his fellow pilots.

"Here you go. You like it black, don't you?"

Kyle took his hands away from his eyes, and nodded, gazing at her long, slender fingers around the white mug. "Black—yes."

She smiled understandingly. "You look like you could use about seventy-two hours more sleep."

"Nah. You know us fighter jocks are as tough as they come." He kept his eyes on her as she walked back to the stove to turn the bacon in the skillet. "It comes with the territory," he said, sipping the scalding hot coffee. The heat burning through him was raging out of control. Didn't he have any command over his feelings toward Gale? How could this have happened? Why?

Glancing over her shoulder, she said, "What? The war?"

"Yeah. Flying missions every other day over Hanoi and back is—" He hesitated, not wanting to use the word *killer* because he saw the worry in Gale's eyes. In a month, Mike

would be joining his squadron. They'd be flying together—
a boyhood dream come true. He and Mike had grown up
in Sedona, Arizona, spending hours dreaming of careers as
military pilots. Trying to disarm the anxiety he saw in
Gale's eyes, he forced a smile. "It's a piece of cake." That
was a bald-faced lie, but there was no sense in further up-
setting her.

She raised an eyebrow. "It's dangerous."

With a shrug, Kyle muttered, "Not to us. Jet jocks are
trained to take the heat."

"Oh, please." She laughed. "You guys are all alike. It
would kill you to admit you're scared, have doubts or any
other human frailty."

He grinned broadly and sipped the coffee. It was good
and strong, just the way he liked it. "The only human frail-
ties we possess are eyes to scope out good-lookin' women
like yourself. Mike sure got lucky."

Gale blushed hotly. There was nothing displeasing about
Kyle Anderson, either, but she kept that thought to herself.
More than anything, she was drawn to the raw confidence
that emanated from him like a beacon.

"How did you get so cocky?"

"You mean confident?"

She grinned. "I don't think the two words have anything
in common, Kyle."

"Sure they do. You can't sit with an F-14 strapped to
your rear carrying a ton of weapons if you aren't a little
cocky *and* confident."

The imagery frightened Gale, although she knew it
shouldn't.

Kyle tilted his head as he saw her expressive eyes
darken. He'd never seen a woman who was so transparent
with her emotions and feelings. It was a delightful and
touching discovery. No wonder Mike had fallen in love
with her. "Sorry," he muttered with a forced smile. "I'll

try and keep the war talk to a minimum. I can see it's scaring you.''

"It does, Kyle." She studied him in the silence. "Doesn't it you?"

"What?"

"Scare you, flying with a load of weapons?"

He shrugged. "I don't know...I never really analyzed it that way before."

It was her turn to smile. "If you did, you probably wouldn't be a fighter pilot."

His grin broadened. "You're probably right. Some things, I learned a long time ago, don't merit being looked at too closely."

"Is that anything like looking a gift horse in the mouth?"

"Exactly." Kyle laughed, his spirits lifting like a fierce wind. He couldn't recall having felt this happy before. He tried to analyze why Gale affected him like a heady wine. Five minutes ago, he'd felt like hell warmed over. Now, all that tiredness and depression had miraculously gone away. Was it because of the kindness he saw in her face? Those dancing green eyes that looked beyond his bravado and saw the real him? Or was it Gale's full, soft lips, which reminded him that there was something left in the world that wasn't hard, harsh or ugly?

"I think Mike's the luckiest guy in the world. Imagine him snagging you."

She turned to the kitchen counter to busy herself. It was too easy to stare into those dark blue eyes that made her go weak and shaky inside. "You're making it out as if he captured the most beautiful woman in the world," she teased. "And I'm not. I'm just an Air Force captain."

"No one said women in the service aren't beautiful."

"Please."

Kyle laughed softly as she turned and gave him a dark look over her shoulder. "Now, that's the *truth*, Gale."

"Sure. Fighter jocks have more lines per square inch than any other male I've ever run into."

"Sounds like an indictment."

"More like a chronic disease with you guys."

He sat back, immensely enjoying her sense of humor. "That's another thing I like about ladies in the military—they have a fine sense of humor."

"And probably the last thing you look at or consider when you meet one."

"Now, Gale..."

"Now, Kyle..." And again, she laughed. The merriment in his eyes stole her breath away. There was more happiness there than she'd ever seen before. "You're just like Mike," she accused gently, "all strut and stuff, but underneath, a very nice guy."

"God, don't let *that* get out! The guys over at Udorn think I'm one mean fighter behind the stick."

Rolling her eyes, Gale got eggs from the fridge, then returned to the stove to cook them. "Here we go again. Make sure no one knows the real guy who wears those pilot's wings. Really, Kyle, did they make all of you out of the same mold?"

"Well, we went through flight school together."

"Instead of teaching you how to fly, I swear they put all of you through the same personality training."

"That's not so bad. I mean, look at us—we're confident, good at what we do and besides that, we're good-looking."

"I give up. If I didn't know any better, I'd say Mike was here and not you."

Sipping his coffee, Kyle smiled recklessly. "Well, Mike and I are like brothers, but there are a few differences. I'm four months older than he is."

Gale knew there were other, more profound differences.

Mike was laid back; Kyle was far more aggressive. She wondered if Mike would turn out the same way after being in combat.

Forcing herself to return to the task at hand, Gale busied herself with scrambling the eggs while the bacon finished frying. Her hands trembled. Trying to laugh at the absurd notion that Kyle's presence was responsible, Gale focused on Mike. She had met him a year ago over at Operations, where the meteorology department was located. He'd come in early one morning, angry over the fact his weather plan hadn't been ready in time for his flight. On his return to base two days later, Mike had taken her out to an expensive restaurant in Sacramento to apologize for his less-than-gentlemanly behavior. Over the next six months, they'd fallen in love. Their happiness was complete until Mike abruptly received orders to Thailand. They had decided to get married before he left.

Frowning, Gale stirred the eggs briskly in the hot skillet. Vietnam. War. Death. She felt her heart contract powerfully with fear. It wasn't fair that Mike was going to be torn away from her a month after they became husband and wife. What in life was fair? Not much. Kyle's face haunted her. Shutting her eyes, Gale took a deep breath. What kind of crazy joke was being played on her? She loved *Mike!* So what were all these new and startling feelings she'd had since she had been introduced to Kyle?

Forcing herself to concentrate, Gale removed the skillet from the burner and put a lid over it to keep the eggs warm. At twenty-three, she thought she knew herself. It was true Mike was the first man she'd fallen in love with, but she'd had a lot of dates throughout college before joining the Air Force. Now, the nights she'd tossed and turned, dreaming of both Mike and Kyle, had left her nerves raw and taut. How could she be attracted to Kyle? Perhaps because he was Mike's best friend and they were similar in some ways.

Reaching blindly for the skillet that held the bacon, Gale bumped the pan containing the hot grease off the electric burner. Unthinkingly, Gale reached out, trying to catch it. Hot grease splattered across her right hand. Pain reared up her arm, and she cried out, leaping back as the skillet crashed to the floor, the grease flung in all directions.

"Gale!" Her scream galvanized Kyle into action. In an instant, he was at her side, his arm going around her shoulders, holding the reddened hand that had been burned.

"Oh, damn..." she sobbed, gripping her wrist, trying not to let the pain overwhelm her. Sinking against his strong, supporting body, Gale felt safe. Kyle's breathing was punctuated, harsh near her ear, his breath moist against her cheek.

"So stupid," she whispered, a catch in her voice. "I— I'm sorry...."

"It's all right. Come on, get over to the sink. Cold water will help," he whispered, guiding her in that direction. The burn on her hand didn't look nasty but still his heart was pounding in his chest and he felt shaky. After fumbling with the handle on the cold-water spigot, Kyle turned it on and forced her hand beneath the stream.

The water hit her flesh and Gale sucked in a breath, then bit her lower lip.

"Lean on me," Kyle ordered huskily as he felt her tremble. She obeyed him. Her perfume, light and delicate, struck his flaring nostrils. It was the way she fitted against him that nearly unstrung him. Her hair, slightly wavy, felt like silk against the hard line of his jaw. Kyle ached to lean down and kiss her. "Take it easy, easy..." he coaxed, his voice low and unsteady.

For several minutes Gale was unable to do anything except feel. Feel the lessening of the pain, feel Kyle's strong, powerful body against hers. His breath was choppy, and she was aware of his heart beating frantically in his chest where she lay against him. His touch was excruciatingly gentle as he placed a cloth over her hand after turning off the faucet.

"Come on, sit down. You're shaky."

Wasn't that the truth, Gale thought, allowing Kyle to guide her to a chair at the table. Her watery knees had nothing to do with the burn, but with him holding her as if she were some fragile, priceless treasure.

Worriedly, Kyle studied her, his hand firm on her shoulder. Gale was waxen, and when she raised those dark, long lashes to look up at him, he felt as if someone had gut punched him. Dizziness assailed him, and his grip tightened on her shoulder momentarily. Large eyes, huge black pupils surrounded by a vibrant green, stared back at him. Gale's cry had torn him apart, ripping away all his pretenses, his good sense.

Kyle went to the sink and dampened a wash cloth. Gale sat with her head bowed. She looked so hauntingly vulnerable, her shoulders slumped forward. Fighting all his rising, chaotic feelings, Kyle crouched in front of her.

"Here, this ought to help," he said. He removed one cloth and laid the new one across the injury. Kyle heard Gale breathe in raggedly, but she didn't cry out. He kept a grip on her arm. His heart refused to stop thudding in his chest, his pulse pounding until every beat was like the beat of a kettle drum being played within him.

When Kyle looked up and saw tears form and then fall down Gale's cheeks, he lost what little control he had left. "Don't cry," he pleaded thickly, cupping her cheek with his hand. He stared deeply into her eyes.

"Oh, Kyle..." she choked out.

Her lips parted, lush and inviting, and Kyle started to lean forward.

"Hey, where's everybody at?" Mike called from the living room.

Kyle froze, his hand slipping from Gale's face. He stood, dizzied and shocked by what had almost happened. "In here, buddy."

Mike appeared at the doorway. Dressed in his blue winter uniform, he took off his garrison cap. Immediately, he went to Gale's side and knelt on one knee next to her.

"Honey?" He gently cradled her hand. "What happened?"

Gale made a frustrated sound. "I made a dumb move at the stove and splashed grease over my hand, Mike. It's nothing. I'll be okay."

Kyle backed away in a daze. What the hell had just happened? He had been ready to kiss Gale! Shocked, he left the kitchen and went to the living room. Hands shoved into his pants pockets, Kyle was angry and upset with himself.

Gale was barely able to think. If Mike hadn't arrived when he had, she knew Kyle would have kissed her. His eyes had been hooded, stormy with unrequited need. She trembled, but it wasn't out of fear. It was out of anticipation of the unexpected. When Kyle had held her, he'd made the pain go away. She shook her head, forcing her attention to Mike, who had retrieved some salve to put on the minor burn.

It was all craziness! It was the stress of the wedding, the war and the fact that Mike was going to leave in a month. The pressures on all of them were great. Kyle was Mike's best friend, Gale rationalized, and he had simply reacted out of loyalty.

Kyle slowly paced the perimeter of the living room, head down in thought. Mike would never know what had transpired. The wedding would go on as planned. Kyle would be Mike's best man, and he would be happy for both of them....

Savagely rubbing his face, he knew it had to be the jet lag, the shock of stepping out of the war in Southeast Asia and returning to the States. It had to be.

Chapter 2

December 24, 1974
Castle Air Force Base, California

Gale sat in the living room of her base home, several letters and a magazine in her lap. The house was quiet. Deadly quiet. She had just gotten off duty at the meteorology department and the holiday stretched out unendingly before her. This year there was no tree in the corner, no decorations in evidence, not even Christmas music to take the edge off the silence that surrounded her. The coolness in her home seeped through her uniform, making her feel chilled more than she should be.

Six months after marrying Mike, he'd been lost over Hanoi during a bombing raid. Was he a prisoner of war—or dead? No one knew. She slowly looked at the first letter, wishing it was from Mike, but it wasn't.

Instead, it was a neatly addressed envelope from Captain Kyle Anderson. Gently, she ran her fingers across the crisp envelope. Kyle... Her grieving, shattered heart filled with warmth and a thread of hope. Kyle had signed up for a second tour so he could be with Mike during his first. When Mike had been shot down by a SAM missile, Kyle had been there. He'd seen the whole thing.

Mike had often said Kyle was like the brother he'd never had. Since the time Mike had been listed as missing in action, Kyle had written to her at least once a week, fulfilling his duties as a friend who wasn't there to help her over the terrible days and nights of loneliness. In his first letter, Kyle had told her that Mike had made him promise to care for her if he was ever shot down and became a POW or MIA Like the Marines, the Air Force took care of its own, Kyle had informed her. And because of his promise to Mike, he would do his best to take care of her, even though they were half a world apart.

With a sigh, Gale saw that the other two letters were bills. Her parents were dead, so there was nothing from family. Her sister, who lived in Haight Ashbury, was opposed to the war and to Gale being in the service. Gale expected nothing from Sandy as a result. They were on opposite sides of an ideology that had divided them for the past four years.

This would be her Christmas present: Kyle's letter was a precious, life-giving gift. Inevitably, Gale's spirits lifted, as they always did whenever she received a letter from him. Opening this one slowly, savoring the fact that it was several pages thick, she settled back to find a tiny shelter from a storm that hovered around her twenty-fours hours every day.

December 16, 1974

Dear Gale,
This is your hot-rock jet jock writing to you from a place where a Christmas tree would *never* grow! I'm sitting here

at a bar in Udorn trying to write to you under some pretty severe conditions: beautiful Thai bar girls dressed in decidedly tight dresses, loud (and lousy) music, cigarette smoke so thick you could cut it with a knife, and a lot of pilots making eyes at all the bar girls.

Of course, yours truly is the only one doing something praiseworthy—writing to you! How are you? In your last letter, you sounded down. Don't give up. I *know* Mike will be back. Somehow, some way. And me? Brazen (to use your word) as ever. Yes, I still fly a mission over Hanoi just about every other day. And no, I haven't had any close calls. Are you kidding me? The ace at Udorn? Come on! This jock has one and a half tours under his belt. I'm considered the Old Man around here. All the younger jocks always gather around me when I sidle up to the bar, wanting stories. So I oblige them.

Thanks for the tin of cookies! My God, they were a hit around here! You know how our post office works don't you? Those enlisted guys have noses on them like bloodhounds. They smell each package. The ones that have cookies in them are somehow detoured or "lost." When the package finally finds its way to the officer, the food that was in it has mysteriously gone. All the guys who work over at the post office are overweight. I wonder why?

However, because you told me ahead of time that you were going to make six dozen chocolate-chip cookies and send them to me for Christmas, I went over and warned all those guys to keep their hands off—or else. Your cookies got through unscathed. How did you know my favorite was chocolate chip? I'd die for those. Between the box my mom sent and yours, I was the cookie king here at Udorn. And don't you think the other jocks weren't wandering over to my hooch to bum a few. Yes, I shared them, like you requested. Would I hoard them? Don't answer that. I carried out your wishes to the letter. You made a lot of jocks happy. I gave some to the enlisted guys on the flight line, too. Those guys bust themselves twenty-four hours a day, and it was a good feeling to make them smile. They thank you, too.

Hey! Gotta zoom off. One of those beautiful Thai ladies is giving me a look I can't resist. Look, you take care of yourself, hear? Your letters are like life to me here at Udorn. I really enjoy getting them. Don't stop! I won't, either. I promised Mike that I'd take care of you, so expect a letter once a week.

Merry Christmas, Gale.

Your Friend, Kyle.

December 24, 1974

Dear Kyle,

I want you to know that your lively letter—which sounded like a buccaneer swashbuckling—was my Christmas gift. I sat here with two bills, a magazine and your letter in my hand. Your letter, by far, was the one I wanted to open and read.

I had to giggle about the Great Cookie Heist! Just to brighten your day, I'm sending another box (air mail, of course, so it doesn't take three months via ship to reach you) of chocolate-chip cookies. Keeping busy is my only way to keep my sanity, and it's nice to be able to cook for someone who loves my cooking so much. So, in your own way, you're helping me, even if it's something as simple as appreciating my cookies. Baking them keeps my mind off so many terrible thoughts I shouldn't be thinking.

Enough of my maudlin musings. I hope the bloodhounds of the Udorn post office can't smell these. I've triple wrapped them in foil, plus wrapped each cookie individually to make sure no odor escapes to get their attention. And I've disguised them in a plain cardboard box instead of sending them in a suspicious round tin, which I'm sure tips them off that it might be cookies or other goodies inside.

Hi, I'm back. I started this letter an hour after getting yours. When I'm lonely, I write letters to my friends here Stateside. Yours is the only one going overseas. It's Christmas Day now, and I got lonely. I'm learning to turn on the radio or television set just so I can hear the sound of another human voice. What hurts is when the nightly news comes on and they show at least fifteen minutes of footage on the Vietnam War. I forget that it's going to come on, and then, some part of me focuses in on it, no matter what I'm doing. I'll hurry to the living room to shut it off, but it's like I'm mesmerized by some power and I just stand there watching and listening to it. What's wrong with me? Why do I have to watch the shooting, the killing they photograph?

It's worse on the radio because I never know when some news flash is going to come over it. At least with the television on—and if I can remember to turn it off—I only have to avoid hearing it at 6:00 p.m. and 11:00 p.m. I'm learning all these little tricks to avoid pain. Amazing what a human being will do, isn't it?

Thanks for listening to me. Just talking to someone, another military person, helps. I don't say anything to anyone around here because they all have a husband, brother, sister, son or daughter over in Vietnam and I don't want to depress them or make them worry any more than they already do. Thanks for being a compassionate ear. Please, fly safe. You're in my prayers every night along with Mike.

Warmly, Gale

December 23, 1975

Dear Gale,

Merry Christmas! I tried calling you yesterday, but the airman over at Ops said you'd just gone home after twelve hours of duty. I was going to call you and tease you unmercifully because I hadn't yet received those chocolate-chip cookies you promised to send this year. Now that I'm Stateside and stationed at Homestead AFB in Florida, I wonder if the cookies really got lost in the mail or if the same guys in the post office over in Udorn are now stationed at Homestead with me. I'll fill out a form at the post office, but it won't do any good.

You sounded better in your last letter. I know it's tough to go on without knowing about Mike, but you're a fighter and I admire your courage under the circumstances. Just hang tough. It's all you can do.

So, you're going to be stationed at Travis AFB, eh? Busy place. You'll be there for three years and get plenty of opportunity to visit San Francisco—lucky lady! Have a bowl of clam chowder down on Fisherman's Wharf for me, will you? It's one of my favorite places. I like the smells, the color, the people and activity. Quite a place. Take a cable-car ride for me, too. I like that bell they ring. Makes you want to get up and dance up and down the aisle while they're ringing it, ha, ha.

I can't believe you want me to tell the story of my life! Me, of all people! All I do is give you a hard time, lady. So I make you laugh a little. Nothing wrong with that. I figured it out: fifty-two installments, one letter a week to you, three or four pages at a time, and I ought to have my autobiography finished in the forthcoming year. Brother, are you a glutton for punishment, but, if that's what you want as your Christmas present, I'll indulge your whim. Next letter, I'll start. Can you see it now?

''I was born in Sedona, Arizona, to a grocer and his wife.

I was red, wrinkled and too long. My mother, upon seeing me for the first time, broke out in tears because I looked so ugly. Of course, she reassures me that as I grew and filled out, I was the cutest kid in Red Rock County.''

Whew, that was close! I'm such a handsome devil now that I couldn't let that info slip out to my flying buddies. I'd never hear the end of it.

Is this the kind of thing you're wanting to hear about in my letters? The down-and-dirty life of Kyle Anderson? Ha, ha. I think you're a real masochist, Gale—a new and provocative side to you I never realized existed. Okay, okay, I can hear you nagging me in the next letter to quit quibbling and get on with it. So—Merry Christmas! You get fifty-two installments over the next year about me and the story behind this fantastic jet jock. It ought to hit the *New York Times* bestseller list, don't you think? Nah, don't tell me now. Tell me next Christmas, okay?

I know you don't have anyone to go home to for Christmas, and you've already said you'll spend it there at base. I really think you need to get away for a while and get some down time. You've worked yourself to a bone this year, Gale. Even I take time off and go see my folks in Sedona once a year. Why not take the thirty days leave you've got coming and get some R and R? I worry about you, sometimes. You're a strong lady with a warm heart, but stop and smell the flowers, huh?

Merry Christmas, Gale. As I hitch my foot up on the brass rail of the O Club bar, I'll lift a toast to you.

Your special friend, Kyle

December 30, 1975

Dear Kyle,
I can't believe you didn't get the cookies I sent! Are you *sure* they're missing? Or do you just want two huge batches

to hoard? Knowing your love of desserts in general—and cookies specifically—I wouldn't be a bit surprised if you fibbed to get a few extra dozen.

I'm so happy you've decided to send me your autobiography. I'm going to do the same thing. Not that I have had a terribly exciting life, but I think that's only fair. As you get writer's cramp and the next letter is hounding you to be written, you can fondly think of me having to write to you, too. Only, I won't see it as a royal pain as perhaps you might as the weeks roll by. Letters have been a life-sustaining source for me, giving me hope and often lifting me out of the depression I allow myself to get into.

Actually this year, I'm doing better. But I want to get on with writing my life story to you, too! I hope you won't be bored to death. I can see you sitting at your desk, feet up on it, letter in hand, snoozing away. Ha, ha.

Okay, here goes nothing. Promise me if you do get bored, tell me. I'll stop my autobiography. As I said before, my life's pretty nonedescript (my opinion).

I was born in Medford, Oregon. Unlike you, I was a pretty baby (according to Mom). She said everyone in the hospital oohed and ahed over me. I don't really remember. However, my star status quickly sank because my older sister, Sandy, really hated me. Sibling rivalry and all that, I suppose. Mom said Sandy (who was four years old when I was born) started having temper tantrums every time Mom picked me up to breast-feed me.

My father, who wasn't long on patience or very tolerant of such childish things, stood about two evenings of Sandy's shrieking and did something about it. He warned her that if she started screaming again, he was going to pick her up by her feet and dip her head in a bucket of water. I guess Sandy believed him because she never ever again had a temper tantrum. I'm not condoning what he did, but I wonder what psychologists would say about it. Sandy is the one who became a hippie in Haight Ashbury. She went to San Francisco when she was eighteen and got into the drugs and flower-children culture. I forget how many times she's been arrested.

I often wonder why she turned out the way she did. Mom said I was the favorite of the family because I was a sweet, quiet baby. Later, I was the ''good girl'' who did what was expected of her, while Sandy started to rebel. I know this letter is supposed to be about me, but I think every person is somehow fashioned and shaped by those around them. I ache inside because Sandy hates the military and, therefore, hates me.

I just wish she could overlook my job, Kyle, and see me, her sister. We got along well as kids. It's just that in our teenage years, Sandy got wild and had awful fights with Dad. When our parents died in that car crash when Sandy was eighteeen, I think it drove her off the deep end. That's when she took off for San Francisco.

Me? Well, I got shuttled between my father's two brothers and their families for the next four years until I turned eighteen. To this day, Sandy and I have never gotten together to talk about the loss of our parents. It would have been nice if she could have stayed around for the funeral. I really needed to be held. Looking back on it, I'm sure she did, too, but there was no one else who could hold us like our parents. I remember standing in front of the two coffins with my aunt and uncle on either side of me.

I never again felt so alone. Well, I should amend that. I felt that alone when I got the telegram telling me that Mike was shot down. The same kind of awful gutting feeling. Looking back on my short life, I wonder if I'm always destined to lose the people I love. I don't mean that to sound maudlin. It's just that I see people live their lives in cycles where things get repeated. I hope the cycle changes. I want Mike home, safe and alive.

Your friend, Gale

December 20, 1976

Dearest Gale,
This letter ought to reach you in Medford, Oregon, hopefully *before* Christmas, not after it.

I was TDY (temporary duty) to Anchorage, Alaska, (where Santa Claus lives) until four days ago. The temperature extreme between Anchorage and Florida is alarming. I'm coming down with a cold. (I can see it now—the next letter I receive from you will tell me to drink lemon juice in hot water, put myself under a lot of blankets, and sweat the cold out of my body. Better yet, I'll probably receive a bottle of vitamin C, along with a finger-shaking letter demanding "why didn't you dress properly so you wouldn't catch a cold?")

This isn't a normal Christmas for me. Usually, I'd be over at the O Club with the rest of the single guys, playing dead bug or something to make the time pass. Getting stuck with duty around here stopped me from going home to Sedona like I wanted to. This year is different. Can't put my finger on it...maybe I'm getting older? Ha, ha. Perish the thought. Older but better-looking. How's that?

I can hear you laughing right now. Did I ever tell you how pretty your laughter is? I like the sound of it. I intend to call you on New Year's Eve, as always. I really look forward to our talks. I don't know if the post office or the phone company makes more money off us.

When I got back to Homestead, your Christmas present was waiting for me. What a great surprise! You knitted this sweater for me by yourself? Dark blue, for the Air Force, of course. Seriously, Gale, it's beautiful. I just sort of stood over the package after opening it, running my hand across it. It felt soft and yet strong—like you. I never expected such a beautiful or thoughtful gift, Gale. Florida weather isn't very cool for very long, but I'll wear it every chance I get. Thanks.

This is the last installment to the story of my life. Letter #52. Here goes.

Presently, I'm stationed at Homestead AFB, in Florida, doing what I do best: flying. Sometimes, though, I get tired of the military machine and some of its stupider management decisions (and God knows, they abound in great proliferation). If I didn't like flying so much, I'd quit. But what else is there except flying?

I live on base, and the sound of jet engines lull me to sleep. I like that. The house is pretty empty to come home to sometimes. Just depends on what kind of mood I'm in, I guess. The television keeps me company—another human voice, to use your turn of phrase. There's no special lady in my life at the present. Maybe I'm looking for the impossible and I've set my sights too high. I like the fact women are coming into their own sense of identity. That's why I've always admired you so much, Gale. You were a strong, independent woman long before it was popular.

My life revolves around my squadron and the duties therein. I'm lucky: I get paid to do something I love, which is to fly. Still, there's a hollowness in me I can't describe, can't seem to fill, no matter what I do. Maybe it's age or I'm mellowing. Possibly, even changing. Gadzooks! Did I say something personal? I *must* be getting old! Or maybe it's you. You're easy to talk to and share with.

There! That's it! So now, you've got the inside scoop on this jet jock. Now that it's all over, I don't feel as vulnerable as I did when I started writing my life story last Christmas. You're right: jet jocks are a flippant, arrogant lot who would *never* reveal their real feelings, their fears, hopes or dreams to anyone else. But I did to you and it felt kinda good. (Don't let that get around, or I'll never be able to live it down here with my squadron.)

On the other hand, I liked getting your letters about your growing-up years, going through ROTC in college and then into the Air Force. Unlike me, you never did have a tough outer image in front of the real you. I always knew you were a softy with a heart as large as this base. You do so much for others, Gale. I know Mike's parents really appreciate the fact you visited them last year. Mom told me it made them happy. I can't know what it cost you in terms of emotions, but I'm sure it was a hell of a lot. They're lost without word on Mike. You've managed to pick yourself up by your boot straps and continue on. God, I admire you for that. Is there a clone of you somewhere? I'd like to meet her.

Take care, sweet lady. I'll call you on New Year's Eve. A special gift for both of us. You're always in my thoughts.

Kyle

December 24, 1976

Dearest Kyle,

I'm going to miss getting your weekly letters. To be honest, your letters and phone calls have helped me stay centered during this awful period. You don't see that, though, do you? That's one of the reasons why I could face Mike's parents and stay with them. It was a cathartic experience, but I think, in some ways, healing for all of us.

Well, here's my Letter #52! Last one. I'm surprised you

haven't fallen asleep over them yet! What a masochist you are at heart!

Right now, I'm living on base at Travis. The base housing here is like it is everywhere: you can hear your neighbors through the walls. I'm surrounded by families on both sides of me and I really like that. Often, when I don't have duty at night, I'll baby-sit for Susan, who has three small children ranging in age from one through four, or Jackie, who has two, ages seven and ten.

I really enjoy the children. They give me so much hope. When I hear them laugh, I remember back to the good times when I laughed like that as a kid—or even as a grown-up. I especially remember laughing at something you had in every one of your letters. You have been wonderful in giving humor as a gift to me on days when I felt lower than a snake's belly, to use Susan's words. (She's from Texas, can you tell.)

This fall, I planted daffodils out front. The soil here is really bad, but I've tried to prepare it properly so I'll have at least three dozen plants poking their heads up in early March. It's nice to have something of home that you can bring along with you, isn't it? That's why I knitted you the sweater. To tell you the truth, that sweater was knitted during baby-sitting time. I'm surprised you didn't find a dab of jelly, a gob of sticky caramel or some other unidentifiable stain on it! The younger children especially loved to sit with me while I was knitting. And they love to touch things at their age. I ended up using a lot more yarn than it should have taken because they loved playing with it so much! Rather than them handling your burgeoning sweater, I let them play with the extra skeins I kept in my basket.

The kids have been good for me in a lot of ways. Nights are usually filled with helping Susan or Jackie (because both their husbands are SAC pilots who fly B-52s and are

away more than they're home—sound familiar?). I've become Auntie Gale to the children, and I rather enjoy my
status. There's something about a child's smile when it's
given to you, or the touch of a child's hand that just can't
be duplicated anywhere else in life. Do you like children,
Kyle? I know you were an only child and never had the
pleasure of sibling company. Let me know. I'm curious.

Take care. And you're right: enclosed is a huge bottle of
vitamin C! You'd better be over your sniffles by the time
the New Year call rolls around or you're in deep you-know-
what. As always, you're in my heart and thoughts.

Your friend, Gale

December 20, 1977

Dearest Gale,
Another Christmas. Life goes on, doesn't it, whether we
want it to or not? This letter will reach you down in Sedona.
I'm sure Mike's folks are delighted you're there again for
them. I don't see how you do it. You've got a hell of a lot
more courage and internal fortitude than I would under your
circumstances. Just your being there has got to lift their
spirits. If you were here at Griffiss AFB, which is near
Buffalo, New York, I'd give you a big hug and kiss for
what you've done for them. You're one hell of a lady in
my book.

Well, I'm finally settled into my new base—I have more
responsibility, less flying time. I don't like that. If I wanted
to fly a desk, I wouldn't have joined the Air Force.

Buffalo is—well, let's put it this way: it's not the most
exciting place for a bachelor. We've already got a ton of
snow. Hell of a change from my Florida base. I guess I
live a life of extremes. I wear the sweater you knitted for
me a lot nowadays when I'm off duty.

Until you told me, I often wondered what your favorite flower was. A daffodil. I pictured you like spring flowers, so I was close. Fall is my favorite time of year. I like the riot of color. Makes me think of some invisible painter who's gone wild with a palette of colors, slap dashing them here and there. I like the smells, too. Funny, since I've known you, you've put me more in touch with my senses. I never used to notice subtle shadings or pay attention to smells in general.

You're right: pilots are put in a little box, certain skills they possess brought out and honed to a fine degree, but everything else just sort of sits there, ignored and untended. You're a hell of a gardener, lady. I like being cultivated by you. I like seeing life through your eyes. It's made me see my world differently. Better.

Because of my transfer to Griffiss, I can't be home for Christmas with my parents. Too bad, I'd promised them I'd make it this year. I know you'll drop by and see them for me, you're that kind of lady. Don't tell my mother that I'm unhappy here. Lie. She tends to worry too much. I think she got all her gray hair while I was over at Udorn flying missions over Hanoi. I don't want to be responsible for any more gray hairs on her head. Worst of all, I can't be there while you're there. If nothing else, I could have offered you fortitude with Mike's parents and been there in case you needed a shoulder to cry on.

Hi…this is a supplement. A KC-135 tanker just slid off the end of the runway during an ice storm and I had to go help. Not much for me to do, but as one of the few officers left on base during Christmas, everyone becomes more important or integral than usual. Luckily, the crew is fine. The 135 is going to need some major structural work, but it could have been worse. Much worse.

God, it's freezing cold here compared to Florida. I think

my blood's thinned too much. It's dark and gloomy here in the office. I really didn't want any lights on, I guess. It's 1600 and the dusk is coming up rapidly. I was sitting here in my new office, leaning back in my chair, my feet propped up on the desk, a warm cup of coffee in hand, and I got to thinking about you. It was a good, warm feeling, Gale.

You've taken the last few years with so much grace. You haven't faltered at work, and you've gone on without Mike. Hanging in limbo must be a special hell for you. It's got to be. And yet, you survive. The last year's worth of letters from you has explained so much to me about you, how you work, think and feel. Reading about your world has affected how I see mine. I've got the best end of the deal, I think.

Maybe I'm feeling guilty...feeling something, that's for sure...hell, I don't know *what* it is. Maybe it's the holiday blues that strike the military people who can't be with the people they love at special times like this. I think I'm feeling sorry for myself because you're home with people I love and I'm not there to share it with you. So, don't get alarmed at my wallowing. I'm just sharing my wallowing with you for the first time.

We've shared a lot of ground with one another, haven't we? That's the good thing about our friendship. I've never had a woman as a friend. (Don't comment on *that!*) I guess I want to say while I'm in this philosophical mood, that these past few years have been the best of my life. I never had a relationship with a woman that ever got to this depth or that I allowed to get past my jock facade. It's not so bad. In fact, it's damn good. Just thinking of you, of what we've shared these years, makes my heart feel like it's exploding in my chest. If you feel one-tenth as lucky as I do, I'll be happy.

Give my folks and Mike's folks a big hug for me, will you? Tell them I'll make it next Christmas or else, okay? And give yourself a big hug from me.

Warmly, Kyle

December 26, 1977

Dearest Kyle,

I'm here in the guest room at Mike's parent's home. Your last letter touched me so deeply, that I cried. Oh, I know, you didn't intend on making me do that, but I couldn't help it. Loneliness is something I know well, and so do you, in another kind of way.

More than anything, I wanted to meet you here so we could have celebrated a Christmas together. Wouldn't that have been nice? We both could have drunk a toast to Mike and been here to help support his parents. They still are suffering so badly, I just don't know what to say or do. I talk a lot with Mom about this, and I think it helps to alleviate some of her fears. This year, she really unloaded and revealed a lot more to me than last year. I think she's really beginning to trust me. After all, I was a stranger who walked in, married her son and then left town. I really like her, but she's gotten so many gray hairs worrying.

Mike's dad has internalized the whole thing. His ulcer (which he got after Mike was M.I.A.) tends to act up at this time of year, according to Mom. I spend time with him down at Oak Creek. You know how he loves to fish. I just sit there on one of those smooth red sandstone rocks and let him do the talking, if he feels like it. For the first time, he spoke about Mike. About the possibility that he was dead, not alive. It hurt to hear him feel that way.

I guess men are more pessimistic than women by nature. I hold out hope he's alive. Dad has not. But Mom has. I really wished you had been here. It got pretty emotional for me with each one of them unloading on me. They didn't mean to, but who else could they talk to? I went for a hike on Christmas Day and wished you were here. I know that I could have cried in your arms and it would have been okay. I didn't dare cry in front of Mom and Dad. They were feeling miserable enough.

Oh, Kyle, I just hope this is over soon. What's wearing me down isn't myself as much as those I love, like Mike's parents. It hurts me to see the pain they carry with them daily. With your help, I've been able to put my pain into a perspective of sorts. I don't know what I'd have done without your care and help through all these years. I'm thankful for your support. And, like you, I love where our friendship is going. It's a privilege to know the *real* Kyle Anderson, 'cause he's a far better guy than that jock facade he wears.

I'd better go. I hear Mom downstairs. I woke up early and wanted to get this letter off to you today. I can hardly wait to hear from you on New Year's Eve! Your parents and Mike's can hardly wait, either. How I wish you could come home for Christmas. Any Christmas! You're dear to my heart, my best friend.... Gale

Chapter 3

December 24, 1978
Travis Air Force Base, California

Any minute now, Major Kyle Anderson was going to walk through the doors of Operations. Gale fidgeted nervously behind the meteorology desk, the only meteorologist on duty Christmas Eve. Her heart speeded up, as it always did whenever she got a letter or received a call from Kyle. How long had it been since she'd last seen him? Five years. Five of the most hellish years of her life. But his letters and later, his frequent phone calls had helped ease her suffering.

Licking her lower lip, Gale moved to the forecaster's desk and sat down. In the other room, twelve Teletype machines noisily clattered away, printing out weather information from around the world. Her mind and heart focused on the fact that within seventy-two hours she would know one way or another whether Mike was alive or dead.

Rubbing her aching brow, Gale closed her eyes, the tears coming. She fought them back, refusing to cry.

Sniffing, she took a tissue, dabbed her eyes and tried to

focus on the wall of weather maps. Operations was ghostly quiet. Across the way, one airman was on duty at the air-control desk. Everyone else was with family on this Christmas Eve. Everyone had someone to spend the holidays with.

Two days ago, the Pentagon had informed her that Mike's dog tags had been supplied by Hanoi as belonging to a POW. The North Vietnamese were releasing some POWs and the remains of other servicemen as a goodwill gesture. As to Mike's fate, sometime between December 25 and 28, the Pentagon would know and Gale would be contacted. Unable to stand the suspense alone, she had called Kyle.

More tears came and she wiped them away. He was supposed to go home for Christmas this year. She'd hesitated calling him. She knew how badly his folks wanted to see him and how much he needed to be home. But the pain of waiting alone had driven her to the phone to ask him to come and wait with her instead.

Kyle hadn't sounded as if he wanted to be anywhere but at her side when the news came from the Pentagon. She felt guilty about taking him from his folks and hoped that they would forgive her moment of weakness.

Gale got up and went to the Teleype room where there was a modicum of privacy. She didn't want the airman across the way to see her like this. Even now, Mike's parents waited, having also been notified. They had looked to her for solace over the past few years, especially since they had both come to fear Mike was dead. But they'd never openly admitted that to her.

Kyle was coming to be with her. He'd always kept up her hope, her belief that Mike was still alive.

"How am I going to handle this?" she muttered, burying her face in her hands. *"How?"*

Right now, her emotions were little more than taut butterfly's wings ready to shatter at the slightest movement. Kyle, flying in from Griffiss AFB, was supposed to land momentarily. A part of her was so weak after the years of terrible waiting and wondering, of being in limbo about Mike, that she ached to simply be held by Kyle. Gale knew she'd feel safe and protected from a world gone mad. The peace she'd felt in his arms five years ago when she'd burned her hand would be there, too. Her emotions were playing tricks on her. Gale thought she had heard longing in Kyle's voice when she'd made that phone call, but that was impossible.

She began to absently tear off and collect the Teletype paper, gathering it from each machine and then clipping it to posting boards. Some of the sheets would be used in plotting the midnight weather map an hour from now. Walking out into the main office, Gale put the weather information on the desk where a clean sheet of map paper lay. Working kept her from thinking. Working kept her from feeling.

Halting, Gale lifted her chin and looked out the windows into the gloomy darkness. The landing apron in front of the building had very few jets parked on it. No one flew during the holidays unless they were on alert duty. It was raining. The gusting wind sent sheets of water across the tarmac. Gale prayed Kyle would be strong enough for both of them. The waiting...the wondering had taken their toll. She was too emotionally drained to be strong any longer.

She moved to the front desk and stood watching the double doors, and she wondered when Kyle would arrive. His letters had been filled with anecdotes about his military life, funny stories about things that had happened to him, stories meant to make her laugh, to pull her out of her depression. During the past year, there had been a wonderful shift in his letters—they were more personal, more about the man, Kyle Anderson, and not the pilot. Those letters were special to her.

Kyle's phone calls weren't frequent. He called on her birthday, Thanksgiving and Christmas, just to check in on her. Kyle knew what it was like to be in the service and alone on holidays. She ached to hear his voice, to listen to him laugh and tell his jokes. There was nothing but good in Kyle Anderson. His loyalty to Mike was unswerving.

The doors opened.

Kyle stepped into the dimly lit Ops area and shook water off his olive-drab flight suit. In one hand he had his helmet bag, in the other, a small traveling bag with two sets of clean civilian clothes inside, including the sweater Gale had made for him. His F-4 Phantom was parked at the hangar, the crew chief having given him a ride over to Ops.

Sensing Gale's presence, he looked up. He hadn't seen her in five years; he hadn't dared. Her heart-shaped face was the same, and so were those haunting green eyes, that full mouth and slender build. Her hair was longer, and he was pleased about that for no discernible reason. The strands were pulled into a French twist behind her head, with feathery bangs barely touching her eyebrows.

It was the look of utter devastation on Gale's pale features that forced him to remain strong, because he could see that she wasn't. This wasn't the Gale he'd met five years ago, the woman who had courage under incredible duress. Five years without Mike had ravaged her in many ways. And still, she was the most beautiful woman Kyle had ever seen. The years hadn't dimmed his memory of her. Like a miser, Kyle had hoarded that precious, sweet memory, pulling it out from time to time to savor it, knowing that it could never be anything more.

Putting a smile of welcome on his face, he strode toward the counter where she stood. He noticed the airman sitting at the control desk, reading a magazine, not even bothering to look up.

"Hi, stranger," Kyle said, setting his helmet bag on the counter and the traveling bag on the floor. An ache seized him, and he wanted to walk around that desk, pull Gale into his arms and simply hold her. The urge was over-whelming. Kyle didn't let his smile slip, being very careful to keep the look of devilry he was famous for in his eyes—and to hide a look of yearning.

Gale stared up at Kyle not believing he was really with her. She moved without realizing what she was doing, com-ing around the end of the counter. The smile on Kyle's face changed, became nakedly vulnerable, and she saw him open his arms to her. Tears blinded her, and she couldn't stop herself. In moments, his arms closed around her. He dragged her against him and held her tightly.

"Oh, Kyle," she said, her voice muffled by his flight suit, her arms going around his waist. She needed to lean against someone for just a little while, to seek protection against the final seventy-two hours of a five-year marathon that she'd run alone. Then the words she had refused to say to herself started pouring out of her. "I'm so afraid...so afraid...."

"It's going to be okay, Gale," Kyle whispered, shutting his eyes and absorbing the feeling of her against him. "Mike's coming home. I can feel it. Everything's going to be okay." Every muscle in his body screamed out for fur-ther contact with her warm, pliant body, but he kept his embrace that of a friend. "Just hang in there," he told her, pressing a chaste kiss to her hair. The clean, faintly fragrant scent of her body sent a painful surge through him. Kyle dragged in a deep breath, rocked her gently in his arms and fought his personal need of her as a woman.

Now beyond words, Gale collapsed into Kyle's arms. The moment his hand stroked her hair, a small sob caught in her throat. She felt his arms tighten around her momentarily. It was as if Kyle knew exactly what she needed, and beyond exhaustion, she capitulated to him. Each stroke of his hand on her hair took away a little more anxiety, a little more pain and suffering. Finally, after a full five minutes, she was able to ease out of his arms and step away.

Wiping her cheeks dry, Gale managed a shy, broken smile. "Thanks for coming, for being here...."

Kyle shrugged self-consciously. "I'm glad you called. I wouldn't have wanted it any other way, Gale."

"Your parents—"

"They understand," he whispered, reaching out, barely caressing her hair. "I *want* to be here."

"It's been so long since I last saw you."

Too long. The words begged to be said, but Kyle held on to them. He managed a strained smile meant to buoy her flagging spirits. "I know."

Gale sniffed and found a tissue in the pocket of her dark blue slacks. "I'm just glad you're here."

"Hell of a thing," he muttered, forcing himself not to reach out to smooth back several strands of hair clinging to her reddened cheek.

"What is?" She stuffed the tissue back into her pocket, then raised her head and met his blue eyes smoldering with dark intensity.

"The Pentagon springing this on you at Christmastime. I wish they'd waited...or something."

With a shake of her head, Gale whispered, "At least I'll know."

The haunted look in her eyes tore at him. Kyle had to

stand there, not touching her, trying not to comfort her beyond the province of an old friend. "Buck up," he coaxed huskily, trying to sound positive. "It'll be good news. Mike will be back in no time."

Rubbing her arm because she was suddenly chilled, Gale forced a slight smile. "I hope you're right, Kyle. So many prayers, so many hopes dashed so many times and ways."

"The kind of suffering the wives and families of the men who went over there is a special kind of hell. I can't really know what it's like for you, except that I know it's agony." How could he tell her he hurt for Mike almost as much as she did? Kyle didn't want to dwell on negatives with Gale.

"Despite everything, you look pretty as ever," he said, meaning it.

Gale touched her cheek, feeling the heat of a blush sweeping onto her face. "Thank you."

"Going to say the same for me?" he asked, beginning to grin.

"You look more mature." The war had carved and etched deeper lines into his face. She saw the pain he carried in those lines.

"Have I changed *that* much?"

Managing a wobbly smile, Gale shook her head. *You look wonderful.* She longed to reach out and touch the hand that rested on the counter. A long, spare hand like the rest of him. Kyle was built whipcord lean, with a deep, broad chest and shoulders. His face was narrow, his smile warm with welcome, his eyes hooded by some undefinable emotion.

"Whew, that was close."

"You're such a clown, Anderson," she joked weakly, trying to get a handle on her escaping emotions and to pick up on his effort to lighten the mood of their vigil. Tears had come, but just the way Kyle was behaving helped her to stabilize. The tears went away and in their place, Gale felt an overwhelming lightness sweep through her. "You haven't changed a bit."

His boyish grin broadened. "The same? Usually, at my age, people say I look a bit more suave or some such thing."

She laughed, a terrible burden sliding off her shoulders. "All pilots know they're handsome devils. You don't need me to add to that confident ego you already own." If anything, Kyle had grown more handsome with age. The crow's feet at the corners of his eyes were deeply embedded, and the laugh lines around his mouth were pronounced. A few errant strands of black hair dipped over his wrinkled brow and Gale yearned to push them back into place.

"Touché, Major Taylor." He forced himself to look around because if he didn't, he was going to stare deeply into her eyes, bare his soul and then destroy the fragile truce between them. "Got a cup of coffee for this tired old jet jock?"

"I'm forgetting my manners. You bet I do. Come on around the end of the counter."

"I'm allowed to tread on sacred meteorology territory?"

"Of course. While I get you coffee, why don't you call the B.O.Q. and tell them you've arrived. I made reservations and they've got a room ready. They'll send over a driver to pick you up whenever you want to hit the rack. The number is 920."

With a nod, Kyle rounded the counter. "Thanks, I'll do that." His eyes narrowed when she turned away and went to the Teletype room, where the coffee pot was kept. Gale was terribly thin. Damn! The uniform hung on her. A deep, startling anger coursed through him. War did terrible things to all people, not just the people who fought it, but the wives and family left at home were equally injured by it. No one was left untouched or unscarred. But surely Gale had suffered more than most.

Gale tried not to let her hand tremble when she placed the mug in front of Kyle, but it did. Tucking her lip between her teeth, she looked away, aware of his sharpened gaze. She leaned against the counter, opposite him, listening to the rich timbre of his voice, a healing balm across her taut, screaming nerves. He automatically allowed her to relax, to feel as if everything would be fine.

Kyle hung up the phone. "Thanks for making the reservations," he said, picking up the mug.

"At Christmastime, the B.O.Q. is empty."

"All the bases are deserted. Only the poor schmuck stuck with the duty is around." Kyle glanced at her critically. "Which reminds me, why are you on duty at a time like this?"

Gale shrugged, crossing her arms against her chest. "Why shouldn't I be? If I wasn't, I'd be going stir crazy over at the house. I couldn't just wait, Kyle. I have to be doing something—anything—to keep my mind off the what-ifs."

The coffee was hot and strong. Kyle nodded, understanding. "When do you get off duty?"

"Christmas morning at 0700. Then, I come back at 1900 tomorrow evening for twelve hours and then get the next seventy-two hours off."

He glanced around. "So you're here holding down the fort by yourself?"

"Do you see a crowd of pilots standing around needing weather?"

"Not a one."

Gale smiled. "In about half an hour, I've got to plot a weather map, is all."

"And you have to take a weather observation from the roof of Ops once an hour?" Kyle guessed. He watch her nod, thinking how the lights gave her hair a golden cast, like a halo around her head. "How long is your hair?" *Damn!* He hadn't meant to get so personal.

"Believe it or not, almost halfway down my back. Isn't that something?"

Swallowing hard, Kyle agreed. The very thought of sifting his fingers through that thick brown mass was too much. He forced himself to think of Mike and his ordeal.

Mustering a smile, Kyle said, "In three days or less, we'll know Mike's fine and coming home to you."

"I wish I had your optimism."

"My stock and trade."

It felt good to laugh—freely and with happiness. Gale shook her head. "You're good medicine, Kyle. You take away my pain and make me laugh when I never thought I would again. Thanks."

You take away my pain. Kyle looked away from her green eyes which were sparkling with life once again. When he'd arrived, Gale's eyes had been flat with pain, dull with fear. Her words tormented him. Well, maybe he could take some of her worry and anxiety away—if only for the next few days. Sitting up, he took a good look around the office.

"What, no Christmas tree? What kind of place do you run here, Major?"

Gale grimaced. "Want to know the worst of it?"

"What?"

"I don't have a Christmas tree at home, either."

He studied her, hearing the underlying strain in her voice. "Probably haven't had one in years, right?"

"How did you know? Never mind, don't answer that."

Gale gave him an exasperated look. "Do you know how disconcerting it is to have someone know me that well?"

Kyle grinned and stood up, stretching fully. Flying in a cramped combat jet from New York to California wasn't his idea of pleasure. "I promise, your secrets are safe with me."

With a smile, Gale reached for his emptied mug. "I don't know how you've put up with me through the years, Major Anderson. I've been a royal pain at times." Some of the depressing letters she'd written to him, in which she'd let her fear for Mike and the real possibility he was dead surface, weren't her idea of chatty letters to a friend. Kyle had fielded her tough, hard questions and issues addressing her trepidation for Mike. He'd counseled her on how to stay sane and try to lead a normal life while she remained in a painful limbo of not knowing.

"Never a pain," Kyle told her, working at keeping his tone light and teasing when it was the last thing he wanted to be with her.

"More coffee?"

"Yeah, please. Hey, you got an old cardboard box sitting around here somewhere?"

She gave him a strange look. "Yes. Why?"

With a shrug, Kyle pointed to the main desk. "I think we ought to put a Christmas tree up, don't you?"

Kyle's enthusiasm was contagious and just what Gale needed. "I think you're right. But cardboard...?"

"Sure." He followed her back to the Teletype room. "When Mike and I were kids in Arizona, we had this tree house in this huge old sycamore in his backyard. A couple of days before Christmas, we'd go up there and make a Christmas tree and leave it in the tree house. You must have seen it when you stayed with the Taylors."

"Mmm. Mike's mother told me how you two used to

spend hours playing in that old tree. The view from their home is breathtaking." The surrounding country—the wide, flowing creek and pine forest—was a salve to her spirit when she visited there. Smiling wistfully, Gale straightened, handing him the mug. "That sycamore is still standing out back, you know."

"It must be at least a hundred and fifty years old." Thoughts of the tree brought back a wealth of good memories.

"What did you two do out there with that sycamore?"

Brightening, Kyle spotted an empty Teletype-paper box in the corner. "As I said, Mike and I would make a cardboard Christmas tree for our tree house every year. We'd sit up there with crayons, paper, glue and string for hours putting it together." With a grin, he walked over and picked up the box. "And we're going to do that tonight. A good-luck charm to get Mike back home alive. Ready?"

Gale didn't have time to protest. With a small laugh, she nodded, walking back to the forecaster's desk with him. She watched as Kyle searched through several drawers until he found some colored felt-tip markers.

"Perfect," he muttered, pulling up another swivel chair and motioning for her to sit beside him. "Come on, we've got a lot to do. Normally, this takes a whole day to do up right, and we only have seven hours left before your watch ends."

Sitting down, Gale watched as he placed the markers and white paper in front of her. "You mean, you're planning on staying up all night with me?" Kyle had to be tired from the flight. She saw dark shadows beginning to form beneath his eyes.

"You've got to stay up all night," he pointed out blandly.

"Well...that's different, I have the duty. Kyle, you've

got to be dead on your feet. Don't you think you ought to go over to the B.O.Q. and get some rest?''

He shook his head. ''No way. I want to be here when you get that phone call telling you Mike's alive. I wouldn't miss that for the world, lady.''

Fighting the urge to throw her arms around his shoulders and hug him for his thoughtfulness, Gale didn't do anything. Instead, she muttered, ''You're such a glutton for punishment.''

Kyle grinned lopsidedly. ''Yeah, I know. Now, come on, you've got to help me here.''

''Do what?''

''Well,'' Kyle murmured, picking up the box, ''we used to make Christmas decorations of things we liked. You know, planes, cars and stuff like that. Whatever we made had to mean something important to us. Usually we made decorations of toys we *wanted* to get for Christmas.''

Laughing, Gale drowned in his amused look. ''So, if I wanted Mike, I draw him—''

''And cut him out and put a string at the top of him and then hang him on the cardboard tree I'm going to make for us. Yeah, you've got the idea.''

Touched, Gale felt the intensity of Kyle's happiness. Suddenly, they were like two children rediscovering the joy of simple things like playing. ''Okay,'' she whispered, ''that's my first decoration, Mike coming home safely to me. To us.''

Giving her a wink, Kyle said, ''I've never given up on him being alive.''

''I—I haven't been as positive as you,'' Gale hesitantly admitted. She began to make an outline of a man, her husband, on the white paper. As much as she wanted Mike to be alive, she just couldn't shake the awful feeling she was a widow. Still, for the Taylors' and Kyle's sakes, she fought her pessimism.

"No one is going to go through five years without having a few bad days," Kyle said gently. Whistling softly, he tussled with the box and cut off the top and bottom of it. Next, he opened it out and laid it flat on the desk. Glancing down at Gale, he saw her completely immersed in her first decoration.

"Hey, you ought to have been an artist. That really does look like Mike."

Blushing, she managed a quirked smile. "Thank you."

Taking a black pen, Kyle drew the main trunk of their "tree," and then four smaller cardboard branches. "I can remember Mike and I laying on our bellies for hours up there in that tree house, making these decorations. Our moms used to call us down for dinner, but we never came, so they ended up bringing it up the ladder to us."

"Mike mentioned that you two spent a lot of time up there."

"Yeah, we used to talk for hours about what we were going to be and do."

Gale sat back, examining her handiwork. She had drawn Mike in his blue officer's uniform.

She sat back, watching Kyle fashion their tree. He took some tape and fastened the four branches to the trunk. With some extra cardboard, he shored up the bottom so the tree would stand—at a bit of an angle.

"There," Kyle said proudly, studying his creation. "It looks a little naked right now, but when we start hanging the stuff on it, it'll look great."

Stifling a giggle, Gale looked at the tree and then at Kyle. "Doesn't it look a little...scrawny?" As a matter of fact, it looked like a multiarmed scarecrow.

"Nah." Kyle sat down, grabbing some paper and a red

marker. "Come on, Major, quit laughing at my artistic efforts and get to work."

Giggling, Gale carefully cut out the drawing. "Now what?"

"You got any string around this place?"

Rummaging around in one of the lower desk drawers, she drew out a small ball of it. "Here you go."

Taking the string, Kyle cut off a small piece. "Just take a bit of tape and put it on the back of Mike, and then hang him."

"Hang him? Do you think Mike would like your choice of words?" She burst out laughing.

"He was always hanging around," Kyle muttered good-naturedly as he showed Gale how to make a loop that could be slipped onto the branch of the tree.

"Mike said you were always on his heels," Gale parried.

"It was the other way around."

"You two were inseparable."

"Yeah, we were shadows to one another, that's for sure."

She surveyed Kyle's handiwork. "Nice. Now what?"

"Well," Kyle said with great seriousness, "we always put what we wanted the *most* on the top limb, and then we'd put other decorations in descending order of importance. The lowest branch represented what we wanted least."

Getting up, Gale gently put Mike on the uppermost limb on the right. "There," she whispered, staring at it.

"Looks good," Kyle said, giving her a game smile. He saw the tears in her eyes. "Come on, what's your second wish for Christmas? A fur coat? A new car?"

She smiled and sat down. "I'm not telling. I'm going to watch you for a minute. What's your first choice?"

Kyle saw flecks of gold in the depths of her green eyes.

Swallowing hard, he tore himself away from his own need of her. These next few days were for Mike and for her, not for himself.

"Kyle?"

Damn, he was staring at her, something he hadn't meant to do. "Uh…oh, I was going to draw Bell Rock, a red sandstone butte that sits out in the village of Oak Creek, near Sedona." He got to work, carefully making an outline of the butte.

"You need to go home for a while."

He shrugged. "Well, sometime."

Gale read between the lines. "Sooner rather than later. Right?" She saw his mouth quirk. "Kyle Anderson…?"

"Sometime," he hedged. If Mike was dead, he wanted to remain here with Gale, to help her adjust. She would need someone, since she had no close family. "I'll get there soon enough. Maybe in the spring. It's no big deal, Gale." He looked at her serious features. "And quit looking like you're the Grinch that stole my Christmas. You didn't. I don't want to be anywhere else but here right now. Understand?"

She sat there for several minutes without saying anything and watched him painstakingly draw the red-orange butte. He'd cancelled his own holiday leave to be with her. There was so much sentimentality to Kyle, and so much he was sensitive about. Compressing her lips, Gale still refrained from saying anything, not wanting to spoil the liveliness of the mood he'd created for them. But someday, after Mike returned home, she was going to sit down and have a long, searching talk with Kyle, telling him how much she appreciated his care, his love, as a friend.

"Mike and I used to climb all over Bell Rock," Kyle said quietly. "It's got skirts around it, kind of like a layer cake, smooth and easy to climb over."

Gale relaxed in the chair, watching him begin to color the formation. "So, you were rock climbers, too."

"Well now, Red Rock County is really hiking country. Bell is a hiking butte, not a true rock-climbing experience."

Gale pulled another sheet of paper to her. "I did a little hiking when I was out there last year. I really liked it."

Kyle picked up the scissors and cut out the butte. "So, what's your next decoration?"

"I'm going to draw my home in Medford, Oregon. I'll use a pear tree to symbolize it, though, because it's a huge valley with nothing but fruit orchards throughout it."

His grin broadened. "Want me to draw the partridge for it?"

She laughed long and deeply, wiping the tears from her eyes. "You have a great sense of humor."

"Thanks. I like the fact you have the good taste to appreciate it." Kyle pointed to the tree she was drawing. "Is that what you want to do? Go back home?" He knew her parents were dead, but that the house was still there, empty and in her name.

Hesitating, Gale looked at the tree with white blossoms. "My enlistment's up in four months. I—I've given a lot of thought to it, Kyle. I'm going to leave the service."

He frowned. "But you've go a lot of time built up toward a twenty-year retirement pension. Why blow it now?"

She shrugged. "I guess I want to have a home...a family."

"Oh."

She met his dark blue eyes. "I'm tired, Kyle. Tired in a way I can't even begin to describe. I need time to get back to basics, back to things that give to me, not take."

"A home and children?" In his opinion, Gale would make a wonderful mother, a spectacular wife.

"Yes. What about you?"

"Me?"

"Sure. Haven't you thought about having a family and kids someday?"

He nodded, trying to contain the pain that mushroomed unexpectedly in his chest. His dreams had been of Gale, of what might have been but would never be. "Yeah...I suppose." And then he made light of it. "You know me, career-oriented all the way. I'll wait until I get my mandatory twenty in, and then hog-tie some good-looking woman who's willing put up with me and my eccentricities."

Gale looked at the clock. It was time to plot the weather map. Rising, she gave him a serious look. "You're far better marriage material than you think you are, Anderson."

Laughing, Kyle sat there, watching her move to the plotting desk. Pulling another piece of paper to him, he glanced at his watch. Time was moving slowly. Didn't it always when something important was about to take place?

December 26, 1978

"How much longer?" Gale asked in a whisper, the question breaking the strained silence. She stood at the window of her base-housing home and stared out at the rainy morning. It was nearly 1000, and still no word from the Pentagon. In the distance, she could hear a bomber taking off, the jet engines creating man-made thunder that reverberated through the overcast sky. Her fingers tightened against the kitchen sink.

"We'll hear soon," Kyle said, sitting at the table. There was a deathly waiting stillness in her home since he'd arrived from the B.O.Q. two hours ago. The tension in Gale's body was apparent.

Slowly, she turned around. Kyle was dressed in a long-sleeved blue-plaid shirt that made his eyes look even darker. Although he was sprawled out on the chair, nursing his third cup of coffee, his long legs stretched out beneath the cherry table, he didn't look relaxed. Searching his composed features, she asked, "Do you think it means bad news if it's taking this long, Kyle?"

He sighed. "They were bringing fifteen bodies back along with twelve POWs. I'm sure they're not releasing any word to the families of the survivors or the dead until they're absolutely sure of identification of everyone," he muttered. "That can take time. They don't want any mistakes."

Gale bowed her head and wrapped her arms around herself because she was cold and shaking inside. "That makes sense." Gale forced a smile, fighting valiantly to look less worried. "They said if Mike was alive, they'd be calling me...."

Gale and Kyle both knew that if Mike was dead, two Air Force officers would come to her house and give her the news in person. It was lousy duty telling the wife and children of a serviceman that he was dead.

The urge to get up, to go over and hold Gale was excruciating, but Kyle fought it. So far, she'd rallied and held her own—until now. "We've got the tree in your front room," he said quietly. He tried hard to keep his tone light, but found it nearly impossible.

She lifted her head. "Does that guarantee a phone call instead of those guys coming to my door?"

"That's a roger."

Turning to the sink, Gale began washing breakfast dishes. Kyle had eaten enough for two men; she hadn't been able to eat at all. The warm, soapy water took away some of the coldness that had been with her since she'd awakened that morning. There was such fear and anxiety pressing in on her, she couldn't shake it—not even with Kyle's caring presence.

Needing something—anything—to do, Kyle got up, collecting the garbage and putting it into a sack. Why the hell were those bastards waiting so long to call her? Why couldn't they let her know the instant the plane had landed if Mike was alive? Was he ill, badly injured? In the hospital? Dammit, they ought to be telling Gale instead of letting her twist in the wind like this!

Needing to calm his rage over the military officials' insensitive handling of the situation, Kyle took the garbage out to the cans that sat alongside the garage. Then he swept the walk, even though it was still raining. The rain was cooling to his anger and frustration.

Reentering the kitchen fifteen minutes later, he found Gale had finished with the dishes. The place was quiet. Maybe some music would help to dissolve the stillness. Shutting the door, he wiped his feet on the rug and put the broom to one side.

"KYLE!"

Tensing at Gale's tortured cry, he quickly strode across the kitchen to the living room. Gale was standing at the picture window, staring out, her hands pressed against her mouth.

"What?" Kyle said in a hoarse voice as he moved toward her, not understanding until he glimpsed two officers coming up the wet sidewalk toward the front door. "No..." he whispered, reaching out, gripping Gale's arm because she was weaving.

The doorbell rang. Once. Twice. Three times.

Kyle cursed beneath his breath, feeling Gale tremble badly. He looked down and winced. Her eyes were dark and narrowed with pain, with denial. "I'll answer it," he said unsteadily.

Gale stood there, her knees watery, watching as Kyle opened the door. Her world exploded as the two men, both somber faced, told her what she already knew: Mike was dead.

She barely heard their apology and their heartfelt condolences. All she could do was stare at Kyle's ravaged features. There were tears in his eyes, and his mouth was pulled into a terrible line of anguish.

Gale was looking faint. Kyle turned to the senior officer. "I'll get in touch with you on funeral details in about an hour, Captain."

"Yes, sir, Major. I'm sorry, sir...."

His attention on Gale, Kyle cleared his throat and said, "We all are. Thanks."

"Yes, sir. Goodbye, sir." The officers turned and left.

Shutting the door quietly, Kyle turned to Gale. She looked small and broken standing there in the middle of the large room, her shoulders slumped, eyes filled with terrible reality.

"Gale?" His voice shook as he took the final steps to where she stood. Tears blurred his vision; her face danced before him.

"Mike's dead...."

Standing uncertainly, Kyle gave a jerky nod. "Yeah... I'm sorry, so damn sorry, Gale—" He couldn't go on. Reaching out, he pulled her into his arms, holding her tightly, holding her hard, as if to take away her pain, her loss.

The gray morning light filtered through the windows bracketed by beige drapes. Kyle felt the first genuine sob rip though Gale, her entire body convulsing. All he could do was hold her, rock her, murmur words, useless words, of apology, of comfort. But nothing was going to help her.

His own pain at the loss of his best friend, someone he'd grown up with, shared his life with, was no less cutting.

They cried together, clinging to each other because nothing else made sense, nothing else existed except the huge walls of pain that battered their hearts.

Eventually, Kyle moved past his first wave of grief enough to think clearly. As he stood there, holding Gale, absorbing her soft, choking anguish, he looked ahead to the next few days. He knew Mike's body would have to be flown to Sedona. Mike's parents would want him buried there, Kyle was sure of that. He'd request emergency leave from his office and make sure Gale had someone to help her with all the details, the endless paperwork that he knew would come.

Sighing, he rested his jaw against her hair, and closed his eyes. Her pain was his pain. So much had been taken from Gale over the years. So much.

Opening his eyes, Kyle stared at the scraggly, leaning cardboard Christmas tree sitting on the coffee table in front of the couch. His gaze moved from the image of Mike to the Bell Rock decoration. Mike was going home. And they'd be going home with him.

His eyes filled with tears, momentarily blurring his vision. Blinking, Kyle shifted his gaze to the second branch, where Gale's pear tree hung. Next to it was the partridge he'd drawn. His arms tightened around her. He knew she'd leave the Air Force and go home to Medford. She would try to pick up the pieces of a life that had been stretched and tortured for five years.

Time...they both needed time to grieve for Mike, to remember him, to cherish all that was good about him and the ways he'd affected their lives.

Taking a deep, ragged breath, Kyle simply held Gale, listening to her sobs lessen with the passing minutes, the first storm of grief, of shock, now passing. There would be many other cycles of tears to come, he was sure.

His gaze remained on the tree. Gale had fashioned a pot of daffodils. They were her favorite flower. She said she was going to plant them along the edge of the house in Medford, a sign of spring, of a new beginning.

Yes, there was a beginning for both of them. Kyle didn't look at his own needs right now. Being there for Gale and for Mike's parents was what was important right now. But he would never forget that pot of daffodils. Never.

Chapter 4

December 24, 1979
Blytheville Air Force Base, Arkansas

Kyle frowned, staring at the mass of paperwork on his desk. It was 0800, and he had all day to plow through it. What did it matter? He didn't have anything else to do over the Christmas holiday, so why not use the time to catch up on paperwork when the office was empty and quiet? December was a lousy month for him, he'd decided that a long time ago. The Air Force had ordered him from Griffiss to Blytheville two weeks ago, and he was still unpacking and trying to get situated at his new command. He'd called his folks, apologizing for not being able to come home as he'd planned. There was simply too much work to do here and the holidays were the only time he'd be able to get things in order before the responsibilities of squadron command rested squarely on his shoulders.

"Major?"

Scowling, Kyle looked up toward his sergeant, who stood at the entrance to his office. "What is it, Dickson?"

"A telegram just arrived for you, sir." He brought it forward and placed it in Kyle's hand.

A telegram? Kyle nodded. "Thanks, Dickson."

"Yes, sir." The door shut quietly.

The yellow envelope stared back at him. Who would send him a telegram? He turned it over and ripped it open, a sense of dread filling him. The only time someone got a telegram was when it was bad news. His heart started an uneven beat as he read the short message.

Kyle. Come Home. Gale.

His hand trembled as he looked at the address. Gale was in Sedona, staying with the Taylors. In the past year, they'd exchanged many letters and phone calls, staying in touch, helping to heal each other in so many ways since Mike's death. She had left the service as she'd planned, moved into her parents' home, and was trying to make a new life for herself.

A deep ache centered in his heart as he mulled over her request. The need to see her was excruciating. Looking around his new office, he grimaced. Stay and catch up on his new workload, or go home? There wasn't any question what he wanted to do. Gently tucking the telegram into the pocket of his light blue shirt, Kyle got up. As he reached for the phone to find out when the next flight left for Arizona, his throat constricted. Why was Gale there?

When the reservations operator answered, it took several seconds before Kyle could speak. He recalled the cardboard tree they'd fashioned together last year. A make-believe Christmas tree filled with dreams and prayers. Some had been answered, others hadn't. He cleared his throat, his voice off-key. "Yes, I need a flight out to Flagstaff, Arizona, as soon as possible."

His need for Gale, the new feelings tumbling through him, made him shaky and unsure. For so long he'd suppressed his feelings for her because they hadn't been right under the circumstances. Now she was a widow. Was she asking him home because he was her friend? Or because she felt similarly? Terribly unsure, Kyle closed his eyes and waited to learn the time of the earliest flight to Flagstaff.

Gale shifted from one booted foot to the other, waiting impatiently at the Flagstaff airport. The small jet from Phoenix had landed, and she knew Kyle was on board. Suddenly she felt an incredible deluge of joy as she saw him emerge from the plane parked out on the tarmac. He walked quickly toward the building, an overnight bag in one hand, a wardrobe bag in the other. Her heartbeat shifted into triple time as her gaze swiftly moved to his face. The past year had deepened the lines, especially around his mouth. There were still remnants of pain there, if she was reading him accurately.

She scanned his tall, lean form. The well-worn leather bomber jacket he wore proclaimed he was a pilot in the Air Force. His light blue shirt was open at the collar, revealing a white T-shirt and a few strands of dark chest hair. He wore a pair of comfortable jeans and, to her delight, a pair of scuffed cowboy boots. Where had he gotten those? Knowing Kyle, he'd probably always had them, a tie to his Arizona roots and heritage. With his tan, he looked more like a Westerner than an Air Force major.

Kyle smiled, the exhaustion torn from him as he saw Gale waiting restlessly at the rear of the crowd gathered at the doors. Christmas music was playing as he entered the small airport lounge decorated with a tree, tinsel and a cardboard Santa Claus waving his hand merrily to all arriving visitors.

It was Gale that Kyle hungrily homed in on. She was wearing a dark green wool dress, the full skirt brushing her knees. The red scarf around her neck emphasized the blush on her cheeks. The festive Christmas colors enhanced the natural radiance of her features.

He hadn't seen her since last year, since Mike's funeral. A part of him breathed a sigh of relief: Gale had regained her previous weight; her cheeks were no longer gaunt. As Kyle slowly made his way through the wall of waiting people, he saw her in an entirely different light. She looked like a rose in full bloom, her parted lips red and filled with promise, her cheeks deepening with a blush that did nothing but make her sparkling green eyes that much more beautiful.

Shyness suddenly seized Kyle. He stopped in front of her, managing a lame smile of welcome. It was impossible to hug her because his hands were filled with luggage. "Hi, stranger," he greeted her, his voice hoarse.

Gale was equally shy. "Hi, yourself," she whispered.

Awkwardly, Kyle looked around. "Where's my folks?"

Gale laughed softly, tying the belt around her camel-hair coat. "They'll see you at home." Gale motioned to the window. "You know they don't like driving in snow, and Flag has had a record amount this year. I told them I'd brave it and come to pick you up."

"Sounds good. Lead the way, I've got my baggage on me."

Gale turned and walked down the crowded hall. She saw how reticent Kyle was and understood. So was she. They were on an entirely different footing with each other for the first time. Was he here as her friend, or as something more? She didn't know, but she had to find out. "I'm so glad you came."

"Your cryptic telegram made me come." He studied her intently, sensing her nervousness and shyness. He felt just as off balance. Trying to make her more at ease, he said teasingly, "What am I going to do around here for ten days?"

A small gasp escaped Gale and she lifted her chin. "You got ten days?"

Kyle didn't know how to read her reaction. "Yeah. Is that too long?"

"Uh, no…no, that's wonderful! I didn't think you'd stay that long."

"Cryptic telegrams make me nervous. I didn't realize you were down here for Christmas and I thought something was wrong that might demand more than a couple of days of my time."

"Nothing's wrong…I changed my mind at the last minute about spending Christmas in Medford—alone. I—well, Sedona just seemed the right place for me to be, Kyle."

He understood. Five years of her life had revolved around the Taylors. She needed their support as she was still easing through the loss of Mike. Yet another part of Kyle was severely disappointed. "Sedona's always a good place to come," he agreed hoarsely.

She smiled. "The best, Major Anderson."

"Why do I have the feeling I'm the fly and you're the spider, Ms. Taylor?" He met her smile, a sharp ache awakening in him. Gale was wearing her hair long and loose, a golden-brown cloak around her shoulders. It gleamed beneath the lights of the terminal. He wanted desperately to sift those strands through his fingers. He gently shut the lid on his heart's urgent request.

Taking a huge risk, Gale curled her hand around his arm

and led Kyle out of the terminal and into the chilly evening air. It was beginning to snow again. "As always, you're perceptive," Gale said with a laugh.

Suddenly, Kyle realized that he'd never felt happier and he laughed with her. Large white snowflakes wafted down slowly from the darkening sky. Taking a deep breath of the cold, frosty air, he shortened his stride to match Gale's. He was home.

"So, what have you got on the agenda for me?" Kyle wanted to say *us*, but decided against it.

Glancing at her watch, Gale said, "Your mom has fixed the two families' Christmas Eve dinner. They're waiting for us. Afterward, we'll decorate both families' trees."

Kyle looked for some hint of unhappiness, of grief, in Gale's eyes, but he found none. Instead, he found excitement and sparkling joy. "That's a nice thing to do," he said, meaning it.

"It's about time we all had something good happen to us," Gale murmured. She squeezed his arm, feeling his muscles tense and then relax beneath her hand. "And for the next ten days, we're going to laugh and have fun, Kyle." Gale held his gaze. "No crying, no tears," she whispered.

"You've got a deal, lady," he returned thickly. Christmas had never looked so good or so hopeful to Kyle. He sensed that Gale had released Mike and put her love for him in a chamber of her heart that held memories. Good, warm memories. Her green eyes were clear, and he saw renewed life within them. Her small hand on his arm felt good—felt great.

"Right after the meal, we'll start with your parents' Christmas tree," Gale said, halting at her bright red sports car. "And then we'll all go to the Taylors'. Mom Taylor has made dessert and egg nog for us." Gale opened the door and smiled. "I have your gift, too. Wait until you see it."

He grinned, hearing the excitement in her voice. Kyle placed his luggage in the trunk of the car. "I already sent you your Christmas present."

"It's tucked under the tree," she said, "and I haven't opened it yet."

"Better not have," he teased. Kyle wanted to lean down and brush her smiling mouth with a kiss. The need to do it was nearly overwhelming. For so long, he'd hurt for Gale, for her loss. The wind swirled, moving her hair restlessly across her shoulders. Snowflakes nestled in the golden-brown strands, and Kyle found himself reaching out, gently removing them one at a time.

Gale stood very still, drowning in Kyle's nearness. When his mouth softened as he lightly touched her hair, she closed her eyes and remembered his gentleness, his ability to give to her. As she opened them, she took a chance and caught his hand in her own, squeezing it because she wanted his closeness.

"Come on, let's go home...."

"Together," he agreed, returning the pressure.

It was nearly 1:00 a.m. before the Anderson household finally quieted down for the night. Kyle led Gale into the den. In front of them was a cheerful fire in the fireplace. Christmas music softly moved through the blue-carpeted room. The laughter, the sharing between the two families, had been nonstop. The Taylors had recovered from Mike's death, obviously happy that both Kyle and Gale were home for Christmas.

It was as if a miracle had occurred in the past year. Kyle remembered how devastated Mike's parents had been. Now, the Taylors were the way he'd always known them—

jovial and sharing. His own parents reminded him of joyous puppies, covering him with kisses, hugs and tears of gladness upon arrival. The decorating of both Christmas trees had been bonding, healing.

He sat on the couch facing the fire. Glancing up, he saw Gale studying him, a pensive look on her face. If nothing else, he was aware of how much he loved her. Did she love him? Or did she still see him as simply a friend? He patted the space next to him.

"Come on, sit with me." How would she interpret his gesture? Probably as one of friendship. The fear he felt at trying to communicate that he loved her, had always loved her, scared him. If he put his arm around her shoulders, what would she do? If he tried to kiss her, what would be her reaction? Kyle was scared to death that Gale would turn away from his advances. The thought was shattering and one he couldn't overcome right now.

She smiled and sat next to him, her hand touching his shoulder. The uncertainty in his eyes kept her on edge. The last few hours of sharing and laughter with both families had been incredibly healing. Incredibly wonderful. Whenever she caught Kyle looking at her, an ache of longing had swept through her like a tidal wave. Gale could barely hang on to the words, *I Love you.* Did he still see her only as a responsibility? Someone to be loyal to because of Mike, because of a promise to always take care of her?

Her hand felt good on him, and Kyle tried to stop the need to return the gesture. Her eyes were filled with caring.

"There are so many good memories here," she said quietly.

He laid his head back and stared at the fire. "Yeah."

She wrapped her arms around her drawn-up legs, the full green skirt like a cloak. "You ate enough for three people,

Anderson. It's a wonder you don't look like a stuffed turkey.''

He grinned, wanting to reach across those few inches between them and put his arm around her. "Tart, aren't we?''

"No more than usual. You just haven't been around enough to see this side of me.''

Kyle sobered, lost in the vision of her upturned face glowing with happiness. "We really haven't spent much time together,'' he agreed, feeling the need to remedy the situation, but not knowing quite how to proceed.

"No, we haven't,'' Gale said softly. Taking a deep breath, she whispered, "I just want you to know how much all those letters you wrote over the years helped me to keep my hope alive, to keep me laughing instead of crying. You shared so much of yourself with me, Kyle—all the silly, human things that were going on in your life while we both waited to hear about Mike.'' Her fingers tightened on her legs. She wanted so badly to reach out and cover his hands. "Each letter was like life to me, Kyle. I lived to get them from you. Your words, how you saw life, helped me grapple with Mike possibly being gone.''

"But...all they were were things about my career and some stuff happening with my squadron. They weren't intimate or—''

"You don't understand, do you?'' Gale gave him a gentle smile, realizing her words were having a powerful effect on him. "Your letters were honest, Kyle.''

"What?''

"You were vulnerable with me. Do you know how rare that is between two people? We're all so afraid of getting hurt, of getting wounded, that we protect ourselves. Your letters over the years bared your soul, how you thought, how you felt on such a wide range of topics that I got the pleasure of knowing the man behind that macho jet jock image. Do you understand now?''

Kyle turned and faced her. ''I think I do.'' Or did he? Had she asked him to Sedona just to thank him in person for his years of loyalty to her? That thought was like a knife cutting him.

Gale saw the pain, the devastation apparent on his features. Did he love her? Or had the flame that burned fiercely between them dimmed and died over time? She was unsure of what she meant to Kyle, if anything, beyond a strong, enduring friendship. She wanted to gather Kyle into her arms, to tell him of her love for him, but the time wasn't right. Perhaps it would never be. Getting to her feet, she laid her hand on his shoulder.

''Listen, I think you need some time to think about what I said. Good night, Kyle.'' She leaned down and brushed a kiss on his cheek. Would he interpret her action as merely friendly, or would he see that she was trying to show him that she wanted much more from him?

Gale saw the surprise flare in his eyes as she kissed him. Why was she being so hesitant when it was the last thing she wanted to be? Why didn't she have the courage to simply blurt out how she really felt?

Deep down inside, Gale knew she was afraid of Kyle's answer. Sometimes the fear of rejection made her less than courageous. Perhaps giving him little hints would help him come to realize what she was really trying to say to him. Perhaps.

Kyle couldn't speak, only feel and feel some more. Gale's hand on his shoulder was focusing his disjointed emotions. Finding his voice, he whispered, ''I'll see you in the morning.'' He wanted to grab her hand, drag her into his arms and kiss her hard and long. The question and hesitation in her darkened eyes made him hesitate. Gale had kissed him. Okay, so it was a chaste kiss. But still, she'd kissed him! Hope flared strongly in his chest. He managed a slight smile, wanting to reach out and at least hold her hand, but he was too afraid. "Good night."

Gale barely lifted her hand. "Good night...."

Kyle watched her leave, the den suddenly feeling empty without her warm presence. The house was dark and quiet. He walked through the living room to the large plate-glass window and looked out over the backyard toward the Taylors' house a mere three hundred yards away. The sky was clear and the stars were large and close, twinkling and dancing.

Thrusting his hands into the pockets of his jeans, he stared at the old sycamore tree standing proud and silent in the darkness. Gale's face lingered before him. Yes, he loved her. The past year had brought that fact squarely to him. He had to make a decision. He realized he'd been waiting, giving Gale time to recover from the news of Mike's death. Now it was clear that she was over her bereavement.

Fresh fear gripped him. Did she love him? Where did friendship like theirs end and a new, different kind of love begin?

Taking a deep breath, he moved away from the window and headed down the hall to his bedroom. The Taylors would be coming over at 10:00 a.m. to open Christmas gifts. And Gale would be with them. Suddenly, the need to see her, talk with her, was overwhelming. It didn't matter how fearful he was of her reaction to his admitting his love for her. He couldn't stand the excruciating wait, not knowing what her answer would be. There was so much to say. The morning couldn't come soon enough....

* * *

"Good morning," Gale said, smiling up into Kyle's freshly shaved face. He'd cut himself, and she wanted to reach up and gently press a kiss to his jaw.

Hungrily, Kyle stared into her lovely forest-colored eyes dancing with incredible life. "Merry Christmas," he whispered. She wore a pale peach blouse and cream-colored slacks. Her hair was a shining cloak across her shoulders. Kyle inhaled the flowery scent of her perfume. A tension, a delicious throbbing sensation, ensnared him.

He saw Gale's eyes widen and interpreted that as her also being aware of the sensual pulsation that had now sprung between them—just as it had the first time they'd met so many years ago. Hope swept through him, making him giddy, nervous.

Gale moved to one side as the two families trooped toward the den where the tree stood laden with gifts. She looked up, drowning in his gaze. Did she dare hope? Did she dare read what lingered in his eyes as love for her?

For the next half hour, gifts were opened amid laughter and joking. Kyle brought a gift from beneath the tree and sat down, handing it to Gale. Would she like it? Or would it make her unhappy. He couldn't be sure.

Gale shook the red-wrapped box. "It rattles!" she cried out to everyone, and then laughed with them.

Kyle managed a nervous smile and watched as she tore into the wrapping like a child. His heart beat harder as she opened the box.

Digging through a mass of crinkly red-and-green tissue paper, Gale found a small, oblong bulb. After finding two dozen more, she tilted her head, giving Kyle a questioning look. "Daffodil bulbs." Tears filled her eyes. She held the bulbs reverently. Memory of their cardboard Christmas tree at Travis slammed through her. And so did the memory of a conversation they'd had about her daffodils and the fact they meant a new beginning for her. Sniffling, she gently placed the bulbs back in the box.

"Here," Kyle mumbled, putting his linen handkerchief in her hands. Embarrassed, he looked at his parents and the Taylors. There was understanding and sympathy in their expressions. Gale was beginning to cry in earnest and Kyle felt the need to get her alone.

"Uh, excuse us for a moment..." he said, rising, pulling Gale to her feet.

"Take her into the living room, honey," his mother said.

Gently, Kyle put his arm around Gale's shoulders and led her to the other room where they'd have a modicum of privacy. Once there, he drew her to a halt, folding her against him. A groan escaped Kyle as she put her arms around his neck, nestling her cheek against his chest.

"I'm sorry," he muttered, absently rubbing her shoulders. "I didn't mean to make you cry, Gale. Not now...God, not after everything you've gone through."

She drew away just enough to see the anguish in his azure eyes. "I'm not sad," she choked out.

"No?" His eyebrows moved upward. "I don't understand."

Managing a small laugh, Gale shook her head. "Oh, Kyle, you're so sweet and good to me. You do things so unconsciously, not even realizing what you're doing."

She was smiling through her tears and he framed her face, feeling the dampness beneath his hands. The urge to kiss those beads of moisture off her thick lashes haunted him. The need to kiss her was more painful than any physical agony he could recall. "Tell me what I did," he said thickly, allowing himself to drown in gold-flecked eyes lustrous with invitation. The thread of hope he clung to grew stronger, and he dared to believe he saw love there.

"My Christmas gift to you is also a set of daffodil bulbs,

Kyle.'' She dropped her eyelids and her voice grew
strained. ''After I got over grieving for Mike, I went back
and reread all your letters. It was then that I realized I care
very deeply for you…that we've always shared something
special.'' She licked her lips, tasting the salt on them, forcing herself to look up at him again. Kyle deserved her courage now, not her cowardice.

''You're honorable, Kyle. More than any man I've ever
known. In the past year, I've realized that although I loved
Mike, there was something you and I shared, too. There
was a lot of caring in your letters to me. How many men
would have written at all, much less as much as you did?
Not many, Kyle.''

Gently, he removed the last of her tears with his thumbs.
''I didn't want to interfere, Gale.'' He dragged in a deep
breath. ''I knew you loved Mike. What I felt…how I felt
about you wasn't important.''

She took a huge risk, sliding her hand across his cheek.
''You did the next best thing, you took care of me in his
absence.'' Her voice grew tender. ''I gave you daffodil
bulbs to tell you in a silent sort of way that I want you
back in my life, I want to share it with you in a new, better
way. That is…if you want to.…''

He stood there thunderstruck, not believing what he was
hearing. Gale stood unsurely in his arms, her eyes giving
away her anxiety, her fear that he would reject her brave
honesty. A tremble passed through him and he closed his
eyes. ''My God.''

''Kyle?''

He opened his eyes and met her gaze. She had called his
name so softly, a plea to him to answer her admission. Her
lips were wet with tears, but they parted, begging him to
kiss her. How long had he wanted to? The ache intensified

within him, and it felt as if his heart were going to be torn apart. Kyle cradled her face with his hands.

Gale stood there, waiting in the silence. Just to touch his mouth, to feel the power and tenderness of Kyle as a man was nearly too much. A fine trembling flowed through her as the world slowed to a halt. She saw hunger in every line of his face, in the stormy blue of his hooded eyes.

He leaned forward, staring at her lovely mouth, and hesitated. It was a dream, a beautiful dream come true.

Tentatively grazing her lips, he felt her breath catch. The second time, he molded his mouth possessively to hers, feeling her fire, feeling her as the young, vital woman she was in his arms. Drowning in the warmth of her lips, Kyle explored her with aching slowness, tasting her sweet, liquid depths. Gale was yielding and hungry, matching his needs, telling him of her desires. There was a lushness to her, a fertileness that made him feel powerful and protective of her. She conveyed so much to him. Kyle felt her love, her commitment to him, unbridled, wild and filled with rich promise. He drowned in a rainbow of emotion.

Kyle gently disengaged from her ripe lips, her half-closed eyes telling him everything. The words, held in abeyance for so long, were torn form him. "I love you...."

Kyle's admission, the emotion behind it, rocked through her. Gale closed her eyes, a whisper of air escaping her lips. He loved her! The words flowed through her heart, and she moaned as she felt his mouth find hers once again.

Surrendering to him in every way, because they each had been denied so much for so long, Gale drowned in the wonderful celebration of his declaration. Gradually, the kiss ended. Looking into his eyes, she whispered, "I love you, darling...so much...."

Words were useless for what Kyle felt for Gale; only holding her, pressing small, heated kisses against her cheek, eyes and lips could convey his joy. His senses were acute, registering each soft breath she took. He could taste Gale on his lips and savor all the sweetness of her, loving her.

"If this is a dream," Gale uttered with a sigh, her head resting on his shoulder, "I don't ever want to wake up."

Kyle leaned over, caressing her flushed cheek. "It's not a dream. It's real...we're real."

How long they stood there in each other's arms, Gale didn't know. Finally, Kyle led her to the dark green couch. They sat down, never leaving each other's arms. She closed her eyes, content to be held, to feel the beat of his heart beneath her fingertips. The silence was like a warm blanket surrounding them.

"I'm glad you had the courage to tell me you wanted me for more than just a friend," Kyle whispered against her hair. "I don't know when I fell in love with you, sweetheart, but it doesn't matter."

"It was the letters," Gale replied, content to be held tightly within his embrace. "This past year, I wondered how we couldn't have fallen in love with one another."

Kyle leaned down, watching as her lashes lifted to reveal her joyous green eyes. "I think the first time I was introduced to you, I fell in love with you. I just didn't admit it to myself. I couldn't."

"Something happened that morning I burned my hand," Gale agreed quietly, "but we both denied it. I loved Mike, I was worried for him...."

"A lot was going down."

"Too much."

He absently stroked her long, silky hair. "This past year, I've been fighting a hell of a battle with myself," he told her, his voice gruff with feeling. "My love for you was growing out of control, and I knew I had to wait. I wasn't even sure if you loved me, Gale. I was afraid to say anything.''

She sat up, caressing his strong, lean jaw. ''I felt the same way. I took a chance and came here, hoping that you would come home when I sent that telegram.''

He caught her hand and pressed a warm kiss to it. ''You had a lot more courage than I did.'' He gave her a smile filled with love. ''Was I ever glad to get that telegram.''

''You had the courage to come. That's all that mattered.''

Her eyes were luminous with tears. Gently, Kyle framed her face and kissed them away. ''Tears of happiness,'' he rasped.

''Yes....''

''Marry me, Gale. Now. Today.''

She blinked and held his intense cobalt gaze. ''Today?''

Caressing her lips, he whispered, ''I don't want to spend another night without you. I want to wake up with you in my arms tomorrow morning...for the rest of the mornings of my life. I'll retire from the Air Force so we could be together always and forever.''

She looked up at him. ''You will?''

He grinned. ''Yeah. I'm getting tired of flying a desk when I've got a lot of good years left behind the stick. What would you think of me starting a feeder airline out of Sedona? Me and two other guys have enough money to buy a small commercial-sized plane to start out with.''

''It sounds exciting.''

Kyle tightened his hands around her. He ached to make love to her, but he stilled his hunger, anxious to see her reaction to his plans. ''Exciting, scary and a real adventure.''

''So we'd live in Sedona?''

''Yeah. What do you think of that?''

"I like it."

"You could be the meteorologist for the airline. We want to call it Red Rock Airlines. What do you think?"

Gale snuggled closer to him. "I like the whole concept, Kyle."

"It's a hell of a leap of faith," he muttered. "And it's chancy. I've got my life savings, including my stock holdings, tied up in the deal." He slanted a glance down at her. "The bank is going to own me for a long time once we get this feeder airline off the ground, sweetheart."

"So we'll be struggling but happy. It's a wonderful idea and I'd love to live here."

"You really mean that?" Her happiness was paramount to anything he wanted.

Leaning forward, Gale kissed him gently. "With my life, Kyle Anderson. So, I'm married to an airline executive instead of an Air Force major. I don't care what you do as long as you're happy doing it. Okay? I just want to share my life with you. That's all I want."

Closing his eyes, he whispered, "I love you so much. As long as I have you at my side, I can do anything, Gale. Anything."

Her smile was soft. "Darling, the best thing is, we'll do this together. We never have to be apart again, and I'm looking forward to living life with you."

"Through all the ups and downs?"

"Through everything. I love you, Kyle. We're going to be happy. I just know it."

Crushing Gale against him, Kyle knew he would never want anything more out of life—ever.

* * * * *

THE GREATEST GIFT

Marilyn Pappano

Dear Reader,

The very basic idea for "The Greatest Gift" came from a a song recorded by the Statler Brothers. "Oh Elizabeth," one line goes, "I'm still missing you."

Six words that started me thinking those two magic words for writers: What if…? What if, in spite of their love, a husband and wife just can't make their marriage work? What if, after they separate, something happens to bring them back together? And what if it happens at Christmas, the season for miracles?

And so Neil and Elizabeth Sullivan were born. I owe them a debt of thanks for my first trip to Montana to research the area for the book. I liked it so much I went back and set several more books there. Ah, this writing life is so hard…not!

I've written nearly fifty books since "The Greatest Gift," and I like to think my writing has improved greatly. But I also like to think that the early stories stand the test of time. I still remember every hero and heroine I've ever written—with great fondness, and with the satisfaction that I gave them the best happily-ever-after I could.

That's my wish for us all this holiday season. May you all find the best happily-ever-after for you and those you love.

Merry Christmas!

Marilyn Pappano

Chapter 1

It was a frigid November dawn, and the Montana sky overhead was leaden, heavy with the threat of snow. Neil Sullivan lay on his back, looking up at the ominous dark clouds, feeling a hundred little aches in his body, each slowly increasing until they equaled the single big ache in his head. Nearby, the stallion that had thrown him to the ground tossed his head and twisted his body, trying to lose the saddle fastened securely to his back. He was a magnificent sight, Neil admitted admiringly—sleek and powerful and filled with fury.

Neil shifted, and the pain doubled in intensity. "If I've broken anything, you worthless son of Satan, I'll kill you," he grumbled while he took stock of his injuries. His forehead had struck an outcropping of rose-colored granite, and blood was flowing steadily down the side of his face. Other than that and an ache in his belly, everything seemed minor—but painful, he thought with a grimace. He was going to be covered with bruises tomorrow.

He gathered his strength to sit up, but at the first movement, the ache in his abdomen exploded into agony, and he fell back against the frozen ground. He swore loudly, viciously, trying to outlast the pain, but it came in waves, fierce, intense, clawing inside him, ripping him apart, destroying him, killing him. He tried to fight it—tried to breathe, to control it, to hold his own against it—but it was defeating him steadily, brutally. He had to hold on. He couldn't die. He was afraid of dying, afraid of giving in, of losing....

An image of Elizabeth, clear and bright and beautiful, appeared before him, and his will ebbed. Elizabeth was the only important thing in his life, and she was gone. He had nothing to lose but life itself, and it was being taken from him anyway, bit by torturing bit.

His belly was on fire, spreading its pain until every part of his body throbbed. Every beat of his heart was like a blow, and every small breath of air he dragged into his lungs was agonizing. The pain was so incredible that his vision went dark, and the picture of Elizabeth disappeared in a swirl of heavy, dark reds and browns and blacks. He tried to speak, but his mouth wouldn't work—tried to move, but his limbs were paralyzed. There was nothing but pain…fear…. And hope. He was afraid of dying…but he was tired of living alone. Death could be his release from a world of loneliness, of emptiness. Death could be his salvation from a life without Elizabeth.

Slowly the strength left his body, and he felt his life going with it. There was darkness around him, and warmth—an enveloping, comforting, close warmth. The pain in his abdomen lessened, and the black, paralyzing fear eased its grip as he gave up the struggle to live.

His eyes opened one last time. His hand clenched, and he whispered one last word.

"Elizabeth."

* * *

Stopping inside the doorway, Elizabeth removed her coat, folding it neatly over her left arm, and took a deep breath to control the trembling inside. She tried to remember the last time she'd been in a hospital, to visit some long-ago friend who'd had a baby. Then it had meant the beginning of a life. Now it might mean the ending of one.

The desk was only a few feet from the emergency entrance, but it took her long moments to reach it. "Excuse me," she said, her voice shaking with emotion. "I got a call that my husband was brought here. Can you tell me where he is?"

The clerk looked up, her expression guarded. "You're Mrs. Sullivan?"

At Elizabeth's nod, the clerk gestured to a nurse to join them. "Carol, this is Neil Sullivan's wife."

The woman extended her hand. "I'm Carol Anderson, Mrs. Sullivan. I'm a critical-care nurse and the health-care administrator for the surgical intensive care unit."

Elizabeth looked blankly at the woman's hand before shaking it, then raised her eyes to her face. The nurse's expression was just as somber as the clerk's, and the panic began rising again. She had been fighting it ever since the phone call had come from Clara, Neil's housekeeper. It had been punctuated with sobs and filled with terrifying words: *accident...bleeding...critical...dying...* Now the panic threatened to overwhelm her. "Where is my husband?" she demanded in a hoarse, frightened whisper.

Carol Anderson shifted the clipboard she held to her other hand, took Elizabeth's arm and guided her down the broad hallway. "He's in surgery, Mrs. Sullivan. I'll take you to the family waiting room outside the surgical intensive care unit. The doctor will meet you there as soon as the surgery is over. Is there someone I can call for you?"

Elizabeth mutely shook her head. She couldn't speak for

fear that the delicate strands holding her together would come apart and let her shatter.

They took the elevator to the next floor, then walked past a large waiting room, where a television was tuned to an early-morning news show. Farther down the hall was a smaller private room, with a window that faced north, a couple of sofas and chairs, a telephone and another television, this one turned off. "Please sit down," Mrs. Anderson said, closing the door behind her.

Elizabeth obeyed, perching on the edge of the worn leather sofa, holding her coat in clenched hands on her lap. She looked around, carefully avoiding the view out the window, focusing on all the questions she needed to ask and the answers she was afraid of hearing. *What had happened? How had he been hurt? What were they doing to him? Would he live? Dear God,* she silently prayed, *please let him live.*

Mrs. Anderson sat in an armchair at an angle to the sofa and leaned forward. "Your husband was injured in a riding accident, Mrs. Sullivan. He has a concussion, and there's some swelling of the brain. The more serious injury, though, is the ruptured liver. That's what they're repairing in surgery now."

Elizabeth tried to remember what the function of the liver was, but she couldn't. All she knew was that you couldn't live without one. Clenching her hands together, she turned away from that thought. "Was he conscious when he came in?"

"No."

"Then how could you do surgery on him? He couldn't give you permission, and you can't operate on someone without permission." It was an awkward and clumsy way of asking, but she couldn't come right out with the real question: how serious is it? Is he going to die?

The other woman drew a deep breath. "When your husband came in, Mrs. Sullivan, his condition was very critical. If the doctors had waited for you to get here to sign the consent form...he would have died."

Elizabeth felt a chill sweep over her from the inside out. How could she live without Neil? How could she live in a world that didn't have him in it?

"This is the consent form for the surgery. Even though your husband is already undergoing surgery, for our records, we need you, as his next of kin, to sign this. I also need you to fill out the admissions form underneath it." She showed Elizabeth the lines for her signature, then held out the clipboard and pen. "Dr. Carter is repairing the liver now. Then, as soon as they're done, they'll take your husband down to radiology for a CAT scan to determine the extent of the head injury. After that, he'll be admitted to the surgical intensive care unit, which is right down the hall."

Elizabeth slowly took the forms. She read a few lines, then raised her eyes. "Is he going to be all right?"

Mrs. Anderson hesitated. She wished she could say yes, of course he would, but it might be a lie. His condition upon arrival had been worse than critical. There had been only a slender thread of life in the man. Finally she shrugged. "After the surgery, he'll be very closely monitored in the unit. We'll know more tomorrow."

"Tomorrow?" Elizabeth sprang to her feet, dropping the clipboard and the pen, knocking her coat to the floor, and paced to the end of the small room. "I can't wait until tomorrow to find out if he's going to be all right!"

Mrs. Anderson picked up the coat and laid it over the arm of the sofa, then retrieved the clipboard and pen. "I'm sorry. I know this is very difficult for you. Are you sure there's no one I could call—a relative or friend?"

Elizabeth shook her head. She hadn't seen her parents, who lived in Texas, in years, and she had no other relatives. Peg White, her best friend and boss, would come the minute she called, but she would be too concerned, too sympathetic, and Elizabeth would fall apart. No, she would be strong for herself, would rely on herself.

Returning to the sofa, she completed the forms, then handed them to Mrs. Anderson. "I'd like to be alone now."

"Are you sure?"

She nodded. She was very sure.

The nurse accepted her decision with a nod. "My extension is next to the phone. If you need anything..."

Elizabeth nodded once more, then waited for her to leave. When the door closed and she was alone in the small room, she placed a phone call to Peg. As she had expected, her friend offered to come to the hospital and wait with her, but Elizabeth politely turned her down. It was enough that *she* would be out of the shop; there was no reason for Peg to close up completely.

After promising to keep in touch, she hung up and sank back against the cushions, shuddering with fear, shock, sorrow. When she raised her hands to cover her face, she saw the slim gold band on her left hand. The matching diamond was at home, tucked away in the back of a drawer. She had removed it the day she'd left Neil and had sworn to never wear it again. But she hadn't been able to take off the wedding ring. Although they were separated, although for all practical purposes their marriage had ended a year ago, removing the ring was a step she couldn't take. In her heart, she would always be married to Neil, would always belong to him, and the ring was a symbol of that.

She rubbed the ring with the tip of one finger, back and forth, until it was warm from her touch. It sometimes seemed that Neil had been a part of her life forever, that she had loved him forever. Since she had first met him, when she was just eighteen and out of high school, on her own for the first time ever, she had loved him. He had been two years older, strong, handsome, with a wicked smile and a sexy drawl and a sensuous, gentle touch. He had promised her love and marriage and happiness for always, but they had been empty promises. Promises that she had lived on for two years, promises that she had dreamed of and prayed for, promises that had finally broken her heart.

With a soft sigh, she stood and walked to the window. Out there in the distance was the Sleeping Giant, a formation of rocky mountains that resembled a man asleep on his back. She could make out his forehead, nose and mouth, the slender column of his neck, the broad chest. It was the most distinctive landmark in the valley. She saw it every morning from her bedroom window, each day when she left her apartment, almost every time she looked outside. It was where Neil lived, where she had once lived with him.

He was a proud man. He'd been poor when she had met him, barely scraping by, but he'd been determined to be a success, to make something of himself. He had succeeded, all right. His ranch was one of the biggest in the state, his stock the best, his business among the most prosperous. He had everything he'd always wanted: wealth, power and respect. And what had it cost him? Nothing but his relationship with Elizabeth—twice. The first time she had left him because she had believed he didn't love her. The second time she'd left him because she had *known* it.

But *she* loved *him*. God help her, she loved him more than life itself.

When the door opened behind her, she stiffened, then, pressing her hands together in a prayerful pose, slowly turned. She was hoping for the best, but expecting the worst. When she saw that the newcomer was a man dressed in jeans, boots and a heavy coat and not a member of the medical staff, she gave a sigh of relief. "Hello, Roy."

Roy Harper, Neil's foreman, closed the door and came hesitantly into the room. He held a cowboy hat in chapped hands, turning it in nervous circles. "Have you heard anything?"

She shook her head. "The doctor's supposed to come here when the surgery is finished."

"You want some coffee or something?"

Once again she shook her head. "What happened, Roy?"

He laid his hat on the chair, then shrugged out of the coat. "It was that damned horse, Elizabeth."

When Mrs. Anderson had mentioned the horse, she had suspected that it was Thunder. "That damned horse" was legendary in western Montana. He was the meanest, most vicious animal she had ever seen, and she had often urged her husband to get rid of him, but Neil had refused. He had loved that horse, had admired his spirit and respected his power.

"Thunder." Roy scoffed at the stallion's name. "Demon is more like it. That horse has a mean streak a mile wide."

Her smile was weary. "About as wide as Neil's stubborn streak." How many times had she pleaded with him not to buy the stallion, not to ride him, not to risk his life on the horse? But he had laughed at her fears, had insisted that nothing could hurt him. And he had been wrong. The horse had damn near killed him.

"We don't know for sure. He rode out alone early this morning. When Thunder wandered home by himself, we went looking for Neil and found him unconscious. I guess that damned horse threw him."

Elizabeth shook her head in denial. "Neil's too good a

rider to just get thrown. He's the only man in the state who can control Thunder.''

"He's been a little…preoccupied lately," Roy said, shifting his gaze away from hers.

She looked away, too. She knew what had distracted Neil this morning—the same thing that had been on her mind for weeks now. Today was November twentieth. The second anniversary of their marriage. And the first anniversary of their separation.

She twisted the gold ring on her finger. "I'm sorry."

Roy moved to the opposite end of the window. "It's not your fault."

She wasn't sure what she was apologizing for, or what he was excusing her for. Neil's accident? Or her leaving? Both, or neither?

Maybe none of it was her fault…but maybe it was. Maybe she had asked too much of Neil, more than he was capable of giving. He had been a good husband to her, had given her everything she'd ever wanted—except his love. When she had left him a year ago today, she had asked for his love, had pleaded for it, had done everything but get on her knees and beg for it, but he had withheld it. He was a proud, honest man—too proud to pretend an emotion he didn't feel, too honest to lie.

"How long do you think it will be?"

"I don't know." She stared hard at the Giant until her vision blurred. "The nurse said he almost died. She said that it will be tomorrow before they'll know if he's going to be all right."

Roy heard the emotion in her low voice and shifted uncomfortably. He didn't know the boss's wife well, but he knew that she loved her husband, knew that she had loved him better the day she'd left than she had the day she'd married him. The breakup of their marriage had come as a shock to everyone at the ranch, including the boss. No one had known what had gone wrong except Neil, and he hadn't been talking. In the past year he had never mentioned his wife's name, had never acknowledged to anyone that he even had a wife living twenty miles away. But he hadn't forgotten. Roy knew *that*, too, from the look in his eyes. "I imagine he'll be all right," he said awkwardly. "He's pretty tough."

She nodded once. He had always been tough. He'd had some bad breaks in his life, but he had made it past each of them, stronger, bolder and more determined than ever. She prayed that he would make it through this.

With a sigh, she looked at her watch. The slim gold bracelet loosely encircled her wrist, and the diamonds that ringed the face winked even in the dreary light. It had been a Valentine Day's gift from Neil, typical—like the diamond ring at home—of his extravagance. Sometimes she thought he had tried to buy her. Since he couldn't love her, he had given her beautiful, expensive gifts, bribes to quiet her demands, to placate her growing unhappiness with their marriage.

But she had never wanted money—not eleven years ago, when he didn't have any, when she had returned his engagement ring and left the state; and not a year ago, when she had turned her back on his beautiful home and beautiful gifts. All she had ever wanted was his love, and that was the one thing, for all his money, that he couldn't give.

"Clara sends her best."

Elizabeth managed a faint smile at the thought of the woman who was Neil's housekeeper and Roy's wife. She was a sweet, gray-haired, motherly type who treated Neil like the mother he'd never known. She had been good to Elizabeth, too. "How is she?"

"She's fine. Says she's missed you." He pushed his

hands in his pockets and rocked back on his heels. ''I reckon everyone has.''

He meant Neil. Elizabeth wondered if it were true. Had he cared that she was gone? Or had she been like the occasional business deal that fell through—just one more venture that didn't work out? She remembered the way he had looked one year ago today, when she'd given her ultimatum: *If you love me, say so. If you don't, I'll leave.* He'd been cold and hard and unyielding, refusing to give an inch, refusing to lie even to save their marriage.

And so she had lost. She had issued an ultimatum, certain that he would tell her what she wanted to hear, and she had lost. As hard as it had been, as badly as it had hurt, she'd had no choice but to leave.

And now she was here, stepping back into the role of his wife as if she belonged. As if he might want her here. But she was used to not being wanted, needed or loved by Neil. She would stay, would wait and would pray, and when he was well, when he had made it through this crisis, then she would go back to her lonely apartment. Back to her lonely life.

Chapter 2

Time passed slowly. One hour, two hours, three. Elizabeth and Roy talked little. He paced back and forth, and she stood at the window, staring at the mountains that marked the location of the ranch. Carol Anderson had returned once, almost an hour ago, to tell them Neil was out of surgery and that the CAT scan, to determine how serious the head injury was, would be done next. She had promised to return with the doctor once Neil was settled in intensive care.

Very critical. That was all she had said when Roy had asked about Neil's condition. Elizabeth had been too frightened to ask the question herself. She had turned back to the window, repeating the answer in her mind, then had closed her eyes in silent prayer.

Now the door opened again. Carol was back, as promised, and behind her was a tired-looking man wearing a white lab coat buttoned over a hospital-green scrub suit. Carol introduced him as Dr. Adam Carter, then suggested that they all sit down.

Elizabeth's legs felt rubbery as she sank onto the sofa

next to Carol. Her eyes were on the doctor, their expression a mix of hope and fear, expectation and dread, all colored by love. "How is Neil?"

The doctor rubbed the back of his neck with one hand. "He came through the surgery pretty well, considering. The ground was rocky where he fell, and he suffered blunt trauma to the head and abdomen. He had an intracranial injury resulting in cerebral edema, along with a stellate fracture of the dome of the liver, multiple capsular tears and a ruptured... Well, Carol can put that in simpler terms for you. We're going to keep him sedated for a couple of days, until the swelling of the brain subsides. His condition is still critical, but at the present it's stable. Your husband is a very lucky man, Mrs. Sullivan."

"So he's going to be all right."

The doctor hedged. "Well, as I said, his condition is stable, and his vital signs are good, so we're hopeful."

Hopeful. That didn't begin to describe the way Elizabeth felt inside. It made her next question easier. "When can I see him?"

Dr. Carter looked at his watch. "You can go in for a couple of minutes in another hour or so."

Elizabeth shook her head. "I want to stay with him."

"No."

"I won't get in the way, Dr. Carter. I just want to be there."

"No." He pushed himself out of the low chair, then looked from her to Carol and back again. "Do you have any other questions?"

Elizabeth shook her head. She wouldn't argue with him about staying with Neil. There were other people who could arrange that for her. She stood up and extended her hand to the man. "Thank you very much."

When he had gone, Carol touched Elizabeth's arm, signalling her to sit down again. "When you see your husband, Mrs. Sullivan, you need to be prepared. He's been through a very traumatic event. He's lost a lot of blood, and he won't be conscious for several days. He's on a ventilator, to help him breathe, and he's full of tubes, numerous IV lines, wound drains, EKG electrodes. It's all going to look very frightening, but it's all there to take care of him."

Elizabeth shuddered uncontrollably, and the fingers of her right hand moved to twist the ring on her left hand. "I want to stay with him, Mrs. Anderson."

"I'm sorry, but that's against hospital policy."

The door swung open once more. Elizabeth turned in her seat to see Karl Nelson, the hospital administrator and a friend of Neil's. Karl was one of those people who could arrange things for her. She greeted him with a faint smile.

Nelson extended his hand, then pulled her to her feet and hugged her close. "Elizabeth, I just heard about Neil's accident. Is there anything at all I can do for you?"

Her response, when it came, was directed to the nurse. "We were just discussing hospital policy. When you donate as much money to places like this as Neil does, you get to make your own policy, don't you, Karl?"

"What do you mean? What's going on here?" he asked, releasing her and taking a step back so he could see her face.

"Mrs. Sullivan wants to stay with her husband in the unit." Carol didn't wait for him to reply, but continued the conversation with Elizabeth. "Try to understand, Mrs. Sullivan, that your husband is still very sick. He's not out of the woods yet. The cubicle that he's in is small and already filled with equipment. There's barely enough room for the nursing team to work. There isn't room for family."

"*You* try to understand: I need to be with him." But it was more than that. For the first time in their lives, Neil wasn't strong, wasn't capable and self-sufficient. For the first time in their lives, he *needed* her, and she had to be there.

Carol was sympathetic, but her first duty was to the patient, not the patient's wife. She tried once more. "Consider Mr. Sullivan's condition—"

Elizabeth's blue eyes grew frigid and dark. "I'm not going to do anything to endanger Neil."

"No, of course not, Elizabeth, that's not what Carol meant," Nelson interjected, laying a soothing hand on her shoulder. "Listen, I'll talk to Dr. Carter and see what can be arranged. Now, why don't you come and have lunch with me, and by the time you get back, you can see Neil."

She knew she couldn't eat, but as long as Karl could arrange permission for her to stay with Neil, she would do whatever he said. She stood, picking up her coat and purse. "Roy, will you come with us?"

He got to his feet, too. "No, Elizabeth, I'd better get back to the ranch. There's work to be done. If you need anything, give us a call, all right?"

"I will. And I'll let you know what's happening." Impulsively she embraced the older man. "It will mean a lot to Neil that you were here." Then she turned from him to the nurse. She felt badly for going over the woman's head to the administrator, but she'd done what she'd had to. "Thank you, Mrs. Anderson."

Carol nodded. "I'll be around the unit. If there's anything I can help you with, let me know."

Karl guided Elizabeth to the cafeteria at the opposite end of the hospital. She accepted a cup of coffee but couldn't bring herself to eat anything, not yet. Maybe after she saw Neil, saw with her own eyes that he was all right...

After lunch, Karl left her in the waiting room again while he talked to Dr. Carter. The doctor was annoyed at having his orders countermanded, but he grudgingly showed Elizabeth to the tiny cubicle where Neil lay. "You can stay for only ten minutes this time," he said flatly, pausing outside the room. When she started to protest, he raised one hand. "Starting tomorrow, you can stay as long as you want, but not today. We've got too much to do."

When she nodded her understanding, he opened the door and stepped back so she could enter.

Elizabeth hesitated. Two more steps and she would see Neil for the first time in a year. He would be on his back, with machines breathing for him, monitoring every heartbeat, every change in his condition. He would be helpless, vulnerable and weak for the first time in his life. When he woke up, his fierce pride wouldn't like the fact that she had seen him this way.

She closed her eyes to gather her strength, then took the two steps.

Even with Carol's warning, she wasn't prepared for the sight that greeted her. The room was dimly lit, and the single bed was flanked by numerous machines. Bags of intravenous fluids and blood hung above the bed, giving life with their steady drips. There were tubes in his nose that were connected to various machines, IV needles in his neck and chest, as well as in one wrist and the back of the other hand. He was pale, his features drawn and still. Oh, God, he was *so* still.

Elizabeth walked slowly to the bed, leaned her arms on the side rails and looked at her husband. Although he was motionless, he was alive. She saw the steady beat of his heart, displayed on the monitor over the bed, and heard the slow, even flow of mechanical breathing to prove it.

She touched his hand, careful of the needle taped to the side of his wrist, and the tears that she'd been damming inside slipped out, hot, salty, full of sorrow and grief and joy. He was alive. Thank God, he was alive.

"Mrs. Sullivan?" Dr. Carter closed the door behind him and approached the bed. "You have to go now."

She had circled to the opposite side of the bed, her fingertips resting lightly on Neil's left hand. "Why is his wedding ring taped?" she asked, her voice soft and quiet and sad.

"They didn't have time to remove it in the emergency room. We'll take the tape off, and you can take it home with you, if you'd like."

Her eyes, when she lifted them to his face, were wide and startled. "No, don't do that." Like her, Neil had always worn his wedding band. If they took it from him, the fragile bond that she shared with him might be broken.

"You have to go now, Mrs. Sullivan."

She ignored his command. "He looks so..." She couldn't say it aloud. Dead. The steady heartbeat and even breathing that had comforted her only moments ago were disturbing now. His heart beat only because he breathed, and he breathed only because the ventilator beside the bed was forcing oxygen into his lungs. "Can he breathe on his own?"

"Yes."

"Then why...?" She indicated the machine with a nod.

"The ventilator assists his breathing—helps regulate it, sort of like a pacemaker helps regulate the heartbeat. We'll take him off it in a couple of days." He paused briefly, then added more softly, "He's critical, Mrs. Sullivan, but stable. That's the best that we could hope for."

"That's supposed to be reassuring, isn't it?" Elizabeth asked, her smile sad. "Because he isn't getting worse. But it also means that he isn't getting better."

"It takes time."

Slowly she drew her hand away from Neil's, gathered her belongings and walked to the door. There she paused to look at the doctor again. "I know you'll only be letting me stay here because Karl Nelson asked you to. I appreciate it very much, Doctor. I won't abuse the privilege."

He looked at his patient for a moment, then went outside with her. "Leave your number at the desk, go home and get some rest. There's no sense in hanging around here any longer today."

She considered his suggestion, but the idea of leaving the hospital—of leaving Neil—was frightening. She shook her head. "I think I'd like to stay here a little longer."

"Mrs. Sullivan—is it all right if I call you Elizabeth?" At her assent, he continued. "I told you, Elizabeth, he's stable and, as you pointed out, that means nothing is changing. Go home. If something happens, we'll call you, and you can be back in ten, fifteen minutes. If you're going to spend tomorrow with him, you need to rest today."

Once again she shook her head. It was too risky. Neil's life was at stake. She had to be there.

The doctor gave a shrug. He had already learned that Neil Sullivan was a fighter—the man should have died, but he was stubbornly hanging on. It seemed that his wife was as strong. "Don't tire yourself out, or you'll be no good at all to him when he needs you."

She thanked him once more, then walked down the hall to the big waiting room. An elderly man sat in a wheelchair in front of the television, laughing at the stale jokes of a game show host. A young mother, her husband and their daughter exclaimed over Polaroids of their newborn baby. A teenage boy, his leg encased in a cast, was flirting with a nurse's aide, who was signing the plaster with a bright red pen.

Elizabeth felt lost, empty. For a brief moment she wished that she could walk past those happy people, down the hall and out the door and just keep on going. She had lived so much of her life for Neil, and what had it brought her besides heartache? The weeks after she had moved out of his house last year had been the most miserable of her life. If she stayed here now, she would fall under his spell again, and it would be more painful than ever to break free again, because their relationship was *stable*, she thought with a grim smile. Nothing had changed. She loved him, and he didn't love her. Simple facts. Cold facts.

But she couldn't walk away, even if it *was* the only way of protecting herself this time. As long as Neil was unconscious and in danger, she would stay with him. She would love him and pray for him and will him to live. When he awoke and no longer needed her, then she would leave. And this time, she promised herself, she would never see him again.

Chapter 3

It was cold on Tuesday morning, the bleak sky promising snow and failing to deliver. Elizabeth stood at the single window in the cubicle that served as Neil's room and stared outside. Neil lay in the bed behind her, looking the same as when she'd seen him yesterday. Motionless. Lifeless.

Everything was fine, Dr. Carter had told her on his morning rounds. Last night had been peaceful, uneventful, and the results of the testing they had done were encouraging. Others besides the doctor went in and out of the room all morning—nurses, a respiratory therapist, lab technicians, the anesthesiologist who had been with Neil in surgery. They tested, examined, checked the equipment, drew blood, and through it all Neil never moved, never flinched, never responded in any way to this invasion of privacy and dignity.

"I'm through now," the nurse said, removing the surgical gloves she wore and tossing them into the wastebasket. When she had begun changing the wound dressing, Elizabeth had watched, curious to see what they had done to him. But when the nurse had removed the soiled Telfa and gauze dressing and Elizabeth had seen the incision, nearly twelve inches long, that cut from the middle of his chest down, she had turned away, sickened with guilt and shock and sorrow. He must have been in so much pain, and she hadn't been there with him.

Now she walked to the side of the bed, touching her fingers to his left hand, looking down at him with teary eyes. He was a handsome man, tall and broad-shouldered, but lean. His hair was black, a soft, hazy, dull-cdgcd color, and his eyes steel gray. They were the most beautiful eyes she had ever seen, quick to laugh, quicker to turn cold and hard. His mouth was finely shaped, softened in the early months of their marriage by a smile, but often fixed in a stern, tight-lipped scowl at the end.

She rubbed her fingertip over his wedding band. The tape had been removed, but bits of adhesive remained, dulling the gold. When she had placed it on his finger two years ago it had been bright, shiny, new, full of promise. Now there were tiny scratches and imperfections, and the luster was gone. It was a fitting symbol of their marriage.

How had they come to this? she wondered sorrowfully. When she had married Neil, she had envisioned fifty or more anniversaries—cheerful, happy occasions that called for joyous celebrations, reaffirmations of their love. Not days like their first anniversary. Certainly not days like yesterday. But when she had married him, she had believed that he loved her. He hadn't mentioned love, but he had talked about marriage and children and forever, and she had been convinced that it meant the same.

How long had it taken her to realize that something was wrong? Six months? Seven? When had her perfect husband grown distant, inattentive, almost bored with her? She had ignored it, had made excuses, had pretended that it wasn't happening. But by the time their anniversary had arrived, she had long since forgotten how to ignore, how to pretend. By then she had been so hungry, so desperate to have his love, that she had gambled everything on it—her own love, her marriage, her future. And she had lost.

"Oh, Neil," she whispered, her voice thick with tears. "I didn't want to leave you, didn't want to lose you. I only wanted you to love me. I couldn't stay without your love. Why was that more than you could give?"

But there was no answer. Just the cadence of his breathing—slow, steady, unchanging.

As she had done the day before, Elizabeth spent all of Wednesday at Neil's bedside, rarely speaking but always touching him, willing him to feel her presence, to come back to life—and to her.

It was late that evening when Dr. Carter stopped in. "We're going to let him wake up tomorrow," he announced, leaning on the bed rails across from Elizabeth.

Tomorrow was Thanksgiving, she realized. How appropriate. If Neil was all right, she would be thankful for the rest of her life. "Are you sure you can do that?" she asked cautiously. "He looks the same as always. Nothing's changed."

"Things *have* changed. The swelling of the brain has gone down, he's gotten stronger, and his body is already starting to heal itself."

But those things were happening inside, out of sight. All she could see was that the outside hadn't changed. There was no movement, no response to the pain, not even an involuntary eye movement. The only outward change was the heavy stubble that now covered his jaw. "Are you sure he isn't in a coma?"

"Actually, he is. It's called a drug-induced coma. There's nothing to worry about, Elizabeth. Today's CAT scan looked good, so tomorrow morning he'll wake up naturally. He'll be in pain when he awakes, and he might not remember what happened right away, but that's to be expected. He's been through a pretty traumatic experience.''

She closed her eyes and murmured a prayer. In one more day Neil would be awake and, thank God, he would be all right.

...And in one more day she would have to leave. She could handle an unconscious, helpless Neil; that way he had no power to hurt her. But awake, flowing with vitality and power—that Neil could destroy her. That Neil had never needed her, had only rarely wanted her. It wouldn't matter to him one way or the other if she was here, just as it hadn't mattered to him whether or not she lived with him.

Careful of the IV, she squeezed his fingers tightly. It would be hard—to not see him again, to not touch him or talk to him, to once again be out of his life—but other things had been hard, and she had survived. She would survive this, too.

''You *will* be here when he wakes up, won't you?''

She looked up at the doctor. ''I'm not sure that Neil would want me here.'' Not sure that she could handle being here.

He considered that for a moment, weighing it against her obvious love for her husband and the heartrending pain that darkened her eyes. ''If that's the case, then he can throw you out when he's strong enough. But I want you here tomorrow, all right? It might be easier for him if there's a familiar face.''

Easier for him...but harder than ever for her. She would have to look at his dear face, into his beautiful eyes, awake and alert, and see once again the cold proof that he didn't love her. But she nodded her agreement anyway, confirming it with her quiet words. "I'll be here. But only until he's awake, until you're sure he's all right. Then I have to go." Then she would go back to her quiet, lonely life, and she would deal with the fresh breaks in her already broken heart.

The powerful sedative that had been routinely injected into the IV in Neil's hand was conspicuous in its absence Thursday morning. Elizabeth waited nervously beside the bed while the nurse finished changing the dressing. The sight of the wound, long and red, with its row of metal clips holding the skin together in place of sutures, didn't disturb her as it had only two days ago. It would leave a long, thin scar, but that was a small price to pay for the return of his life.

"How long will it take him to wake up?"

"Probably a couple of hours," the nurse replied. She gave Elizabeth a smile. "We're having Thanksgiving dinner in the cafeteria today. You're welcome to join us."

It was a tempting offer. Maybe she could arrange to be out of the room when Neil was finally awake. She could avoid having to see him, having to hear him say that he didn't want her with him. She could get the bad news from the doctor; then she could go home and mourn in private. "No, thank you," she murmured anyway. "I'll stay here."

If pain had a color it was white—bright, blinding, take-your-breath-away white. It surrounded him, burned him, set his entire body aflame. He tried to move to ease it, but his body refused to obey. He tried to groan, but there was no sound. There was only the pain.

He was alive, Neil thought with a vague sense of relief. He had to be—he couldn't be dead and hurt this badly. He tried again to move and failed, tried again to speak. When his voice refused to work, he felt the panic growing inside him, expanding, filling his chest. What was wrong with him? Why was his mind so fuzzy, his body so uncooperative?

He tried to calm himself, rationally, logically. He was alive, but maybe he wasn't awake. Maybe this feeling of helplessness was all part of a dream. If he opened his eyes, he would know.

His lids moved, then fluttered open. His vision was blurry, the colors washed out. He blinked several times, struggling to bring the objects before him into focus. There was a white sheet covering him, a beige wall in front of him, a tiled ceiling above him and machines beside him. He was in a hospital, he realized. At least that explained the pain.

Slowly he folded the fingers of his left hand into a fist, enclosing his thumb in the center so that he could feel the cool metal of his wedding ring. The movement caused the tape on the back of his hand to pull tautly, tugging at the skin and hair.

A sound echoed around the room. A sigh, he thought. His body might not be working very well, but his ears were better than ever, amplifying that faint exhalation several times over. He became aware of another sound, rushing like the wind, in and out, matching the rhythm of his breathing, and identified it as the machine beside his bed. He must have been in pretty bad shape, he acknowledged, to merit all this equipment.

Shifting his eyes to the left, he looked for the person who had sighed and found her standing in front of the window: tall, slim, blond-haired. Elizabeth.

He must be dreaming after all, he thought sadly, because Elizabeth had left him. He had disappointed her, had cheated her once too often, and she had left him, and nothing he could do would ever bring her back. Once she had loved him, but he had turned that love to hate. Once she had wanted him, but he'd destroyed that, too. She would never come back to him now, except in his dreams.

The door on his right opened, but he didn't turn to look at the newcomer. His eyes, still a bit unfocused, were on the woman who looked so much like his wife.

"For once I timed my visit just right," Dr. Carter said when he saw that his patient was awake. He came to stand beside the bed. "Can you hear me, Neil?"

At the doctor's question, Elizabeth whirled away from the window and found Neil's gaze, unsteady, dazed, locked on her. Tears came to her own eyes, but she blinked them away and hesitantly approached the bed.

"Talk to him, Elizabeth," the doctor urged.

She looked down at him and felt the tears returning again. "Neil…" How could she talk to him when all she wanted to say was, "I love you"?

She touched his fist, and he uncurled his fingers long enough to accept hers. He lacked the strength to grasp her hand tightly, but he held on the best he could.

God, she was really here—and even more beautiful than he had remembered. Her hair, swinging past her shoulders, was blond and as soft as silk. Her eyes were lowered, but he had never forgotten their clear blue shade, their warmth, their gentleness, their love. If he could see into them now, would he see the love still there, or had it been replaced by hate—or, worse, nothing at all?

He tried to speak, to say her name. The noise that came from his throat was his voice, but it didn't form "Elizabeth." It was only a sound, hoarse, harsh, painful, and it frightened him.

"Don't try to talk," Dr. Carter instructed. "You have a couple of tubes in your throat. You can't talk until we take one of them out, and even then your throat's going to be sore for several days.'' He slid his hands into the pockets of his lab coat. ''I'm Dr. Carter. You were brought here four days ago after a riding accident. Do you remember that?''

Slowly Neil nodded. It had been cold that morning, and he'd been thinking about Elizabeth when suddenly, somehow, the stallion had thrown him. There had been such pain, then... He couldn't remember what had happened next.

''You had a concussion and a ruptured liver. We repaired the liver in surgery, and we've been keeping you sedated because of the head injury. Elizabeth has been here with you the whole time,'' Carter filled in. ''Are you feeling any pain now?''

Once again he nodded, and he felt Elizabeth's fingers tighten around his. The doctor gently touched his belly, asking, ''Here?'' and Neil winced.

''It's going to be tender for a while. What about your head? Does that hurt?''

He remembered the blood flowing down his face and the ache that had centered in his forehead. It hurt now, but not badly, so he shook his head.

''We can give you something for the pain—''

He signaled no again. He had lost four days—four days that Elizabeth had spent at his side. He wouldn't lose another minute with her.

Dr. Carter nodded approvingly. It was a good sign that the pain wasn't bad enough to require medication. ''I'm going to send a lab tech in here to draw some blood. If we find that everything's all right, we'll disconnect the ventilator and remove the nasotracheal tube, and you'll be able to talk soon.''

There were a million things he wanted to say, Neil

thought, shifting his gaze to Elizabeth again. He wanted to tell her how glad he was to see her, how sorry he was for hurting her, how much he loved her. He wanted to ask her to forgive him, to ask her, plead with her, to go home with him, to make a life with him.

"Any questions?" Carter looked from Neil to Elizabeth. When they both gave negative responses, he spoke again in his most authoritative manner. "All right, then, Neil, I want you to get some rest. You're going to be weak for a while, and once the tube comes out I imagine you'll have a few things to say to your wife, so rest. Elizabeth, you're going down to the cafeteria to eat. You've been skipping too many meals the past few days, and if you don't start eating, you're going to end up in a bed here yourself. Understand?"

She started to protest, to tell him that she wasn't hungry, but on second thought, she closed her mouth on the words. Eating lunch would give her a little time away from Neil, time that she needed to prepare herself. When he could talk, he probably *would* have a few things to say to her—very likely unpleasant, hurtful things. She leaned over the bed, hoping that he was still too disoriented to read anything in her eyes, and asked softly, "Do you mind?"

Selfishly he wanted to say yes, to insist that she stay with him. Even if he couldn't talk, he could look at her, and, after more than a year without her, just looking was a gift to be treasured. But grimly he shook his head and released her hand, signaling her to go.

He looked like a lost little boy, left behind by all his friends, Elizabeth thought, and it made her smile faintly. "I'll be back."

She left the room, followed closely by the doctor, his hand on her shoulder. Neil willed the tension at that sight to leave his body and turned his mind to more pleasant thoughts.

Elizabeth was still in love with him. She might deny it later or put it down to emotion, but he knew that had been love in her eyes when she leaned over him. He hadn't seen it in a long time, but he would never forget it, and this time he wouldn't lose it.

He was awfully optimistic for a man lying helpless in a hospital bed, unable even to speak, he thought with a hint of bitterness. He was already a two-time loser with Elizabeth; why should this time be any different?

Because this time nothing was going to stand in his way—not his pride or his ego or Elizabeth herself. This time he was going to love her so thoroughly that she could never, not even in her darkest, weakest moment, doubt him. This time he was going to give her everything she'd ever wanted: his heart, his body, his soul, his self.

Besides—he managed a weak smile as his eyes closed—the third time is the charm.

She was dawdling, Elizabeth admitted, setting her mouth in a firm line as she hung up the phone. More than two hours had passed since she'd left Neil's room—time she'd spent in the cafeteria, sharing Thanksgiving dinner with two of his nurses, lingering over pumpkin pie and coffee and on the phone, placing calls to the ranch, to Peg and to her parents. She gave details of Neil's condition to Clara and Peg and somberly wished her parents a happy holiday.

She was afraid to face him again. If he couldn't talk yet, the silence would be awkward and uncomfortable. If he could talk...well, she was afraid of what he would say. Whether he wanted her to stay or go, to care for him or to get out of his life, she was afraid. If he wanted her to stay, she would say yes, and she would be lost in the heartache once more. If he wanted her to go, she would leave, but the heartache would still be there. Could she possibly protect herself from him, one way or the other?

She went to his room, slowly pushing the door open. She was so used to seeing him there unconscious, motionless, that it was something of a surprise to see his head swivel around, his dark gray eyes open and alert, watching her enter. She saw immediately that the ventilator was disconnected, and the tube hooked up to it removed. Now he could talk. Now he could tell her to go or stay. She didn't know which she would rather hear from him.

"Elizabeth." His voice was a hoarse, harsh parody of its normal low, smooth-as-silk self.

Protect herself? she thought, closing the door and approaching the bed. What a joke. With one word, one rasping, rough word, he had her trembling inside and out. He could destroy her, and she couldn't stop him.

She stopped a safe distance away, too far for him to touch her, and clasped her hands together. "How do you feel?"

"Awful." He paused, swallowing carefully over the soreness in his throat, then continued. "It hurts."

That brought her a few steps closer. She knew that it hurt, knew that he wouldn't even have mentioned the pain if it hadn't been strong. "Do you want me to call the nurse?"

"No." He lifted his right hand, extending it to her. "Please," he murmured when she hesitated.

She took his hand, lacing her fingers through his, feeling the weakness in his grasp. His vulnerability touched the love deep inside her, filling her with it to overflowing. Lord, how could she love him so much when he had hurt her so badly?

"Thank you for coming back." She had been gone so

long that he'd begun to suspect she had run away, leaving him and the hospital behind. That was what she always did when she was hurt or angry or fed up. The first time she had fled to Wyoming, then Colorado, then drifted to California before returning here to Helena nine years later. The second time she had run only twenty miles, to a tiny apartment and a job in Peg's shop. If she left him a third time, how far would she go?

With her free hand, she brushed his hair, thick and heavy, from his forehead. "Maybe you shouldn't talk, Neil. Dr. Carter said your throat would be sore. Let it heal."

"Then you talk." He was tired again. His eyes wanted to close, but he struggled to keep them open, to keep Elizabeth in focus. "Tell me that you'll stay…. Please… stay…"

She continued to stroke her fingers across his forehead in slow, soothing movements. When his eyes closed, so did hers, to hide the tears. "I'll stay, Neil," she whispered. It was a decision that might cost more than she could bear to pay, but whether it was only a few days or—please, God— a few weeks, as long as he needed her, she would stay.

Chapter 4

Being with Neil again was easy—frighteningly easy, Elizabeth realized when she returned each night to her apartment. He was weak and often slept, but when he was awake... Oh, when he was awake, she found such pleasure in his company, just like before. She found herself hoping that this time the pleasure would last, but such hopes were futile. It hadn't lasted the first time, or the second. Why should this time be different?

But she still hoped, still prayed. She had to, because she was in such danger. Every hour she spent with him, every time he looked at her or spoke to her or touched her, she fell a little farther into the trap of her love. She was so close to forgetting that he didn't love her or, worse, deciding that it didn't matter. All that mattered was being with him.

At the sound of his voice, still faintly hoarse but raised in irritation, she turned from the window. He was feeling better today, the one-week anniversary of his surgery. She could tell, because he had argued with every nurse and aide foolish enough to enter his room, about everything from the soft diet they were feeding him to the gown he was forced to wear instead of pajamas to the question of whether or not he could shave himself.

"Neil, quit being so difficult and let the woman do her job," Elizabeth said, going to stand beside the bed. She gave the nurse a sympathetic smile. "He was much better behaved in intensive care."

Neil scowled at her. "I was unconscious then."

Laughing, she laid her hand on his arm. "Precisely." She extended her other hand to the nurse. "Let me shave him. I've done it a time or two before."

The nurse gladly handed over the supplies and left the room, mumbling to herself.

"I can shave myself," he grumbled. "I've been doing it since I was sixteen."

"You heard what she said. You're still weak." She smoothed handfuls of lather over his beard, cleaned her hands and picked up the razor.

"I'm not that weak, sweetheart," he muttered as she sat on the mattress facing him. He definitely wasn't too weak to appreciate the scent of her perfume as she leaned over him, or the touch of her hands on his face, or the warmth radiating from her body, and he wasn't too weak to respond physically to those things. He shifted uncomfortably under the covers, bringing a frown to Elizabeth's face.

"You have to be still," she chided, lifting the razor from his throat. "I'd hate to give Dr. Carter another cut to sew up."

"How do you expect me to be still when you're this close?"

"Hush."

For once he obeyed her, closing his mouth and his eyes. He inhaled deeply of her sensual fragrance, wondering how much of it was perfume and how much was Elizabeth. It was a scent that, even after a year, seemed to permeate his house, his bedroom, his bed, even though he knew it existed only in his mind. In his dreams.

Elizabeth made long, clean strokes with the sharp blade, shaving away the black beard, revealing the dark, smooth skin underneath. His face was too handsome, too dear, to hide under a beard, she had decided long ago, and he had remained clean-shaven ever since. "There," she said softly, using a damp towel to wipe away the remaining traces of shaving cream. "Without even a nick."

She started to draw back, but Neil stopped her with the gentle touch of his hand. "Elizabeth..." His eyes held hers while his fingers traced lightly over her jaw, down her throat to the pulse at its base. There were so many things he wanted to say, but none of them would come, nothing but the sweet sound of her name. "Elizabeth."

Taking his hand in hers, she lifted it away, laying it on the covers as she stood up. "It's time for your walk," she said, her voice soft and unsteady, her hands unsteady, too, as they picked up his robe. "Let's see how far you can go."

That was exactly what he intended, Neil thought as he let her help him with the robe and slippers. He wanted to see if he could go all the way. With her. Forever.

Tuesday afternoon Dr. Carter came in to remove the wound clips. Neil watched, his attention divided between the incision and Elizabeth's reaction to it. She had always managed to be elsewhere when the wound was uncovered, because it bothered her. Was she one of those people who couldn't bear physical imperfection? Or did it upset her because it was evidence of the pain he'd suffered?

Elizabeth stood beside the bed, viewing the scar for the first time since that day in intensive care. That day she had reacted with guilt, sorrow. Since then, she had avoided seeing it for other reasons. When the scar was exposed, so was a good portion of his body—his strong chest, hard stomach, flat abdomen. She was having enough problems without dealing with her physical response to his body.

Dr. Carter removed the clips, replacing them with narrow strips of porous tape. "We'll use the Steri-strips for a few days, just to make sure that the wound edges don't separate," he explained, then surveyed his handiwork with obvious pleasure. "I do good work, don't I?"

It was Elizabeth who replied. "Very good. It looks nice." Strong. Masculine. Erotic.

The thick mat of black curls that had covered his chest and abdomen had been shaved during surgery, but was now growing back. Neil rubbed his hand over his chest absently. "You don't need to tape a bandage on again, do you?"

"No. We'll just check to make sure it's not draining." Carter flipped his surgical gloves toward the wastebasket, grinning when they landed inside. "In another week or so we'll be letting you out of here. I bet you'll both be glad to see the last of this place."

Elizabeth smiled vaguely, but Neil wasn't sure how he felt about leaving. Of course it would be great to go home again, to be able to wear clothes and eat a regular diet and not have to follow any bossy nurse's instructions. But he hadn't yet figured out how to convince Elizabeth to go home with him. It was just possible that in leaving the hospital, he would also be leaving her, and that was something he couldn't bear to think about.

He waited until the doctor was gone and they were getting ready for another walk around the hospital corridors to broach the subject. "I'm probably going to need someone to stay with me for a while when I get out of here," he remarked casually. "Just for a few days or so, until I get back to work."

Elizabeth knelt to slide the rubber-soled slippers onto his feet. "You have Clara." The housekeeper was already busy, but she would be more than willing to take on the extra mothering duties. She already treated Neil like a son, anyway.

"Clara only spends a few hours a day at the house. The rest of the time she's got to take care of her own house and her own husband."

Standing, Elizabeth extended her arm to him, steadying him as she always did when he first stood up. In spite of his progress, a fall now would be disastrous. "Her own husband?" she echoed. "I suppose that means that your own wife should be taking care of you?"

His grin was boyish and charming and untouched by guilt. "It would be nice."

"You know, you could hire a nurse to live in for a few weeks." She stopped in the hallway and asked, "Which way?"

He was scowling as he turned to the right. "I've had enough of nurses here."

Elizabeth gave him a teasing, commiserating smile. "You haven't won a single argument with them, have you? It must be hard on your ego. But they all think you're the handsomest patient on the floor."

"And what do you think, Elizabeth?"

His voice had grown low, intimate, reminding her of long-ago nights and long, easy loving. It made her warm inside, made her ache with a need that she had tried for more than a year to forget. Staring straight ahead, painfully aware of her flushed cheeks, she answered with a lightness she didn't feel. "Fishing for compliments, Neil? I thought you were too sure of yourself for that."

"But I've never been too sure of you." He had always known that she loved him, but he had never known how to keep her, how to make her happy, how to please her. The day she had married him, vowing to stay with him forever—even then he had known that someday she would leave him. And she had, because he couldn't say, "I love you."

And he couldn't say it now, either. Then it had been a foolish promise that had kept the words inside, a vow made eleven years ago in anger, a vow that he would never say those words to her again. Now it was fear that, even if he found the courage to say them, he would see only sadness and disbelief in her eyes. After all that had passed between them, how *could* she believe him?

"Come home with me, Elizabeth."

She looked sharply at him. She had expected this, somewhere deep inside, had even planned how she would respond—with a polite, firm, unemotional, "No thanks." But she was surprised, too, because the refusal didn't come automatically. Because tantalizing images of the ranch, of being home with Neil, filled her mind. Because, more than anything in the world, she wanted to say yes.

He didn't love her, she reminded herself harshly. The last months of their marriage had been miserable ones for her, because she'd kept looking for signs that the love she'd taken for granted really existed and kept finding nothing. How could she condemn herself to that kind of life again?

But she wasn't looking for love this time. This time she knew that he didn't love her. He felt fondness, affection, lust, desire—there were a dozen different names for the way Neil felt about her, but none of them was love. As long as she didn't expect miracles, she couldn't be hurt by their failure to occur.

Encouraged by her silence, Neil continued. "You could

give up your job for a while, move back home, see your friends there. We could try again, Elizabeth.''

She gave a soft sigh and turned her head away from him as they walked. ''We've already tried twice, Neil, and failed both times.''

''Haven't you ever heard? The third time's the charm.''

''Yeah. I've also heard another old saying. Three strikes and you're out.''

Taking her arm, he steered her into the waiting room, empty at this time of day, and over to the windows. ''Look out there. There's hardly a place in Helena where you can't see the Sleeping Giant. Tell me you don't think of the ranch every time you see it. Tell me you don't miss living out there.''

She remained silent rather than lie.

Gently he forced her to look at him. ''Tell me you don't miss *me*, Elizabeth. Tell me you don't wake up in the middle of the night wondering where I am, that you don't miss the rides we used to take, the picnics, the winter nights in front of the fireplace...the loving.''

''It's easy for you to talk about trying again, Neil, because it's different for you,'' she replied, her voice immeasurably sad. ''You didn't risk anything. You didn't lose anything. *I* lost everything.''

His hand fell away, and he took a step back, so cold inside that he felt nothing else. He had played his role so well, had protected himself so well, that she believed what she was saying. She didn't know that her leaving had almost killed him, that he, too, had lost everything because, without her, nothing else mattered. She didn't even suspect that he had loved her.

He walked away, and after a moment Elizabeth followed him. They remained silent until they reached the nursery window. Neil stopped there and watched the babies. He had always wanted children, at least half a dozen, and so had Elizabeth, but they hadn't been so lucky. Maybe a baby would have strengthened their rapidly failing marriage. Maybe a baby would have given him the courage to break that foolish vow and tell Elizabeth that he loved her.

Then again, he admitted with a sigh, maybe not. He had been stubborn. Those first months he had shown her in every way he knew how that he loved her, but she had refused to recognize it. It had been in his actions, his attitude, his eyes, his touch, but without the words, she had refused to believe. By the time she'd asked for them, it was too late. There was nothing left of the marriage to save. She had already drawn so far away that he couldn't reach her. They didn't talk, didn't touch, didn't make love. Even if he had swallowed his pride and sacrificed his honor, he still would have lost her. Too much damage had been done.

He looked tired, Elizabeth thought. His gray eyes were bleak, his face drained of color. She knew the weariness was emotional this time, not physical, but she responded just the same. "We'd better go back, Neil. You need to rest."

He nodded in agreement, accepting her arm around his waist. They made the trip in silence. At the door of his room, Neil paused, gazing down into Elizabeth's face. "If you've already lost everything," he asked softly, "then what more could you lose by going home with me?"

While she searched for an answer, he moved away, shuffling over to the bed and climbing in. He settled on his back, closed his eyes, turned his face away from her and left her to consider his question.

What *did* she have to lose? Her hopes? She didn't have any. Her dreams? She'd forgotten how to dream a long time ago. Her heart? It was already broken into a million tiny pieces; it couldn't break any more. So what could she lose? Maybe nothing.

Or maybe whatever little bit of pride, of life, he'd left her.

The only visitors that Neil had during the week were the ranch employees, the closest thing he had to a family. But on Sunday afternoon people began showing up. It seemed to Elizabeth that every friend he had in the city had chosen today to drop by and see how he was—and to see her. The news that she had spent the past two weeks at his bedside had circulated quickly, she thought with some bitterness, and more than a few of his "visitors" had come to see for themselves if it was true.

After several uncomfortable hours she excused herself and went to the cafeteria for a cup of coffee. She was alone at a table when Dr. Carter joined her.

"I went by to see your husband, but he had a roomful of friends."

She simply nodded as she stirred sugar into her coffee.

"You know he's being released tomorrow."

Again she nodded.

"Are you going home with him?"

"He's asked me."

"But you haven't decided." He paused to take a bite of his sandwich. "If you decide to go, meet me in his room tomorrow morning around eleven. We'll go over the restrictions he'll be under for the next few months."

Elizabeth's forehead wrinkled into a frown. Of course Neil had talked about needing someone to stay with him at home, but she had assumed that he was simply playing on her sympathies to get his own way. "What sort of restrictions?"

''On his activities. No driving, no heavy lifting, no working, no strenuous activity at all. That sort of thing.''

She thought of Neil's comments a few days earlier, when he had asked her to go home with him. *Just for a few days or so. Until I get back to work.* ''How long until he'll be able to ride again?''

''Probably three or four months from the time of the accident, provided that everything heals nicely.''

She looked appalled. ''You can't keep Neil off a horse for three or four months! He rides every day.''

''Well, he's going to have to give it up for a while if he wants to stay alive.'' He studied her curiously. ''Do you think he'll follow the restrictions?''

''I don't know.'' She was still dismayed by the notion that Neil couldn't ride again until spring. ''Are they really necessary? He looks so much better and he's getting stronger every day.''

''The body needs time to heal, Elizabeth—in this case, a lot of time. The liver is fragile, easy to injure and difficult to repair. Until it's completely healed, he can't do anything that will present the slightest risk of further injury.''

She tasted her coffee, found it cold and pushed it away, folding her hands together. ''He thinks he'll be able to go back to work when he gets out of here.''

Dr. Carter shook his head solemnly. ''He might be up to handling paperwork in a few weeks. As far as physical labor around the ranch...two and a half months, *maybe* two.''

''What is he supposed to do until then?'' she asked in disbelief.

''Rest. Slow down. Heal.''

She shook her head emphatically, setting her hair swinging. ''No...no. Neil doesn't rest. He doesn't slow down.

He's worked hard all his life. He doesn't know *how* to slow down.''

The doctor loaded his empty dishes onto his tray. ''Then he'd better learn. Elizabeth, we're not talking about a matter of choice. The man was more dead than alive when he came in here, and it's a miracle that he's still alive. If he wants to stay that way...''

The unfinished warning made her shiver ominously. She looked up at him, her eyes shadowed and confused. ''But you're releasing him. I thought that meant everything was fine.''

''No, it just means that he doesn't need hospitalization any longer. He *does* need common sense and good judgment. If he doesn't have it, Elizabeth, you'd better provide it for him, or he still might make a widow out of you.''

As he walked away, she called his name. ''Is it okay if I talk to him about this today?''

He gave a shrug. ''If you think it will help. I'll go over it with him tomorrow anyway.''

She remained at the table long after he left, staring sightlessly at her hands. *Do you think he'll follow the restrictions?* Not on your life, she thought with a bitter sigh. Then she winced at her choice of words. Not unless he had changed drastically in the past year, and she'd seen no evidence of that. He was the same as ever—teasing, pleasing, charming, determined and stubborn as hell. If he decided to return home and pick up his regular duties right away, no one could stop him.

Except her. She was the only one here at the hospital whom he hadn't argued with, the only one he had willingly obeyed. If she made it a condition of her return, if she traded her presence at the ranch for his best behavior, maybe that would keep him in line.

Caution. She needed to handle this with caution. She

would tell him what the doctor had said, would judge his response to it before she made any decision. Before she committed herself to something she might not come out of in one piece.

"What do you mean, I can't ride again for three or four months?"

Elizabeth winced at the thunder of Neil's voice. He wasn't taking this any better than she had expected. All his life he'd worked long hours and hard jobs. Sitting out the next few months couldn't seem very appealing to him. "It's the doctor's orders."

He faced her, his expression stormy and disbelieving. "You're kidding, aren't you?"

Slowly she shook her head.

"Is this Carter's idea of a joke?"

Another shake.

He exhaled deeply, tugging his fingers through his hair in frustration. "When can I go back to work?"

"Sometime in February."

Her quiet response brought another explosion. "That's ridiculous! I feel perfectly all right."

"Sure you do. That's why you sleep all night and half the day. That's why walking down the hall to the nursery and back wears you out. You don't have any choice in this, Neil."

Her calm fed his anger. He forced himself out of bed and walked across the room to her, stopping only inches away, glaring down into her cool blue eyes. "*All* the choices are mine," he said in a low, cold voice. "If you think I'm going to spend twenty-four hours a day alone in that house with nothing to do for the next three months, you're crazy—and so is Carter."

"I didn't know you had a death wish."

"Nothing is going to happen to me. He's just trying to scare you!"

For the first time in months, her hold on her temper broke, anger spilling out, fueled by two weeks of intense emotion. "Let me tell you about being scared! I was here while you were in surgery! They couldn't even wait for me to get here to sign the consent forms because you were *dying*, Neil! I stayed in that room with you, with the tubes and the lines and the machines keeping you alive, and I talked to you when you couldn't hear anything and held your hand when you couldn't feel anything, and I prayed—I begged God to keep you alive!" She didn't realize she was crying until the tears fell on her hand. She touched her fingers to her face, and they came away wet. "I can't go through that again, Neil," she whispered sadly. "I *can't*."

Reaching out, he pulled her into his arms, pressing her head into the niche of his shoulder. "It's all right, Elizabeth," he murmured, stroking her hair. "Sweetheart, it's all right."

He held her for a long time, his eyes closed, his words soft and soothing. There had been times in the past two weeks when the pain had been unbearable, but now he knew that he'd had the easier role. For the first time he put himself in Elizabeth's place, considering how he would feel if *she* were near death, not knowing if she would survive, if she would ever be all right again. He couldn't cope as well as she had. He wasn't that strong.

When the tears stopped, Elizabeth lifted her head, wiping ineffectually at the damp spot on his robe. "I'm sorry," she said, still sniffling.

Neil brushed her hair from her face, his hand lingering on its softness. "No. Don't ever apologize for caring."

It would bc so easy to kiss her now, to bend his head the few inches that separated them and touch his lips to hers. He did it slowly, to savor the moment, to give her time to pull away. But she didn't pull away, and then his mouth was on hers. Her taste filled him, streaking through him, making him want and need, making him live. He teased her lips open, then her teeth, and was welcomed by her tongue into the moist warmth of her mouth. He sampled, stroking, thrusting, feeling the hunger spread through his body, through hers.

Then, suddenly, she was gone.

He watched as she gathered her defenses, a slight smile touching his lips. "Elizabeth?"

Swallowing hard, she risked a glance at him. "We...we can't do that."

He nodded once. "With all the other restrictions Carter has on me, I'm sure he must have one against feeling that good."

She smiled nervously, uneasily, then looked out the window at the darkening sky. "I'd better go home."

"It's still early."

"I have some things to do." The talk with Carter, the argument, the kiss—all were pulling her in different directions, but one thing had become clear. If she had any influence at all on Neil, if her presence would have any effect on his behavior, she would go home with him. Because one other thing was clear: she couldn't lose him again. She might never have all of him, but God help her, she would take what he chose to give. "I'll see you tomorrow," she said, managing a bittersweet smile. "We'll go home tomorrow."

Chapter 5

Only showers instead of baths until the incision was completely healed. Extra care on the stairs and lots of rest. No driving for two weeks. No work for two weeks. No heavy lifting for two months. No physical labor for two and a half months. No riding for three months.

Neil listened to Carter's instructions, his face impassive, determined not to show his dismay. He had followed orders for the week and a half he'd been conscious in the hospital, and by God he would follow them at home, even if the boredom and frustration killed him. He would do it for Elizabeth.

She was late this morning. She had called to say that she needed to take care of a few things before she picked him up. He still hadn't quite accepted that she was going home with him. He knew that she loved him, but he also knew that she didn't want to live with him. Hadn't her leaving proven that? He would have preferred to have her back because she wanted to be with him, but he would take her any way he could get her. Pity, concern, worry—those were all right if they brought her back to him.

"Ah, let's see...there are no restrictions on your diet, no medications.... Do you have any questions?" Dr. Carter asked from his seat on the bed.

Neil leaned back in the only chair, stretched his legs out and leveled a blank gaze on the doctor. "You left out one thing."

"What's that?"

It was difficult to ask. Carter knew that he and Elizabeth had been separated for a long time, probably knew that she wasn't thrilled about going home with him. He'd probably left out that one restriction, figuring that it wasn't necessary to include it.

Neil's silence was easy to read, making the doctor smile. "As for resuming...intimate relations with your wife, it will be all right in another week or two, provided that she takes the...ah, superior position. Anything more...vigorous, you'll have to wait a couple of months."

A couple of months. Would she even be with him in a couple of months? Neil wondered bitterly. Or would she leave him again when she saw that he was being a good patient and was convalescing well?

"Anything else?" Dr. Carter waited but got no response. "I would like to see you in my office in two weeks, and again two weeks after that. If you have any problems before then, don't hesitate to call me." He stood up and extended his hand. Neil cautiously rose and accepted it. "I guess that's it. You're free to go as soon as Elizabeth gets here. Take care of yourself, Neil. I don't like patching up the same patient twice."

"Thanks for everything, Doctor." He remained standing until Carter left the room, then turned the chair so he could see out the window and sat down again. He was going home today. To the ranch. With Elizabeth. He had dreamed of this day, but now that it was here, he didn't know how to feel, how to act. Was she coming for a few weeks, or even a few months, only to keep an eye on him? Or was she accepting his offer of another chance, another try at being husband and wife? He didn't know if he had the courage to ask her.

The door swung open with a whoosh, and Elizabeth dropped a bag, her purse, coat, gloves and scarf on the bed. "Hi," she greeted him breathlessly. "Did I miss Dr. Carter?" She had rushed through her errands this morning, fearing that if she took her time, she would change her mind. She had given notice on her apartment, quit her job with Peg. They were big steps to take, but if she was going to risk trying again with Neil, she was going to risk everything.

"He just left." He stood up and turned from the window to look at her. Her cheeks were flushed from the cold, giving her face a rosy glow. She wore a simple royal-blue dress that was belted at her slender waist and made her look elegant and incredibly beautiful. It was a long moment before he remembered to speak again. "He laid out the rules."

"Good." She picked up the bag and began removing clothing for him. "Do you think you can follow them?"

He reached for the jeans she'd laid down, running the worn, faded denim through his hands. He recognized the shirt, too, and even the old running shoes. She'd gone to the ranch, either last night or this morning. Had she taken her own clothes out there?

Elizabeth touched his hand, prompting him. "Neil?"

"You know, except for our honeymoon, I haven't taken any time off work in…seven years," he remarked in a distant tone, then sighed. "Yes, I'll follow his rules." Dropping the jeans, he turned his hand over, capturing hers. "What about your rules, Elizabeth? Are you going to tell me that I can't touch you, can't kiss you or try to seduce you? Are you going to remind me that you're doing this only because you feel obligated, because you're concerned about my condition?''

She held her head high, her eyes clear and honest when they met his. She had given this decision a great deal of thought last night and had acknowledged that she had no other choice. She loved Neil and needed to be with him, was happy only with him. It meant living without love, being satisfied with his affection, his caring, his desire. But she could accept that. She didn't expect love anymore, didn't hope for it, didn't dream of it.

So did she have any rules to live by? Not for him. Only for herself. ''No,'' she replied simply. Leaning forward, she brushed her lips across his, then laid the rest of his clothes on the bed: briefs, socks, a coat. ''Do you need any help getting dressed?''

The smile he gave her was slow, teasing, sly. ''You can wait in the hall.''

When the door closed behind her, he drew the drapes at the window, then removed his robe and the plain cotton gown. He had never realized how much bending and maneuvering were required to get dressed, with each movement pulling at the tender, foot-long incision. By the time he finished with the clothing, he was sore and, to his dismay, too tired to bother with his shoes. Sinking into the chair, he called Elizabeth back in.

Without being asked, she knelt on the floor in front of him and slipped his feet into the shoes she'd brought. The boots he normally wore had been unsuitable—too much tugging for a man in his condition—so she'd had to rummage through two closets to find the scuffed, worn tennis shoes.

Neil watched as she efficiently laced them. Her hair fell

forward to hide her face, and reaching out, he captured a swinging strand of it between his fingers. It was soft and smelled of shampoo, the scent faint, sweet, clean. He loved its color—blond in regular light, but gleaming gold in sunlight and silver in moonlight—loved to touch it, to feel it, to simply look at it.

"Elizabeth?"

"Hmm." She didn't look up from the second shoe.

"Thank you."

Then she did look up and smile. "For tying your shoes?"

"For everything. For coming here, staying with me...for going home with me."

She cleared her throat to ease the tightness, then rose lightly to her feet. "I didn't have much choice, did I? I don't think you could have hired a nurse to do it. You now have a well-deserved reputation as the best-looking and most ill-tempered patient in this hospital's history."

He stood up and drew her close, bending his head to breathe in the scent of her perfume. "I'll be good for you," he promised huskily.

"Be good *to* me. That's all I ask."

His eyes darkened to match the sunless sky outside. It wasn't so long ago that she had asked for love, for forever. She had lowered her expectations quite a bit, it seemed. But before he could comment, a nurse came in, pushing a wheelchair, ready to escort him out. He released Elizabeth and scowled at the chair. "Is that for me?"

The nurse nodded.

"For a week and a half you've been telling me to walk, even though it hurt like hell, and now that I feel better, you want me to ride in that?" Dismay echoed in his voice, along with resignation. He knew he could argue until he turned blue, but he would never win. Still glaring, he reluctantly lowered himself into the wheelchair.

Within ten minutes he was settled into the passenger seat of Elizabeth's car and she was driving out of the parking lot. He tilted his head back, closed his eyes and gave a deep sigh of relief. "I thought I'd never get out of there. Let's stop someplace for lunch and celebrate with some food."

"You know darned well that Clara will have lunch waiting for us—probably all your favorite foods."

"Does she know you're staying?"

This time it was Elizabeth who sighed as she pulled onto the interstate. "She knows I'm bringing you." She hadn't known what to say to the housekeeper when she'd called yesterday, hadn't known what her status would be. Was she returning to the ranch as Neil's wife, his friend or simply his nursemaid? Was it temporary or permanent? Would he continue wanting her this time, or like before would it end all too soon?

Neil stared out the window at the Sleeping Giant. Occasionally it disappeared from sight as the highway dipped and curved, but it always reappeared, coming closer, holding the promise of home. When he could see, in the distance, the cluster of buildings that was his ranch, he smiled slowly, gratefully.

Elizabeth glanced at him. She knew what he was feeling, because she felt it, too. The ranch was the only real home Neil had ever had, the happiest home she'd ever had. Coming back like this, together, was enough to quiet her last few misgivings about her decision. "You've missed it."

He met her brief gaze. "Not as much as I've missed you. It's not the same without you, Elizabeth."

"Well, I'm back now," she replied with forced cheerfulness.

But Neil couldn't help wondering: for how long? How long would she stay this time? How long before he lost her again?

She'd been right about lunch. Clara had the meal on the table within minutes of their arrival. Elizabeth hadn't had a chance to bring in her suitcases, to ask Neil about sleeping arrangements, even to take a look around her old home. The housekeeper welcomed her with a kiss and a hug and fussed over her as much as Neil, urging her to eat, then to relax with Neil in front of the fire in the living room.

She stood in the doorway, reluctant to enter. Their last conversation in this house had taken place in this room, and the memories were still strong. He had stood at the window, she at the fireplace, and he'd watched her in cold, cruel silence while she had asked, pleaded, practically begged for his love. Even now she could hear the ghostly echo. *Do you love me?*

Neil turned from examining the fire, saw that the color had drained from her face and knew that she was remembering. For weeks after that night he'd been unable to come in here without seeing her, hearing her, in his mind. Her question had haunted his dreams and tormented his waking hours. *Do you love me?*

Lord, yes, he had loved her, more than life, but he hadn't told her so. When she'd left him ten years earlier, he had sworn that he would never again say those words to her. Then he had been poor, and all he'd had of value was Elizabeth and his word, his honor. He had lost her, but he wouldn't lose his honor. He had made a promise, and by God he had kept it. But it had cost him his marriage. It had meant losing her again.

It had been such a simple conversation, Elizabeth thought, moving slowly into the room. She had pleaded, and Neil had said nothing. *Nothing.* Without a word, he had ended their marriage, shattered her dreams, broken her heart.

He met her halfway, wrapped his arms around her, held her close. "Don't think about that night," he whispered against the softness of her hair. "Forget the past."

"I have too many good memories to forget." Slowly she settled her arms around his waist, linking her hands together behind him. "There's just a lot of pain...."

"I know. But we can make it go away."

She wasn't sure about that. Affection and desire could ease a lot of hurts, but not the hurt of finding out that the love she'd believed in, had gambled her future on, didn't exist.

She turned her thoughts away from that. She wasn't expecting miracles, wasn't living in dreams. If affection and desire were all she could have, they would have to be enough.

"Where do you want me to sleep, Neil?" There were three guest rooms upstairs, rooms that they had planned to fill with children, but unfortunately—or was it fortunately?—the marriage had ended before they'd started their family. She doubted that he had a preference as to which room she used, but there was no harm in asking.

The simple question sent a sudden need trembling through him. His breathing was uneven, his skin grew flushed and hot, and lower there was the impossible-to-hide swelling of long-unsatisfied hunger. He wanted her in his bed, at his side, where he could touch her, feel her, love her. "Do you have to ask?"

She felt his hunger, felt a corresponding need inside herself. It had been so long, and she had missed so much. She would like to share his room, his bed...but not yet. Not until they were used to each other again. Not until she was certain that he really cared, that all his sweet talk in the hospital about trying again hadn't been just talk. Not until she knew that they could make it work.

Lifting her head from his shoulder, she gave him a long, chiding look. "You just got out of the hospital, Neil. How can you possibly be thinking of that?"

His grin was easy and natural, his gray eyes sparkling. "It was my liver that was damaged, Elizabeth, not my—"

She cut off the rest of his reply with her fingers over his mouth. "I'll ask Clara to prepare the front guest room, all right?"

Neil gave a heavy, put-upon sigh. The front room was across the hall from his—*their* room. But it was better than the alternative; she could have chosen the room at the opposite end of the house. "All right," he agreed, letting her go as she pulled away. He watched her walk toward the door, admiring the graceful sway of her hips. "Elizabeth?"

She paused, glancing back at him.

"Welcome home."

The days passed quickly for Elizabeth. The first week was hardly different from the days at the hospital—Neil was still weak, still tired easily and spent long daylight hours asleep or resting on the sofa—but the second week he was stronger, more impatient to return to his normal activities. Only his promise to be good for her kept that impatience under control.

"Take a walk with me," he demanded crossly Friday afternoon.

She could tell by his frown that he expected her to refuse, so she closed the book she'd been reading, got to her feet and extended her hand to him. "Where do you want to go?"

"To the stables."

She'd known that, sooner or later, he would want to see the stallion, though she certainly hadn't intended to go along with him. But, without comment, she bundled up and went out into the cold, walking alongside him, holding back only when they came near the horse.

Thunder. One of the previous owners had given him that name, the story went, because his hooves when he ran sounded like rolling thunder. Because he was as powerful, as vicious, as savage as the fiercest storm, Elizabeth thought privately. She flinched when Neil left her and went to the animal, talking softly to him, stroking him.

Neil glanced over his shoulder at her and grinned. "Isn't he beautiful?" It didn't bother him that she didn't answer. He knew her feelings toward the horse. "By the time I get to ride him again, he'll have forgotten what it's like to have a saddle on his back."

Spinning around, Elizabeth left the building, stepping into the frigid cold, not feeling the bite of the wind on her face. She heard Neil call her name, but she didn't turn back, didn't stop for him.

When he caught up with her, he grabbed her arm and swung her around to face him. "Where the hell are you going?"

"That damned horse almost killed you, and you're planning to ride him again! Why don't you get rid of him?"

He gazed down at the concern, the anger and the love that filled her eyes. "The accident was my fault, not Thunder's. I was careless. I was thinking about you, wondering if you would ever come back, if the emptiness you left behind would ever go away, if the pain would ever stop. I was missing you and not paying attention to the horse. It was my fault, sweetheart."

"Why do you have to ride him again?" she whispered, her eyes glistening with unshed tears.

He rubbed his fingers over her cheek until they rested on her lips, soft and full and sweet. "Everyone deserves another chance, Elizabeth. Even Thunder." He replaced his fingers with his mouth, brushing his lips back and forth over hers. "Even me."

Burning with the emotions that swirled inside her, she slid her hands into his hair and pulled his head down, forcing him to deepen the kiss immediately. She craved the sweet, hot taste of him, needed it to satisfy the longing that had been building inside her these past weeks. These past months.

Neil's groan was low, broken. There had been kisses, embraces, caresses, in the past two weeks, but none like this, fueled by this desperate hunger that made him tremble, that made her quake. For the first time he allowed himself to hope that finally he could make love to her, finally he could ease the ache that left him hard and throbbing for her every night, every day.

He freed the buttons of her coat and slid his ungloved hand inside, over the heavy knit of her sweater, to cup her breasts. Her nipples were hard, aching, needing his kisses...but not here. Not outside where anyone could see.

Reluctantly he ended the kiss, dragged his hands from her breasts and refastened the buttons of her coat. "Come inside with me," he suggested in a thick, unsteady voice. "Let me make love to you, sweetheart. Let me—"

Elizabeth clasped both his hands in hers, her gloves warm against his cold skin. Her face was flushed, from need, from hunger, and her breathing was uneven. She wanted him—Neil could see it in her eyes—but he could also see that her answer was no.

"What is it you want from me, Elizabeth?" he asked grimly. "Promises of forever? Vows of love?" He could give those. She might not believe them—yet—but he could offer them.

"No," Elizabeth answered bluntly, gently. He couldn't give her the certainty that this was right—that could only come from within herself—and, at this moment, she simply wasn't sure.

His eyes intently searched her face, but he saw nothing to help him. "Will you answer one question for me?"

She nodded.

"Is the time going to come when you'll say yes?"

Again, slowly this time, she nodded.

Neil slid his arm around her shoulders as they walked to the house. What had she just said yes to? he wondered. Making love? Or accepting his love?

Chapter 6

When Elizabeth came downstairs from an afternoon nap Saturday, she found Neil in the living room, surrounded by boxes, studying a tall, fat tree in the corner whose branches reached to the high ceiling. "Where did that come from?"

He looped his arm around her waist and pulled her close. "It's called a tree. It grows outside, in the ground."

She gave him a withering look. "We don't exactly have a surplus of trees in this part of the state. You shouldn't be cutting them down."

"It wasn't cut down—it was dug up." He showed her the root ball, securely wrapped. "After Christmas I—" At her disapproving glance, he amended that. "The men will plant it at the side of the house. Will you help me decorate it?"

She looked at the boxes, the tree and then him, and smiled. "Sure. I haven't decorated a tree—"

"Since the Christmas after we got married. Neither have I." He'd found no joy in the Christmas season last year, not without her.

The boxes were filled with ornaments—some cheap, some costly, some plain, some breathtakingly beautiful— but each one special. Each one filled with memories. Elizabeth handled them carefully, remembering the hopes and dreams and joy and, yes, love that they represented. So much love...

She lifted a shiny glass ball from its box. It was one of the cheap ones; it had come in a set of six for under a dollar. They had bought them that first year, when money had been tight, when Neil had worked two jobs full-time to scrape together enough for them to get married. Their holiday that year had been simple, because of lack of money, but they'd had something more important; they'd had love.

The logs in the fireplace crackled and fell as she gently replaced the ball in its box. Neil laid another ornament in her hand, folding her fingers over it. "Remember this?"

It was leaded glass in Montana sky blue, poured into a metal frame that formed the ranch brand. On a whim she'd had it made for him two years ago, because he was so proud of his ranch. Just as he'd been so proud of his wife... "Yes," she murmured, turning it in her hands. She slid a hook through the loop and hung it on a branch sturdy enough to support its weight. "Do you remember our first tree?"

His smile, bright and warm and so damn charming, chased away the gloom that had settled over her. "That was the sorriest-looking excuse for a Christmas tree I've ever seen."

"It was a beautiful tree," she disagreed. "It was perfect."

Calling it to mind, Neil grinned. It had been barely four feet tall, lopsided, crooked and had lost most of its needles on the way to her apartment. But she was right. It had been perfect, because *they* had been perfect. They hadn't had any money or any of the material comforts that surrounded them now, but they'd had each other, and a love they had thought would last forever.

Maybe it still could.

"Your dream came true," she murmured as she hung a fragile glass angel on a high branch.

"I had a lot of dreams, Elizabeth. Which one are you referring to?"

"You used to say that someday you would have a big Christmas tree in a beautiful house, with the money to buy all the gifts you'd ever wanted." She indicated the room around them. "You've got all that."

He stopped her as she reached for a tiny wooden Santa. "When I had that dream, I thought you would be here to share it with me. You were in all my dreams, Elizabeth."

"You were in my dreams, too, but you weren't in my life." In spite of her best intentions, bitterness crept into her voice, subtly shading it. "You were so busy working to save money for us that I never saw you. I didn't exist for you anymore."

He traced one fingertip over her jaw. "I wanted to give you everything. A nice home, a good life…" The kind of life that she'd deserved, and for that he had needed money. She had never understood that he'd worked so hard for *her*, that he had, for a time, been forced to neglect her so that he could build a future for them. Instead she had seen his neglect as evidence that his words of love were a lie. By the time the future had been built, she was gone. "I'm sorry…"

She clasped his hand, pressed a kiss to his palm, then returned to hanging decorations on the tree. "I'm not criticizing you. It was a long time ago. It doesn't matter anymore."

But it *did* matter. Everything that had ever happened between them was still affecting them today. She had left him a year ago because he wouldn't tell her that he loved her, and he hadn't told her because, when she'd left him eleven years ago, he'd sworn never to say those words again. It was the only promise to her that he'd ever kept.

He lifted an ornament from its box, letting it dangle by a thin gold cord. It was a sturdy porcelain heart—white, painted with a delicate holly-and-berries motif. He had bought it for Elizabeth two years ago, for their only Christmas together as husband and wife. "Do you remember—" As he turned toward the tree, Elizabeth bumped him, and the cord slipped from his fingers. Together they watched as the heart hit the wooden floor and broke into four jagged pieces.

Elizabeth stared at the heart for a long, still moment; then, blinking against the tears that filled her eyes, she knelt and picked up the pieces, standing again with Neil's help.

"Honey, I'm sorry," he said, pulling her close. "I didn't mean to break..." Laying his forehead against hers, he muttered a curse, then thickly whispered, "Oh, God, Elizabeth, I never meant to break your heart."

Hours later, Elizabeth lay in bed, her eyes open, staring into the darkness. Neil's apology had continued, the words rushing out in an uncontrolled flow—words of regret, of promise, of sadness. She had listened as long as she could, as long as she could bear the pain of what he was saying; then she had fled the room in tears. Now, safe in her own room, the words echoed in her head until she wanted to scream.

You were my wife, my life. I wanted to make you happy,

*wanted to live with you forever, wanted you to love me
forever.... Sweetheart, I never meant to hurt you.*

He was saying that he had loved her. Even though he
had denied her the words, even though he had let her walk
out of his life rather than say them, he had loved her.

She didn't believe him. She *couldn't* believe him. It had
taken her too many painful months to give up her hopes
of love, her dreams that someday he would love her the
way that she had always loved him. If she began to believe
again, began to hope and dream again, she would be destroyed once again. *As long as she didn't expect miracles...*

But it was Christmas. The season of miracles.

Rolling onto her side, she looked at the nightstand
where a shaft of moonlight touched the pieces of her ornament with its cold, silvery glow. The porcelain heart
was a fitting symbol of her own heart. Broken. Irreparable.
No miracle in the world could make it as good as new
again, and no miracle in the world could fix *her* heart,
either.

Neil stuffed an extra pillow under his head, crossed his
propped feet at the other end of the sofa, laced his fingers
loosely together and sighed loudly. Dramatically. In the
easy chair across from him, Elizabeth looked up, as he'd
known she would, and offered him a warm, gentle smile.
"What's wrong?"

"I'm bored."

She glanced at the television, tuned in to a football
game with the sound turned off. "You can listen to that,
if you want. It won't bother me."

He shook his head. He didn't like football, didn't like
any sports. Rodeo was the only one he could identify with.

"What would you like to do?"

He would like to lift her in his arms, he thought with a sly smile, and carry her upstairs to his room—to their room. There he would strip off her clothes, lay her on the bed and make love to her sweetly, tenderly, thoroughly. Then the smile faded. He couldn't lift her, couldn't carry her, couldn't make love to her. In fact, since Friday, he'd been lucky to get more than a few chaste kisses from her. "Let's talk."

"All right. About what?"

About how long she was going to stay with him. About when she would be ready to accept his lovemaking. About whether she would ever accept his love. But he didn't have the courage on this dreary, cold Sunday afternoon to ask questions that would upset the snug, cozy warmth they shared. "Do you date?" He deliberately made his tone light, casual, so she wouldn't take offense.

Elizabeth left the chair, lifted his feet from the sofa and slid underneath, leaning against the arm to face him. He automatically shifted, making room for her legs on one side, so her feet could stay warm beneath his back, then settled his own feet comfortably across her stomach. It was a familiar position, one that allowed them to share their warmth, to be close without being intimate. "Do I date?" she asked when she was settled. "What kind of question is that to ask your..."

"Wife," he supplied, annoyed by her hesitation. What had she wanted to say? Estranged wife? "You're still my wife, Elizabeth, and it's a nosy question, but I think I'm entitled. Do you?"

"No." She paused only a moment before asking curiously, "Do you?"

"No. If I can't have you, I don't want anyone."

She tried to ignore the shiver of pleasure that coursed through her at his matter-of-fact statement, but it touched

every part of her. She understood what he meant. Occasionally Peg had pointed out various single men to her,
offering to arrange introductions or dinners, but Elizabeth
had always refused. No explanation had been necessary,
because Peg had understood; however nice and attractive
these men were, they weren't Neil. "Is that why you still
wear your wedding ring?"

He held up his hand and gazed at the gold band. "I
wear it because I'm a married man. Because, even if you
don't want to be my wife, Elizabeth, I will always be your
husband."

Always. It was one of those little words that made her
squirm, like love and forever. One of those words that
made her want to believe, however foolishly, in miracles.

"Always, Elizabeth," he repeated. "Whether or not
you believe me, whether or not you stay with me, whether
or not you love me."

To keep her hands from trembling, she began rubbing
his feet, encased in thick, white socks. She couldn't think
of some light comeback, of any easy way to respond to
what he'd said. "Sometimes 'always' doesn't last very
long, Neil, does it?"

"It will last as long as I live."

"Will it?" she asked cynically.

"The problem with us, Elizabeth, is *your* 'always.' *I*
never left you. *I* never walked away. *I* was the one who
got left behind."

She shook her head in disagreement. "By the time I
left, I had already lost you in every way that counted."

This time it was Neil who disagreed. "You never lost
me, Elizabeth. You threw me away."

Their gazes locked for a long, tense moment; then
slowly, coolly, she smiled. "They say that if five people
witness an accident, they'll give five different versions of

what happened. I guess we're not different from anybody else.''

He wasn't amused. ''What are you looking for, Elizabeth? Why did you agree to come back here? What do you want from me?''

Again she smiled. ''I've learned one lesson in my thirty-one years: if you don't ask for anything, then you can't be disappointed when you don't get it.''

''I disappointed you, didn't I, Elizabeth?'' he asked quietly, sitting up so he could touch his fingers gently to her face. ''I didn't give you what you wanted, what you needed.''

''No, you didn't. But you taught me another lesson.''

''What? How to live without love? How to quit trusting in it? How to settle for nothing when you could have everything?''

She sat up, too, catching his hand in hers. ''You taught me that there's a time when you have to quit dreaming and be satisfied with what you can have.''

''No,'' he disagreed solemnly. ''No one should ever give up their dreams.''

She rubbed her finger over his wedding band for a long time before meeting his gaze. ''I don't have any dreams, Neil.''

''Then share mine.'' He searched her face for any sign of unwillingness before kissing her sweetly, fiercely, his tongue probing her mouth, giving, taking, arousing. His caresses shared the same sweetness and fierce urgency as his hands slid beneath her sweater to cover her breasts, teasing her nipples into aching crests, making her heart thud, her blood rush.

She shivered when he leaned back and pulled the sweater over her head, letting it fall to the floor. His fingers trembled over the clasp of her bra; then it fell, too, leaving her breasts naked and hungry for his touch.

Neil's gray gaze moved like a caress over her satiny skin, her rose-peaked breasts. "You are so beautiful," he murmured, laying his hand flat across her stomach. "Do you know how long I've wanted you? How many nights I've dreamed about loving you?"

There it was again—one of those little words. If only he did love her. If she could have his love, she could... She closed her eyes on his dear, handsome face. If she believed in his love, she'd be believing in miracles, and she didn't. She couldn't. For the sake of her sanity, her heart, her life, she couldn't believe in miracles.

He felt her withdrawal like a chill through his soul. He clasped his hands together so he wouldn't reach for her, wouldn't try to change her mind, wouldn't consider taking her away.

When she opened her eyes, she avoided looking at him as she retrieved her sweater and tugged it over her head, pulling it down to cover her suddenly cold flesh.

"How long do I have to wait?" he asked, his voice hard and edgy and barely controlled.

Like him, Elizabeth laced her fingers tightly together. "Until it's right."

"Until it's right?" he echoed derisively. "And, of course, that's some arbitrary decision that *you* get to make, isn't it?" He didn't wait for her to answer before he continued accusingly. "I've been waiting for more than a year, Elizabeth. For more than a lifetime."

"For what? To have sex?"

"I want to make love with you."

"But *I'm* not ready to make love, Neil! All I have to give right now is sex." She stood up and paced the length of the room, stopping at last in front of the fireplace. "I'm sorry. I thought it would be easier. I thought I could forget about everything that's happened and move in here and be your wife again, but I can't.'' She leaned against the heavy stone mantel, resting her forehead on her arm, closing her eyes against the tears that burned. "I need..." Time. Reassurance. Love. God help her, she needed love.

This time it was Neil who found the easy way out. He came to stand beside her, wrapping his arms around her, hugging her close. ''You'd never believe from the way I've been acting that I turned thirty-three on my last birthday, would you?''

She turned in his arms, hiding her tear-stained face against his chest. ''Neil, I'm sor—''

''Don't apologize, Elizabeth. *I* was wrong. I can't take what you can't give.'' He raised her head so he could look at her. ''Come on, sweetheart, don't cry. We just had our first real argument, and we're still speaking—that counts for something, doesn't it?''

She didn't answer. She couldn't. All she could think of was how she had fooled herself into believing that she could be happy living with Neil and knowing that he didn't love her.

It seemed she still had her own dreams, after all.

Following Neil's appointment with Dr. Carter Tuesday morning, they went shopping, then made the long drive back to the ranch. Elizabeth had gifts for Clara, Roy and Peg in her bags, along with two small presents for Neil: the newest book by his favorite author and an ornament, a beautiful horse in delicate, tinted glass. She had felt awkward shopping for him—she was his wife but not his lover, his companion but not his friend. So many gift suggestions had seemed too personal for the circumstances, so she had opted instead for the impersonal.

While she put her packages in her room, Neil went into the living room. It smelled sweetly of pine and was bright and warm, a pleasant contrast to the stark view outside the big window. This was the dreariest winter he'd ever seen—all dark skies, heavy clouds, bone-chilling cold. They should have had snow by now, but all the sky offered was empty promises.

Sort of like him.

With a deep sigh, he turned away from the window as Elizabeth came into the room.

''That sounds ominous,'' she commented lightly. ''What are you thinking about?''

She was a vision to brighten even the bleakest day. In a royal-blue sweater and navy corduroy slacks, with her blond hair pushed back behind her ears, she was achingly beautiful, and she made him long to hold her, to love her, to please her. But he couldn't. Not until she could accept what he had to give.

She'd been pretending since Sunday afternoon—pretending that nothing was wrong, that the situation between them was comfortable and light and easy, that the scene that afternoon hadn't affected her at all. But he could see through her act. He had spent the past two nights awake in his bed, remembering the things that she'd told him.

If you don't ask for anything, then you can't be disappointed when you don't get it. There's a time when you have to quit dreaming and be satisfied with what you can have.

She had asked for his love once, and it had broken her heart when he hadn't offered it. Had he taken her dreams from her, too?

As much as he hated to admit it, he knew that the answer was yes. Now he wanted to give them back, along with so much more. He wanted to give her everything. To do that, he had to explain why, a year ago, he had denied her everything.

Elizabeth asked her question again, and he answered it quietly. "Do you remember the first time you left me?"

His question caught her off guard, in the middle of removing her shoes. She paused before letting the second one fall to the floor with a thud. Stalling for time before answering, she sat down in the chair, tucking her feet beneath her, spreading one of Clara's hand-crocheted throws over her legs. "The first time?" she echoed. "You make it sound as though I made a regular habit of it."

He sat down on the raised hearth, rubbing his hand over the rose-colored granite. "Didn't you?" he asked dryly, then shook his head impatiently. He didn't want to criticize, to lay blame, to anger her. "That night you said, 'You're the man who claims to love me, but all you've given are the words, and words mean nothing.'" It was an exact quote. The hurtful accusation had been burned into his soul, and he would never forget it.

She clasped her hands together in her lap, holding them so tightly that her fingertips turned white. She didn't want to remember. She had enough unhappy memories without going back that far for more.

"Do you remember what *I* said?"

"No," she lied. "I don't want to play 'remember when?' with you."

"It's important," he insisted. He left his seat and knelt in front of her, forcing her hands apart so he could hold them. "Elizabeth, we can't have a future together until we settle the past."

She tried to pull her hands away, but he held them tighter. "The past is settled. It happened the way it did, and nothing we say can change that."

Stubbornly he continued, forcing her to listen. "Words

mean nothing, you said, and my answer was, 'You'll never hear them from me again, sweetheart.' Do you remember now? Do you remember the rest of it?''

Closing her eyes, she could hear his voice from that long-ago night—cold, cruel, threatening. Words that had been uttered in anger, that had been intended to hurt. Words that had broken her heart.

'''I swear before God...''' Even after eleven years, it was hard for Neil to say it aloud. '''...I'll never say *I love you* to you again.''' He looked up, his dark eyes shadowed with pain. ''Do you understand, Elizabeth? Do you understand why I couldn't answer your question when you left me last year? Do you understand what I'm trying to say?''

She stared at him, the color drained from her face, her blue eyes just as pained. A promise—that was why he'd let her go. That was why he'd destroyed their marriage with his refusal to tell her that he loved her. A stupid, angry promise.

''I've made a lot of promises to you, Elizabeth. Love, happiness, children. A perfect life with no wants, no needs. But I've only kept one, and it was the wrong one. And I am so damn sorry.''

''Why didn't you tell me?'' Her voice was unsteady, laced with sorrow and dismay. ''Why didn't you break that promise and answer my question?''

Releasing her hands, he stood up and walked over to the Christmas tree, touching a miniature bell, making it tinkle. ''Companionship, consideration, tenderness. That's how I was supposed to prove my love to you. Not with words, but with actions.'' He glanced over his shoulder at her and saw that she remembered that part of their long-ago conversation, too. ''So that's what I did when we got married. I spent time with you, I talked with you, I made you the center of my life. I treated you the best way I knew how, but it wasn't enough. The actions weren't enough. You demanded the words—the words that, eleven years ago, meant nothing to you.''

She got to her feet, unable to sit still any longer. ''I didn't demand anything until the day I left you, when our marriage was already dead!''

He tilted his head back to study the angel on top of the tree. With her beautiful face and lovely blue eyes and golden halo of hair, she reminded him of Elizabeth. That was why he'd bought it years ago. ''Didn't you?'' he challenged mildly. ''What about when you started telling me that you loved me, then waited expectantly for me to say it, too, and looked so disappointed when I didn't? What about all those nights you pretended to be asleep when I went to bed, so I wouldn't touch you? What about when you *stopped* telling me that you loved me? You didn't want to talk to me, to spend time with me, to look at me or make love with me, unless I said I loved you. Those were demands, Elizabeth. Maybe not as plain, as blunt, as the day you left, but demands just the same.''

''That's not true,'' she protested weakly. But it was. How had she ignored the truth for so long? How had she viewed the same situation that he'd seen and considered herself blameless? She had rejected the very things that she had demanded of him the first time, had pleaded for the very words that she'd once thrown back in his face as meaningless. *She* was responsible, too. This last year of misery had been her fault as much as his.

''But, Neil…why didn't you tell me?'' she asked again.

''It was too late. Everything between us was already falling apart. You would have believed that I said 'I love you' only to keep you with me, not because I meant it. It never would have been enough to replace what we'd already lost.''

Her protest died unspoken. Maybe he was right. She had been so insecure, so unsure of him and herself. Eventually she would have wondered if he'd really loved her, or if he'd given her the words only to placate her, and the uncertainty would have torn her—and them—apart. ''Oh, Neil...''

''We can have another chance, Elizabeth.'' He walked over to her and raised his hand to her hair. In all the years, with all his money, he'd never found anything as soft, as silky, as beautiful, as her hair. ''It isn't so hard. If something breaks, it can be put back together. Problems can be resolved, promises renewed, dreams rebuilt.''

That meant trusting—in Neil, in love, in miracles. Could she afford to take that risk? Could she believe in promises and dreams and miracles, only to be destroyed once again? Could she survive another disappointment, another heartache?

She didn't think so. This time it had to be forever...or not at all. She couldn't risk her heart—her very soul—only to lose again.

Neil watched her consider his plea. The thoughtful look in her eyes was replaced by fear, pain, then sorrow. There was no hope there, just the memories of two heartaches, of two painful endings. Sadly, he knew what her response would be.

''I'm sorry, Neil.''

Her whisper sliced through his heart like a blade. He tried to think of a response that would ease their pain, but there was nothing he could say, nothing he could do. He raised his fingers to her cheek, but, her eyes damp, she quickly stepped back and walked away.

He wanted to chase after her, to plead with her, to beg her, but he remained where he was. Even though it broke his heart...he let her go.

Chapter 7

It had been a long, draining week, and Elizabeth went to the privacy of her room Saturday night, as she had the previous four nights, with a feeling of great relief. Neil hadn't started any more intense discussions since Tuesday—in fact, she'd seen very little of him. He had spent every day in his office, catching up on the paperwork that had been neglected since his accident. To fill her suddenly empty hours, she had offered her services to Clara, helping with the housework, the cooking and the seemingly endless holiday baking. She had decorated so many sugar-cookie trees, snowmen, Santas, stars and wreaths that she could do it with her eyes shut. It certainly hadn't been enough to keep her mind occupied.

And all she'd been able to think about was Neil. She was a coward, she had decided, pure and simple. He was offering her the things that she'd dreamed of most of her life—a future, a happy marriage. Maybe even love. All she had to do was accept them—reach out and take them.

But she couldn't. She was afraid—afraid to dream when her dreams had been so cruelly shattered twice before.

Afraid to believe that this time could be right, that this time could be forever. Everything she wanted was right there before her, but she was too afraid to take it.

She sat down on the bed to remove her shoes. There on the nightstand, never out of sight, was the porcelain heart. She really ought to throw it away, she thought, rubbing the tip of one finger over the largest piece. It had once been so beautiful, but now nothing could be done to save it. The fragments were just a depressing reminder of how easily— and how permanently—things could break. Hearts, marriages, dreams, people.

She scooped up the pieces, intending to carry them to the wastebasket across the room, but impulsively she laid them on the bedspread in front of her, fitting them together, careful of the sharp edges.

For a long time she sat very still, staring at the heart, her eyes damp and stinging with tears. It was beautiful. Oh, tiny chips were gone, marring the perfection of the painted surface, and thin, jagged lines showed the path of the cracks, but it was still beautiful. It would never be as good as new again, but none of the flaws would diminish its value. It would always be precious to her, would always be Neil's gift to her. It would mean even more, because she had thought it was ruined, and now it was whole again.

If something breaks, it can be put together. Problems can be resolved, promises renewed, dreams rebuilt.

Was Neil right? Could their broken marriage be put back together? Could it be just as good as—maybe even better than—before? Could she, with his help, renew her promises and rebuild her dreams?

It was a risk. If she took it and was disappointed again, she feared the damage would last forever. She would never find the courage to love again. But could she live the rest of her life like this—wanting, needing, craving love, but too fearful to accept it?

She could have it all—or she could end up with nothing. The choice was hers.

Gently she returned the pieces to the nightstand, then left the room, closing the door with a quiet click behind her. Underneath Neil's door across the hall, a narrow line of light revealed that he was still awake, too.

She found the bottle of glue that she needed in the kitchen and made her way through the darkness to her room. Settling in on the bed, she opened the bottle, picked up the heart and set to work.

Across the hall, Neil heard Elizabeth leave her room, then return a few moments later. He wondered why she was up at this hour of the night, but he didn't leave his position sitting on the hearth to check on her. The stones were warm, the fire hot against his bare back, the room still. If he thought there was any chance of sleeping, he would be in bed now—he could use the rest—but sleep had been hard to come by these last few nights.

It was Elizabeth's fault, he thought with a scowl. She made his days as perfect, as pleasant and comfortable as could be, then made his nights hell, while she slept like a baby across the hall. When he slept, he dreamed of her—of the love and the sorrow—and woke up feeling more tired than the night before. He didn't know how much longer he could go on like this.

The worst part of it was, he'd done it to himself. She loved him—he was as sure of that as he was of his own love—but he had hurt her so badly that she couldn't believe in him. She didn't have the luxury of certainty, like he did. She would have to accept him on faith, when he had betrayed her faith twice before.

He let his head hang limply, stretching the taut muscles in his neck, then grew very still. Lifting his head, he saw that he hadn't imagined the faint click. The door was open, and Elizabeth was standing there. He sat straighter, but didn't rise from the hearth. Silently, his heart pounding, he waited.

She took great care in closing the door before she approached him. Stopping a few feet in front of him, she knelt on the floor, her robe settling around her like a cloud. "Neil."

Her voice was breathy, a soft, insubstantial whisper of need, and it made his hunger unbearable. If she walked away from him again, this time he would surely die from the ache.

He raised his hand to her hair, and it trembled. How long had it been since he'd made love to her? He couldn't remember. *Too long.* But tonight she was asking him to. He didn't know why—whether she wanted that chance they had talked about, or if her longing had finally gotten the better of her judgment—and right now he didn't care. He would accept this precious gift that she was offering and worry about the reason later.

He moved to his knees in front of her, fumbling fingers undoing the buttons of her robe. It was heavy, soft, white, warm, and her skin underneath it was warm, too. He slid it off her shoulders and pushed it away, then slipped his hand beneath the thin straps of her nightgown. Her breasts were heavy, her nipples swollen, hard against his palms. Impatiently, he pulled off the gown and tossed it aside.

The firelight turned her skin golden—warm, soft gold. Neil gently laid her back on the braided rug, and for a long moment, he simply looked at her, his throat too tight to speak. He had known her, had loved her, for nearly half his life, and he had never tired of looking at her. She was so beautiful, so incredibly perfect, so deeply loved…and she didn't even know it.

She grew warm under his heated gaze, and the warmth fed her hunger. She reached for him, but he brushed her hands away. When his mouth closed over her nipple, she gasped, arching her back. He suckled it, dragged the rough wet surface of his tongue back and forth over it, sending shudders of desire that were almost painfully intense through her. At last, gritting her teeth over a low moan, she pushed him away and rose again to her knees, facing him.

For the first time since his release from the hospital, she saw his scar, extending six inches above his jeans. Her fingers gently grazed over it, following the thin line to his waist and the wide leather belt there. She opened the buckle, then reached for his jeans. They were fastened with a row of buttons, and she took great pleasure in loosening each button, her questing fingers sliding between cool metal, warm fabric and the hard flesh beneath.

The weakness that troubled him in the last month was back, and he laid his hands on her bare shoulders for support. Opening the last button, she slid both hands inside the worn denim, underneath the soft cotton briefs, and with his help pushed them away, her hands leaving a hot trail down his hips and legs, then up again. She found the hard, heavy length of him and gently caressed him at the same time that she lifted her head to claim his mouth with hers.

"Now." Her whisper shimmered between them, then faded as Neil kissed her.

Finally he released her and pulled her, protesting, to her feet. "In bed," he murmured, then kissed her again, his tongue exploring the warmth of her mouth, as he guided her with his hands at her waist to the bed, gently lowering her, following her down. She tugged impatiently at him, but he refused to be moved. Reluctantly he leaned on one arm and gazed down at her, his free hand stroking over her, his eyes dark and hungry. "I can't..."

Her fingers closed around him once again and she wet his nipple, once flat, now hard, with the tip of her tongue. "I need you, Neil."

It was a simple, pure statement that made him swell even more. "Oh, sweetheart, I need you, too, but...the doctor said...not for a couple of months...."

Slowly she smiled with understanding. As she rose from the bed, she pushed him down, flat on his back, and shifted until she was astride him. "Did the doctor say that this is all right?"

His groan was the answer as she took him inside herself, slowly, deeper, tighter, until he filled her. She sat still, her eyes closed, savoring, feeling, loving. She had never forgotten this perfection, this glory. She never would.

In the light from the fire, Neil saw the tear that slipped down her cheek and lifted his hand to wipe it away. His fingers slid to her chin, their slight pressure encouraging her to meet his gaze. "You are my life, Elizabeth," he solemnly promised. "Always. Forever."

Those words again, she thought with a teary smile. Only this time she believed them. This time she accepted them.

Careful to support her weight above him, she gave him a long, sweet kiss. Her breasts rubbed tantalizingly against his chest, and he raised his hands to capture them, to stroke them, to fan the flame burning low in her belly. When she could stand it no longer, she moved her hips against him, returning the torment, feeding his own need, until it exploded in bright, heated light, then faded to a warm, soft, golden glow.

Mindful of his injury, Elizabeth moved to Neil's side, and he pulled her close, his arm possessively around her, his shoulder her pillow. His heartbeat beneath her stroking hand was still rapid, erratic. Pressing a kiss to his damp skin, she asked huskily, "Are you sure Dr. Carter said this was all right?"

"Oh, it was better than all right, sweetheart," he teased, stroking her hair. Turning onto his side, he kissed her. "You are so beautiful.... God, I've missed you."

"I won't leave again." She offered the assurance quietly, without hesitation. There were few things in life that she was certain of, but that was one. She would never stop loving him, never stop needing him, and never again leave him of her own will.

"You'll give up your apartment and your job?"

"I've already done that."

"You'll be my wife? Live with me? Have my babies? Grow old with me?"

She nodded solemnly. "Yes."

He opened his mouth to ask the next question, faltered, then finally, in a husky, thick voice, asked it. "You'll love me?"

It took her as long to answer. "Always," she whispered. "Always, Neil."

He held her tightly, hiding his face in her hair, as the wonder of her promise swelled through him, wrapping around his heart, weaving into his soul. When he drew back, he raised his hand tenderly to her face. "Elizabeth..."

She knew what he was going to say, could read it in his eyes even in the dimly lit room, but she covered his mouth with her fingers. "No demands, Neil." She had made demands before, and it had almost destroyed them. She wouldn't let it happen again. "Just accept my love. Let me love you, and that will be enough."

He wanted to tell her that it wouldn't be enough, not for him—wanted to tell her that he loved her so much that he thought he would die with it—but she was touching him, kissing him, stroking and arousing him, and the words died unspoken, forgotten in the torment of need.

No demands, she'd said. Neil was scowling as he tugged on the jeans he'd discarded the night before, then added another log to the fire. Couldn't she see that he wanted— *needed*, after so many years—to acknowledge his love? Was she afraid that he would feel obligated, that because she'd said she loved him, duty would drive him to make the same claim? Was she still unable to believe in his love?

When the fire was burning brightly, he sat down on the hearth, his back to the flames, and studied Elizabeth across the room. She lay on her back, her hair a delicate tangle across his pillow, her expression as she slept one of complete satisfaction. God, she was so beautiful that looking at her made him ache. What was he going to do with her? he wondered forlornly. She was offering him everything…and asking for nothing in return. Not even his love.

Warmed by the fire, he went to the nearest window, pushing the curtain back. It was gray and cold and dismal outside. They should have had snow by now, he thought with a sigh. Snow for Christmas.

"Having regrets?"

As he turned to look over his shoulder, his smile came slowly, gently. "I have a lot of regrets," he replied. "I regret each time I lost you. Each time I hurt you. Each time I could have made you smile but didn't. Each day I spent without you."

She sat up, holding the sheet in front of her. "Do you regret last night?" she asked softly, fearful of his answer. She had assumed so much when she'd come here last night—that he would want her as much as she wanted him, that it would mean as much to him as it had to her. Had she been wrong?

He turned to face her then, folding his arms over his chest, leaning against the window frame, slowly, confidently shaking his head. "Not one second of it." Well... just one, when she had stopped him from telling her that he loved her.

Her shoulders rounded with relief, Elizabeth sank lower beneath the covers. "Then what was that sigh for?"

"I was just wishing it would snow. After all, tomorrow is Christmas." The last word echoed in his mind. Christmas—a time of joy, of celebration, of miracles. Also a time of gift-giving. He had bought Elizabeth gifts—foolish, expensive gifts calculated to bribe a woman who couldn't be bribed, to buy love from a woman who gave it freely. But he had another gift for her, he realized. One more important than the emerald earrings, one more valuable than the diamond necklace, one that she wouldn't demand, wouldn't ask for...but surely she would accept it if it was given the way she gave—freely, honestly, sincerely.

Elizabeth watched him. She knew there was more on his mind than the lack of snow for Christmas, and she suspected what it was—her unwillingness to hear any words of love from him last night. She wished she could explain to him that she didn't need the words any longer. Oh, they would be nice, of course, but the real proof would come in his actions—in the way he kissed her so sweetly, in the way he looked at her so warmly, in the way he touched her so tenderly. In their lovemaking, their meals together, their quiet evenings in front of the fireplace—in all the hours they spent together, loving or talking or laughing or fighting or doing nothing at all, she would find the proof of his love.

He was such a handsome man. Standing there barefoot, bare-chested, the metal buttons of his jeans undone, he made her pulse flutter unevenly, made her throat tighten, made her think about loving, about heat and possession. He made her ache.

''Neil?''

He knew what she wanted before she spoke—knew because he wanted it, too. He couldn't remember a day in his life when he hadn't wanted her, couldn't imagine a day in his future when he wouldn't need her. He walked to the bed, stepped out of the jeans, ready and hungry for her, and joined her in the bed.

''Love me, Elizabeth,'' he muttered hoarsely as he shifted her into position above him. ''Oh, God, sweetheart...please love me....''

Elizabeth sat at Neil's desk, measuring wrapping paper to fit the small, flat box she'd found in the attic, smiling at the faint creaks above her. Neil was moving her things from the guest room to his room—*their* room. She had slept her last night in any bed other than his, he had insisted over dinner, and he was making the move himself while she wrapped this final small gift.

Although his office had never been off-limits to her, this was the first time she'd entered it in well over a year. Surprisingly, nothing had changed. Their wedding picture still sat on his desk, and another photo, of her alone, still hung on the wall. She wouldn't have blamed him if he had destroyed every memory of her in this house, but he hadn't. Because he had loved her.

Smiling serenely and humming Christmas carols to herself, she folded the edges of the paper, making tight, neat corners and taping them securely. It was a small package, wrapped in green and gold stripes, sporting a tiny, shiny gold bow. Neil would never notice it under the big tree until she was ready to give it to him.

She took the gift to the living room, adding it to the pile already beneath the tree, then stepped back to admire the scene. Neil stopped in the doorway to do the same. With the decorated tree, the brightly wrapped presents, the blazing fire and Elizabeth in a rich green dress, it was the perfect Christmas scene. All it needed was half a dozen small children and a loving husband and father.

Sensing his presence, she turned, a welcoming smile on her lips. "Are you finished upstairs?"

He nodded, coming to wrap his arms around her. "Have you looked outside? It's snowing."

Her gaze followed his to the window. At the sight of the fat, white flakes falling heavily, she smiled again. "Merry Christmas."

He bent to nuzzle her throat, then kissed her mouth. "Merry Christmas."

She turned back to the tree. "Sit down and let me give you your gifts now."

"But it's only Christmas Eve." He said it with a grin, knowing that it didn't matter to her. In her family, gifts had always been opened at home on Christmas Eve, so Christmas Day could be spent at her grandparents' houses. Since he'd had no family traditions, they had adopted hers, including this one.

Elizabeth gave him a look of mock annoyance, then smiled so sweetly that he willingly obeyed her, taking a seat on the sofa. She retrieved the three packages, leaving the smallest one on the end table, then handing him the book. It had been so suitable when she'd bought it only a week ago, but now, considering the changes between them, it seemed too impersonal; not even the inscription inside the front cover could change that.

The ornament came next. "It reminded me of Thunder," she said softly as he cradled the delicate glass in his big hands. "I guess, since I'm going to live here again, I'm going to have to get used to the beast...but I'll never like him."

He gently laid the glass horse on the coffee table, then leaned forward to kiss her. "He can't be all bad, can he? He got us back together again.... Thank you, Elizabeth."

He collected her gifts from under the tree and returned to sit beside her. Holding two of the three packages in his hands, he looked somberly from one to the other. He knew that, when she saw the expensive jewels, she would smile and tell him that they were lovely, but they wouldn't excite her. They wouldn't touch her heart.

And she did smile, told him that they were beautiful, admired their cold, icy sparkle. She would treasure them, not for their beauty or their monetary value, but simply because they were from Neil. But he had been right; they didn't excite her. They didn't touch her heart.

He offered her the third package.

It was a small box, and Elizabeth's fingers fumbled over the ribbon. Finally she uncovered the box and lifted the lid, giving a gasp of pure pleasure. "Oh, Neil..."

Inside was a Christmas ornament, a small white porcelain heart. It was identical to the one he'd given her two years ago, the broken one, but was painted in a mistletoe-and-berries motif instead of holly. She lifted the heart by its gold cord and let it dangle from her finger, her hand cupped underneath to protect it from harm.

He reached over to touch it. "I broke your other heart, Elizabeth," he said, though he knew the reminder was unnecessary. "I wanted to give you a new one—one that's never been broken and never will be."

She knew she would cherish this heart as much as the

broken one. Together they symbolized her own heart, her marriage, hope and courage and understanding. Blinking back tears, she replaced it in its box and reached for her final gift for Neil, but with his hand on her arm, he stopped her.

"I have one more thing to give you. This one couldn't be wrapped and placed under the tree. You can't hold it in your hands or see it with your eyes, but it's something you can feel...something you can trust...something that will be with you for the rest of our lives." His hands were trembling, and he stilled them by grasping hers tightly. "I love you, Elizabeth. I loved you the day we met, and in all the years since, whether we were together or apart, I've always loved you. I always will."

Elizabeth stared at him for a long time, until her sight blurred. There were a dozen things she wanted to say to him, starting and ending with "I love you," but her throat wouldn't work. All she could get out was his name on a soft sigh. "Oh, Neil..."

He couldn't judge anything by her whisper, and her eyes were closed so the tears could flow. Was she happy because she believed him, or sad because she didn't? "I know I've given you good reason not to trust me, sweetheart, not to believe in me, but—"

"Don't, Neil," she interrupted. She pulled free and got the last package from the end table, thrusting it into his hands. "Before you say anything else, open that."

His eyes dark and confused, he ripped the paper off the box and opened it. When he saw the heart inside, he looked at Elizabeth, even more confused.

"I was so afraid to try again, Neil. Our marriage was broken, my heart was broken, *I* was broken, and I was convinced that none of it could be fixed. But you told me that if something breaks, it can be put back together. This heart is proof of that; it was broken, and now it's whole again. It gave me the courage to try, to hope, to dream.'' She smiled through her tears. ''No one should ever give up their dreams. You've given mine back to me.''

''Then you believe me.'' The wonder he'd felt when she had come to him last night was back. He had hoped, and he had prayed, but he hadn't known if she would ever accept his love. ''You believe that I love you.''

''Yes, Neil,'' she said, going into his arms. ''I believe. And I love you.''

He held her close and kissed her, with all the gentleness and tenderness and love inside him. When he released her, she remained in his embrace, her head on his shoulder, her left hand with its shiny gold ring flat against his chest, above his heart.

He had given her so much, she thought with a contented sigh—the gift of trust, the gift of faith, the gift of dreams. They were precious, and she vowed that she would never lose them again. But being loved by him, hearing him say those words that she hadn't heard in eleven years—that was the greatest gift of all.

* * * * *

CHRISTMAS MAGIC

Annette Broadrick

* * *

To Nancy, who has a special magic of her own

Dear Reader,

Christmas has always been a magical time for me.
This is a time for family visits, glittery decorations,
mysterious packages and, for me, it is the time when
I think of the reason why we celebrate. Regardless of
weather, I look forward to the candlelight service on
Christmas Eve where we are graphically shown that
from one lone candle, each of us can add to that light
by carrying that sense of peace, love and goodwill
with us wherever we go.

I also enjoy reunion stories. Innocent love that's
separated then found once again. Reunions are magical,
as well.

May you find this time of year magical in some way,
especially in your heart, and share that magic with
others.

Annette Broadrick

Chapter 1

Natalie Phillips patiently made her way through the crush of Christmas shoppers in the large department store. The store and the mall surrounding it had been built during the six years since Natalie had left Portland, Oregon. This was the first time she had returned to the city where she'd grown up, and thus far she had found the visit to be as painful as she had feared it would be. Poignant memories kept intruding on the present.

In quiet desperation, Natalie had borrowed her brother's car that afternoon and had gone shopping at the Clackamas Town Center, a large mall near I-205. Surely she would find nothing there to remind her of other times—of happier and more innocent times.

Natalie had learned a great deal about people in the six years she had been gone. Never would she be so gullible again, so willing to believe in fantasies—in happy-ever-after.

She could sense the anticipation and excitement in the very air she breathed. Christmastime—a time to spend with loved ones; a time of suppressed excitement and secrets; a

time of smiles and laughter, of family warmth and giving;
a time of peace.

Unfortunately Natalie hadn't been able to find much
peace. Not in Portland. She had another life now and no
longer wanted any reminders of the past. She had left the
unhappiness of six years ago behind her and was determined not to allow it to influence her future.

Natalie watched as a young child paused to exclaim over
a Christmas display at the store's wide entrance to the rest
of the mall. The excited child pointed, calling his mother's
attention to the glitter and animated figures.

Natalie glanced around, unconsciously searching for
someone with whom she could share the small scene. Her
gaze caught and held for a moment, and she stared at the
broad back of a man standing in front of a jewelry display
counter.

There was something about the wide shoulders, the confident stance and the way he held his head that reminded
her of the one man she had worked hard to forget.

Tony D'Angelo.

Surely not. She must be imagining a likeness that wasn't
there. After all, she hadn't seen him in six years. No doubt
the Tony she remembered no longer existed. He had probably never been as attractive as her memory had recalled
during the many nights she'd lain awake thinking about
him.

Natalie moved closer, drawn to the man who seemed to
be intently studying the jewelry beneath the glass display
counter. He turned his head so that she saw his profile, and
Natalie froze, no longer able to deny what her senses were
telling her.

There was no mistaking that beautiful profile that looked
as though it belonged on an ancient Roman coin. Black
curly hair fell across his forehead, and he impatiently

shoved it back, a familiar gesture that almost brought tears to her eyes.

Hesitantly, Natalie cut through the crowd toward him. Should she speak to him? Would he even remember her? Wouldn't it be better to leave all of her fantasies and memories intact? Surely speaking to him would only destroy any of her remaining illusions.

But could she walk away and not at least give herself the opportunity to speak to him once more? While part of her seemed to be in a perpetual debate, her feet continued to move toward him until she stood an arm's length away.

"Tony?"

She watched as he seemed to tense, then slowly turned to face her.

"I wasn't sure it was you," she said, trying to smile. "Hello, Tony."

The six years had been more than kind to him. His body had matured and filled out. At twenty-two he had been tall and slender with a wiry strength that she'd found impressive. Now his arms and chest were wide, tapering down to a narrow waist and hips.

His face looked more chiseled. There were lines around his mouth and eyes that hadn't been there before. And his eyes—those beautifully expressive black eyes—no longer told Natalie what he was thinking. He stared at her with no discernible expression.

"Don't you remember me? I'm Natalie—"

"I remember you," he broke in. "I was just surprised to see you."

"Yes. It's been a long time, hasn't it?"

"Has it?"

His gaze flickered over her as though automatically registering any changes in her. She wondered what he would see. She had just turned eighteen the last time she had seen him. She'd been so young then—too young to have known how to handle the situation she'd found herself in. Would she ever be able to forget the last time she'd seen him? He'd been angry then, watching her with snapping eyes as she'd walked away—out of his life and away from the future that they had naively planned together.

It was obvious he'd never forgiven her for her behavior. Those expressive black eyes were now shuttered, reflecting nothing of his thoughts or feelings.

"Do you live around—" Natalie started to say when someone brushed heavily against her and knocked her off balance and against Tony. She stumbled, and he automatically put his arms around her to keep her from falling.

Being suddenly jarred was not responsible for the way her body reacted to his touch. How many nights had she dreamed of being in Tony's arms once more, of having him hold her close, murmuring soft love words in her ear? How could she ever forget the hard-muscled length of him, the familiar scent of his after-shave lotion that continued to haunt her whenever she caught a whiff of it being worn by someone else—and the way she fit so well against him, her head nestling into his shoulder?

Natalie placed her hands on his chest and tried to collect herself. "I'm sorry," she muttered breathlessly. "I'm afraid—"

He cut her off by growling, "Let's get out of here." Taking her arm he guided her out of the store and across the mall to the ice-skating area. Food franchises circled the upper level, and he moved with her toward the small tables and chairs that overlooked the rink. Motioning for her to sit down, he asked, "What would you like to drink?"

In some respects Tony hadn't changed. He was still in charge, not even asking if she wanted something—just giving her a choice. Six years ago he probably wouldn't have bothered asking that—he would have known her so well he would have automatically ordered for her.

"A hot chocolate, please," she said, and met his gaze.

She saw his eyes flicker briefly at her familiar selection, then whatever emotion had washed over him was gone. "I'll be right back."

Natalie watched as Tony weaved his way through the crowd to the nearest window and ordered.

Now that she could catch her breath, Natalie observed other changes in him, changes that surprised her.

His clothes, for one thing. Tony had always worn jeans, motorcycle boots and a black leather jacket, only one of the many reasons her father had disapproved of him. She smiled at the memory. She remembered how her heart would race whenever she heard the sound of his motorcycle pulling into the driveway.

Even then Tony hadn't cared what anyone thought of him, not even her father. He had dressed the way he wanted.

He'd worked in construction back then, and his wardrobe hadn't lent itself to formal attire. Tony had worked hard—doing heavy physical labor, taking on tasks that others shirked.

Whatever he was doing now for a living was certainly not hard on his clothes. He wore well-fitting slacks that accented his hips and thighs and a pullover sweater that made a pleasing contrast to the long-sleeved shirt he wore.

But no tie.

That was in keeping with the Tony she remembered. She continued to watch him through the crowd as he patiently waited in line. Patience had never been one of Tony's biggest virtues, either.

But then she'd never considered patience particularly appealing herself. Yet now she was content to sit and watch him, speculating on his life in the past few years.

Was he married? He didn't wear any rings, but then he'd once explained to her that rings were dangerous in his business. Maybe he'd never gotten into the habit of wearing one.

Natalie had long ago convinced herself that she would not get upset when the time came that she heard Tony D'Angelo had married someone else. How could she possibly blame him? If she hadn't been so frightened and so unsure of herself, perhaps she could have better withstood her father's terrible anger.

She shook her head. Dwelling on the past was such a waste of time. There was no way to go back to undo the damage that had been done. Instead she forced herself to bring her mind back to the present and to the fact that, despite everything that had happened between them, she could think of no one she'd rather be with. For a short space out of time, Natalie was reminded of the magic of Christmas, the magic that Tony D'Angelo had brought into her life so many years before.

To most people, Natalie Phillips's childhood would have seemed to be blessed with a plentiful supply of wealth and advantages. Her brother, ten years older, had never had much time for her, and her mother had been very cautious about her playmates.

Consequently she had been a rather lonely child. She'd learned early in life to amuse herself by reading or playing with her dolls. Later she had enjoyed swimming and tennis, whenever she could find someone who was willing to play.

Natalie could remember exactly when she first laid eyes on Tony. She'd been ten years old.

It was summertime, and she had spent the morning in the house. She'd been upset that day, she remembered, because her parents had refused to allow her to go to summer camp. Or more precisely, her father had refused. Her mother had acquiesced to his decision as she always had, even though she had better understood Natalie's desire to go.

Henry Phillips had learned early in life that his only vulnerability was through his family, and he guarded them jealously. He knew that he'd stepped on many people getting to the top. He'd made enemies. He didn't care, but he wasn't going to take any chances that his family would suffer for any of his decisions. Consequently, Natalie was given very little freedom.

That day she had felt rebellious at her father's restrictions and had stomped outside, looking for a way to vent her anger and frustration.

Instead, she had fallen in love.

Fourteen-year-old Tony was riding a large lawn mower in the area behind her home. Two men were trimming the hedge that surrounded the swimming pool, but she never even noticed them.

He wore a pair of cutoffs that left his bronzed body bare. A red bandanna tied around his head kept his hair and the perspiration out of his face. He was so intent on what he was doing that he was oblivious to the people around him.

He looked like Adonis to the impressionable Natalie. She lost track of time as she watched him. Eventually the heat of the day penetrated her preoccupation. That's when she came up with the idea of bringing the gardeners something to drink.

Natalie rushed into the house, made a pitcher of ice water, found some freshly baked cookies and hastily returned to the back lawn.

Tony had stopped the mower and was checking the grass catcher when she came out.

"Hi! I bet you're thirsty, aren't you? I brought you some water and some cookies," she said.

She would never forget the way he had turned around, looked at her standing there so eagerly holding the tray and smiled.

"That sounds great. Thanks." She watched him untie the bandanna and rub it over his face before retying it around his forehead. Then he walked over to where she had set the tray on one of the tables by the pool. "What's your name?" he asked with a grin, after promptly emptying one of the glasses.

"Natalie."

"Thanks for the water, Natalie. That was very thoughtful of you." He glanced over at the house. "You live there?"

She nodded.

"Nice place," he said, studying the lines of the house as though they meant something to him.

"Would those men like something to drink?" she asked, nodding to the men who were at the far end of the pool.

"I'm sure they would." He raised his voice. "Say, Uncle Pietro, do you and Grandpapa want some water?"

The younger man glanced up. "We have a jug of water, Tony, and you know it. Don't bother the little girl."

Natalie flushed.

Tony glanced around and grinned. "He's right, but the ice has long since melted. And we certainly didn't bring any cookies!"

His black eyes danced mischievously as though she would understand and share the joke.

"How old are you, Natalie?" he asked, after he'd finished off two of the cookies.

"Ten."

"Ah, that's a good age."

"How old are you?"

"Fourteen."

"I'll be glad when I'm fourteen!"

"Why?"

"Because then maybe my father will let me do more things. He never lets me go anywhere!"

Tony smiled. "Maybe he just wants to protect you."

"From what?"

"From the world. From life. You're a very pretty girl, Natalie. If you were mine, I'd want to protect you, too."

His flashing smile in his dark face caused her breath to catch in her throat. He thought she was pretty? He would want to protect her, too?

She smiled, unable to think of anything to say.

"Get back to work, Tony. We don't have all day," one of the men hollered.

Tony shrugged and grinned. "I gotta run. Thanks again, Natalie."

She had watched him as he'd walked away with a spring to his step. She remembered thinking that day that she had never met anyone like him. She found him fascinating.

Nothing had ever caused her to change her mind.

"Here you are."

Startled, Natalie glanced up to see Tony sitting down across from her at the table. He carried two steaming insulated paper cups.

"It's good to see you again, Tony," she managed to say, her voice sounding husky to her ears.

He sat there for a few moments in silence, studying her. Finally he spoke. "Six years is a long time, isn't it?"

"Yes."

"You look very different from the young girl I watched grow up. I didn't think you could ever be more beautiful than you were at eighteen. I was wrong."

He spoke in a quiet, matter-of-fact tone, as though he

were discussing the weather or skiing conditions on Mount Hood. He was making it clear that no matter how he'd reacted to her in the past, she had no effect on him now.

"How have you been, Tony?"

He took a sip of his drink. "You're a little late in asking, aren't you?"

"Yes, I suppose I am. I have no excuses to make for my behavior back then. I behaved very badly."

"Not really. You were young. You'd been sheltered all your life. Your actions were predictable."

"Perhaps. But I can see that you never forgave me for leaving."

"It wasn't a matter of forgiveness. You made your choice, that's all."

They sat there for a few moments in silence, sipping their hot drinks. Natalie discovered that she couldn't meet his gaze. She recalled that he had always had a direct gaze. He'd stood up to her father and brother, never showing any sign of being intimidated by them. Natalie had always felt as though Tony had the ability to look deep inside her, to see her innermost thoughts and feelings.

If only she had the knack of doing the same thing with him.

"How's your family?" she finally asked.

"Fine. Mama is busy cooking and baking for the holidays." He shook his head. "Now Angela is working right along with her. They could feed everyone around us for blocks."

"Is Angela married?"

He tilted his head slightly. "As a matter of fact, she is. Why?"

"I just wondered. I wrote to her a couple of times after I went back East to school. But she never answered." Natalie shrugged. "I've wondered if she decided to go on to school."

"Yes, she did. She met Paul in one of her classes. They were married two years ago."

"I think of Christmas and remember your family, Tony. I always thought they had such a wonderful way of celebrating—all the cooking and preparations and the fun they always had with the younger children." She shook her head. "I used to envy you your family."

"You envied us? That's funny, with your background."

"Everything was always so formal at our home. The traditional tree and trimmings, the carefully wrapped gifts for Tom and me. The formal meal. There was never any laughter, any surprises. We seemed to go through the motions without experiencing any of the feelings of Christmas."

"And what feelings were those?"

She sighed, and her expression became wistful. "The love, the laughter, the sharing, the giving. All the wonderful things that your family seems to take for granted."

He shook his head. "Never for granted. We've always known what we had. I suppose I never realized before that you could see and appreciate all that we shared." He studied her for a moment, then asked, "When did you arrive in town?"

"Last night."

He glanced around the busy mall. "And now you're trying to get your shopping done, I take it?"

She shook her head. "Actually, I've already done that back in Boston. No, I just wanted to get out of the house today."

"How is your mother these days?" he asked politely, ignoring the undercurrent between them.

"Busy, as usual. She's so pleased that I decided to come

to Portland for Christmas. She and Tom have always flown East each year, since my father died.''

''I'm sure your brother was just as pleased that you came home.''

''I suppose. Tom and I don't talk much.''

''I see.''

There were so many questions she wanted to ask him, so many things she wanted to know. But how could she? It was none of her business. Tony D'Angelo was no longer a part of her life. It was obvious that he had accepted that. Natalie had thought she had accepted it years ago. And she had. Of course she had. But only when she had the entire continent between them.

''How long are you going to be here?'' he was asking her, and she forced herself to concentrate on his question. ''I'm leaving the Monday after Christmas.''

''Then you won't be here for New Year's.''

''No. I have to get back.''

How was it possible that they could be carrying on this perfectly normal conversation, like old friends who had been out of touch for a while, as though there was nothing between them?

But of course there *was* nothing between them now.

Her father had seen to that—six years ago.

Chapter 2

"Look, I've got to go," Natalie said, gathering her purse and packages. "Mother will be wondering about me. I borrowed Tom's car, and he's probably irritated that I've been gone this long."

Tony got to his feet. The smile he gave her didn't quite reach his eyes. "I'm sorry you have to rush off. I was rather hoping to hear about your life since we last saw each other."

She looked up at him, surprised by his interest. "Most of the time I was in school."

He seemed to hesitate. "I'm sure my family would be pleased to see you again. Would you like to come over some evening while you're here? I could pick you up."

Natalie's pulse began to race. Was this actually happening? Did Tony D'Angelo want to see her again, to spend additional time with her, after all that had happened between them?

Was there such a thing as a second chance?

"I'm not at all sure that you're right, Tony. I doubt that they want to see me after all this time."

"You might be surprised. Of course, it's up to you."

"I'd like to see them again, Tony. I'd like that very much."

His slow smile set up a vibration within her that caused her to almost visibly tremble. "Good. When could you go?"

"I really don't have anything planned."

"Then how about tomorrow night? I could pick you up at seven, if that would be convenient."

"That would be fine," she heard herself saying, as though from far away.

They parted, and only after Tony disappeared in the crowd did Natalie face the fact that except for the time when she'd been accidentally knocked into him and when he'd guided her through the crowd, Tony had carefully refrained from touching her.

What was she doing to herself? This was going to be some kind of refined torture, to become a part, once again, of the D'Angelo gathering at Christmastime.

Torture or not, she couldn't resist. How could anyone resist magic?

That night Natalie disgustedly punched her pillow and tried to straighten her rumpled bedclothes. She was tired. Fighting holiday crowds and traffic was always wearing, and she had gone to bed early, hoping to get some rest.

It was no use. Every time she closed her eyes she saw a pair of black eyes watching her. Sometimes their expression was warm and loving. At other times they held no expression at all.

Tony had handled their unexpected meeting today so well, without showing any shock or surprise. Was that an indication of how little his emotions had been affected by their meeting?

Natalie reminded herself that he had been standing at the jewelry counter—the *women's* jewelry counter, which strongly suggested there was definitely a woman in his life.

What else did she expect, anyway? Tony was extremely attractive. He always had been. She smiled, remembering…

She would never forget the summer she first met Tony, when he came to help his family take care of the sloping lawns and gardens of her home. Natalie had counted the days in between.

Not that she got to spend any time with him. That part didn't matter. It was enough for her to be able to watch him as he worked. As the weeks passed, she managed to find out more things about him.

He was the oldest of five children. She discovered that he had three sisters, one of whom, Angela, was Natalie's age, and a brother who was only a few months old. It was plain to Natalie that he loved his family very much.

By the time Natalie started high school she knew that there would never be any man who could possibly take Tony's place in her heart. In six years she had watched him become a man. He'd stopped working at her home after a couple of summers, but Natalie was able to see him occasionally because of Angela.

She had met Angela her first day of high school. The school was large, covering a vast district. As soon as she saw Angela she knew that the girl was related to Tony, with her curly black hair and dark eyes.

Angela had been shy but pleasant. Natalie and she quickly became friends. Although she could never convince Angela that she would be welcome in Natalie's home, eventually Angela had begun to invite Natalie to the D'Angelo home.

Natalie didn't deliberately lie to her mother about her

whereabouts. It was true that Natalie was busy with school-related activities. However, there were times when meetings and other activities ended early, and luckily for Natalie the D'Angelos lived close to the school.

Not that she was ashamed of Angela or the D'Angelo family, but Natalie had learned early in life that her family had decided ideas about who she should spend time with. Her father, especially, had set stringent rules about her dating and the young men who he would consider worthy of her attentions.

Because of Natalie's shyness, most of those young men soon lost interest and went in search of more lighthearted friends. Natalie was content to help Angela with her younger sisters and brother. And when Tony happened to come home while she was still there, Natalie's day was complete. She lived for the times when she happened to see him.

Even the fact that he treated her much in the same way he treated Angela made no impression on her. He was Tony, and that was enough. His flashing smile and teasing remarks were cherished like a priceless treasure.

It was the summer between her junior and senior years, when she was seventeen, that everything changed between them.

Natalie had finally coaxed Angela into meeting Natalie's mother. Her mother seemed relieved that the two rather quiet girls had formed a friendship. She had heard enough stories from her friends about some of the wild parties and problems occurring around their children.

Consequently Natalie spent most of her summer at the D'Angelos' home with her mother's silent blessing.

She would never forget the first time that Tony asked her for a date. She and Angela had just come from swimming at Natalie's home. They were late and rushed back to the D'Angelos' because Angela had promised to cook dinner for Tony since the rest of the family had gone out of town for the weekend.

Tony was working full-time in construction, his only means of transportation a rather beat-up motorcycle. They had just gotten home and hadn't had time to change out of their suits when he walked into the house, looking hot and very tired.

"Oh, Tony," Angela wailed, "I'm sorry. The time just slipped away from us. I'll make you something to eat right away."

He sat down at the table. "Don't worry about it, Angie. It's too hot to eat right now, anyway." His gaze slid from his sister to Natalie, who was self-consciously tugging at her suit. Why hadn't she worn the new one she'd purchased the week before? This one was last year's and too small. It hadn't mattered to her when they'd first gotten the idea to get some relief from the unusual heat of the day.

Now she wished she'd taken the time to have searched for the new one instead of standing there wishing she could disappear.

Tony grinned, the mischief in his eyes apparent. "Hi, Natalie. That's a lovely shade of red you're wearing."

She glanced down at her faded blue suit, then looked up, puzzled.

"I'm talking about the color in your cheeks. No doubt you got too much sun today. You'd better be careful with your fair skin."

His eyes seemed to assess the condition of her skin, from her face down to her toes, lingering along the length of her legs.

"Uh, Angela, I'm going to go change clothes. Then I'll help you with dinner."

"I have a better idea," Tony said. "Why don't both of you go change, and I'll take you out for pizza."

"Oh, but Mama said that I was supposed to feed you," Angela replied.

"She won't care, as long as we eat. And it's too hot to cook."

Angela didn't need much coaxing, and the girls scurried to Angela's room.

Natalie could still remember that night. They had laughed and talked. Tony had seemed content to listen to their chatter. He'd subtly questioned Natalie about her activities, her interests and the boys in her life.

Angela had embarrassed her by pointing out that Natalie showed no interest in the boys *at school*. The emphasis was made for Natalie's benefit, and was the closest that Angela would come to letting Tony know where Natalie's affections lay.

It hadn't taken Angela long to discover Natalie's secret crush on her older brother. Since she quickly learned to love Natalie, Angela could think of nothing better than for her to love Tony. Angela worshiped her brother and always had.

But she had been zealous in never alluding to Natalie's feelings for Tony. Until that night.

Natalie retaliated by kicking her under the table, which elicited a spate of giggles from Angela. Tony looked mystified.

And later it was Tony who insisted on taking Natalie home—on the back of his motorcycle. He found her a helmet and made sure that she had a good grip around his waist before they left. Angela's sparkling smile when they drove off was filled with glee.

Natalie had never been that close to Tony before, and she reveled in it. He'd showered before taking them out for dinner, and she could distinguish the slight scent of soap and after-shave. She rested her head against his back and closed her eyes. Natalie didn't care how long the trip took. She could have stayed that way forever.

When they pulled into the driveway, Natalie noted that her parents were gone. Tony followed the driveway to the back, coming to rest near the garage.

After he helped her off, Tony turned as though to get back on the motorcycle again. Natalie found herself saying, "Do you have to go?"

He looked up, surprised.

"I mean, well, it's such a beautiful night and all. Wouldn't you like to sit out here and talk for a while?" She gestured toward the tables and chairs by the pool.

He glanced around. "Where are your parents?"

"They were invited to a dinner party tonight."

"And they left you here alone?"

She laughed. "Hardly. Charles and Harriet live up there." She pointed to the apartment located over the garage. "Charles always waits until my parents are home before making sure the house is locked and going home."

"What does Harriet do?"

"Cooks and does some of the light cleaning."

"Is that why you're always over at our place, learning to cook?"

She nodded, shyly. "Yes. Harriet doesn't like me messing around in her kitchen. Besides," she said with a toss of her head, "she doesn't know how to cook Italian."

Tony stroked one of the loose blond curls that lay on Natalie's shoulders. "And you want to learn how to cook Italian?"

Natalie was thankful that the moonlight concealed her blush. "Yes, I do."

"Why?" he asked bluntly.

She shrugged and glanced around, desperately looking for another topic of conversation. Spying the pool, she blurted out, "Would you like to go swimming?"

He laughed. "Sure. Unfortunately I don't have anything to swim in."

"That's no problem. We have extras." She grabbed his hand. "I'll show you." She led him to the cabana at the end of the pool. Holding up her bag, she said, "I'll slip my suit back on and meet you out here in a few minutes."

Natalie was trembling so, she could scarcely get undressed. Tony was there, and they were going swimming together...in the moonlight. It was the most romantic moment she could possibly imagine.

By the time she came out of the dressing room, Tony was already in the water, swimming laps. The moonlight glinted off the water, bathing him in a glow of light as he moved rapidly through the water.

Natalie quickly joined him, and he began to pace her, matching his strokes to hers. When she could not swim another stroke Natalie grabbed the edge and gasped, "I give up! I'm going to drown if I don't stop!" Her breath came in short pants.

Tony laughed. "I'd never let you drown, Natalie. You know that." He placed his hands on the side of the pool, one on each side of her, so that she was boxed in.

Her heart was racing so fast it was almost painful in her chest, and Natalie couldn't seem to get her breath. Tony was no longer smiling. In fact, she had never seen him look at her so seriously.

"You are so beautiful, Natalie, you seem almost unreal to me. Those silvery-blue eyes staring at me so innocently almost unman me completely." His voice was low, and he spoke haltingly, as though the words had been dragged out of him.

"I'm real," she managed to say softly.

He groaned. "Don't I know it." He glanced around. "I don't think this was such a good idea, after all."

"Why not?"

He shook his head. "Come on, let's get dressed."

Tony was only a few inches away from her, and Natalie couldn't resist the temptation to find out what it would be like to kiss Tony D'Angelo.

Before he could pull away, she let go of the side of the pool and placed her hands lightly on his shoulders. Then she leaned over and kissed him very softly on his lips.

She felt his start of surprise, then her body floated against his, touching his bare chest and legs. His mouth opened slightly, and he began to return her kiss without ever letting go of the side of the pool.

Natalie felt safe in the circle of his arms, and she relaxed more fully against him. Tony deepened the kiss, nudging her lips apart with his tongue. Natalie thought she would faint from the joy of sharing this intimate act with him.

When he finally pulled away, they were both breathing hard. Tony grasped her firmly around the waist and lifted her to the side of the pool, then vaulted up beside her. Without saying a word he pulled her into his arms again, this time holding her tightly against him as he repeated the lesson he'd just given her.

Natalie was eager to learn all that he taught, and she wrapped her arms around his neck, luxuriating in the feel of his crisp curls beneath her fingertips.

Tony's hand eventually slipped from her back to her breast. Natalie couldn't conceal her gasp, and Tony abruptly let go of her.

"What am I doing?" he muttered. "I must be insane." He glanced down at her. "I'm sorry, Natalie."

"I'm not," she replied. "I've dreamed of kissing you

for years.'' Then she realized what she'd admitted to him and covered her face with her hands.

''Natalie?'' he said in a wondering tone.

She refused to look at him.

''Natalie?'' he repeated. ''What are you saying? That you want to go out with me, spend time with me? What?''

Slowly she removed her hands from her face and looked at him. ''Only if you want to be with me.''

He shook his head. ''I've spent years reminding myself that you aren't for me, that I shouldn't show my interest in you, and now you're telling me that—''

''You mean you don't think of me as just another sister?''

He almost choked with his laughter. ''Hardly.''

They stared at each other in silence. Then Tony brought his hand up and rested it against her cheek. She felt the tremor in his fingertips and vaguely recognized the restraint he was placing on himself. ''Oh, Natalie. Do you have any idea what you do to me?''

She shook her head.

''I've got to go. Now.'' He stood up and strode to the dressing room. She sat there and stared at the door that had cut off her view of him until he reappeared. Then she slowly came to her feet. He walked over to her. ''Against my own sense of self-preservation, I'm going to call you for a date. I'll borrow Dad's car. We'll go to a movie or something. We'll go someplace where there are people and where I'm not so tempted. But I've got to see you again, Natalie. Do you understand?''

She smiled. ''I'm glad.''

He ran his hand over her damp curls. ''I've got to be out of my mind.''

''If so, then I've joined you,'' she said with a shy smile.

He pulled her to him and gave her a brief, hard kiss, then

set her away from him. "Good night," he said, and turned away. The sudden sound of his motorcycle in the quiet night seemed to bring a touch of reality to the fantasy evening. Natalie watched Tony pull away. She stood there until he disappeared down the driveway, then turned away to go upstairs to relive the past few hours.

For the next two and a half months she saw Tony every day. She no longer cared what her mother thought, or her father. When her father made his disapproval of their relationship clear, she ignored him for the first time in her life.

She loved Tony. She had loved him for years. And now she had the opportunity to be with him as much as his work schedule would allow. Natalie refused to think of the future. She wanted to enjoy her time with Tony that summer. In her mind's eye each day spent with him was another pearl of memories that she collected until a beautiful strand of shared moments linked them to each other.

Natalie floated through the summer in her own dreamlike state of contentment, until the end of August when her father announced that she would not be returning to the public high school for her senior year. She would be going back East to a private girls' school.

Chapter 3

Tony D'Angelo lay awake for hours the night he saw Natalie at the mall. He went over each and every word that was spoken, looking for clues to how she felt about him.

The changes in her were not surprising. Six years was a long time. Was it too long for feelings to last? She had loved him at one time, that much he was sure of. But what about now?

She had seemed glad to see him, hadn't she? He wasn't sure how he had appeared to her. He'd been too busy guarding his reaction to the sudden, unexpected sight of her.

After six years, he had given up hope of her returning to Portland. He had known that sooner or later he would have to make the effort to contact her one last time, but he had continued to put off that inevitable meeting for as long as possible.

Now he had no choice. She was back, and he had to talk with her. He owed her some explanation regarding his silence for the past six years. Would she understand? Would she even care?

She hadn't asked him why he hadn't attempted to contact her nor had she given any explanations for her silence. He wasn't sure he was ready to hear that she had long ago dismissed him from her life. But then, what could he expect from her?

Six years was a long time. But he had kept his word to her father, long after the man was gone. Tony considered his word his honor. Her brother, Tom, had kept her family's side of the bargain.

Now was the time to bring their situation to an end and hopefully use it as a new beginning.

Tony turned over and lay on his stomach, his thoughts full of memories.

He would never forget the first time he'd ever laid eyes on Natalie. She'd been a shy little girl who looked like an angel to him, the kind that always sat at the very top of the D'Angelo family Christmas tree. She'd worn her hair long, the golden curls cascading down her back in a saucy ponytail. But it was her eyes that had drawn him to her. Those clear blue eyes that seemed to be the window of her soul, as though she had no secrets to hide. The dark fringe of thick lashes had appeared to be almost artificial with her light hair and fair skin.

Tony knew that he'd fallen in love that very first day, when she'd shyly offered him something to drink and some cookies.

How old had she been then? Ten or so, probably. She'd looked like a little porcelain doll, and he'd wanted to wrap her up and take her home with him, to protect her against all the hard knocks that life had to offer.

He still felt the same way. He just wasn't sure what course to take. Perhaps she only needed protection from him. At least her father had always felt that way. Perhaps he had been right.

Well, now she was back in Portland again, and she had agreed to visit his parents with him the next night. That was a start, anyway. He would just have to play it by ear.

He fell asleep thinking about her clear-eyed gaze smiling at him with love.

"Mama, look who I found out shopping yesterday," Tony said, motioning for Natalie to join him in the hallway of the family home. He had kissed and hugged his mother when she opened the door.

"Natalie! What a surprise! Come in, come in. You must be freezing out there." Serena D'Angelo waved her arms and hurried Tony and Natalie into the other room where a merrily dancing fire in the fireplace added to the warmth of the atmosphere.

"Hello, Mrs. D'Angelo. I hope you don't mind that I came along."

"What nonsense. Of course I don't mind. You have been a part of this family for years. Besides, you know me. I always cook enough to feed a couple dozen people." She turned and hurried out of the room. "Papa, you will never guess who Tony brought home with him!"

They stood and listened to the voices from the other room. "What did I tell you?" Tony asked with a grin.

From her place in the center of the room, Natalie slowly turned, taking in everything. Tears filled her eyes. So much was familiar—the decorations and ornaments, the Nativity scene on the mantel, the gaily decorated fir tree in the corner that she knew the family had found and cut down as part of their traditional Christmas celebration.

And yet, she saw signs of change as well—new drapes, a new sofa and chair. The place looked homey and lived in—in addition to being well loved.

For the first time since she'd arrived in Portland, Natalie felt as though she had finally come home.

"What's wrong?" Tony asked, concerned.

She shook her head. "Nothing. It's just so good to be here. I didn't think I'd ever see any of this again."

He held out his hand. "Let's go find the others. I forgot to ask if Angela and Paul were coming."

Natalie soon found herself accepted into the laughing circle of the family as though she had never been away. The changes were more apparent at the dinner table. There were only two children still living at home, and they had changed so much that Natalie wasn't certain she would have recognized them. Tony's brother was now fourteen and bore a distinct resemblance to the boy she'd met so many years before.

The D'Angelos were such a warm, loving family. She enjoyed watching the banter and teasing that seemed to be a part of their conversation.

At one point, Serena turned to Natalie and said, "I called Angela and told her you were here. She said that Paul was working late tonight but they would try to come over in time to have coffee and dessert with us." She patted Natalie's hand. "Angela was very excited to know you were here. She has lots of news for you."

Natalie had missed Angela. She had never made another friend who had been as close to her as Angela. Natalie felt as though she'd lost so much that was irreplaceable when she moved back East.

She wondered how Angela would treat her now.

"So tell us what you've been doing, Natalie," Serena continued after making certain that everyone had all that they wanted to eat.

Natalie glanced around and saw that the whole family was waiting for her answer.

"Mostly going to school. I've been doing some graduate work, learning how to help children who have learning disabilities."

"Where do you intend to work when you're through with your schooling?" Serena asked.

Natalie shook her head. "I don't know."

"I'm sure you could find something in the Portland area if you wanted," she pointed out.

Natalie's gaze met Tony's intent one. "That's true," she said softly, wondering what would happen if she were to move back to Portland. Two days ago she would never have considered the idea. Now that she had seen Tony again, her mind seemed to be coming up with some rather unusual ideas.

Serena went on. "I know you must be proud of Tony. Hasn't he done well?"

Natalie looked at Tony sitting there so relaxed beside her. His hand rested alongside hers, and she had an almost uncontrollable urge to touch him. "What do you mean?" she asked, reluctantly forcing her attention toward Serena.

"Hasn't he told you?" Serena asked, beaming. "Tony has his own company now."

Natalie looked at him once more. "Your own company? I don't understand."

He shrugged. "Construction is what I know. I've been going to night school, learning the technical information I needed to build. I started remodeling old homes until I got enough capital to buy one. After that it became a matter of selling the remodeled homes and buying more. I've been doing some new construction as well."

"Oh, Tony. That's wonderful."

"I doubt that your father would have been impressed."

His words seemed to echo and reecho around the room. Her father. Yes, her father's influence on her life still lingered. How different things would have been now without his interference.

"Natalie! You're really here!" Natalie glanced up in time to see Angela rushing toward her. "I couldn't believe it when Mama said you had come to visit." She hugged Natalie, then whirled around. "Paul, come meet Natalie."

A tall blond-headed man had followed the diminutive brunette into the room and had stood there watching the reunion with a smile on his face. "Hello, Natalie," he said with a nod. "I'm glad to finally meet you."

Serena motioned to two empty chairs and said, "Sit! Sit! You're just in time for some cake and ice cream."

"Oh, no, Mama, I can't. I'm having to watch everything I eat these days."

Natalie looked at her slim friend in surprise. "Surely you're not dieting, Angie?"

Angela chuckled. "Not exactly. But I'm still having trouble with nausea in the morning, and I've discovered that it's much easier to eat lightly the night before."

Natalie looked from her friend's face to those seated around the table. "Is this news to anyone besides me?"

They all burst out laughing. Serena explained, "Angie insisted that she wanted to be the one to tell you. I thought we managed to stay off the subject very well, didn't you?"

"Oh, Angela. I'm so happy for you." Flashes of previous conversations they had had over the years came back to her. They had both wanted large, happy families. It looked as though Angela was well on the way to starting hers. Natalie felt a flash of envy at her friend's good fortune. She glanced at Tony and found his intent gaze on her. She dropped her eyes, unable to face him.

Once upon a time she and Tony had talked about the family they wanted to have some day. That was another life ago, before she had decided to train to help other people's children.

She looked at Serena. "So you are going to have a grandchild, are you?"

Serena laughed. "Yes. I can hardly wait."

No one mentioned that Tony, being the oldest, had been the most likely candidate to produce the first grandchild. Natalie glanced down at her hands, which restlessly twisted in her lap.

Tony reached down and touched her hands lightly, as though gently soothing her. She looked up at him, startled by the gesture. What she saw in his face made her realize that he, too, remembered their plans.

The conversation continued with numerous interruptions and hilarious anecdotes as each family member shared with Paul some of the situations that Natalie and Angela used to find themselves in while trying to learn to cook.

Natalie couldn't remember the last time she had laughed so hard nor felt so loved and accepted. After clearing the table and cleaning the dishes, the family returned to the living room where Natalie found herself sandwiched on the small sofa between Tony and his younger brother.

Tony had pulled Natalie against his side with his arm around her shoulders as though it were normal and a routine they had established in front of his family. She smiled at the thought. He had always treated her with such careful distance whenever they'd been around the family in the past, making sure that they understood he was taking no liberties with her.

Now he seemed to be making a silent claim on her, one that was deeply affecting her. How had she possibly stayed away from him this long without making some effort to know if what they had once shared was salvageable? Because if it was—if his body language this evening was any indication—Natalie knew that God in His mercy was willing to give her another chance at happiness.

"Are you ready to go?" Tony asked Natalie some time later, after Angela mentioned that she needed to get home and get some rest.

Natalie smiled. "I'm never ready to leave this place," she said, coming to her feet and hugging Serena. "But I do need to get home. It's been so wonderful, seeing everyone again and sharing one of your marvelous meals. Thank you so much for dinner."

"You're quite welcome," Serena replied, hugging her back. "What are you planning to do for Christmas, Natalie?"

"We haven't discussed anything, actually. My brother's tied up in some big business negotiations and is seldom home. Mother's been busy with Christmas plans for some of the organizations she works with, but she hasn't said anything about our family plans."

"Well, you're welcome to come over here. You know we still have the open house on Christmas Eve, and we all go to the church services at midnight." Serena glanced at her oldest son. "You were planning to come, weren't you, Tony?"

"Of course, Mama. I've never missed spending Christmas with you, now have I?" he said, giving her a hug.

One of the many things that Natalie had always admired was the freedom the D'Angelo family had with each other to express their affection. She had never seen her father, or even her brother, hug her mother. She couldn't remember the last time either her mother or brother had touched her.

There was so much she missed about this family. Watching Tony she knew that she would give everything she owned to be a part of it now.

Tony was quiet during the drive to Natalie's former

home located in the west hills overlooking Portland. Natalie wanted to say something, anything to break the silence.

"I take it you're no longer living at home," she finally said.

Tony glanced at her, then returned his gaze to the road in front of them. "No. I'm living in one of the houses I'm currently remodeling."

"Would it be possible for me to see it?" she asked.

"Now?"

Her heart seemed to be thundering in her chest. What did he think she meant? She wasn't sure, herself. She'd just been trying to fill in some of the silence between them, trying to overcome the tension that had appeared as soon as they were alone.

"I don't think that would be a very good idea," she said, knowing that she was admitting a great deal more than she'd wanted to by her statement.

Tony didn't reply but continued toward her home.

They pulled into the long driveway that followed the hillside up to the large home. Instead of parking in front, Tony continued around to the back entrance. He turned off the lights and engine of the car, then turned to her. "If you really want to see my place, I could take you over there after I finish working tomorrow."

The light over the garage created shadows across his face, and she couldn't read his expression. "I'd like that," she admitted softly.

Tony looked at the garage, the house, the swimming pool, then back at her. "This feels very familiar, doesn't it? Bringing you home like this? Wondering if we woke up your parents?"

She smiled. "You have to admit that this car is considerably different from your old pickup or the motorcycle."

He grinned. "True. I doubt that anyone in the neighborhood heard us drive in this time."

They stared at each other in silence. Tony placed his hand on her cheek and gently brushed his thumb across her slightly parted lips. "I've missed you," he finally said in a husky voice.

"I missed you, too. I guess I just assumed that you never wanted to see me again."

He stroked along her ear and down her neck as though relearning the shape and feel of her. "Why would you think that?"

"Because of what happened. Because I never heard from you after I left."

He tilted her chin so that she had no other option but to look at him, unless she closed her eyes. She was tempted by the thought—to close her eyes and move the necessary few inches to kiss Tony again, to experience the wonderful magic that only he seemed to evoke. But she had to know. Why hadn't he tried to contact her through the years? She had asked Angela to have him write to her, but she hadn't heard from either of them.

He leaned over and placed a gentle kiss at her temple, his touch feeling like butterfly wings brushing against her sensitive skin.

"I couldn't contact you. That was part of the agreement."

She stared up at him in confusion. "What agreement?"

"The one I made with your father."

"I don't know what you're talking about."

"I'm not surprised."

"He told you to leave me alone?"

"What else did you expect from him? He never accepted me in your life. He made his disapproval very obvious, particularly that last time I saw you."

She could feel the heat rising to her face, but could not control it. How many years had she tried to forget that last time she'd been with Tony? She shook her head. "I was so frightened."

"I know. I even understood your reaction at the time. But it still hurt."

She placed her hand on his arm. "I never wanted to hurt you, Tony. Please believe me."

"I know. I understood that at the time. You were very young. You were faced with a decision you weren't prepared to make."

"You're right. I thought I'd made all the decisions that were necessary." She could feel her heart racing in her chest. She wanted him to kiss her and hold her, to reassure her that his feelings hadn't changed for her. If he were to ask her to stay in Portland, she would willingly do so. But how could she understand how he felt if he didn't say anything?

He leaned over and lightly kissed her on the lips, then pulled away from her. "I'd better get you inside. It's late."

Natalie tried to hide her reaction, hoping that the shadows masked her expression. What had she expected, anyway? They were both too old to sit out in the car like a couple of teenagers.

"Why don't I come by tomorrow early enough to show you the house before dark? Then we can have dinner together somewhere."

She smiled. "I'll be ready whenever you say." Tony got out of the car and walked around to her side. She waited until he had opened her door, then said, "I want you to know how much I appreciated getting to see your family tonight. Being with them brought back so many happy memories."

"Yes, it did. We used to enjoy teasing you and Angela so much. I'd almost forgotten."

They reached the screened porch and paused. The cold night air seemed to move around them in swirls. "Sleep well," he said with a smile, holding the door open for her. "I'll see you tomorrow."

Natalie nodded. "You do the same," she said, and hurried inside to the warmth of the house.

Natalie slowly climbed the stairway to her room. Memories of her last Christmas in Portland continued to stir around her, as though insisting on being recalled and acknowledged.

After going through her nightly ritual of getting ready for sleep, Natalie stretched out on the bed and pulled the covers up around her.

If only she could understand the man that Tony had become. He acted so natural around her, as though he were comfortable with her. Was she the only one feeling the tension that seemed to hold her prisoner whenever he was present?

What had happened to the young man she had known, the one she had fallen so much in love with? Did he still exist somewhere beneath that calm and controlled exterior?

The hovering memories swooped down around her, eager to gain her attention once again.

Chapter 4

After almost four months away from home, Natalie still hated the boarding school. She missed Angela and her friends at school. But most of all, she missed Tony. After having seen him every day during the summer, the sudden jolt of being away from him had been almost more than she could handle. Her father had not even allowed her to come home for Thanksgiving, insisting she take the time to get better acquainted with her new classmates before coming home for Christmas.

With only another week before Christmas, Natalie hurriedly packed so that she would be ready to catch her ride to the airport. She felt like she'd been away from home for years instead of months.

She'd written Tony almost every day that she'd been gone. He had managed to respond to a few of her letters, admitting that he wasn't very good at corresponding, but that didn't mean that he wasn't counting the days until she arrived home for Christmas vacation.

Natalie had kept a large calendar hanging over her desk and had drawn a large X through each day before going to bed. At long last she would be able to see him again, even though she wasn't sure how.

Her father had refused to be swayed from his decision to send her away last September. She had cried. She had pleaded. Never in her life had Natalie wanted so desperately to stay home, but he would not relent.

He made it clear that his daughter was going to have a proper education and meet the right kind of people. Her summer rebellion was now over.

She hadn't even been given the opportunity to tell Tony goodbye. Instead, she'd had to send a message through Angela.

Natalie had learned a great deal in the past few months. She had learned not to be so open and trusting. She had always thought that her parents respected her, including her beliefs and opinions. She had learned that she was wrong. She would never make that mistake again.

Natalie had no intention of telling her family that she was going to spend any time with the D'Angelos. She had made sure that her letters were full of the new people she'd met and all of her activities. As far as her parents knew, she had forgotten her old friends.

By the time she'd been home for two days, she could tell that she had convinced them of her lack of interest in anyone in Portland. She made a great many remarks about how boring it was to be home and how she could hardly wait to return East. Watching the satisfied glance her father gave her mother convinced Natalie that she could have a career in acting if she chose. She had managed to cover her true feelings.

Consequently she was given a great deal of freedom to come and go as she pleased, which suited her just fine. She spent every available minute at the D'Angelo home.

Tony was the one who wasn't pleased when she refused

to allow him to take her home. He was much harder to convince that what she was doing was the only way she could still see him without creating all sorts of difficulties with her family.

They even argued about it.

"Don't you see, Tony? This is the only way I can see you!"

"Don't give me that! We aren't in the Dark Ages, you know. You're eighteen years old, Natalie. Your father has no say-so over you."

She nodded. "But he does. I'm still in school."

"So what?"

"I have no choice but to go by his rules as long as he's taking care of me."

"Then let me take care of you."

They were in his car at a secluded lookout near the Columbia River, and she looked at his shadowed face in surprise. "What do you mean?"

"Marry me, Natalie. I can take care of you. Then you can go to school here. We have the community college and Portland State if you want to go further. Just don't go back East."

"Oh, Tony," she whispered, her heart seeming to pound in her throat. "Do you really mean that?"

He pulled her into his arms. "Of course, I mean it. I can support you. I love you. I want to marry you. I can't stand the thought of your being so far away."

His kiss made it clear to her that he wanted her in every way that a man could want a woman. Natalie surrendered to his touch, trembling in his arms. When he drew away, they were both having trouble breathing.

She shook her head. "You know they'd never allow that," she managed to say.

"They can't stop us."

"What do you mean?"

He nodded to the other side of the river. "We could go over to Washington and get married. They wouldn't have to know anything about it until it was already accomplished."

"Are you serious?"

The kiss he gave her removed any doubt in her mind. When he finally raised his head, his voice was husky with longing. "I've never wanted anything more in my life."

"But what will they do when they find out?"

"What can they do? They'll just have to accept the fact that we're married." He brushed a stray curl away from her brow. "It's the only way I know to keep them from sending you back East after the holidays."

The thought of being married to Tony D'Angelo caused Natalie's heart to triple its rhythm. To actually be married to him, to live with him, sleep with him, have his children was more than she'd ever envisioned.

She couldn't think of anything she'd rather have happen in her life. "All right," she managed to say, her voice quavering.

This time it was Tony who needed reassurance. "Do you really mean it, Natalie?" She nodded her head, and he hugged her to him. "You'll never regret it, Natalie. I promise. I'll make you happy, I swear."

She laughed. "You don't have to do anything to make me happy, Tony. Being with you is all that it takes."

He stroked her cheek. "I love you so much, Natalie. I can't begin to tell you how much."

"I love you, too."

He shook his head. "But you're so young. Maybe we should wait awhile. Maybe until after you've graduated."

She pulled away from him. "You want me to spend five more months away from you?"

He shook his head. "No."

She grinned. "So what do we have to do?"

He was silent for several minutes. "Tomorrow is Christmas Eve. We always have an open house and go to midnight services. Are you going to be able to come?"

"I think so. My parents are having some people in, and I told them I'd be going to church. They probably won't know when I leave."

"If you could get away early, say around noon, we can go to Vancouver, get a license and find a judge to marry us. Then we'll spend the evening with my parents. Instead of taking you home, we'll go to a hotel. I'll take you home Christmas morning, and we'll tell your family."

"When will we tell yours?"

"Not until after we've told your family. We'll go back home and spend Christmas with my folks."

"Your family is going to be hurt at our doing it this way."

Tony was quiet for a moment. "I know. And you won't be having the kind of wedding that you and Angie have always talked about, I'm afraid."

"I don't care," she said, tracing his jawline with her finger. "All I care about is being with you." Her voice broke. "I can't stand being away from you, Tony."

"Then this is the only way I know to keep you here." He held her so close that she could feel his heart beating, its rapid rhythm telling her better than words how she affected him.

Tony had been so careful with her ever since he'd first started seeing her. She had been aware of the tight rein he'd kept on his reactions to her, but she wasn't so naive that she hadn't understood what a strain he'd been under.

By this time tomorrow night, they would be married. He wouldn't have to keep such a rigid control over his actions.

The next day there was talk of snow for Christmas, and her mother warned her about driving in the bad weather. Natalie laughed at the idea. She wouldn't be going far. She explained that she had some last minute errands to run and some gifts to deliver and that she wasn't sure when she'd be home.

She met Tony at noon.

They were in the clerk's office in Vancouver by one o'clock and by two had found a benevolent judge who agreed to marry them.

By two-thirty they were back in Portland. Natalie couldn't believe it. She was actually married to Tony. She was now Natalie Phillips D'Angelo, and she had the ring to prove it. "It's beautiful, Tony," she said, touching the wide gold band on her third finger.

"Not as beautiful as you. Someday in the near future I'm going to buy you an engagement ring to go with it."

"I don't need one, Tony. This is all I need."

He took her hand and placed it on his thigh. "I wasn't sure you'd be there today."

"Why?"

"I thought you might have second thoughts about the idea."

"All I could do was to count the hours."

"Where did you tell your mother you were going?"

"I had some last-minute shopping. If I go home now, she won't think anything of my leaving later."

"I'm not sure I can let you leave me, even for a few hours," he said, pulling up beside her car in the parking lot where she'd left it earlier.

She threw her arms around him. "This will be the last time. I promise."

He hugged her tightly against him. "I'll see you at our place this evening."

"Yes."

"I love you, Natalie."

Those words echoed in Natalie's mind all that afternoon. She hurried home and helped her mother prepare for their guests. She made sure the gifts she'd brought from school were under the tree so that her parents and brother would find them the next morning.

For just a moment she had a strong desire to tell them about her marriage, but Tony had cautioned her against that. He wanted to be with her when they heard the news.

Besides, she wanted this particular night with Tony before they told anyone. For a little while they would share their special secret only between the two of them.

By the time she quietly left the house, her parents' guests had begun to arrive. She had no difficulty in slipping outside with her overnight case.

The sky had cleared, and the twinkling lights from downtown Portland were no competition to the bright stars that seemed to be specially polished for this particular night.

Natalie drove slowly through the streets, enjoying the many decorated homes. The crisp air seemed to shimmer with the echoes of church bells and carols being sung.

Such a special night. One that she would never forget. She and Tony had picked a beautiful time to be married, to share the love they felt for each other with the love that had been brought to the Earth almost two thousand years before.

Tony met her at the door of his parents' home, giving her a brief, possessive kiss before escorting her into the room filled by members of their family and a collection of laughing friends.

"I missed you," he whispered. "Are you sure you want to stay here all evening?" He couldn't hide the desire in his eyes.

"Don't you think we should?"

"Yes. But I don't know how much longer I can be around you without shouting to the world that you now belong to me."

She hugged him tightly, thrilled at the leashed control he was keeping on his emotions. When he finally let go, she would be able to show him how much she loved and wanted him as well.

"None of that, you two," Angela warned with a grin. She was carrying a large tray of food to the buffet table set up near the Christmas tree. "You don't want to be shocking anyone with your behavior now, big brother."

Tony grinned, refusing to remove his arms from around Natalie.

The rest of the evening passed in a blur to Natalie. When it was time to leave for church, she and Tony managed to slip away in his car without offering to take anyone with them. They didn't intend to return to the house. Natalie had placed her bag in his car when she arrived.

The church bells were ringing as family clusters went through the front doors of the church. Once inside each person was handed a candle.

The service, as always, touched Natalie's heart. After the story of the Nativity was read aloud, the lights in the church were dimmed and each candle was lit. The smiles around her were so beautiful. The shared love was so tangible that Natalie felt that she could reach out and almost touch it.

She was so glad to spend this time with Tony, to be reminded of the magic of Christmas, that time of year when people took time out of their busy lives to remember the wonderful gift they had been given, the example they had been shown on how to love one another. It was a gift that could be carried with them throughout the new year.

After the service Tony quietly took her hand and led her

out of the church. Silently they walked to the car and drove to one of the luxury hotels downtown that overlooked the Willamette River.

He carried their small cases and went inside. Without pausing at the desk he walked over to the elevator.

"Don't we have to register?"

He glanced down at her. "I checked in earlier."

"Oh."

When he opened the door to the room, Natalie walked in and stopped, awed by the view.

The moonlight shone brightly over the city and high-lighted the snow that coated Mount Hood in a pristine white blanket.

"I left the drapes open. I thought you might appreciate the view."

"It's beautiful, Tony," she murmured, moving over to the window and staring outside. The lights along the many bridges spanning the river were reflected in the water, so that the entire city seemed to be a gigantic ornament lit up for their pleasure.

Tony pulled her against him, her back resting against his chest. "I hoped you would like it."

She turned in his arms. "Thank you. Thank you for being who you are, for being so thoughtful and considerate. Thank you for loving me."

"You don't owe me any thanks, love. I got to marry the Christmas-tree angel. What more could any mortal ask?"

His kiss was gentle, as though he didn't want to frighten her. At last, after all these months together, there were no more restrictions between them.

Natalie felt so loved and protected. She had loved this man since they had both been children. Now they were grown. Now they were married.

Now they belonged to each other.

Tony dropped his arms and stepped back. "I don't want to rush you. I want this night to be special."

"It already is."

He nodded to the bathroom where the only light they had glowed. "You can change in there if you'd like."

She could feel herself blushing, despite everything she could do. Why should she feel shy with Tony? She loved him. She wanted him to show her how to express that love physically.

Somehow he must have known how she felt. He touched her cheek softly and smiled. Turning away, she opened her case and pulled out her gown and robe. "I'll only be a few minutes," she whispered, picking up her bag of toiletries.

"There's no rush. We have the rest of our lives together."

When she came out, she turned off the bathroom light. Moonlight poured through the large expanse of glass, illuminating the room so that she could see Tony was already in bed, waiting for her.

Natalie moved silently toward him. She let the robe slide from her shoulders and fall to the floor beside the bed. Then she shyly slid under the covers beside him.

Tony turned onto his side and leaned on his elbow. "You are so beautiful, I'm afraid to touch you for fear you're not real."

She rested her hand on his bare chest. "I'm real enough." She could feel the heat of his skin almost burning her fingertips.

He touched her hair lightly, brushing it out over the pillowcase. Then he traced the shape of her ear with his forefinger.

Natalie turned her head so that she could see him. His dark eyes glittered in the moonlight, and she could see the tension in his face.

For the first time, Natalie realized that he was as nervous as she was. Recognizing that fact helped her to relax. She tilted her head so that she could kiss him.

His mouth felt so familiar, so dear to her. She remembered the months that she had lain awake at night, wishing he were there to kiss her good-night. Now her dreams had come true on this most magical of all nights. Tony was there to share his love with her.

As the kiss continued, the soft gentleness began to change. It became heated, moist and more demanding. Natalie felt as though she were igniting. Everywhere he touched, Tony's caressing hands seemed to set off tiny explosions of excitement within her.

He began to explore her face with his kisses while his hands followed the contours of her body. Although he had never taken such liberties before, Natalie felt no qualms about allowing the intimacies. This was Tony, and he was turning her into an inferno.

She could no longer lie still and restlessly began to trace the well-developed muscles of his shoulders and back.

When his kisses moved down along the low neckline of her gown, Natalie shivered. He raised his head and looked at her. "Did I hurt you?"

She shook her head. His hand cupped her breast. "Would you rather I not touch you?"

"I love you to touch me, Tony."

He slid his hand under first one strap, then the other, then slowly pushed the gown down until it was around her waist.

Natalie had always been shy, and yet she loved the expression that Tony had on his face when he looked at her. When he leaned over and kissed the rose-tipped surface of her breast, she almost cried out with the pleasure of his touch.

She ran her hands restlessly across his chest, then around his back and up through his hair. The curls clung to her fingers as though returning her soft caress.

Natalie clung to him as he worshiped her body. By the time he moved so that he was lying between her legs, she was almost whimpering with longing without understanding what it was she needed.

He showed her—with infinite gentleness he showed her the beautiful ecstasy that two people can share. With patience he allowed her to adjust to him before he began the age old rhythm that brought them ever closer to each other and to the pinnacle of sensation.

His murmured love words filled her mind and heart. She clung to him as though he were the only thing that prevented her from being swept away with all the new sensations. He waited for her to respond, to ignite, to take the lead in finding their goal.

His patience was rewarded. When she gasped, he felt the contractions begin deep within her and could no longer postpone his own reaction. With a soft cry he gave a convulsive lunge and held her as though he never intended to let her go.

"Oh, Tony," she whispered when she could get her breath. "I never knew it could be like this. I never guessed making love would be so wonderful. How could we have waited so long?"

He had rolled to his side, holding her tightly against him. "I had to wait, love. I could never have loved you so intimately, then walked away from you. I had to know you were mine to hold all night, every night."

She smiled, kissing him. "If only I'd known."

"I'm glad you didn't. You were enough of a temptation as it was."

They lay there, sharing memories of the separation they

had just gone through, planning for their future, talking about their family. He had been careful to protect her from pregnancy, and they had discussed the need for waiting until she was through with school before starting a family.

Then they had made love once again. This time they took their time—the urgency was gone. There was time for exploration and experimentation. Natalie was eager to learn all about him and what affected him. When they finally fell asleep it was almost dawn, and they were exhausted.

Which was why they did not hear the key in the lock or the door being opened the next morning.

The first thing they heard was the sound of Natalie's father demanding that they get up, get dressed and get ready to leave.

Chapter 5

With a sob Natalie came awake, shaking. She sat there for a moment, trying to get her breath. She'd been dreaming again, the same dream that had haunted her for years. Why did her subconscious persist in reminding her of the past when she'd worked so hard to forget it?

Instead, she continually relived the nightmarish feeling of waking from a sound sleep to find her father yelling at her and Tony, calling them names she'd never heard coming from her father.

She could still remember the horror of that moment as she scrambled to find the robe she'd discarded the night before beside the bed. She could still hear her father's angry words, threatening Tony.

She had tried to explain that they were married, that they had done nothing wrong, but instead of appeasing him, her explanations called forth an even louder denunciation, most of it aimed at Tony.

Her father had reminded Tony of her youth, her lack of education, her family's plans for her. Then he told them that he intended to have the marriage annulled and that if either one of them gave him any trouble over it, he would see that not only Tony but his entire family would never be able to find work in the entire Pacific Northwest.

Then he'd demanded that Natalie get dressed and come home with him, that her brother was waiting downstairs.

Her humiliation was complete. She felt like a rebellious runaway as she ran into the bathroom to get dressed. She could still hear her father's voice as he continued to roar at Tony. She could hear Tony's attempts to break into the tirade, but without success.

When she had replaced the clothes she'd worn the day before, Natalie had reentered the bedroom. The first thing she noticed was that Tony was up. He wore the pants he'd had on the day before, but was still barefoot and without a shirt. In the bright morning light streaming through the window he looked like a marble statue that could be found in Rome. She was forcibly reminded of the night they had just shared, the intimacies, the passion, and she found herself moving toward him.

"Leave him alone!" her father ordered. "Go on downstairs and wait for me, Natalie."

Tony's calm gaze met hers. "You don't have to leave, Natalie. There's nothing he can do to us, you know."

"The hell there isn't!" her father interrupted to say. "You don't know what trouble is, young man, until you've tangled with me. I've got enough clout in this area to see that you and your father are hounded out, forced to move clear across the country. I'm telling you to leave my daughter alone!"

Tony continued to watch Natalie, waiting for her response.

All she could think about was what her father was saying. It was true. She had seen what he could do. She knew how he had destroyed competitors. What could he do to the D'Angelos if he really set about bringing them down? It didn't bear thinking about.

"Tony?" she whispered, uncertainly.

"Don't go, Natalie. He can't hurt us. You belong to me now!"

Her father blew up with that remark, shouting words that made Natalie cringe. Tony didn't understand. He didn't know the kind of man that her father was capable of being.

But Natalie did. How could she do something that would hurt not only the man she loved but his wonderful loving family as well?

She began to cry. "Oh, Tony."

Tony started toward her, but her father blocked his way.

"Go downstairs, Natalie. Now!" her father said. He looked as though he were ready to strike Tony. "I want you out of her life, D'Angelo. Do you understand? Completely and totally out of her life. I don't care what sort of ceremony you think you went through, there is no marriage. I'll see to that!" He turned to Natalie. "Now get out of here."

Years later, Natalie could still feel the awful pain in her chest. She remembered starting to the door and looking back. The anguish in Tony's eyes was unmistakable. His murmured, "Don't go, Natalie," as she slowly went out of the room continued to haunt her all these years.

She had never seen him again. Not until two days ago when she'd recognized him at the mall.

Her father and brother had driven her home. She'd been hysterical. Her father had told her to forget about Tony and any marriage. The marriage was no longer in existence, he would see to that.

He had sent her back to school the day after Christmas. She had never talked to him again. Three months later her father had had a sudden heart attack and died before they could get him to the hospital.

She had flown home for the funeral, but hadn't attempted to contact Tony or his family. After three months of silence in response to her letters, she had gotten her answer from the D'Angelos. None of them wanted anything more to do with her.

Now, here she was, six years later, back in their lives. They had all been kind to her, including Tony. He had treated the past as though it had never happened, as though they had never spent that marvelous night together, as though he hadn't taught her so much about his own sexuality and hers.

She had stayed in the East once she finished school for the year, taking summer courses and planning her college curriculum. It was as though she could bury herself in a heavy schedule so that she wouldn't have time to think about what she had given up.

Natalie knew that she was responsible for the present situation. The choice had been hers, and she'd made it. If she had it to do over again, she would probably have done the same thing. Even with her father gone, it was too late to go back and attempt to make amends.

She knew that walking out on Tony at that vulnerable time in their relationship had been a betrayal of all that they had shared.

Now he was treating her like a friend. He was relaxed and easy around her. And it was slowly killing her. When she had attempted to discuss what had happened, he had excused what she had done as though it were no longer important.

She glanced at her bedside clock. It was almost four o'clock in the morning. He was coming by later that day to take her to see his home. What did it mean? Why was

he willing to spend time with her without discussing anything personal between them? Natalie wondered how she
could possibly continue to be around him without betraying
her feelings.

She felt as though the past six years had been wiped
away and she was once more the eighteen-year-old girl
whose bones seemed to melt whenever he appeared.

Some things never change.

When Tony arrived to pick her up, both Tom and her
mother were there. Natalie brought him into the living room
with her.

"Mother, Tom, I believe you remember Tony D'Angelo,
don't you?"

Natalie was surprised to see Tom promptly get up and
stride over to Tony. "Hello, Tony. It's good to see you.
It's been a while," he said with a smile.

Tony nodded. "I've been busy."

"So I understand. I read in the paper that your company
won the bid on the Crandall property."

"That's right."

"Congratulations. Your growth in the industry has been
phenomenal."

Natalie could scarcely believe her ears. Tom was talking
to Tony as though they were old friends, although Tony
was much more reserved. And it was obvious that Tom had
been keeping tabs on Tony's company. Why?

"Hello, Tony," her mother said quietly. "How is your
family?"

"Doing very well."

"Would you like to join us? We've been having coffee
in front of the fire and enjoying a quiet moment. We don't
seem to have many of them these days."

He smiled at the older woman. "Not today. I promised

Natalie I would take her over to see my latest project, then we're having dinner.''

"Yes, she told me. I know she's enjoyed seeing her old friends after such a long absence.''

Tony glanced at Natalie from the corner of his eye. "I've enjoyed seeing her as well,'' he offered in a noncommittal tone.

After Natalie put on her coat, they left the house and walked down the steps to the curving driveway where his late-model sports car waited.

"Quite a different reception than I'm used to from your family,'' he pointed out quietly after they'd started down the driveway.

"I don't think either my mother or brother shared my father's animosity toward you, Tony.''

"So I noticed.''

"Tom seemed to be very interested in you.''

She noticed that he hesitated a moment before answering her. "Yes, well, we've run into each other occasionally over the years.''

"He's never mentioned you whenever we talked.''

"There was no reason for him to, was there?''

She shook her head, trying to pull her thoughts away from the past.

She noted that Tony was headed south along the Willamette River, toward Lake Oswego. After several turns and winding streets he pulled into a driveway that was marked Private. They followed it through the dense trees until the driveway split, forming a circle in front of a large home.

Natalie looked at the two-story structure, then back at Tony. "This is where you're living?''

He nodded. "It had been neglected for several years and needed some major renovation. I decided it was worth saving. I've finished up most of the inside work. Now all that needs to be done is cosmetic repair to the outside.''

Natalie slowly got out of the car and walked to the door. ''This is beautiful, Tony.''

And it was. It looked like an English country home, with weathered red bricks and large windows with small panes of leaded glass. She could almost feel the warmth that seemed to radiate from the place.

''The house had been tied up in probate proceedings for years with no one taking proper care of it.''

''It has such a happy feel about it, as though you can almost hear the laughter of children,'' she said as he opened the door into the wide foyer.

He pointed to the curving staircase. ''I'm certain that more than one person slid down that railing, aren't you?''

''It certainly is tempting, isn't it?'' she said with a grin, running her hands over the smooth-grained surface.

Each room was open. Tony had done an excellent job of lightening the look of the place, painting pastel colors on the walls and refinishing the hardwood floors.

When they walked into the breakfast room, Natalie paused, touched by the view from the multipaned windows. A garden sloped down to the edge of the lake. The profusion of rhododendrons, azaleas and rosebushes told her that the spring and summer would be filled with riotous colors. An arched trellis indicated climbing roses made their home there during the blooming season.

''Oh, Tony,'' she whispered, enchanted.

''Do you like it?''

''I love it. I've never seen a more homey, comfortable place.''

He took her hand and led her through the kitchen that had been thoroughly modernized, then back into the hallway. ''Let me show you upstairs.''

The upstairs contained four large bedrooms. The master suite had a built-in bath and dressing area that had been completely modernized.

The furniture in the room was distinctively masculine, but not heavy. She caught herself staring at the massive bed that was located on a dais. How many women had shared that bed with Tony? Of course she didn't want to know. It was no longer any of her business. She had walked out of his life.

She turned away, trying to cover her reaction to the room. "This is marvelous, Tony. You've done a wonderful job. Do you intend to put it on the market now that you've completed most of the work?"

"I'm not sure at this point what I intend to do."

"I see."

She wished she did. Tony had not mentioned another woman in his life, and yet she knew that he was entirely too attractive not to have someone. She had listened carefully to his family's conversation, hoping a name would be dropped in the conversation that would give her a clue to his personal life.

If she were more brave, she could question him, but she knew it was none of her business, and she wasn't sure she would be able to handle his answer when she heard it.

"Are you ready to go? I have reservations at one of the restaurants overlooking the river."

She nodded and started toward the door.

"Natalie?"

She turned. He still stood there in the middle of the bedroom, watching her.

"Yes?"

"Do you think I should keep this place?"

She attempted a casual shrug. "I can't really say, Tony.

It seems to be a rather large home for one person to occupy.''

''I don't intend to live here alone.''

A lump seemed to form in her throat, and she had trouble swallowing. ''Then you need to ask the woman you intend to share it with.''

He was by her side in a few long strides. Gripping her forearms he gave her an intense look. ''I'm asking *you*.''

Before she could form any words, he pulled her up against him and kissed her, a long, slow, mind-drugging kiss that took her far back into the past to other times, other kisses and to the one unforgettable night they had spent together.

Her arms curled up around his neck, holding him close. She had never forgotten the feel of Tony's arms around her, his powerful body molded tightly against hers. His kiss revealed that the restraint he'd shown around her was merely a facade, and Natalie reveled in the knowledge that she could still affect him so strongly.

When he finally raised his head, his face was flushed and his eyes glittered.

''Let's get out of here now,'' he muttered, ''or I'll never be able to let you walk out of here.''

Without looking at it, Natalie was aware of the presence of the large bed waiting only a few feet away. It would be so easy to let him know how much she wanted him again, after all this time.

But giving in to her feelings wouldn't solve anything. After a few hours with Tony in bed, she would once again be faced with a life without him. She didn't need the reminder.

They walked out to the car in silence. When Tony slid behind the steering wheel beside her, she glanced at him and smiled. "You're wearing more lipstick than I am at the moment," she said, handing him her handkerchief.

He glanced in the rearview mirror, then took her handkerchief and slowly removed the color from around his mouth.

"I'm sorry. I didn't mean to do that," he said without looking at her. He returned the handkerchief and started the car.

Natalie decided to be honest. "I'm not. I've wanted to kiss you like that since I saw you the other day in the mall."

He glanced down at her in surprise, then a smile slowly spread across his mouth. "No kidding?"

"No kidding."

He began to laugh. "And here I've been trying to be so careful with you."

"Why?"

"I didn't want to scare you away."

"Tony, there is nothing you can do that would scare me away."

She watched his reaction to her statement. He reflected on it for several moments in silence. Then he spoke. "We need to talk."

"Yes."

"But not tonight. I wanted a quiet evening with you, a chance to get reacquainted." He paused, as though searching for words. "Tomorrow is Christmas Eve."

She knew that they were both remembering what that day meant, but she could find no words to express what she was feeling.

"Natalie, would you spend tomorrow evening with me? We could go to my parents' open house and to church...." He paused, as though unsure of himself.

"I'd like that."

"Would you come back to the house with me, afterward?"

Her heart felt as though it was going to rocket out of her chest at his words.

"We need to talk. There's so much to say, but I'd rather wait until we have enough time and privacy."

He waited, and Natalie knew that a great deal rested on her response. "Yes, Tony. I'll spend as much time with you as you'd like me to."

They both knew what she was agreeing to without further words. He took his hand from the steering wheel and without looking at her, brushed his knuckles gently against her cheek. "Thank you."

How could he possibly be thanking her for agreeing to something she wanted so badly? She was the one who had walked out on him.

When they arrived at the restaurant they were immediately shown to their table. She had never been there before but was impressed with the decor and the privacy afforded each table. They were seated near a wide expanse of glass so that they could see the river and a nearby bridge. A fat candle in an oval glass holder flickered on the table, casting a warm light that created a halo effect to enfold them.

After they had ordered, Tony took her hand in both of his. Looking deep into her eyes, he said softly, "Tell me about you, Natalie. About school, about your friends, your hobbies. Help me learn about the woman that has grown from the young girl I once knew."

Haltingly at first, Natalie described her life. Tony quietly asked probing questions that she answered easily. Her life was open, free of secrets, almost boring.

By the time she had answered all of his questions, they were being offered dessert. She shook her head, sighing. "I couldn't eat another thing." They both ordered coffee, and when the waiter left, she said, "How about you? When are you going to tell me about you?"

"I will. Tomorrow night. I promise." He glanced away for a moment, and once again she was aware of the perfection of his profile. Then his dark eyes met hers once more. "It's getting late, and we both need our rest. I'll pick you up tomorrow to go to the open house."

She nodded, her thoughts flying ahead. Their plans for the next day were so similar to that day six years ago that she had a frightening sense of déjà vu. This time her father wasn't around to make changes in any of their plans. This time Tony was not suggesting marriage. This time she was not a foolish girl with stars in her eyes.

She knew he wanted her, there was no way to miss that. She wanted him, too. If this was all she could have, she was determined that it would be enough.

After all, the Christmas season was once more with them. During that magical time anything could happen. Love could grow and become whole once again.

When Tony took her home he walked her to the front door, refusing her invitation to come in. "They're predicting snow tomorrow. I hope not. There'll be so many people traveling."

"Drive safely," she said, going up on tiptoe and kissing him softly on the mouth. "Take care of you for me."

He grinned. "Always. I'll see you tomorrow."

When she walked inside the house, Tom came out of the living room. "I thought I heard you."

"Where's Mother?"

"She went up to bed. She's tired. Would you like a glass of sherry or wine before going to bed?"

"Sure, why not? Sherry would be nice." She wandered into the living room behind him and walked over to the fireplace. "The fire feels good tonight. I understand there's a chance of snow."

"Yes." He handed her a glass, and she sat down opposite him in one of the chairs in front of the fire. "Did you enjoy dinner?" he asked, watching her.

She nodded.

"Do you intend to spend tomorrow evening with him?"

"Yes, why?"

"I just wondered. You've never talked about Tony to me since you left Portland. I wasn't sure you'd even see him when you came back."

"I probably wouldn't have. We ran into each other accidentally."

"I don't believe in accidents."

"What do you mean? There's no way either of us could have known the other was shopping at the mall that day."

"But you would have seen him, sooner or later." He took a sip of his drink. "I know that you think Dad was very harsh with you and Tony back then."

"'Harsh' isn't the word. He was brutal, and you know it."

"He was concerned about you."

"He had no reason to be."

"Dad loved you very much, Natalie. He wanted what was best for you."

"Except he seemed to think he was the only one who knew best."

Tom shook his head. "Getting married in the middle of your senior year didn't make much sense, did it?"

She looked away from him, watching the fire dancing along the logs. "I loved him. It was the only way we could be together. Besides, I would have gone on with my schooling."

"Unless you had gotten pregnant. There's always that chance."

She shrugged. "What difference does it make now?"

"Do you still love Tony?"

She looked at him, surprised at the personal question. "Of course I love Tony. I always have. I always will. That isn't the issue."

"And what exactly is the issue?"

"Tony has put me out of his mind and life. He doesn't even bring up what happened, as though it means nothing to him."

"Natalie, he's right. You can't continue to live in the past or let the hurts of the past hang around you today. What happened, happened. You can't undo it or change it."

"I know. I really thought I had put it all behind me until I saw him again. I lost so much."

"I don't think 'lost' is the proper word. 'Postponed,' perhaps, would better describe the situation. You're both young yet. You can have so many happy years together, now that he's successfully established in business and you have your education."

"Except for one minor detail."

"What's that?"

"Tony never brings up a future for us. He talks as though we'll both continue on our separate paths."

"He's never suggested that you consider moving back to Portland?"

"Not once."

"Interesting."

"What do you mean?"

"Nothing. I just find Tony D'Angelo an interesting character study." Tom finished his drink and stood. "Then you won't be home tomorrow evening?"

She shook her head. "Not until very late, anyway. I'm

not sure what time I'll be home.'' She couldn't quite meet his eyes. How could she tell her brother that if Tony suggested she spend the remainder of Christmas Eve with him, she would do so, without any qualms?

Natalie set her glass down and got up from the chair. ''I'll see you in the morning, Tom. Good night.''

His murmured good-night was barely audible as she walked out of the room.

Chapter 6

When Natalie came downstairs the next evening she discovered that Tony had already arrived. He and Tom were standing in the foyer in the midst of a discussion when she came out of her room and started down the stairway. Both men stopped talking and looked up.

She caught her breath. Tony wore a black suit that fit him like a glove, the white of his dress shirt showing up in a splendid contrast, emphasizing his tanned skin, black hair and eyes.

He looked wonderful to her, and from the look on his face as he watched her descend the stairs toward him, he was having a similar reaction to her.

She had chosen to wear a white dress with silver threads interwoven through the fabric so that the dress sparkled with every move she made. The style was simple so as not to detract from the beauty of the cloth. It swirled around her legs as she moved toward the two men.

''I'm sorry to keep you waiting, Tony. I wasn't aware you were here.''

He glanced at Tom. "I just arrived. You look beautiful, Natalie. All you need are your angel wings."

She looked at Tom and winked. "I'm not sure I'm ready for my halo just yet. What do you think, Tom?"

In an unusual gesture, he put his arm around her and hugged her close to him. "I have to admit there's a glow about you, sis, that I haven't seen in a very long time. Who knows? Maybe the halo comes next."

Surprised at his show of affection, she kissed him on the cheek. "Where's Mother?"

"She hasn't come downstairs yet. I'm taking her over to some friends' home a little later."

Tony picked up her coat and laid it across her shoulders, carefully lifting the hood so that it protected her head.

"I'm not sure when I'll be home, Tom," she began when Tom interrupted her.

"Don't worry about it. Just have a wonderful Christmas celebration, all right?"

She smiled. "I will." Glancing at Tony, her smile widened. "I know I will."

It was already dark when they stepped outside. Once again a sense of déjà vu swept over her. The night was so clear that the stars seemed to be within reach. The air felt clean and fresh, and Natalie took a deep breath, as though to draw in some of the magic of the night.

Tony tucked her into the car before closing the door and joining her.

"Mama is so excited. She and Angela have been baking all day. Several of my aunts and uncles came over from the coast to join us. So the house will be full." He glanced over and grinned at her. "As usual."

They had to park several houses away from the D'Angelo home. Every window was brightly lit, and as they approached the front porch they heard the music, voices and laughter of happy people.

Just before he opened the door, Tony paused and placing his hands lightly on her shoulders, he leaned down and kissed her softly on the lips.

"Merry Christmas, Natalie."

She knew her face was flushed when they walked into the house. Everyone greeted them boisterously, teasing them unmercifully about arriving late. Within minutes Natalie felt as though she'd been embraced by every member of the clan as they hugged and kissed her, exclaiming how beautiful she looked. Tony never loosened his hold on her hand as they moved through the crowded rooms. Instead, he stood beside her grinning, refusing to respond to the teasing they were receiving. To his father he shrugged and said, "I was late getting away tonight."

His father patted his shoulder. "I know. This is a busy time for you."

The hours seemed to run together as the family gathered around the old upright piano while Serena D'Angelo played. Tony's father had a rich baritone voice and led the rest through several carols.

Even the small children joined in, their treble voices occasionally off-key but always enthusiastic.

Before Natalie realized the time, Tony was placing her coat around her once more. That was when she saw that the rest of the family members, Angela and Paul included, were gathering up coats and hats in order to go to the midnight services at the church.

There was no question about anyone riding with them, since the sports car only contained two seats. Tony wrapped his arm securely around Natalie, and they hurried to the car. Snowflakes had begun to fall all around them.

"The children will all be happy if this stuff sticks,"

Tony said as soon as they were on the way. "But right now it's fairly slick to be out driving."

The peaceful serenity of the night seemed to surround them as they drove slowly through the residential streets. Most people had gone to bed by now. For a moment Natalie felt as though she and Tony were the only people awake. The illusion dissipated when they pulled into the full parking lot at the church. Many people had chosen to spend this night in quiet contemplation of the meaning behind all of the festivities.

Tony and Natalie found places toward the back of the church and sat close together to give room to others arriving behind them.

Natalie had never dreamed that she would be able to reenact that night with Tony once again. Looking at him, she knew that there were vital changes now. They were both adults. They knew what they wanted in life. At least, she did. What Natalie realized as she sat there through the moving story of the very first Christmas was that what she wanted more than anything was to spend the rest of her life with the loving, tender, compassionate man beside her, to share many more moments like this one with him.

She could visualize the years to come when they would have children who would participate in the observance of Christmas, a family they would be able to share with and teach to appreciate what it meant to have been blessed with such love from God.

When the service was over they left the church without speaking. They drove to Lake Oswego in silence, although Natalie felt as though there were unseen carolers singing in the far distance, just out of range of her conscious hearing.

When they pulled up in front of the house, Natalie noticed that the snow had dusted the shrubs around the doorway, as though even they needed to be decorated in order to fully celebrate the occasion.

They entered the hallway, and Natalie noticed a light coming from upstairs. She looked around at Tony. "Did you mean to leave a light on?"

He helped her out of her coat and then took her hand. Leading her toward the stairway, he nodded. "Yes." When he started up the stairs, she followed.

He paused in the doorway of his bedroom and motioned for her to go inside.

A small Christmas tree sat on a table between the large picture windows that overlooked the lake. Twinkling lights blinked on and off. Gaily colored decorations hung on the tree. Perched at its point, a tiny angel with long blond hair and a white gown waited for them.

"When did you do this?" she asked in surprise.

"This afternoon. I wanted us to have our own special tree."

"What a lovely idea."

He walked over to the tree and picked up a small package. Without saying anything he handed it to her.

Natalie's hands were shaking so hard she wasn't sure she was going to be able to pull off the paper. When she finally did, she almost dropped the small case. Inside was a glittering ring, a sparkling blue stone surrounded by diamonds.

"Oh, Tony. It's beautiful."

"The color matches your eyes. I was told that it's called a London blue topaz. All I know is that I thought of you when I saw it."

He lifted it from the box, then slipped it on the third finger of her left hand. "Merry Christmas, love," he whispered, and kissed her.

When he loosened his hold a few minutes later, Natalie couldn't hide the tears in her eyes.

"What's wrong?"

"Nothing's wrong! Everything is so right I can't believe it. Tony, does this mean you want to start all over again? That we have a chance to build a life together?"

"Is that what you want?"

"More than I've ever wanted anything."

"Do you mean you're willing to move back to Portland?"

"I want to be with you, Tony, wherever that might be."

"Would you want to live here in this house?"

"If that's what you want."

He picked her up and carried her to the side of the bed. "That's what I want."

She watched as he loosened the unaccustomed tie around his neck and slipped off his suit jacket. Then she glanced down at the ring. "This time we're doing everything in order."

"What do you mean?"

Holding up her hand, she said, "The engagement ring first."

Tony paused as he unbuttoned the top two buttons of his shirt. "Well, not exactly." He turned away and walked toward the windows. "Do you remember that I told you I made an agreement with your father six years ago?"

"To leave me alone?"

"Yes. To let you get on with your life and your education. I promised him that I would not do anything to influence you to come back to me." Without turning around he added, "I believe I kept that promise."

"Yes. You did. I never expected to hear from you again."

"You would have, at least indirectly, if at any time you

had made any indication to your family that you were interested in another man.''

''I don't understand.''

Tony continued to stare out the window. ''I agreed to leave you alone. In exchange, your father agreed not to have our marriage annulled.''

She stared at his back in astonishment, trying to make some sense out of what he was saying.

''You mean—'' she walked over to him, trying to see his face ''—there was never an annulment?''

''That's right.''

What he was saying was unbelievable. Did he mean that during all this time—while she was away at school and he was here—

''Tony?''

Slowly he turned to face her, his hands in his pants pockets, his expression guarded. ''The marriage was valid, Natalie. Your father made sure of that. He hoped to find some way to get out of the agreement we made, so he had it all checked out.''

''Then you and I are married.''

He nodded.

''And no one ever told me.''

''Your mother doesn't know. Only your father, Tom and I. Then after your father died...'' His voice faded off.

''All this time Tom knew, and he never said a word?''

''No. He wanted to see if it was an infatuation with you. I promised him that if you ever met anyone else, I would immediately start proceedings to dissolve the marriage.''

''I was never interested in anyone else.''

''That's the only thing that has kept me going all these years, love. I got reports third hand—through your mother to Tom, then to me.''

''So that's why you seem to know him so well.''

"Not well. But we've stayed in touch. You see—" Once again he turned away, this time to the little tree that blinked so merrily beside the window. "You were my wife, and I wanted to be responsible for you. I insisted on paying all of your school expenses."

"You what! But that wasn't fair. My family had the money. You didn't."

"Maybe not at first," he admitted wryly, "but I was determined to show your family that I could do whatever it took to take care of you." His grin slowly appeared. "The hours I put in at work and school kept me too tired to think about anything else—like the fact that I had a wife that didn't know she was my wife. Like the fact that I didn't even know if you'd ever want me again. Like the fact that your refusal to return to Portland had almost convinced Tom that I was wasting my time and money in hopes of your wanting me."

"Oh, Tony," she cried, throwing herself into his arms. "If only I'd known! All these years we could have been together. All of these years so wasted."

"Not wasted. We both needed some time. Proving myself to your family made me more determined than ever to succeed. You had never treated me as the gardener's grandson, someone to look down on. I wasn't going to tolerate that treatment from your family."

She hugged him tightly, her cheek resting against the softness of his silk shirt. "Oh, Tony, I love you so much."

He sighed, his arms going convulsively around her. "There were nights when I would lie in bed wondering if I'd ever hear you say that again." He tilted her chin so that his mouth found hers, and all the longing, the uncertainty, the love that he'd carried within him for her all of these years seemed to pour from him, filling her heart and soul with gladness.

When the kiss could no longer properly express what he was feeling, Tony picked her up once more, this time laying her tenderly on the bed without breaking the kiss. He came down beside her, his restless hands exploring her, loving and adoring her.

All of the uncertainty she had experienced since seeing him that day at the mall disappeared in the passionate intensity of his kiss. She couldn't seem to get close enough to him, and Natalie hastily tugged at the buttons on his shirt, trying to reach the warm flesh hidden beneath the silk.

She felt the zipper at the back of her dress move down, and she willingly moved away from him long enough to remove the beautiful gown. Tony pulled away from her in order to slide the silken underwear from her body, so that she was bathed in the twinkling light coming from the tree.

"My Christmas angel. Happy anniversary, darling," he whispered. He quickly dispensed with the remainder of his clothes and stretched out beside her once more.

Natalie could more readily see the changes that had taken place in his body—the wide chest and heavy shoulders were revealed to her in all their silken splendor. She followed the curve of his chest down to his waist, then smoothed her hand across his abdomen and down his thigh. His skin rippled beneath her touch, and he pulled her over until she lay on top of him.

"Do you have any idea what you're doing to me, woman?" he groaned.

"I seem to be having a similar reaction," she admitted.

"Six years is a long time to wait, you know."

"I know that. I'm not asking how you spent those years, love. How can I possibly ask?"

"But I can answer. I didn't want anyone but you, Natalie. My thoughts and dreams have always been filled with you. I never wanted anyone but you. Never." His hands encircled her head and gently brought it down to him so that his mouth could touch hers. He ran his tongue along the surface of her lips, then plunged deeply inside—taking possession.

There was never any doubt how his body reacted to her nearness, and Natalie could no longer ignore her position on top of him. Raising herself slightly, she moved so that she could enfold and absorb him, her action causing him to gasp at the pleasure of joining with her once more.

Fiercely he held her as she moved over him, at long last able to enact some of her many fantasies over the years.

Eventually she collapsed on his chest, too weak to continue. Tony rolled so that she was tucked beneath him, bringing her to repeated peaks until at long last he joined her in that wonderful feeling of total satiation.

Not wanting to crush her, he stretched out beside her, holding her close. Her eyes drifted shut, then popped open again. She didn't want to waste a moment of this time.

The Christmas angel kept a watchful eye over the proceedings, her kindly smile indicating that all was well. Once again the magic of Christmas had brought to Natalie her heart's desire.

This time she knew it would last forever.

"Are you awake?" Tony whispered a few minutes later.

"Mmm-hmm."

"Are you hungry?"

"Not really, why?"

"I thought we could raid the refrigerator. I stocked up on everything I could think of before I left here today."

"Do you think I should call Tom so he and Mother don't worry about me? The roads are going to be treacherous tonight."

With his forefinger, Tony traced a trail from her chin down her throat, between her breasts and finally paused at her abdomen. "Tom knew you weren't coming back home tonight."

"Is that what you two were talking about in the foyer?"

"Yes. He told me that there was no reason not to tell you the truth now. I'd already decided I couldn't wait any longer, anyway. Whatever the outcome, you had to know."

"I can't believe that both of you kept this from me all these years."

"Your mother is going to be the one in shock. She never knew what had happened. Your father told her that he had found you at my parents' home, that you'd stayed overnight with Angela."

"And she believed that, as upset as I was?"

"I suppose. So now we're going to have to explain to her why you aren't going to be home until a few days after Christmas."

She ran her fingers through his black curls. "A few days?"

"I don't intend to let you out of my bed any longer than I can help it. Why do you suppose I'm offering food? I want you to keep your strength up."

"What about you?"

"I've been doing that for six years, love." His slow kiss made it clear that he was more than willing to demonstrate.

Natalie settled contentedly into his arms. In a contest of this nature, there were definitely no losers.

With Christmas magic, anything was possible.

* * * * *

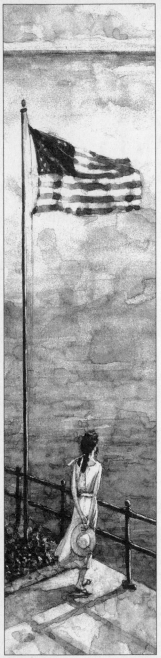

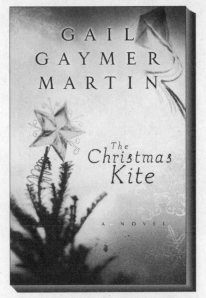

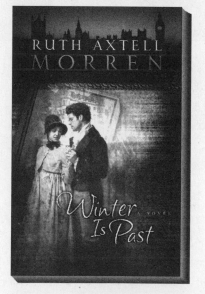

The Wolfe twins' stories—
together in one fantastic volume!

USA TODAY bestselling author

JOAN
HOHL

Double
WOLFE

The emotional story of Matilda Wolfe plus an original short
story about Matilda's twin sister, Lisa. The twins have
followed different paths...but each leads to true love!

Look for DOUBLE WOLFE in January 2004.

**"A compelling storyteller who weaves her tales
with verve, passion and style."
—*New York Times* bestselling author Nora Roberts**

Where love comes alive™

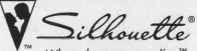